Crime Files Series

General Editor: Clive Bloom

Since its invention in the nineteenth century, detective fiction has never been more popular. In novels, short stories, films, radio, television and now in computer games, private detectives and psychopaths, prim poisoners and overworked cops, tommy gun gangsters and cocaine criminals are the very stuff of modern imagination, and their creators one mainstay of popular consciousness. Crime Files is a ground-breaking series offering scholars, students and discerning readers a comprehensive set of guides to the world of crime and detective fiction. Every aspect of crime writing, detective fiction, gangster movie, true-crime exposé, police procedural and post-colonial investigation is explored through clear and informative texts offering comprehensive coverage and theoretical sophistication.

Published titles include:

Maurizio Ascari
A COUNTER-HISTORY OF CRIME FICTION
Supernatural, Gothic, Sensational

Hans Bertens and Theo D'haen
CONTEMPORARY AMERICAN CRIME FICTION

Anita Biressi
CRIME, FEAR AND THE LAW IN TRUE CRIME STORIES

Ed Christian (*editor*)
THE POST-COLONIAL DETECTIVE

Paul Cobley
THE AMERICAN THRILLER
Generic Innovation and Social Change in the 1970s

Emelyne Godfrey
MASCULINITY, CRIME AND SELF-DEFENCE IN VICTORIAN LITERATURE

Christiana Gregoriou
DEVIANCE IN CONTEMPORARY CRIME FICTION

Lee Horsley
THE NOIR THRILLER

Merja Makinen
AGATHA CHRISTIE
Investigating Femininity

Fran Mason
AMERICAN GANGSTER CINEMA
From *Little Caesar* to *Pulp Fiction*

Linden Peach
MASQUERADE, CRIME AND FICTION
Criminal Deceptions

Alistair Rolls and Deborah Walker
FRENCH AND AMERICAN NOIR
Dark Crossings

Susan Rowland
FROM AGATHA CHRISTIE TO RUTH RENDELL
British Women Writers in Detective and Crime Fiction

Adrian Schober
POSSESSED CHILD NARRATIVES IN LITERATURE AND FILM
Contrary States

Lucy Sussex
WOMEN WRITERS AND DETECTIVES IN NINETEENTH-CENTURY CRIME
FICTION
The Mothers of the Mystery Genre

Heather Worthington
THE RISE OF THE DETECTIVE IN EARLY NINETEENTH-CENTURY POPULAR
FICTION

R.A. York
AGATHA CHRISTIE
Power and Illusion

Crime Files
Series Standing Order ISBN 978–0–333–71471–3 (hardback)
978–0–333–93064–9 (paperback)
(*outside North America only*)

You can receive future titles in this series as they are published by placing a standing order. Please contact your bookseller or, in case of difficulty, write to us at the address below with your name and address, the title of the series and the ISBN quoted above.

Customer Services Department, Macmillan Distribution Ltd, Houndmills, Basingstoke, Hampshire RG21 6XS, England

Masculinity, Crime and Self-Defence in Victorian Literature

Emelyne Godfrey

First published 2011 by
PALGRAVE MACMILLAN

Palgrave Macmillan in the UK is an imprint of Macmillan Publishers Limited, registered in England, company number 785998, of Houndmills, Basingstoke, Hampshire RG21 6XS.

Palgrave Macmillan in the US is a division of St Martin's Press LLC, 175 Fifth Avenue, New York, NY 10010.

Palgrave Macmillan is the global academic imprint of the above companies and has companies and representatives throughout the world.

Palgrave® and Macmillan® are registered trademarks in the United States, the United Kingdom, Europe and other countries.

ISBN 978–0–230–27345–0   hardback

This book is printed on paper suitable for recycling and made from fully managed and sustained forest sources. Logging, pulping and manufacturing processes are expected to conform to the environmental regulations of the country of origin.

A catalogue record for this book is available from the British Library.

Library of Congress Cataloging-in-Publication Data

Godfrey, Emelyne.
  Masculinity, crime and self-defence in Victorian literature/Emelyne Godfrey.
      p. cm. — (Crime files)
  Includes bibliographical references and index.
  ISBN 978–0–230–27345–0 (alk. paper)
    1. English literature—19th century—History and criticism.
  2. Masculinity in literature.   3. Crime in literature.   I. Title.

  PR468.M38G63 2011
  820.9'3521—dc22   2010034132

10   9   8   7   6   5   4   3   2   1
20   19   18   17   16   15   14   13   12   11

Printed and bound in Great Britain by
CPI Antony Rowe, Chippenham and Eastbourne

To my Grandad, Peter Godfrey B.E.M., who was always a gentleman

Contents

List of Figures

Acknowledgments

My thanks to: Clive Emsley, Laurel Brake, Mark Turner, Deborah Parsons, John Harding (Officer for Safety, Newham Borough Council), Lizzie Richmond of the Richard Bowen Collection at the University of Bath, Victoria List, Ellen Moody, John Jackson, Catherine Cooke (Curator of the Sherlock Holmes Collection at the Marylebone Library) and Yuichi Hirayama of the Japan Sherlock Holmes Club.

Punch Ltd and the Mary Evans Picture Library.

London Metropolitan University: Anne Hogan and Lucy Bland.

Roy Edwards of *Health and Strength* and the team at *History Today*.

Toynbee Hall, the British Library, the Senate House Library, the London Library, James Smith and Sons Umbrella Shop, New Oxford Street, and the Intellectual Property Office.

Joe Svinth, Shihan Kevin Garwood and the Bartitsu Forum. Special thanks go to Tony Wolf who always responded to my queries at lightning speed from across the pond and guided me through the intricate aspects of martial arts history.

The Tower of London and Royal Armouries Leeds: Bridget Clifford, Mark Murray Flutter, Chris Streek, Stuart Ivinson, Rob Temple, Keith Ducklin and Robert Woosnam-Savage.

I am grateful for kind support from the Japan Foundation Endowment Committee in the preparation of this book and to Clive Bloom for giving me this wonderful opportunity.

Many thanks to local historian, Bill Tonkin, of the Exhibition Study Group, for introducing me to his impressive collection of postcards and for his helpful advice on the Japan-British Exhibition of 1910.

I must mention the remarkable individuals at the Metropolitan Police Stores for their warm welcome and cups of tea: Paul Dew, Camilla Lawrence, Phillip Barnes-Warden (for solving what I will call 'The Adventure of the Missing Life-Preserver'!) and Keith Skinner.

Finally, I wish to express my gratitude to my mother, who has been particularly supportive, and to Jonathan Fry for his friendship. A special thank you goes to Martin Kolmar whose loving support, level-headed advice and proofreading have been invaluable during the final stages of writing.

Note on the Text and Abbreviations

All references to the Palliser novels are derived from the Oxford World's Classics series. The Sherlock Holmes stories are taken from the *Penguin Complete Sherlock Holmes* (London: Penguin, 1981).

In English alone, 'jujitsu' has a variety of spellings, including 'jiu-jitsu', 'ju-jutsu', 'jujitsu' and 'jujuits'. I have used the Japanese spelling of 'jujitsu' instead of the Westernized form, 'ju-jitsu'. Japanese names are anglicized, with forenames first, followed by the surname, as this is how they were often referred to in the Edwardian texts I have examined.

In the text I refer to *The Text-Book of Ju-Jutsu as Practised in Japan* as '*Text-Book*' and 'Uncontrolled Ruffianism as Measured by Rule of Thumb as 'Uncontrolled Ruffianism'.

Introduction

Keith Ducklin strides onto the stage, darkly clad in Victorian garb. He looks every inch the gentleman about town. As he tells us, he is about to give his friend Rob Temple a few lessons in an exciting new style of self-defence. But Rob is already feeling the heat inside his tweed jacket and when Keith lunges at him with his walking-stick, he catches him unawares in a manoeuvre called 'Guard by Distance'. The audience is dazzled by a flash of scarlet; the lining of Keith's coat shimmers flamboyantly as it catches the light. In another moment, Rob finds himself felled to the ground when his ankle is trapped in the crook of Keith's Alpenstock.

'Dr Watson, you must be quicker off the mark!'

'Holmes, you are just too fast for me', Rob admits, smiling. Amused, the audience applaud and salute the pair with their digital cameras. After the show, a small group gathers around the two highly trained fight interpreters. Despite their busy schedule at the Royal Armouries, Leeds, Rob and Keith still have time for questions.

The performance we have just seen had its origins in the nineteenth century and arose from the demands created by the perceived perils of urban living. Self-defence in nineteenth-century Britain is an account of conflict, of the tussle between civilians and adversaries and the struggle between competing visions of manliness. If masculinity is a socially constructed role, changing over time, then the responses men took towards attack were influenced by cultural shifts. Middle-class manliness was defined by self-control, and adherence to the principles of the law was seen as highly commendable, although the move to a less belligerent response towards violent crime was increasingly characterized by hand-to-hand self-defence. This book explores crime from the perspective of the city-goer and is set against the works of popular playwrights and the fiction of two literary giants of the mid- and late-Victorian era, Anthony Trollope and Sir Arthur Conan Doyle. At the time this book was written, *The Pallisers* and the Sherlock Holmes canon were serialized on BBC Radio and the BBC also showcased a new television series entitled *Sherlock*, a fast-flowing, playful twist on the Holmes adventures, crafted for the iPod generation. This suggests that while Doyle's stories have been the subject of another fresh interpretation, Trollope's Palliser novels have also been reawakened for a larger audience.

Historians have observed that the latter half of the nineteenth century witnessed fewer incidents of violent crime.[1] As Clive Emsley has shown, the number of homicides committed dropped continuously from the mid-Victorian era to the end of the century, although a general fear of violence, committed by the 'dangerous classes', remained.[2] Periodicals, plays and fiction produced in the decades after 1850 reflect a heightened awareness of personal vulnerability and a growing fascination with forms of urban self-defence. The mid-nineteenth-century garotting panics (robberies involving strangulation) prompted widespread investigations into methods of self-defence and are therefore the starting point of this book. They persist as a leitmotif, influencing the reportage of crime in the late-nineteenth century and in Edwardian writing. This is not to argue that the respectable classes prior to the 1850s did not consider themselves affected by the spectre of street violence in the form of, for instance, the London Monster panic of the 1790s or the Spring-Heeled Jack scare. Actually, the garotting panics were distinguished from earlier crime scares in that they were perpetrated by a number of offenders against a sizeable amount of the population and precipitated a larger response than earlier crime panics. The London Monster attacks were perpetrated on a select number of female victims in the metropolis while, as Jennifer Westwood argues, Spring-Heeled Jack was 'an imaginary bogeyman, rather than a serial killer'.[3] The widespread and sharpened interest in personal protection, which is the subject of my investigation, was occasioned by the garotting scare, which was itself fuelled by changes in print culture. The panics presented themselves as the culmination of a variety of concerns relating to the changing urban make-up. While the police force offered a means of apprehending criminals, civilians were nonetheless influenced by ideas of 'self-help' and clearly still felt obliged to protect themselves.

The opinions of the majority of civilians on violent crime between 1850 and 1900 did not stem from personal experience. Rather, their views were formed by information conveyed by the press.[4] Publication was facilitated with the removal of advertising tax in 1853, newspaper stamp duty in 1855 and newsprint paper duty in 1861. Thanks to technological advances, newspapers cost less to produce and could be printed and distributed faster to an ever-widening readership. In fact, from 1855 to 1860 – the years of the garotting scares – the circulation of daily newspapers increased threefold.[5] Consequently, anxieties were transmitted to a greater readership, while manufacturers and martial arts practitioners, respectively, were able to advertise weapons and defensive techniques to a larger clientele and use the printed press to debate methods of tackling violent crime.

Changes in perceptions of the metropolis impacted on the ways in which danger was conceptualized. Lynda Nead argues that Victorian London was perceived as a new 'Babylon', a vision which embodied the idea that London, in the throes of modernization in the 1860s, was still 'haunted by the image of ruin'.[6] Concerns over Victorian Babylon were also manifested in attitudes to crime, a topic not extensively covered in Nead's study. Sindall observes of the mid-nineteenth century that: 'We are presented with a situation in which the central class in a society has a growing feeling of security in all aspects of life except that of physical confrontation, primarily on an individual level and secondly on a class level.'[7] The garotting panics demonstrated that middle-class anxieties about personal threat on the street were certainly not unfounded.

As Richard Sennett has famously observed, the aversion to physical threats became embedded in the structure of the modern city, in the building of walls, highways and 'spaces which remove the threat of social contact'.[8] Urban planning aimed at the separation of morally upstanding citizens from the criminal underclass. However, nineteenth-century novels and articles emphasize the ease with which these defences could be breached. In 1860, the population of London was around three million and by the end of the century, this number had more than doubled. The way in which the rapidly expanding city was imagined influenced perceptions of the self and informed attitudes towards physical threats. At the turn of the century, over one million pedestrians, including employers, employees (both female and male) and visitors, entered the City of London on a daily basis,[9] forcing commuters into packed spaces. The daily commute was represented as a hazardous ordeal in which 'all the murderers, forgers, embezzlers, and assaulters whose crimes escape detection altogether' brush past respectable pedestrians 'in the streets of this and other towns every day of [their] lives'.[10] The respectable citizen was free to roam where he pleased; so too was the violent criminal. Therefore, increasing urbanization inspired a greater awareness of physical danger. For Sennett, 'the fear of exposure' (which Sennett defines as a horror of injury) is 'in one way a militarized conception of everyday experience, as though attack-and-defense is as apt a model of subjective life as it is of warfare'.[11] The conceptualization of this 'attack-and-defense' model altered in that, from the 1850s to 1914, civilian self-defence had shifted from an approach virtually resembling an armed attack to a physically defensive, corporeal response.

The culture of self-defence was in the main a reaction to the perceived limitations of the police force in their responses to violent crime. By the 1850s, London 'Bobbies' had 'already acquir[ed] an affectionate image in the perception of many of the respectable and propertied classes'.[12] However, despite the presence of the police force on the streets, a size-able number of individuals nevertheless considered it necessary to equip themselves with methods of self-defence. This was because the police force was limited in its response to violent crime. Officers were slow, forced to run to destinations and raise the alarm using only a rattle or, from the late 1880s, a whistle. In addition, the police could not prevent a crime by arrest, but only by apprehending the offender whilst he was committing the deed. It is also likely that tracts and articles on personal protection were influenced by notions of 'self-help', a key middle-class value emphasized by Samuel Smiles in 1858. The defensive arts thus instructed individuals on how to set their own protective barrier whilst offering them the opportunity to assert physically and figuratively their own space in the city.

This study of self-defence is contextualized against the depiction of male violence in nineteenth-century literature. The increasing interest in personal protection was an attempt to adapt to the tightening of legisla-tion regarding interpersonal violence during the nineteenth century, laws which were premised on the understanding that men were naturally aggressive. The passing of specific laws showed that attitudes towards the punishment of violent offenders changed throughout the century. These developments influenced how the individual was required to respond to threats. As recent historiography has affirmed, the first decades of the nineteenth century saw a focus on the establishment of suitable punish-ments for a plethora of newly created offences. This action was seen as representative of the British response to the spectre of mass violence raised by the French Revolution abroad or the Peterloo Massacre of 1819 at home.[13] The 'Six' Acts (1819) passed in the wake of the Massacre gave magistrates the power to seize arms and prevented civilian organizations from training with weapons. While their purpose was to curtail the activities of political extremists, they problematized the use of weapons and thus formed a basis for the regulation of armed or unarmed male violence. The legislative changes in the early nineteenth century led to a wider range of offences against the person and to an increase in the severity of the sentences which could be handed down. Under Lord Ellenborough's Act, which was passed in 1803, the death penalty was extended for a wider variety of assaults (such as attempted murder) and attacks perpetrated using knives and other weapons. By 1837, we see a change in attitudes with the result that assault was now considered a non-capital crime. Later, under the Offences Against the Person Act 1861, the death penalty was abolished for all crimes except murder and high treason.[14] This last piece of legislation in this list provided a backdrop against which other specific laws relating to interpersonal violence were passed in the 1860s.

Trollope and Doyle's work – particularly the Sherlock Holmes canon – are exposés of the maltreatment of women. Martin Wiener emphasizes the progressive criminalization of male violence during the nineteenth century and discusses the passing of nineteenth-century laws aimed at protecting women and children.[15] The Act for the Better Prevention of Aggravated Assault Upon Women and Children 1853 was the first law to tackle violence towards wives directly. Assaults on those under 14 years of age that resulted in actual bodily harm could now punished with six months' imprisonment. Further amendments in 1861, 1878, 1886 and 1895 consolidated such legislation. Wiener argues that novels including Anne Brontë's *The Tenant of Wildfell Hall* (1848; hereafter *Wildfell Hall*) and Wilkie Collins's *The Woman in White* (1860) fostered a 'victimisation tradition' and 'plac[ed] men's treatment of women in the dock'.[16] The violent treatment of household animals was employed in fiction as a metaphor for male violence towards women. This is apparent in *Wildfell Hall* and is strongly emphasized in *The Wing of Azrael* (1889), a novel by the anti-vivisectionist Mona Caird. In 1822, the maltreatment of animals was first made illegal, while 1824 saw the founding of the Society for the Prevention of Cruelty to Animals. Notably, Trollope uses the trope of animal cruelty to hint at his hero's demise into irascibleness and Doyle employs it as a marker of physical and mental degeneration.

Attempts to regulate the ownership of firearms met with very little success. Apart from the introduction of licences in 1870 and the restriction of the sale of firearms to adults over 18, radical attempts to control gun ownership were unsuccessful until the 1920s. This is a conclusion drawn by more than one historian, and it has been argued that this fact points to the popularity of aggressive forms of civilian self-defence.[17] However, such an account is not a hegemonic interpretation of nineteenth- and early-twentieth-century British cultural attitudes to violence. While novelists and self-defence instructors alike advocated the avoidance of violence, if confrontations did ensue, they exhorted the defending party to defend themselves with non-aggressive physical vigour. Contemporary writing increasingly questioned the association between the recourse to firearms and middle-class masculinity.

There has been much scholarship on the theme of masculine restraint, from the oft-quoted *Violence and Crime in Nineteenth-Century England: The Shadow of Our Refinement* (2004) by John Carter Wood to Karen Volland Waters's lesser-known but wide-ranging study of literature, *The Perfect Gentleman: Masculine Control in Victorian Men's Fiction, 1870–1901* (1997). In the 1830s and 1840s, restraint and abstinence from violence became a marker of the bourgeois persona, while in the latter half of the nineteenth century, notions of what constituted 'civilized' behaviour were predicated on a disavowal of the perceived barbarism of the lower classes and foreigners.[18] The shift in the nineteenth century away from violence has been identified as an integral product of what is referred to as the 'civilizing process'. A key symbol of restraint was the self-assured and composed perfect gentleman, yet this ideal was riddled with paradoxes. Looking at the years 1870 to 1901, Waters examines the psychological and physical fragmentation of the figure of the gentleman as a method of asserting patriarchal control during the latter half of the nineteenth century. Inherent in the concept of the perfect gentleman were, she argues, destabilizing dichotomies: control of one's destiny/the restrictions of one's station; masculine forcefulness/feminine reticence; and conformity/individuality.[19] She sees these qualities unravelling in Robert Louis Stevenson's *The Strange Case of Dr Jekyll and Mr Hyde* (1885), a warning of latent aggression under the civilized façade. As Peter Gay has written, 'manliness was a potentially volatile compound of desperate restraints and ferocious desires barely held in check, the whole ready to burst into flame if combined with other alibis for aggression'.[20] Jerome K. Jerome spooked his readers with the idea that 'underneath our starched shirts there lurks the savage, with all his savage instincts untouched'.[21] It is the tendency to pass from iron self-control to wanton aggression which render Jekyll's nature and, by inference, the nature of the gentleman unstable.

Wiener's well-received *Men of Blood: Violence, Manliness and Criminal Justice in Victorian England* (2004) provides a helpful way of looking at the Jekyll-and-Hyde side of nineteenth-century thought and will be used as the framework of analysis in this book. Wiener divides Victorian attitudes towards aggression into two main stances: one considered to endorse displays of passionate anger – the 'man of blood' mentality – the other, the 'ordinary reasonable man', characterized by forbearance.

Self-restraint was a key product of what Norbert Elias famously conceptualized as the 'civilizing process'. This process was occasioned by industrialization, the spread of the middle class and the increasing interdependency of the individual and the state, which resulted in the transition of 'social constraint towards self-constraint'.[22] One significant aspect of this transition was the stigmatization of violent behaviour, what Wiener calls the 'civilizing offensive', which elicited a backlash from men of all levels of society. However, the keynote to Wiener's work is not bloodthirsty aggression but restraint. In every chapter, Wiener emphasizes the legal and social consequences that followed acts of violence (for instance, spousal murder or duelling) and therefore underlines the penalties incurred at the expression of passionate anger.

Men of Blood looks at men not simply as perpetrators but also as victims of violence. Prior to his book, three key works of the 1980s and 1990s had considered middle-class masculine vulnerability: Jennifer Davis's 'The London Garotting Panic of 1862: A Moral Panic and the Creation of a Criminal Class in Mid-Victorian England' (1980);[23] Geoffrey Pearson's *Hooligan: A History of Respectable Fears* (1983)[24] and Robert Sindall's *Street Violence in the Nineteenth Century: Media Panic or Real Danger?* (1990).[25] Considering the depiction of vulnerability with specific relation to Victorian moral panics, these works are frequently found on class reading lists and in bibliographies on crime, and will play a part in the following chapters. Sindall's study does not appear to have directly informed *Men of Blood,* yet it demonstrates that during the garotting panics, a number of middle-class men articulated themselves violently in response to the threat of interpersonal aggression without apparent fear of legal consequences. These panics suggest that a transition between the ideals of the 'man of blood' and those of the 'ordinary reasonable man' took place in the 1850s. Sindall and Davis discuss the reasons behind the beginning of the garotting panics, while Pearson's study seeks to 'explode mindsets of good old England' and debunks the notion that there was ever a 'golden age of order and security'.[26]

This book responds to Wiener's invitation for a study of textual sources beyond statistics and government reports.[27] As Wiener's important overview of the treatment of violence in law courts shows, one major site for societal transformation is gender relations. Therefore, it will be argued that the cultivation of vulnerability by the media, together with a shifting of gender values, contributed greatly to the perpetuation of crime panics themselves. Literature provides an excellent source for investigating such attitudes. Sindall highlights the 'inexactitude' of statistics and at the same time argues that literary resources do not provide 'an alternative method to the truth about the state of crime in the nineteenth century', in that 'many literary sources are either reworkings of the criminal statistics or rewrites of received myths and as such are a poor substitute'.[28] However, if the main aim of Sindall's research is to gain an understanding of what people 'believed' was occurring in the world around them, surely literary, particularly fictional resources are an extremely useful form of gauging people's reactions to events and assessing what the presentation of these events tells us about gender and society? Furthermore, a gendered analysis of journalistic writing and fiction offers a way of assessing encoded attitudes to vulnerability. More work needs to be done on men as victims of, for example, sexual violence. For instance, Eve Kosofsky Sedgwick's work on metaphors of male rape in Charles Dickens's *Our Mutual Friend* (1865) points to the way in which nineteenth-century fiction could explore a form of danger which could not be openly expressed.[29] Novelists were aware of currents of thinking, and therefore views on the threat of interpersonal aggression and other topics unfit for official airing in the drawing room found their way into works of fiction.

Waters briskly argues that 'there is a very fine line between the driving force of a man directed toward work and the industriousness of a man turned toward aggression, and one sees in popular literature toward the end of the century a growing emphasis on self-defense and belligerence'.[30] This needs further investigation. While aggressive means of protection abounded in the mid-Victorian era, it is particularly at the end of the nineteenth century that self-defence began to be differentiated from *violence* and aggression. Unfortunately, she says little on the outlets offered to the gentleman to challenge social convention.

The dichotomies of conformity and reticence on the one hand and individuality and forcefulness on the other hand are discussed by Waters and are examined by James Eli Adams in his study of the writings of Thomas Carlyle, Walter Pater and Oscar Wilde. As Adams observes, 'Wilde's "transgressive desire" is enacted through "conformity to rule," not against it; it is enacted through Wilde's insistent staging of the contradictions that beset the ideal of the gentleman in Victorian culture'.[31] This is a helpful insight as it shows the ways in which individuals could stretch the boundaries of societal norms by working within them. My study of the interiority of the characters in Trollope and Doyle demonstrates that engagement with forms of assertive self-defence offered a means for the expression of heterosexual flamboyancy and stretched the limits of individual subjectivities.

Contributions on the debate centring on the dichotomy of masculine restraint and expression have not only emanated from literary and social studies but also from the discipline of fashion history. Two studies provided by Christopher Breward and John Harvey in the 1990s have placed the male consumer within the scope of scholarly research.[32] In his study of nineteenth-century masculine City fashions, Breward shows how sartorial restraint, a gentlemanly attribute, was paradoxically widely exploited to dramatic effect. Compared with earlier styles of clothing, 'the dulled moleskin and broadcloth frock coats of the mid-century decades […] were no less self-conscious in their attention to form'.[33] Therefore, the sartorial *display* of modesty and reserve in itself constituted a 'performance of professionalism', communicating a man's value to his contemporaries. The colour black is a symbol of conformity but is also often worn as a marker of rebellion, as is apparent when we watch Keith perform on stage at the Royal Armouries. A colour associated with restraint, black was also imbued with the potential for fluidity.

Studies on middle-class manly self-expression have also focused on sport as a mechanism for the building of masculinity, of the containment of aggression and the promotion of self-restraint.[34] Naturally, field games require the employment of improvisational skills and even self-display and assertion. However, the self-defence scenario was the ultimate challenge faced by the civilian. It has often been maintained that the middle classes did not subscribe to notions of heroism in everyday life. As Gay maintains, the bourgeoisie confined 'heroics to the opera house or the sports stadium', preferring domesticity to 'the warrior's militancy'.[35] Again, Antony Simpson's damning conclusion of the mid-Victorian era is that 'instantaneous heroism is not a concept that exists in middle-class thought', being incompatible with bourgeois values such as restraint and reliability.[36] Wood notes that bourgeois culture 'emphasised self-restraint, aspiring at least to the appearance of control over "passion", which was often linked directly to violence'.[37] In fact, as I will show, there was much interest in the figure of the heroic average urban man and he can be found in the large body of writing on self-defence, and that, in fact, the spectre of urban violence startled mainstream middle-class masculinity into displays of physical action.

E. Anthony Rotundo has shown how American writers sought a return to nature in order to test modern physical manliness. However, this does not take into account the presence of masculinities based on the articulation of emotion. Rotundo posits three models of middle-class manliness: the Masculine Achiever, the Masculine Gentleman and the Masculine Primitive. The last category 'asserted its power in the private writings of the middle class' in the 1860s and was a response to sedentary, bourgeois, white-collar professional life. The rugged Wild West provided the inspiration for the formulation of such 'Primitive' masculinities based on physical strength and the capacity to survive. As Rotundo points out: 'Suddenly passions and impulses had become a valued part of a man's character.'[38] Although it was statistically unlikely that the ordinary city-dweller would become a victim of violent street crime, the encounter with violent criminals was nevertheless a legitimate risk. As Wood argues, 'savagery brought clarity to the civilized identity' and 'shadows' served to define civilization.[39] As he points out, confrontations between the British bourgeois and the Other were opportunities for self-definition; therefore, it was easier to define gentlemanliness by juxtaposing the ideal with its 'ruffianly' polar opposite. Furthermore, the invention of 'savagery' could also be seen as an aggressive act of Othering. The lower-class ruffian was still present in fictional narratives of the self-defence scenario at the end of the century, yet in fiction the emphasis on the prevention of lower-class interpersonal violence was moving towards an investigation of aggression perpetrated by other groups placed higher on the social scale. This development correlates with the increasingly frequent appearance in fiction of the violent gentleman-villain at the end of the nineteenth century. Such a scenario, which took the form of a battle waged between the 'civilized' versus the 'savage' set against a familiar backdrop of urban development, would have resonated strongly with the ordinary reader in the 1850s and 1860s.

So, self-defence was more than just the protection of purse and person. The self-defence scenario involved the appreciation and assessment of risk. Elaine Freedgood's riveting book *Victorian Writing About Risk: Imaging a Safe England* (2000) considers numerous means devised by Victorians to understand a world laden with peril. They assuaged fears over industrial unrest, threats to personal security and public health by either finding a solution to the problem – collecting data or enforcing sanitary measures – or confronting a fear in person by climbing mountains and intrepidly venturing into the ether above the Victorian city in a hot air balloon. How did the middle classes respond to the threat of crime? Could the means that they used provide them with a sense of safety and, moreover, a feeling of self-aggrandizement?

One can also look at self-defence from the female perspective. Judith Walkowitz, Deborah Epstein-Nord and Lynda Nead have considered the ways in which middle-class women negotiated their own safety *and* their own identity in the urban environment.[40] Furthermore, Deborah L. Parsons has questioned the stability of the male gaze and *flâneur,* and has advanced the argument for the existence of its female equivalent, the *flâneuse.*[41] While Wiener contends that 'notions of female helplessness became ever stronger',[42] the existence of the phenomenon of the *flâneuse* suggests that a number of women, whilst aware of their vulnerability, may not have considered themselves to be weak and helpless. However, this is a vibrant topic in itself and is beyond the scope of this book.

We often hear about heroes of the Empire – for instance, the national hero General Charles Gordon, who was killed by rebels during a siege on Khartoum in 1885 and acquired the status of martyr in the eyes of the British public. What of domestic heroes? Narratives of civilian self-defence have aspects in common with military propaganda – both, for example, drew on nationhood as a galvanizing force – yet in the civilian self-defence scenario, belligerence was often considered to be un-British. The way in which a man responded to a threat was a barometer of his character. Self-defence took various forms, from the preventative, such as walking in the middle of the road, to the retaliatory. What becomes apparent is that many of these approaches are complemented by middle-class forms of knowledge, for example, the cerebral response, which involved assessing one's enemy through the use of such means as the science of physiognomy or by mentally outwitting them. This act of reading the body is abundantly apparent in the Sherlock Holmes canon. A modern literary example of this cerebral assessment of risk and of the enemy is Ian McEwan's *Saturday* (2005), in which a neurosurgeon, a 'pedestrian diagnostician', stalls his attacker by revealing to him that he has a neurological condition and that the neurosurgeon can assist him.[43] While some types of crime tended to follow the same form and were therefore predictably similar to each other, literature still focused on the element of surprise. A possible life-and-death situation, the outcomes of which are wholly unforeseeable, required almost superhuman resolve and temerity coupled with a very human awareness of the constraints of the law and the ever-tightening influence of the civilizing offensive. It is no wonder that the assault scene furnished writers and journalists with opportunities to explore and stretch masculine identities.

Very few significant studies focus solely on violent encounters in nineteenth-century British literature, although the number is gradually growing. Wiener's *Men of Blood* and Peter Gay's *The Cultivation of Hatred* (1993) investigate nineteenth-century manifestations of and attitudes towards interpersonal violence, and do consider nineteenth-century fiction, but instances of self-protection are not their central points of reference. Frederick Edwin Smith's early *Fifty Famous Fights in Fact and Fiction* (1932) is by no means comprehensive. Many of his examples of fights (not exclusively self-defence scenarios) are gleaned from literature across the centuries. By focusing on a tighter timeframe, my book examines scenes of confrontation in a historical as well as a literary context. Surprisingly, none of the nineteenth-century works considered in this book feature in Smith's collection. There are a small number of key articles on martial arts in the Sherlock Holmes canon,[44] but none look at the metaphorical significance of, for example, jujitsu or place this art within a gender context. The only literary study thus far to take such an approach is Douglas M. Catron's analysis of the function of jujitsu in relation to male bonding in D.H. Lawrence's *Women in Love* (1920). Catron argues that jujitsu 'with its ancient philosophical base and ethical code, would likely have been attractive as a symbol of the search for self-hood and wholeness [Lawrence] is depicting throughout *Women in Love* and in many other works besides'.[45] Catron provides a list of Victorian and Edwardian self-defence manuals in his footnotes; however, there is little space in his article to examine the significance of such printed material and its relation to popular fiction produced in the 1900s. I will add to Catron's study by considering how Victorian and Edwardian authors employed the self-defence scenario and martial arts to promote 'selfhood' and also to further their own political purposes.

This book shows how studying objects throws light on cultural atti-tudes towards crime and violence. Over the last ten years, the academic world has shown a growing awareness of the role of 'things' in literature. At the start of the millennium, Bill Brown coined the term 'Thing Theory'[46] and raised some pertinent questions about the way in which our conscious encounters with all kinds of objects – even the human body itself – result in the transcendence of objects into 'things'; that is, objects of strangeness. Brown's work has elicited a flurry of conferences, scholarly books and articles which have taken material culture as their central theme. While this book is not designed as a response to Brown's theory, it nonetheless works within the spirit of this burgeoning explo-ration into the adventures and contemporary perceptions of what Asa Briggs, in his classic book *Victorian Things* (1988), once called 'emissaries of the Victorian era'.

Appreciating objects deepens our understanding of a writer's creation, giving us further insights into how a work of fiction was to be read at the time in which it was produced. That an author has chosen to refer to certain objects, particularly if it is more than once, is itself worthy of our attention. This elicits a rediscovery of what these items actu-ally were. Fortunately, most of the weapons encountered in this book are displayed in museums or boxed in stores, open to the inquisitive researcher. For instance, the life-preserver is an object whose cultural meaning has become dusted over with the change in attitudes towards self-defence since the end of the nineteenth century. Being able to see this object at close range, to note its weight, size and texture and to glean information about the manner in which it was produced is invaluable. With such knowledge we can understand who would have owned certain objects and how these were perceived. Elaine Freedgood's key study *The Ideas in Things: Fugitive Meaning in the Victorian Novel* (2006) explores *Jane Eyre* (1847) and *Great Expectations* (1861) to uncover subtexts of slavery and ecological damage, anxieties which are hidden to us now but were quite possibly readily apparent to many readers of the time through the consumer items in these novels. The hardy mahogany furniture with which Jane Eyre furnishes her home (mahogany being symbolic of its owner's robust character) also cost lives in its production.[47] Since the publication of Freedgood's book, David Trotter has highlighted the need to consider at whom such anxieties were aimed, as well as the need to appreciate the changing ways in which novelists refer to items: 'The objects described in detail in eighteenth- and early-nineteenth-century novels are often objects laid low by accident or neglect.' The description of objects within the text is an apathetic pause in the plot. However, by the middle of the nineteenth century, objects became commodities and were treated with more attention. Trotter argues that a commodity 'is an object raised in and through its preparedness for exchange – its abstraction from the sensuous human activity of which it is the product – to the status of an idea'.[48] The things featured in this book, whether handmade or purchased, were commodities. They were discussed principally by male writers whose opinions on these items were directed, by and large, at the middle-class male reader. What is also important to note is that the meaning of things could be fluid. This is certainly true of the everyday items which were turned into protective shields. At the same time, other objects are dangerous to handle and illegal to purchase at auction nowadays. Through literature, we can see this increasing apprehension towards these objects, with the result that things that were once reassuring are now seen as dangerous, imperilling, rather than protecting, the owner's life. Certain objects even appear to embody sheer evil, while others in this book have been rendered preposterous objects of the satirist's imagination. Yet some of these weird implements were real items, patented and produced by named individuals to satisfy a demand for street weapons. While the existence of certain offensive weapons may inspire the conclusion that nineteenth-century British masculinity was characterized by aggression, the representation of these weapons in literature leads us to an entirely different conclusion. They are associated with states of mind and the character of their owners; however, their appearance in fiction is not only a literary device but is also prescriptive, telling us about anti-weapons attitudes. In the nineteenth century, perceptions towards the body itself were subject to revision. As Martin Wiener says: 'In the modern world, one of the most fundamental obstacles to social order and peace has been the nature of males.'[49] From being a site of anxiety, the masculine body was restyled into – contradictory as the term appears – a highly defensive non-weapon, its movements declaring a new mode of thinking about problems of vulnerability in the urban space. Therefore, the things and commodities discussed here are not only ideas, but are sometimes also ideals.

Part I of this book examines the depiction of bourgeois masculinity in hitherto neglected plays written in response to the garotting panics during the mid-Victorian era. Gay argues that acts of aggression were shaped by the need to invigorate middle-class masculinity through physical exertion.[50] Although he does not devote any space to the garotting panics, these moral scares are excellent examples of the manufacture of hatred towards the Other, accompanied by an initiative to stir the pedestrian into action. This section of the book compares these farces alongside satirical portrayals of overly armed civilians in the periodical press to argue that the over-use of weaponry is frequently linked to masculine hysteria. At the same time, I juxtapose such an analysis with a study of the emergence of the assertive non-violent English bourgeois. In summary, this part demonstrates that the literature produced during the 1850s and 1860s occasioned an interest in non-armed self-defence which continued into the beginning of the twentieth century.

Anthony Trollope's two Palliser novels, *Phineas Finn* (1869) and *Phineas Redux* (1874), are the focus of Part II. These novels have been considered to be the most political works of the whole Palliser series, as a large part of the plot revolves around parliamentary events in the late 1860s. However, it is clear is that while Trollope was deeply absorbed in political matters, he also found the problem of personal danger compelling and he not only used it to add extra suspense to his novels but centred the plot around encounters with the darker side of human nature, drawing a link between the management of aggressive impulses with the entitlement to vote. What emerges from his interweaving of mid-Victorian political and social themes is an exploration of the kinds of violent encounters in which, in his opinion, the mid-nineteenth-century man could find himself. He then offers a vision of an ideal of masculinity in which not only self-control but also charisma and self-expression are the key virtues. In *Phineas Finn*, Trollope tells his male readers how to respond to threat, but in the sequel he elaborates on the consequences of resorting to weapons for self-defence. He has much to say on the possible causes of violence between men, laying the perpetration of violent acts on a lack of character and manliness. He certainly complicates the demarcation between the man of blood and the 'reasonable' man, showing how a man's character could change for better or worse. Furthermore, he temporarily sacrifices his hero in order to underline the importance of the measured response to aggression. Ultimately, Phineas's use of a popular street weapon – ironically termed a 'life-preserver' – almost ends in his own death.

The Sherlock Holmes canon is more than a set of narratives about the investigation and solving of crime with all the attendant pleasures of detective fiction. As Part III shows, the adventures are also a collection of lessons expressive of Doyle's views on reasonable force in response to violent crime. A cultural shift from the use of weaponry to the employment of physical strength and prowess is reflected in Doyle's Sherlock Holmes stories. The types of martial arts Holmes employs were very popular around the turn of the twentieth century and their inclusion in the stories hints at Doyle's involvement with the 'physical culture' community. Doyle shows how the middle-class gentleman could flaunt his superiority over the aggressive criminal using the 'art' of self-defence in which the hero's masculinity is underscored by his powers of improvisation and the gracefulness of his defence. Victorian and Edwardian articles on boxing, jujitsu and other forms of self-defence tell us about the operation of these arts, their mode of execution and the principles on which they are based. In five adventures Doyle promotes the cause of measured self-defence. 'The Adventure of the Speckled Band' (1892; hereafter 'ASB') depicts Holmes as the antithesis of the man of blood, yet his assertiveness disqualifies him from being merely categorized as Wiener's 'peaceable home Englishman'. Seen against a backdrop of gun crime perpetrated from the 1880s onwards, 'The Adventure of the Empty House' (1903; hereafter 'AEH') and 'The Valley of Fear' (1914–15; hereafter 'VF') delineate the worst excesses of firearms use, while in 'The Adventure of the Solitary Cyclist' (1903; hereafter 'ASC') Doyle explores the possibilities of boxing for personal protection. This adventure questions the use of even regulation firearms, while 'The Adventure of Abbey Grange' (1904; hereafter 'AAG') gives a favourite self-defence weapon a bad name. The keynote to this section is 'AEH'. Holmes dies in 'The Adventure of the Final Problem' (1893; hereafter 'AFP'), with, as the *Daily News* put it in December 1893, 'his name ringing in men's ears'. In 'AEH' he is resurrected, with a little help from an obscure martial art. As I will show, in this story Doyle indicates his support for reasonable force by describing how Holmes defeats his nemesis through the use of a mysterious martial art, 'baritsu'. Are hand-to-hand combat techniques merely another tool in his arsenal of knowledge or does their appearance in the Holmes canon reflect greater forces at work in society at the time this story was published? This question requires us to step beyond the text and consider the social context around Doyle's works. As it transpires, the curious Edwardian martial art which Holmes employs to save his own life in 'AEH' changed the face of martial arts in Britain.

Part I
The Garotting Farce: Armoured Masculinity and its Limits: 1851–67

1
Foreign Crimes Hit British Shores

The 'garotta' and the garotte

The story of England's mid-Victorian moral panic of garotting began with the gruesome death of an insurrectionist in Havana on 1 September 1851, thousands of miles from Britain. An anti-Spanish filibuster, General Narciso Lopez, had invaded the island in the summer of that year with the intention of severing Cuba from Spanish rule. However, lacking vital local support, his troops were surrounded and he was arrested and put to death by a 'Spanish' method of execution. He was seated on a wooden chair attached to a column against which his head rested, while an iron collar was passed around his neck and his face was covered. As he sat before a public audience, he would have felt the collar around his neck be screwed ever tighter and his windpipe eventually crushed. The lengthy article in the emerging American *Harper's New Monthly Magazine* in 1854 described the method of torture as 'the hateful collar', the 'fatal screw' or, as the *New York Times* called it, an 'infernal machine'.

This form of capital punishment by strangulation was known as the 'garotta' and it is from this that the verb 'to garotte' was derived. With stunning alacrity, the term became used to describe a new type of robbery with strangulation, incidents of which appeared to be becoming alarmingly frequent on British streets, particularly in London where the crime was given extra news coverage. During the nineteenth century it became increasingly *de rigeur* for the middle classes to rely on the police force for protection and the apprehension of criminals. Yet the plethora of letters to the press and the fictional depictions of the crime show that when it came to tackling the garotter, the middle classes widely believed in hand-to-hand combat. The garotting panics have been frequently studied by crime historians, with Jennifer Davis's 1980 article on the outbreak of the 1860s and Rob Sindall's book *Street Violence in the Nineteenth-Century: Media Panic or Real Danger?* (1990) being the standard works on the subject. However, there has not yet been an attempt to consider the panics from a literary angle, an approach which shows why the panics commanded such attention during the 'Age of Equipoise'. As I will show, the garotting scares sparked debates about the nature of middle-class heroism which preoccupied prominent novelists and playwrights until the end of the nineteenth century.

The execution of Lopez occurred at a time when the public was readily encouraged to associate images of Spanish history with brutality. Crime by strangulation was obviously not new to 1850s Britain. An entry in the *Oxford English Dictionary* from 1622 demonstrates that the term 'garotte' had been used in the English language prior to the garotting panics. The Victorian periodical *Notes and Queries* traced strangulation back to the criminal activities of seventeenth-century street rogues, while the *OED* provides an example of a garotting from 1622: 'Throwing a cord about his necke, making vse of one of the corners of the Chayre, he gaue him the Garrote, wherewith he was strangled to death.' From the early 1850s the garotte was no longer a stationary object confined to the torture chamber and, as the meaning of term became more fluid, the danger of strangulation found its way onto the streets.

Journalists understood the potent effect of drawing a link between crimes and methods of torture and so, in the wake of Lopez's execution, the word 'garotting' made increasingly frequent appearances in the press. Detailed descriptions were given in the British and American papers of the Spanish 'garotta', which appears to have been both a method of torture and execution. Pain and torture were emphasized in the depictions of garotte attacks in Britain. The first known reference to violent robbery with strangulation as a garotting occurred on 12 February 1851, when the Great Exhibition was in full swing and Hyde Park glittered majestically, showcasing Britain's industrial and imperial pre-eminence. The startled lawyer James Brockbank warned *The Times* that 'an application of this human garrotte to an elderly person, or to anyone in a bad state of health, might very easily occasion death'. By the December of that year, *The Times* noted that the 'frequency of these attacks' was causing 'great alarm to the inhabitants'. C.J. Collins's *The Anti-Garotte: A Farce in One Act* of 1857 depicted the link between newspaper reportage and the heightened awareness of crime. As Collins's character, Commodore Rattlin, told audiences at the Strand Theatre that Spring: 'I'm sick of reading in the newspapers about this system of garotting as it is called. One can't take up a newspaper but one is sure to meet with half a dozen letters from poor scribes about the frights they suffer in going home at night.'[1] In a later but unlicensed play set in Kentish Town, *The Garotters* (1873), the protagonist of the piece, William Whiffles, reads a newspaper and immediately exclaims: 'It's truly dreadful – its its [*sic*] horrible! The Garrotte [*sic*] robberies seem to stand alone – enough to shake the strongest nerves.'

At first glance, it is curious that the garotting outbreaks occurred in the 1850s. After the threat of Chartism had passed, levels of violent crime appeared to be declining and an era of optimism was ushered in, symbolized by the Great Exhibition.[2] Yet the execution of Lopez took place just before the virtual cessation of transportation to the colonies in 1852 (Western Australia still took a number of convicts). The highly controversial Penal Servitude Act of 1853 allowed a greater number of convicts to be given 'tickets of leave', conditional pardons on grounds of good behaviour, which resulted in their being released at the end of their term not on Australian soil but in Britain. The terms 'garotter' and 'ticket-of-leave man' soon became conflated. It was alleged that garotting – used as a method by which to subdue prisoners – was learnt by ticket-of-leave men onboard convict ships who had personally experienced its effects. The general belief was that the men practised this technique on each other. A commentator on the penal system, Thomas Barwick Lloyd Baker, later remarked on garotting panics of the 1860s that the appeal of garotting among convicts was that it could be easily learnt in one week.[3] This was an apprenticeship of a ghastly character.

At the end of the first garotting panic, the Chaplain of Pentonville Prison, Reverend Joseph Kingsmill, described a garotte attack for the benefit of the readers of *The Times* in January of 1857:

> Sir, – it may be of some service to the community at large to be told how garotte robberies are usually perpetuated, and how best prevented. The robbers work in a gang, which consists generally of three persons. The tallest and most muscular comes from behind the intended victim, and, rapidly throwing his arm around the neck, presses the throat almost to strangulation. The others rifle the pockets and otherwise assist.

It seemed therefore that this form of street violence was not spontaneous, but was choreographed or performed.

Published near the end of the panics, Henry Wilkinson Holland's 1863 soberly titled feature 'The Science of Garotting and Housebreaking' offers the most detailed and therefore the most engaging account of the crime and its perpetrators. A modified version of this article, authored by Alfred Guernsey, was also adapted for American readers in *Harper's New Monthly Magazine,* which had printed G.P.R. James's eerie description of the garotta in 1854. In his article, Holland utilizes his prior experience as a prison chaplain to persuade criminals to confess to him their methods, although his journalistic interests and loyalty to his readership predominate. The purpose of his interviews is less an attempt to rehabilitate offenders and understand their motives than an attempt to glean material for *Cornhill Magazine* on 'the most approved and successful methods of burglary and the garotte'. In 1862 Holland had written a piece for *Cornhill Magazine* on the modus operandi of professional thieves and his 'The Art of Self-Protection Against Thieves and Robbers' appeared in the religious journal *Good Words* in 1866. Holland devotes much space to listing and depicting housebreaking equipment, both entertaining and instructing his readers. In this manner, his article prefigures the catalogue of tools – panel cutters, crowbars, skeleton keys, lanterns – which Sherlock Holmes uses to break into the residence of the blackmailer Charles Augustus Milverton in Doyle's thrilling story of 1904. As *The Times* had said in 1862, the ticket-of-leave man 'took to burglary, to robbery and at length to garotting'. Thus, all these crimes were considered to be part of an offender's repertoire.

The aim of Holland's article was not to raise alarm, yet his manner of discussing the 'epidemic' of garotting was hardly likely to pacify readers. According to his findings, garotters allegedly hunted in packs of three, stalking their victim for several days in order to pinpoint the location of his residence and ascertain his daily habits. The attack itself occurred late at night. The 'first stall' walked in front of the victim and raised his hat to the other two ruffians behind him to indicate that the road ahead was clear. The 'back stall' walked near the victim, giving the semblance of ignoring him. He was followed by the 'nasty man' who stealthily crept up behind the victim, struck him on the head and applied pressure to his Adam's Apple with the paraphernalia of the garotter's trade: a handkerchief, a stick or his own wrist-bone. The 'back stall' rifled through the unfortunate man's pockets, while the 'front stall' and nasty man kept the victim incapacitated, loosening or tightening the hold on his throat to maintain a steady level of unconsciousness. Holland reminds us that it is a 'scientific operation, abundantly cruel, but not absolutely murderous' where the 'intention [is] neither to kill nor to maim'. Of course, as Holland ominously adds, the growing numbers of copycat garotters who imitated the original convicts were more likely to make mistakes, with fatal consequences.

Despite the decline in crime rates in the latter half of the nineteenth century, some types of offences appeared to be rising during the garotting panics (although this could, as a number of historians suggest, be attributed to increased police activity). In 1862 the Metropolitan Police recorded 96 robberies with violence, as opposed to 33 and 32 in the previous two years.[4] This translates to 2.2 robberies per 100,000 in 1862 as opposed to 174 in 1982, suggesting that London was a far safer place in the mid-Victorian era than a century later.[5] Yet even a glance at the papers – particularly *The Times* – suggests that garottings were occurring on a daily basis. At the same time, it was common that any form of violence involving theft was described as a 'garotte' attack, as Rob Sindall has pointed out. Nevertheless, a startling number of attacks did loosely conform to the staged garotte robberies described by Kingsmill and Holland.

Neil R. Storey's book on Victorian London concludes that garotters were mainly female criminals who, as prostitutes, gained the trust of their victims and strangled them (with the help of a male colleague) in a dark alleyway.[6] *The Times* did record a small number of garottings involving female accomplices who acted as decoys; however, the act of garotting was overwhelmingly portrayed in the popular press as a crime perpetrated by groups of men against male pedestrians. The images of male garotters and their male victims, which made a frequent appearance in the press in the mid-Victorian era, are so prominent that they can be readily found using internet search engines today. Moreover, criminals who operated during the mid-nineteenth century would not have regarded muggings involving female offenders as 'garottings'. An ex-garotter interviewed in the 1880s by the social explorer and journalist James Greenwood informed him that operations whereby the victim is fooled into following a 'prostitute' only to be attacked by her accomplice were referred to as the 'dark lurk'. I draw on what I describe as classic garotte attacks, as illustrated by two examples from *The Times*: in 1852 a clerk received a nasty Christmas present when he was seized and robbed by two men who 'held him tightly by the throat', while in May 1862 a compositor was 'grasped by the throat' as his accomplice 'rob[bed] him of all the money he had in his pocket'. These particular attacks strongly suggest the ways in which middle-class gentlemanliness was perceived as being under threat from lower-class brutishness.

The skulking garotter represented the antithesis of gentlemanliness, and this rough villain's underhand and violent actions provided the opportunity for the display of middle-class acts of heroism. The journalistic treatment of the convict would have informed the audience response to the garotter-villain. In the early 1850s and to a greater extent in the 1860s, the garotter and his crimes symbolized the untamed savagery of the British Empire. A public outcry was provoked by the way in which offenders were allowed to roam the streets with tickets of leave and perpetrate ghastly attacks on law-abiding citizens. Ticket-of-leavers were unsurprisingly depicted as boorish, ungainly and unintelligent. The caricature was so well known that in 1857, social explorer J. Ewing-Ritchie could allude to a group of public house regulars possessing 'a nasty ticket-of-leave look'. The ticket-of-leaver excited interest among mid-nineteenth-century journalists and writers including George Augustus Sala and Henry Mayhew.[7] Charles Dickens appears to have been interested in the crime and its victims. He included lengthy articles on garotting and thuggee in *Household Words* and *All the Year Round*, which he ran until his death in 1870. At the end of the nineteenth century there are references to garotting and garotters in the works of Greenwood in *The Policeman's Lantern* and Doyle's 'The Adventure of the Empty House'. Furthermore, the prolific American playwright and journalist William D. Howells expressed an interest in the panics, shown by his play *The Garroters*, which was staged in the late 1890s (the British Library keeps an edition of this play, published in 1897). During that time, he was writing editorial pieces for *Harper's New Monthly Magazine* and may have been aware of Alfred Guernsey's article on garotting. The play was written in 1885 and the London performance of the play was renamed *A Dangerous Ruffian*. George Bernard Shaw found the farce 'quite amusing', but other reviews deemed it 'wholly destitute of ingenuity of construction'. It was, perhaps, not the high point of Howells's career.

Thuggee

Dissatisfaction with the ticket-of-leave system was articulated through imperial imagery. In the mid-Victorian era, the violence of the Empire, in the form of robbery with strangulation, was brought to the doorsteps of the ordinary British civilian. The manner in which this invasion was depicted served to encourage a strong verbal and physical response. During the winter of the 1862–3 panic, *The Times* quotes one reader who argues that 'to go into the streets right now was safe as going into a tiger's den'. In an article on garotting in December 1862, *All the Year Round* claims that the London streets are filled with tigers, 'specimens of the true Bengal breed'. The professional City gentleman was thus considered an innocent victim, while the garotter was represented as wild and scheming.

British journalists readily linked garotting to the religiously-motivated form of robbery practised by the Indian cult of thuggee, in which death by strangulation preceded the act of theft. The term was derived from the Hindu word 'thag', meaning 'deceiver'. Garotters were, alleged the *Globe* in November 1856, 'street Bedouins [who] lurk[ed] in the highways', while it appeared to *The Times* in the same month that the 'metropolitan and provincial Thugs' were intent on waging a 'predatory war against society'. A parliamentary debate reported in *The Times* in 1857 revealed that it was widely considered that 'the new species of offence', garotting, was more 'allied to the Thug system than anything else'. This is what Guernsey also hinted to his readers. The activities of thuggee involved the murder and robbery of travellers in India. The taking of life was not viewed as murder but as a sacrifice to the goddess Kali. Once the act was committed, the victim's body was disposed of by burial or it was thrown into a well. Thugs did not carry weapons but instead became adept at using a scarf (the rumal) to choke the victim and were therefore known as Phansigars, or 'noose-operators'. Like garotting, thuggee was perpetrated by gangs of criminals who were co-opted into the practice, although in contrast to garotting, the cult of thuggee was much more extensive and was governed by large networks. Thuggee had posed a significant challenge to the British administration of India in the early nineteenth century. The practice was successfully eradicated by the 1840s under the aegis of Major William Henry Sleeman, 'hero of the Raj', who was responsible for the capture of 3,000 thugs. The exact number of fatalities is a moot point. In 1933 Sleeman's grandson, James Sleeman, calculated the death toll to be one million; however, the historian Mike Dash has recently posited a slightly more conservative estimate of 50,000. Dash's theory is based on the premise that thuggee was not in existence until approximately 150 years before the extensive manhunt supervised by Sleeman.[8]

Despite the suppression of thuggee, popular culture, mainly film and fiction, has fuelled a fascination with the cult which continued in the twentieth century. An example of the garotta can be seen in the film *The World is Not Enough* of 1999, in which the villainess tortures James Bond with the device. This was not Pierce Brosnan's only experience of being garotted. Eleven years earlier, in Nicholas Meyer's lesser-known *The Deceivers*, Brosnan's character, William Savage, is a British thuggee hunter and learns the art of manipulating the rumal from its exponents. As Meyer emphasizes, the anti-thug Christian mission in India was rapacious: by desisting from killing Feringhea's son, Savage has condemned him to a life of playing the servant to British officers, yet Meyer condemns the cruelty of the thugs and the slyness of their leader, Feringhea, and his filial protégé. This depiction of the Phansigars was in keeping with the presentation of thuggee in the nineteenth-century press. Thuggee had caused a stir in the 1830s and 1840s with the *Illustrated London News* providing detailed accounts of the crime. *Confessions of a Thug* (1839) by Captain William Meadows Taylor, a resident in Hydrabad during the anti-thug campaign, was published to great critical acclaim at the beginning of Queen Victoria's reign. Based on Feringhea, the novel's anti-hero, Ameer Ali, robs and kills for his own gain. Ali tells the reader that for him the taking of human life is mere sport, and he exploits and murders those who show him kindness. He is shown to exploit and murder those who show him kindness. Feringhea also appears in Eugène Sue's bestseller *The Wandering Jew* (1844), where he is portrayed as devious, sensual, 'half-feminine' with 'delicate joints' that hide 'muscles of steel'. The Indian thug-murderer concealed his power, unlike the British boxer whose strength could easily be read on his body, as an extract from *Tom Brown's Schooldays* suggests: 'Tom [...] though not half so strong in the arms [as Slogger Williams], is good all over, straight, hard, and springy, from neck to ankle [...] you can see by the clear white of his eye, and fresh bright look of his skin, that he is in tip-top training.' The thug's strength is hidden and this characteristic suggests he does not play 'fair' as it were.

Household Words described thuggee to lower-middle-class households in November 1857. To readers who had read Reverend Kingsmill's description of a garotte attack in *The Times* in January that year, it was instantly apparent that thuggee differed from garotting in one key aspect: 'There was the unsuspecting traveller with his bundle; the decoy Thug, who engaged him in conversation; the two men, who at the given signal, were to seize; the executioner, standing behind with the handkerchief, ready to strangle the victim.' The 'executioner' was a sinister addition to the garotte formation. Unlike garotting – where murder was not the intended outcome of the attack – death through strangulation was an integral process of a successful thug attack. *Household Words* alleged that 'it is a part of a Thug's religion not to rob a live body' and that 'the crime of murder must precede that of theft'. It was this casual attitude towards death that still excited a shock of repugnance in the British press during the 1850s, a decade after the suppression of thuggee. In an interview with a young former thug, a journalist writing for *Household Words* demonstrates to readers that the thug feels no remorse. His interviewee tells him that 'Heaven will hold us all, Sahib'. The journalist cannot 'reason with' the young woman but gives up, realizing that the interviewee takes pride in the fact that she has killed 21 people. While an effort is made to interact with the thugs, they are still portrayed as remorseless killers, whose values are opposed to those espoused by the white, British, Christian readers of *Household Words* over the sanctity of life and the respect for private property. This portrayal was in harmony with Charles Trevelyan's earlier assertion in the *Quarterly Review* of 1837 that: 'If we were to form a graduated scale of religions, that of Christ and Kalee would be the opposite extremes.'[9]

The mode of killing involved in thuggee and its purported relation to garotting was extensively examined in the periodical press. Against a background of mounting tension in India, the Chaplain of Newgate famously persuaded the British Museum in early 1857 to remove displays of figures engaged in thuggee from public view to prevent British criminals from learning the art for themselves. *The Times* quotes the Chaplain's words:

> I have often thought, and still think, that the origin of garotte robberies took place from the exhibition of the way the Thugs in India strangle and plunder passengers, as exhibited in the British Museum. However valuable as illustrations of Indian manners such representations may be, I could heartily wish that these models were placed in some more obscure position, and cease to be that which I fear they have been, the means of giving to men addicted to crime and violence an idea how their evil purposes may be accomplished.

The same statement was reprinted in *Household Words* in the spring and its large readership would have been aware of his concern that thuggee could infect the minds of British criminals.

2
The Ticket-of-Leave Man

Contagion of crime

A poem that appeared in *Punch* in December 1862 entitled 'The Song of the Garotter' expresses the way in which garotting was equated with underhand thuggee:

> H, meet me by moonlight alone,
> And then I will give you the hug,
> With my arm round your neck tightly thrown,
> I'm as up to the work as a Thug.

The illustration to *Punch*'s song highlights the vulnerability of the individual. As Jennifer Davis notes in her classic study of the 1860s garotting panic, '*Punch* added a biological dimension to the composite picture being drawn of the dangerous classes (thirty years before Cesare Lombroso) by invariably portraying convicts in its cartoons as beetle-browed, simian-featured louts'.[1] In the illustration, the characters of the sinister and even carnivorous garotter and the fragile, somewhat foppish, gentleman pictorially prefigure H.G. Wells's predatory, chthonic Morlocks and decadent Eloi in his novella *The Time Machine* of 1895. As Daniel Pick notes of the 1870s, the 'condition of England question was now centrally concerned with the condition of the English body'.[2] Yet such apprehensions were very much alive in the 1850s and early 1860s, as demonstrated by the illustration in *Punch* (which is representative of many such images). The obsession with masculine fitness and the health of the nation was quite likely responsible for stoking the fascination with street violence, despite the downturn in crime which historians have observed.

At the same time, images from melodrama were deployed in the creation of the garotter-villain on stage. Jennifer Jones shows how actors playing the villain on the Victorian stage would blacken their faces and apply wrinkles, which though they 'may seem a strange characteristic for a villain' were 'thought to be the traces left on a face that was perpetually fixed in the expression of anger or hatred'.[3] She has related this observation to Watts Phillips's portrayal of villainy in *A Ticket of Leave: A Farce in One Act* (1862) – the only secondary reference to the garotting farces – in which Quiver declares of the appearance of a guest who he suspects is secretly a ticket-of-leave man: 'What a farce – there's a criminal in every wrinkle, and it's full of them!'[4] The extract from the play also suggests that the image of the sinister, frowning garotter (an impression created by the media) possibly found its way onto the stage. The concern with degeneration, heightened by elements of melodrama, sparked a culture of self-defence, a manly response to a danger that was perceived not only to emanate from further down the social scale but also from abroad. The attempt to conjure up and then physically contain foreign and antiquated forms of violence was apparent in Watts Phillips's farce: 'Servants are the vipers we warm in our bosoms [...] "There are traitors in your house! You have a Guy Fawkes in your cellar!" [...] The reign of terror is inaugurated, and garotted or guillotined, what does it matter?' These acts of violence stood in contrast to new middle-class ideals of civilized behaviour and were the 'shadows' of bourgeois refinement.[5] Through humour, the author invites his audience to link garotting to images of revolutionary violence in order to incite unease in the minds of his audience that the disturbances initiated by the aggressive lower classes, the ticket-of-leavers, could have far-reaching effects if unchecked.

In the winter of 1862, readers of *All the Year Round* were invited to 'consider the great analogy between crime and disease' and, like the *Illustrated London News*, to adopt the view that 'like disease, [crime] occasionally takes an epidemic form'.[6] Crime has often been likened to a disease, an attack on the 'body politic', but the metaphorical link between sewage and disease to garotting was a particularly explosive synthesis during the mid-1850s and early 1860s. The garotting panic surfaced in the wake of the cholera outbreak of 1854 and the Great Stink of 1858, when the causes of crime as well as the causes of cholera were repeatedly debated. Julia Kristeva has famously argued that an abject object which has been cast out can haunt the perpetrator of its expulsion. Building on Kristeva's theory, Anne McClintock's *Imperial Leather* posits that abject zones of conflict and social groups can represent abject objects.[7] McClintock's observation can be readily applied to an examination of press depictions of ticket-of-leave men. Here the ticket-of-leave man is clearly envisaged as belonging to an abject group. His arrival on British shores is framed as a return of bodily waste to the origin of its expulsion, the British body politic. In 1856 *The Times* argued that the return of convicts to the streets of London was comparable to the way that 'the garbage and other horrors' that are disposed of 'on the Thames with the ebb [...] revisit our metropolis with the flow, making day hideous'. *All the Year Round* particularly exploited public concerns in order to alert readers to the gravity of the crime of garotting and sell more copies in the process. In autumn 1862 *All the Year Round* protested that Australia, the 'useful drain' into which convicts could be 'flushed', had sent its waste back to Britain, 'much as the tide sends our London pollution back by river every six hours'. Therefore, the nightmare image of expelled waste returning to the shore is symbolically related to recurring cholera outbreaks. A particularly violent epidemic preceded the first garotting panic in 1854. In the 1850s medical authorities believed the cause to be 'miasma' emitted by decaying animal and human waste. In October 1862 *All the Year Round* likened prisons and Houses of Detention to hospitals, while the ticket-of-leave man/garotter was described as a 'plague to himself and to every one else', with the potential to 'infect' British citizens. Holland particularly favoured such imagery when he discussed the science of garotting and housebreaking: 'A few years ago the garotte broke out suddenly, like a new plague, infested the streets with danger, infected the community with half-shameful apprehensions. [...] The epidemic has come upon us again, and we are just as unprepared and as helpless as before. The doctors who are appointed to regulate our social system are taken by surprise, and the public dread has almost become a panic.' The threat to public safety is magnified by the way in which the infrastructure erected to handle outcast groups is depicted as being at breaking point.

Some attempt was made to portray ticket-of-leavers as human beings and to comprehend their difficulties on returning to Britain. Henry Mayhew convened a meeting with ticket-of-leavers in 1856 for the men to 'say a word to society'. The accounts given by ex-convicts regarding, for instance, the difficulties in finding work or false re-arrest were then discussed by Mayhew in *The Times*. However, Mayhew's account is mediated by his own perceptions. His account of the meeting is nonetheless the closest we come to hearing working men's opinions on a subject relating to the garotting panics, but his portrayals were not always sympathetic to the ticket-of-leaver. The fourth volume of *London Labour and the London Poor*, published in 1862, contains a 'narrative of a returned convict'. The excerpt describes the process of garotting not through the third person, but through the eyes of a convict who maintains that he is an honest character. He describes stalking his victim for several weeks in the City. One 'dark wintry' and 'very stormy' night, the convict and his accomplices follow the victim 'to a quiet by-street by London Bridge then "garotte" and "plunder" him of his bag'.[8] Therefore, by using imagery and language associated with the garotte attack, the writer John Binney authorizes the typical depiction of the violent and ruthless garotting criminal as expressed in *Punch*'s 'The Song of the Garotter'. The convict might describe himself as 'honest' and reformed, but the account given in Mayhew's *London Labour* invites the reader to draw the conclusion that the convict and the garotter are one and the same man.

The contradictory attitude towards the ticket-of-leaver is reflected in two nineteenth-century plays which were written during the garotting panics. Tom Taylor's well-known nineteenth-century play *The Ticket-of-Leave Man* (1863) aimed to highlight society's prejudice towards reforming criminals who were trying to struggle towards a livelihood. In the process, he hoped to encourage sympathy with the mid-Victorian convict. Taylor was a civil servant, lawyer and contributor to *Punch* during the garotting panics, and he could not fail to have been struck by the negative press surrounding the ex-convict. He brought his knowledge of the law and his journalistic experience into practice, guaranteeing the audience a heady theatrical experience. His play is concerned with the rehabilitation of Robert Brierly, duped into a forgery scheme by the miscreant of the piece, Dalton, and wrongfully sentenced to transportation. *The Ticket-of-Leave Man* is one of the most famous melodramas, appearing in the Olympic Theatre in 1863 and playing for an impressive 407 nights.[9] The BBC radio play was broadcast in 1937 and the stage play was revived by the Victoria Theatre, Stoke-on-Trent in 1966. Its initial run exceeded 400 nights. Henry Neville, the actor who played Brierly, made his name with this role, playing it until his retirement in 1910. However, as Watts Phillips's play shows, it was not the first to take the ticket-of-leave man as its central theme. There were also flaws in the plot. According to the June 1863 edition of the *Athenaeum*: 'He has not exactly firmly stated the case, for his hero is an innocent man, who has been unjustly accused, and is, accordingly more "sinned" against than "sinning".'[10] Like Oliver Twist, Taylor's hero is a good character who is thrown into a bad situation. As he is innocent, he is also not a typical convict. Moreover, the presence of the play's villainous ex-convict only serves to underline popular stereotypes of the duplicitous ticket-of-leaver.

This was certainly the case with Phillips's now obscure *A Ticket of Leave* (1862) which, in view of its portrayal of the convict, may have inspired Taylor's piece. Phillips wrote 25 plays, including a stage adaptation of *Barnaby Rudge* in 1866. *A Ticket of Leave* was his only farcical piece. A number of his works, including *A Ticket of Leave*, found their way into *Lacy's Acting Edition of Victorian Plays,* which was very popular with the amateur market and was used by provincial theatre companies, which put on productions after the London showing. Phillips's appearance in Lacy's publication suggests that his work was considered to have commercial merit. It certainly enchanted the audience at the Adelphi and was advertised in the *Illustrated London News* and given a highly favourable review in *The Age We Live In,* which excitedly described it as a 'real roaring farce'. Although only appearing between December 1862 and February 1863, the play was performed at the Adelphi 61 times, which, compared to other plays of that year, was a generous airing.

A Ticket of Leave is set in a middle-class household in Clapham which is invaded by both innocent and guilty ticket-of-leavers. The miscreant of the play is known as Bottles who, disguising himself as a butler, plans to garotte and rob his master, Mr Aspen Quiver, whose nervous disposition can be readily guessed by his name. The actor who played Quiver, John L. Toole, delighted reviewers with his portrayal of a crazed civilian who is 'all of a tremble'. While the farce ridicules Quiver's terror, the presence of Bottles makes clear to the audience that fears of encountering malevolent criminals in one's private space are not unfounded. Bottles is prevented by a convict, Thomas Nuggetts, who has been wrongly transported and, in another comic turn, reveals himself as Mrs Quiver's cousin. Like Tom Taylor's more sombre play which graced the stage of the Adelphi a year later, Phillips's farce failed to redress common misconceptions of the ticket-of-leaver. Nuggetts's inherent good character is justified by his blood ties with the middle class, while Bottles, whose diction betrays his lower social standing, is beyond reform. The hero saves the day in this lighthearted play, although Bottles contributes some sinister, valedictory advice: 'Dear Brethren, here's as how you'll forgive me my many transgressions and I'll promise to meet you every day not only here but at your own house if you'll give me a ticket of leave.' These words were significant. Henry Holland's *Cornhill Magazine* article had focused on exposing the arts of the housebreaker and the garotter; in Phillips's play, garotters and burglars are one and the same person. *A Ticket of Leave* appeared in the same year as what is arguably the most famous garotte attack, the assault and battery of the Member of Parliament for Blackburn, Hugh Pilkington, in July 1862. I will discuss this incident in further detail in Part II, but it is sufficient to point out that the event effectively relaunched the danger of garotting in the public mind.

At the time when *A Ticket of Leave* was shown in the theatre, calls for the return of transportation were issued in *The Times* and Joshua Jebb, the Director of Prisons, desperately attempted to express his support for the ticket-of-leave system and to exonerate the ticket-of-leave man of the crime of garotting. Public opinion was against him. In December 1862 a Royal Commission on Penal Servitude and Transportation was set up by George Grey which, as Sindall tells us, led directly to the passing of the Penal Servitude Act of 1864.[11] Also stemming from these initiatives was the draconian Security Against Violence Act which was passed in July 1863 and stipulated that offenders guilty of garotting be punished with 50 strokes of corporal punishment over and above other penalties meted out to perpetrators of violent robbery. Widespread indignation was so successfully fomented that the laws passed in the 1860s remained in force until the twentieth century. Jennifer Davis adds that apart from assaults upon the monarch, only robbery with violence was punishable by whipping, which, she argues, suggests how grave the threat of garotting was considered to be by law-makers and the public.[12] In the original script submitted to the Lord Chamberlain, Bottle's words form the last lines of the play, but in Lacy's version it is Quiver who is permitted to close the play, stating his confidence in the work done by Richard Mayne, the Commissioner of the Metropolitan Police Force, and expressing his doubt as to Bottles's entitlement to a ticket-of-leave. As *The Times* had announced that August: 'An end must be put to the present mode of granting tickets-of-leave.' The message is therefore that the state and individuals should fight against rather than understand the criminal and that they could, by force of public opinion, destroy the ticket-of-leave system. To listen to the pleadings of Bottles and his ilk would be very risky indeed.

Garotters and their prey

Tom Brown's Schooldays is generally considered to be representative of popular notions of middle-class physical capability, promoting the idea that the English gentleman was expected to be able to defend himself with his fists if called on to do so, to 'speak up, and strike out if necessary for whatsoever is true and manly, and lovely, and of good report'. As Dennis W. Allen observes, the athletic body becomes 'a class body, the body of the bourgeoisie', and symbolizes Englishness.[13] Quite possibly,

Thomas Hughes attempted to redress the problem that, as Antony Simpson has observed of the 1840s, spontaneous outbursts of valour were not associated with the middle class. By contrast, 'heroic reputations are built upon rare public exhibitions of courage and coolness, and impose no strictures regarding appropriate conduct between wars, duels, or brawls'.[14] Concerns persisted over the middling man's inability to protect himself, a worry which was apparent in the sheer number of sensational press depictions during the garotting panics of mainly middle-class victims. However, when it did come to self-defence, there were, at this time, no 'strictures' as to how a man responded to crime.

This point was pressed home in a satirical and fictitious piece written by a garotter, 'A Retired Practitioner of the Science', which appeared in *Fraser's Magazine* in 1863. While darkly humorous, the piece is nonetheless a serious tract on the benefits of exercise for self-defence: 'When I behold a sleek and pursy city magnate with a heavy watch-chain and jingling pockets, I say to myself, "Here is a business-grazing, profit-ruminating animal that can neither fight nor run, and who insults the harmonies of nature and outrages the fitness of things by carrying valuables".' The street becomes the site of a 'struggle for existence' against the 'pecuniary phlebotomist', an observation well-timed to coincide with the publication of Charles Darwin's *The Origin of Species* only four years earlier. In an 1864 article on rooks and herons, *All the Year Round* used the theme of garotting (by then well known) to describe the 'dishonest' behaviour of birds of prey: 'The crows attacked the heron from three opposite points: one from above darted down on his head; a second assailed him in front, or sideways; and the third, from behind, seized the outstretched feet of the heron, and turned him topsy-turvy.' This, of course, echoes the observations of Holland and Kingsmill. The message was that 'garotting is always, among birds as among men, a cowardly and rascally business', a neat comment on the perceived similarities of street crime to the struggles in the natural world. As Samuel Smiles said in *Self-Help*, also published in the same year as Darwin's trailblazer: 'An easy and luxurious existence does not train men to effort or encounter with difficulty; nor does it awaken that consciousness of power which is so necessary for energetic and effective action in life.'[15] In *Fraser's Magazine* the garotter is presented as a vampire, preying on the life-blood of the economy, stalking individuals who have become flabby grazing animals, meat for the brutes and the streetwise. Therefore, in what appeared to be a Darwinian struggle for existence, the lowly criminal was gaining ground.

Victims were overwhelmingly male and middle class, although other victims, namely working-class men and women, have been omitted from research. There are few examples of working men falling prey to the garotter's hand – a sailor, a scissor-grinder, a labourer and a power-loom weaver. Additionally, crime studies have not paid attention to the representation of female victims. This was because, as the press reports suggest to us, garotting was a crime perpetrated mainly against men. Women are depicted as what *The Times* described as 'anxious mothers and timid daughters', praying into the small hours of the morning that the man of the house has not been garotted. In *Phineas Finn*, Robert Kennedy's wife, Lady Laura, is cast in the role of the concerned spouse. Holland attempts to convince the readers of *Cornhill Magazine* that it is unusual for a garotter to come upon a middle-class woman who is alone and carrying 'money or jewels worth the risk of penal servitude', and notes that it is 'safest altogether to allow her to go unmolested', as a woman's neck is more fragile than a man's, with the risk of causing serious injury or death. As *Cornhill Magazine* was intended to be a family periodical (suitable for women readers), Holland was most likely to be wary of alarming readers of the 'gentler sex'. According to him, a garotter would rather concentrate on temporarily stunning men who were most likely to be carrying objects of greater worth, while the criminals' aversion to attacking women could be attributed to 'some last spark of manly and generous feeling which even a garrotter might cherish'.

However, there were a small number of female victims or, rather, a small number of reports relayed to the press. During his trial in 1856, an offender confessed that he had garotted a woman, although her social status was not revealed. In the same year, the *Illustrated London News* printed a much more detailed account of an attack on two 'respectable' women. Elizabeth Bensen was walking near Southwark Bridge when she was throttled, rendered unconscious and robbed of her gold watch and other gold and silver in her possession. Surprised by the speed of her attacker, she was unable to call out and her attacker disappeared. There is no explanation of why this female victim took the imprudent decision to carry valuables about her person whilst walking on her own at night at the height of the garotting panic, but it is none-theless important to note that she is portrayed as a helpless, swooning victim, especially at a time when gender differences were emphasized.

Sindall cautions us to remember that 'the panic produced and was fed by rumours and plain fiction masquerading as fact' so that 'every attack was published as a garotte'.[16] Indeed, as the *Illustrated London News* observed in December 1862: 'Fear, of course, exaggerates the danger; nevertheless, the danger is real, and exists in fact as well as in fancy.' Despite Sindall's assertion, there were a large number of 'garottings' depicted in the press which conformed to the model outlined by Holland, forming what I will call the narrative of the garotte attack. Male pedestrians of the middle classes were considered to be more profitable targets whose very clothing and accoutrements advertised themselves. Clerks were particularly perceived to be at risk as they walked home late at night. In 1857 a group of attackers were put on trial at the Old Bailey and were sentenced to 15 to 20 years' transportation for committing a garotte outrage. Charles Hogan, a clerk at the Board of Works, was lost in the environs of Old Kent Road late one evening. He asked two local women for directions and promised to reward them with drinks and cake if they could assist him, which they did. En route, the party was approached by garotters, although Hogan was the only individual to be garotted. His statement to the Old Bailey is possibly one of the longest existing testimonies and is worth quoting at length for its dramatic and typical description:

When I went down the street, the first sensation I had was blindness; I was thrown on my back, and the sight was taken from my eyes, by strangulation; I found my tongue protruding—I do not know the cause of it; all I know is I was nearly choked; I do not know whether it was by a hand, or cloth, or cord, or what it was; before I had time to think of myself, I was on my back, and choking; I could not breathe—there were men about me; I heard their feet pattering about me—there were no words spoken until I was nearly dead, and then a man, about two yards to the right of me, said, 'Don't choke him outright'—there was a hole made in my tongue, I do not know by what means—I remember my tongue protruding, and endeavouring to scream, and I could not—there was a hole next morning; it was not quite through my tongue—it was sore for about a week; it has healed now, but there is a hole still—as soon as one of them said, 'Don't choke him outright,' I found myself relaxed from their grasp a little, and I could then breathe, but I was unable to move—simultaneously a hand went into my right hand pocket, and took my watch, and about 15*s*. in silver—I then heard them depart—nothing was said— I was unable to move; I was on my back—I lay there for about twenty minutes, I should think—I was insensible, but conscious of what had happened—one moment longer would have killed me—my impression is that one man held me by the neck, one by each arm, and one was on my breast, and I fancy that I threw that man off into the mud by my exertions—I should say I remained there about twenty minutes, but I cannot say exactly—as soon as I was able I got up and ran, and cried out, 'Police!' and 'Murder!'[17]

The press warned readers of the dangers of garotte attacks by dramatically representing the ways in which victims were physically and mentally humiliated at the hands of lower-class ruffians. A large number of attacks featured in *The Times* depict men sprawled on the ground, dis-possessed of their middle-class accoutrements, namely their watches, money and hats. Contemporary media reported various incidents; for instance, a lieutenant, a barrister and a tobacconist were robbed of their watches. A German teacher's spectacles were stolen and a prosperous merchant's spectacles were 'knocked off his face' during a garotting. In such cases the smashing of the spectacles serves as a metonymy of the victim's downfall. According to *The Times*, one 'elderly gentleman' was struck so hard on the head that 'his hat was sent some dozen yards, and that at the same moment he was seized violently by the throat and was forced backwards down on the ground'. A barrister was also robbed of his hat. According to Asa Briggs, 'the tall black hat, the "topper" […] became the indispensable symbol of good form'. Therefore, the victim's social status is undermined by the removal or destruction of the articles that identify his financial, social and possibly even his intellectual achievements.

The Times is profusely embellished with sensational images of middle-class masculinity defeated. A 'retired gentleman and invalid' was 'found in a most exhausted state' in the entry to a street; a banker's clerk, Edward Mason, was 'thrown upon the ground with great violence'. One victim was 'left lying on the ground in a state of insensibility, and his wounds bleeding fearfully', while a theatrical assistant, Joseph Simpson, was 'forced to go to the ground in a half-strangled position'. The description of Mason and Simpson being hurled to the ground as if they were defeated boxers or wrestlers in the ring suggests that the garotte attack was not just a form of assault but was also represented as a sport, a test of masculine fitness.

At the same time as the Adelphi audience was watching Mr Quiver barricade his house against garotters, the fictional 'Mr Goodman' was set upon by ruffians in a graphic tale in the pages of *All the Year Round*. Goodman is 'harmless and necessary', a man who plays a vital role in the running of the city and is therefore 'entitled to our respect in every way'. He sits at his desk all day and all week, which is why the author says that 'his muscles are unaccustomed to much exercise'. He has 'not used his fists since he was at school' and, unlike Thomas Hughes's Tom Brown, he 'knows nothing of brawls and fighting'. He bears a relation to Arthur who abhors conflict and cannot bear to see Tom fight. By his name, Goodman is a defender of family values. This is symbolized by the way in which, when he is attacked by the garotters, he vows to protect the toy horse he has bought his child in case it is broken during the attack. He would rather risk injury in protecting the trinkets of family life. However, he does not possess the physical and mental prowess to defend himself against the assailants. Goodman suffers not only the loss of his possessions – indeed, the attack does not just affect his body and mind but also his role as the provider of his family: 'His hat flies off, his umbrella springs into the air, the blood rushes into his ears, flashes of fire appear before his eyes, and as he falls backward from the effect of a heavy blow somewhere about his head, his last thoughts are of a warm liquid trickling down his face, of his wife at home, of his hat – which is a new one – of his youngest child.' The theft of the toy horse he has bought his youngest child symbolizes an incursion on the domestic home and hearth, an indirect attack on middle-class family life.

The garotter threatened the victim with the rape of cherished notions of self-help, independence and masculine self-control. However, in the journalistic account of the garotting of Edward Mason, the boundaries between symbolic and actual rape are blurred. The attack was described in *The Times* three times within the space of a winter month in 1856, suggesting not only that a large readership was exposed to the material but that journalists were interested in the case. Mason's ordeal represents a method in which lower-class violence could overpower the middle-class man: 'He resisted and kicked at them, but they forced up his over-coat, unbuttoned all the buttons of his trousers, and pulled out his shirt. While this was going on one of the men called out "Squeeze him tighter," and his neck was then pressed more forcibly and he became insensible for a short time, and when he came to himself all the men were gone.' It would be impossible to ascertain exactly what took place while Mason was unconscious. Nonetheless, the account of the way in which his clothes were pulled from his body is suggestive.

The incident – in which the victim loses consciousness – recalls the key 'nonscene' of Heinrich von Kleist's *The Marquise of O* (1808). The sexualized description of a garotting implies that through his helplessness, the victim becomes feminized and subject to dominant masculine violence. R.W. Connell has argued that 'women are unable to compete in the masculine world of violence and are not legitimate participants in the exchange of physical aggression'.[18] The clerk not only loses the battle between himself and the garotters but, furthermore, his implied violation serves to suggest that he has been rendered passive, stripped of the physical ability to compete further in the masculine arena.

The physical and psychological trauma undergone by the victim is feminized when it is alleged that Goodman will most likely suffer a form of male hysteria in response to his physical ordeal. As *All the Year Round* elaborates: 'It is long before a man recovers from such an attack. Perhaps he never entirely recovers from it. Besides the risk of actual injury to the bodily frame, there is the nervous shock, which in these cases is very severe, and not soon or easily got over.' This is perhaps hardly surprising, as *The Times* reported that in November 1855 during one garotte attack, 'a stiff but pliable noose' was 'placed round the victim's head and pulled so tight as nearly to strangle' the victim. The hole in Charles Hogan's tongue is a bizarre but tangible effect of the garotting yet, mostly, the symptoms described by victims suggest that the victims suffered from mental trauma. An elderly accountant was ill for a week following the attack, while Joseph Simpson felt pain in his throat eight days after being garotted. By the time of the trial, Edward Mason's throat was 'still sore in consequence of the injury inflicted upon him, and he frequently felt dizziness in his head, and his stomach and arms were also severely bruised at the time of the transaction'. When Henry Holland requests a jailed garotter to strangle him, he suffers a shock which lasts longer than the duration of the attack: 'The operation [...] occupied a few seconds only [...] and yet, had I been held a few seconds longer, I must have become insensible. As it was, I was wholly help-less, and my throat was not easy again, for several weeks afterwards.' Given their excessive duration, it is likely that Mason's 'dizziness' and Holland's uncomfortable throat were imaginative and post-traumatic responses to garotting. Indeed, in the farce of 1873, simply titled *The Garotters*, a paranoid gentleman grasps his throat, exclaiming he can 'feel now all the sensation of Garrotting'. Thus, Holland legitimates his account of male hysteria or 'nervous shock' by blurring his mental suf-ferings with a tangible source, pain incurred on physical confrontation with the Other.

A condition sometimes associated with fright in garotting farces was delerium tremens. There was a concern that the symptoms of shock could overspill into this mental condition. In *Men of Blood*, Martin Wiener argues that while delirium tremens was often used as a legal device for excusing male violence, a widespread aversion towards inebriated offend-ers meant that the majority of pleas were unsuccessful. Delirium tremens was considered an unmanly condition, particularly in an environment which emphasized self-control. The physical symptoms of the potentially fatal condition resulting from a sudden withdrawal of alcohol include anxiety, tremors and hallucinations. As Frank Rahill points out, on the stage, attacks of delirium tremens were often articulated by dramatic facial gestures and the affliction was used as a 'melodramatic device' to express devastation and loss of control. Certainly during the 1850s and early 1860s, the delirium tremens sufferer was made to look ridiculous. *The Garotters* of 1873 offers a good example of the way in which delirium tremens was deployed to depict unhinged masculinity. It is a badly written manuscript in which the author is clearly confused by the names of the play's characters and one wonders whether this shaky, schizophrenic submission may well have dissuaded the Lord Chamberlain's office from granting a licence. Having read the newspapers, Mr Whiffles is so terrified of being attacked or burgled by garotters that he suspects everyone to be involved in a 'grand Garrotting league'. The papers inform him that garotters have taken to disguising themselves as women. While on the way to the railway station, Whiffles mistakenly attacks his aunt and runs home believing he has indeed been garotted. From the start, we realize that he has taken leave of his senses: 'My medical adviser tells me to keep calm, very calm, and quiet. [...] Those horrible Garotters. [...] What a turn that Knock [on the door] gave me. I'm getting fearfully nervous. I hope it won't turn into delirium tremens.' He is 'all in a perspiration' and 'in such a nervous state of excitement that [he is] hardly sure [his] heads [*sic*] on [his] shoulders'.[19] John Toole captivated his audience with his 'whimsical and extravagant humour' in his portrayal of the shivers and ravings of the frantic alcoholic Mr Quiver: 'Ring the alarm bell! [...] barricade the premises – communicate with the world through the medium of the coal hole [...] Dear me, how my hand does shake, to be sure!'[20] The *Illustrated London News* was most impressed by Toole's performance: 'The excess of nervous irritability is taken on its humorous side, and thus we have a comic portrait which stands out in the midst of the dark shadows with which the dramatist has invested it.'[21] As the phrase 'dark shadows' indicates, there is a more sinister aspect to this otherwise comic play – the violence of unhinged masculinity.

3
Tooled Up: The Pedestrian's Armoury

'A danger to their owners'

'I, for one, deem it incumbent on me to protect myself in the best way that I can.' This bold statement of intent appeared in 'War to Garotters', a rousingly titled piece which was published in *The Times* in 1856, written by 'An Antigarotter'. Furthermore, in an article which appeared in *The Times* entitled 'The Noble Art of Self-Defence' in 1856, the writer who calls himself 'Tyburniensis' (which probably reflects his desire to punish and hang the criminals) reflects on the problems involved. Believing his house to be watched, he keeps a loaded revolver and carries knives and other weapons. In his article on garotting and housebreaking in *Cornhill Magazine*, Holland observed that there was 'no immediate remedy beyond the courage and caution which every man may exercise in his own defense'. It is impossible to comment on how widespread such notions were. As Sindall's book suggests, the police force was not particularly perturbed, while civilians demonstrated anxiety through an obsession with self-defence methods. Permeating a variety of periodicals and contemporary plays, the fascination with anti-garotting pursuits stemmed partly from a reluctance to rely on a seemingly incompetent police force. As Simpson's article on duelling points out, heroism was not automatically linked with middle-class values. Yet, according to his study, it is also explained by a need to create middle-class masculine heroes. The garotting panic shows that there was some confusion as to what the ideal type of bourgeois civilian gallant should be.

Despite Simpson's assertion that middle-class heroism was not apparent in the 1840s, by the 1850s accounts of both real and fictional bourgeois heroes embellished newspapers and literature alike. The garotting panic staged a clash over opposing attitudes on the nature

41

of manliness between those advocating medieval-inspired forms of defence and punishment and ideals based around the cultivation of the body. As Kestner has argued of Victorian painting, 'for the Greeks, it was the naked male that constructed masculinity; for the Victorians, it was the armoured male'.[1] This observation is certainly true of the 1850s and 1860s when discussing the influence of the Gothic revival on the construction of street weapons.

The Middle Ages had become a reference point for discussions on gentlemanliness. In the 1840s the Young England Movement, headed by Benjamin Disraeli, exemplified an aristocratic approach to the medieval era. One of the most potent symbols of this particular interpretation of the age of chivalry was the Assault at Arms tournaments, which culminated in the Eglinton Tournament in 1839. A reviewer of the Great Exhibition of 1851 wistfully told readers of *The Times* that 'the martial spirit and the showy equipment of generations that have long passed away are reproduced in miniature for the decoration of our apartments, and we, the wearers of broadcloth, who clothe ourselves in garments of sombre hue and hats of unsightly proportions, are taught to wonder at the changes which time and fashion create in the habiliments and pursuits of man'.

While street crime is usually a domestic phenomenon involving civilians and criminals, garotters and garotting were seen as an invasion; the cause of the defence of the realm was felt by some to sanction the civilian to display his own skills at arms in response to an attack on British values. The garotting panic provided middle-class professionals with an excellent excuse to clothe the desire to indulge in fancy dress of a bygone era as the necessary *duty* of tackling crime. Images of the bizarre anti-garotte weapons are well known today and are printed in classic texts such as Geoffrey Pearson's *Hooligan: A History of Respectable Fears* (1983) and Sindall's work on crime panics. Yet, far from being figments of fantasy that appear in *Punch*, many of the weapons did exist and respectable middle-class professionals were involved in their design and manufacture.

The volume of printed letters featuring anti-garotte inventions, ostensibly submitted by readers of *The Times*, suggests that the manufacture of urban armour was heavily influenced by the notion that science and technology could provide a solution to the problem of personal vulnerability. The issue of science and domestic security had been the subject of publicity events at the Crystal Palace in 1851. Firstly, a three-foot high 'wedding-cake' of locks, the Aubyn Trophy, was designed for and presented at the Exhibition. The display included a Chubb recording lock which documented attempts made to break it and a lock which shot a harpoon into the would-be lockbreaker's hand. Although an object of curiosity and decoration, the Aubyn Trophy can nevertheless be seen as a business venture, an artistic and scientific solution to the problem of crime, even if only short-lived. At the same time, Alfred Charles Hobbs's extensive feats in breaking the Chubb and Bramah locks were extensively covered in numerous articles in *The Times* in 1851, the latter taking 51 hours to crack. Therefore, an engagement with crime was transformed into a spectacle in which the ingenuity of the individual was challenged and rewarded by public appreciation.

Emily Brontë's *Wuthering Heights* (1847) has not been studied for its depiction of weapons, but the novel is nonetheless an early example of the literary depiction of the kinds of personal arms used during the garotting panics and the pitfalls of employing multiplex gadgets for self-defence. Earnshaw uses a 'curiously constructed pistol' with 'a double-edged spring knife attached to the barrel' against his enemy Heathcliff. The weapon literally backfires on Earnshaw and he is injured to the extent that he 'falls senseless with excessive pain'. Heathcliff is brutish and taciturn, and treats those around him with contempt, but it is Earnshaw's sly use of the weapon which is punished in this scene. It is likely that Emily Brontë's own childhood experience of firearms inspired her to present their use with scepticism. As Elizabeth Gaskell wrote in her 1857 biography of Charlotte Brontë and her sisters:

> Miss Brontë never remembers her father dressing himself in the morning without putting a loaded pistol in his pocket, just as regularly as he puts on his watch. There was this little deadly pistol sitting down to breakfast with us, kneeling down to prayers at night, to say nothing of a loaded gun hanging up on high ready to pop off on the slightest emergency.[2]

According to her account, Patrick Brontë's firearm 'lay on his dressing-table with his watch; with his watch it was put on in the morning; with his watch it was taken off at night'. As firearms historian Guy Wilson has shown, Brontë's obsession with firearms inspired him to submit illustrated suggestions, based on his own research into pistols used for civilian self-defence, to the Board of Ordnance for improvements in military firepower. Published in the mid-1850s, Gaskell's biography was a timely negative portrayal of the use of firearms at a time when civilians enthusiastically experimented with pistols against garotters.

Multiplex weapons were obviously not new to the nineteenth century. Catherine Dike's overlooked yet marvellous pictorial presentation of modified walking-sticks mentions pre-nineteenth-century weaponry, discussing an ornately spiked cane carried by Henry VIII. However, during the 1850s it was the manufacture, sudden abundance and media coverage of weapons carried by ordinary civilians which gave rise to excited press commentary. For Richard Sennett, 'the fear of exposure' (which he defines as a horror of injury) leads to 'a militarized conception of everyday experience as though attack-and-defense is as apt a model of subjective life as it is of warfare'.[3] Sennett's 'attack-and-defense' dynamic was readily discernible in the design of what I argue constituted nineteenth-century 'body armour'.[4] With reference to Sennett's observations on city divisions, such armour effectively walled in the civilian, protecting him from the violent attacker. The *Daily News* remarked upon the strange appearance not of medieval knights but of modern men and announced that 'no exaggeration that the most fanciful pantomime author can indulge in will caricature the armed condition of our citizens'. According to the paper, alternatives to revolvers and Bowie-knives were 'elaborate knuckle-dusters [...] containing one sharp stiletto protruding from the side [...] bludgeons that shoot out bayonets, and sticks that contain daggers and swords', arms which were 'sold more openly on the city streets than oranges and chestnuts'. How many self-defence weapons were sold is unknown, but Anthony Trollope gives an impression of their availability by also making references to popular foodstuffs. In *Phineas Redux* he writes that 'there had been a run upon life-preservers [bludgeons roughly six inches in length, which I will describe in more detail in Part II], in consequence of recommendations as to their use given by certain newspapers; – and it was found as impossible to trace one particular purchase as it would be that of a loaf of bread'.

The 'Anti-Garotte Glove or Gauntlet' was described in *The Times* in 1857 as 'a simple and effective weapon', 'patented' and 'armed with pointed steel blades, and strengthened to resist any desperate assault'. According to its maker, it was 'cheap and portable' and 'the only weapon capable of instantaneous application when in the grasp of the garotter'. It was ostensibly sold in London, Reading and Birmingham, and one of the inventors appears to have been a medical doctor from Hertfordshire. Like Patrick Brontë, Frank James Wilson Packman was a part-time weapons enthusiast. The plans for the improvements of airguns and projectiles that he submitted to the Patent Office in 1855 were approved. In 1856 he joined forces with a Charles Frederick Pike, described as a 'gentleman', and applied for provisional patent protection for the 'Armed Glove', a glove fortified with claws, hooks and blades. For an unknown reason, full protection was not granted (possibly because there were many similar devices on the market already) but the gauntlet, credited to Packman, did feature in *The Times* and *Mechanics' Magazine*.

Readers were prepared to make improvements to existing patented inventions. In February 1857 'Detector' criticizes the anti-garotte glove, most likely the one designed by Packman, which was advertised in *The Times* in January's classified section as the 'Anti-garotte glove or gauntlet'. 'Detector' argued that this much-coveted weapon failed to 'disable at a blow' and had 'the inconvenient tendency of fastening or hooking the enemy's clothes, thereby depriving the user of administering more than one blow'. It was 'a thing, indeed, that you cannot at all depend upon on a cold or wet night'. In its place he invented what he named the 'highway protector'. The writer points out that it can immediately stun the enemy in whatever position he makes the attack, as the highway protector is both a knuckleduster for striking forwards and a dirk for striking backwards or sideways. His invention therefore appears to be a Victorian design with a medieval twist. As for Packman's gauntlet, the weapon was not sold in considerable quantities and did not bestow on him the riches and fame he may have desired – in 1857 he was declared bankrupt.

One anti-garotte weapon has survived and is kept at the Self-Defence Gallery at the Royal Armouries, Leeds, which is open to the public. It was described in the *Daily News* thus: 'One belt at least has been seen the buckle of which is loaded like a pistol, and which, when a string is pulled under the coat of the wearer, will shoot anyone in front in the stomach.' This was the 'Anti-Garotter' or 'belt-buckle pistol' as it subsequently became known in gun collecting circles in the twentieth century.[5]

Figure 3.1   Henry Ball's belt-buckle pistol of 1858, Royal Armouries, Leeds.

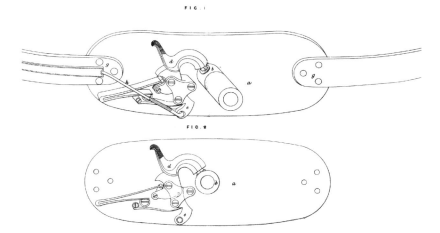

Figure 3.2   Belt-buckle pistol, patent design by Henry Ball, 1858.

A patent for this device was taken out by Henry Ball on 8 February 1858. Very little effort was required to use this weapon, yet in the hands of a gentleman who could not control his fears or his weapons, an object like the belt-buckle pistol was deadly. Its existence demonstrates that a number of proponents of self-defence believed that maiming or killing was justified in the name of personal protection. This is apparent in 1856 when a reader of *The Times*, 'An Anti-garotter', expresses his reluctance to rely on the police force and devises an alternative method of laying down the law:

> I have had manufactured the accompanying weapon, without which at night I now never stir from my house. I send it for your inspection, and you will see on examination that it is quite as efficient as either revolver, bowie-knife, or life-preserver, and that whoever comes in contact with it stands an excellent chance of coming off second best ...

The editor remarks at the bottom of the letter that 'the weapon forwarded is certainly of a very formidable nature, and likely to leave such ugly marks on any garotter as must speedily lead to his detection'. The weapon in question is designed to play a vital role in bringing the criminal to justice. Of course, such a weapon may never have existed and the article might merely have been aimed at disconcerting potential attackers. Nevertheless, all kinds of bizarre street weapons were legally permitted, although the bellicose stance and reliance on weaponry would increasingly become unfashionable as the century progressed.

The tendency for individuals to invent their own self-defence weapons is lampooned in C.J. Collins's *The Anti-Garotte*. Alarmed by newspaper reports of muggings, Commodore Rattlin announces that he will offer his niece's hand in marriage to the man who can invent the perfect anti-garotting device. The play's scientist, Datum, attempts this task, but it is ultimately the character Tomkins, an ordinary man, who crafts the contraption in his forge and wins the hand of Rattlin's overjoyed niece. In one scene, Tomkins is described as holding 'a hammer in one hand and a newspaper in the other'.[6] This spoof image suggests the compatibility of intellectualism and physical action, turning the passive act of reading into an active enterprise. While Tomkins manufactures an offensive weapon, his action is nevertheless preferable to other characters in the garotte plays. In farces such as Phillips's *A Ticket of Leave* (1862), *The Antigarotte/My Knuckleduster* (1863), *The Garotters* (1873) or Howells's *The Garroters*, the main characters over-estimate danger and react hysterically to the information they receive in the papers. Tomkins's inventive response is representative of the scientific approach to crime manifest during the Great Exhibition. The character of Tomkins symbolizes the achievement of the everyman, the individual, just two years before Samuel Smiles wrote on self-help.

In 1857 an engineer, Andrew Peddie How, had submitted an application for patent protection on his interpretation of what he called the 'anti-garotte cravat'. These items had attracted considerable attention in various circles. For instance, the Lambeth Anti-Garotting Association, active in the early 1860s, was sent letters by individuals who strongly advocated the wearing of spiked collars. One correspondent claimed that he had been garotted seven times; the only time he had forgotten to wear this device, he was throttled. However, How was unsuccessful in submitting a patent application as these weapons were already on the market to the extent that they found their way onto the London stage. While its characters are sympathetic, Collins's *The Anti-Garotte* nevertheless lampoons the armoured, neo-medieval response to garotting. Tomkins performs a chivalric endeavour and succeeds in winning the hand of the fair maiden. The audience would have seen the anti-garotte device, but the playwright does not offer us any description of the weapon. Judging by contemporary papers, 'anti-garotter' was a generic term, used to describe weapons employed against garotters. In Collins's play, the weapon is likely to be an anti-garotte collar, as we know that while Rattlin embraces

48

DO YOU WISH TO AVOID BEING STRANGLED!!

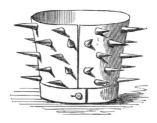

IF so, try our Patent Antigarotte Collar, which enables Gentlemen to walk the streets of London in perfect safety at all hours of the day or night.

THESE UNIQUE ARTICLES OF DRESS

Are made to measure, of the hardest steel, and are warranted to withstand the grip of

THE MOST MUSCULAR RUFFIAN IN THE METROPOLIS,

Who would get black in the face himself before he could make the slightest impression upon his intended victim. They are highly polished, and

Elegantly Studded with the Sharpest Spikes,

Thus combining a most *recherché* appearance with perfect protection f.om the murderous attacks which occur every day in the most frequented thoroughfares. Price 7*s*. 6*d*., or six for 40*s*.

WHITE, CHOKER, AND Co.

EFFECT OF THE ANTIGAROTTE COLLAR ON A GARROTTEER.

Figure 3.3 'Do You Wish to Avoid Being Strangled!!' Cartoon from *Punch*, 27 September 1856, p. 128.

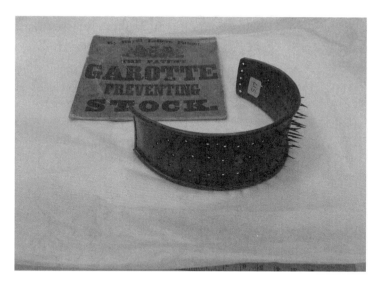

Figure 3.4 Anti-garotte collar and advertisement.

Tomkins, he is 'prickled' by Tomkins's anti-garotter.[7] In Wilson's *The Antigarotte*, A.H. Smith shows his landlady the weapon he has been concealing around his neck, a piece of 'leather filled with spikes'.[8] As *The Age We Live In* tells us, John Toole wore one during his performance as Mr Quiver, choking himself in the process. This device is first mentioned in Sindall's book and while he points out where it is kept, he does not elaborate on it. Since his book was published, the items housed in the Metropolitan Police Historical Collection have been exhumed for public viewing, now providing an engaging visual representation through weaponry and uniforms of the changes in policing through the last three centuries. A surviving example of an 'anti-garotte collar' kept at the Metropolitan Police Historical Museum shows that the stock consisted of a plate of small, thin, metallic spikes to be worn by a gentleman under a cravat at the front and held in place with a bow at the back of the neck.[9] The wearer would have held his head stiff and upright at all times in case of contact; however, self-injury was likely.

Gung-ho responses that are so radically disproportionate to the threat of violence can become targets for the comedian. The Monty Python team demonstrated this in their 1969 sketch 'Self-Defence Against Fresh Fruit', in which John Cleese plays the part of a highly-strung physical education instructor with a maniacal obsession with the dangers of fruit in all its forms. Yet, when he has one of his pupils attack him with a banana, the instructor abandons his martial arts credentials and shoots his would-be assailant. The portrayal of the over-armed male particularly delighted Victorian metropolitan audiences and readers. Phillips's *A Ticket of Leave* (1862) was so memorably hilarious that the *Athenaeum* described the play as 'one of the funniest farces ever acted'. According to *The Age We Live In*, Quiver 'takes every possible precaution against thieves or garotters' and 'follows *Punch*'s prescription by wearing an antigarotte collar and keeps a fierce mastiff; but the one nearly chokes him in the street, and the other assails his calves in the house'. His fearful disposition threatens his mental state in general. As the *Athenaeum* notes, Quiver's wife suspects that her husband is 'becoming insane, and that his excessive agitation is owing to incipient hydrophobia'. Therefore, what is a temporary crime wave can have a lasting impact on its victims.

Crawford Wilson's farce *My Knuckleduster* (1863) was, according to the *Athenaeum*, 'received with approbation' from its audience at the Royal Strand Theatre. The farce illustrates how weapons like 'antigarotte collars, revolvers and knuckledusters, without skill and courage, are mischievous only to their owners'.[10] The play revolves around the blunders that befall a Manchester traveller, Augustus Smith, staying at Highgate, London. The quiet neighbourhood unnerves him and he is in constant fear of lurking burglars. The *Athenaeum* review tells us that 'our hero sits down on the collar, and suffers from its sharp points, pricks his fingers with the knuckleduster; and is alarmed at the possible explosion of the revolver'. A satirical extract from the play argues that an impressive collection of weapons did not always result in an increased level of personal safety:

A. H. SMITH: 'I'm as full of spikes as a porcupine, (*takes off muffler, Antigarotte*). So far, so good – now for the fastening, and here it is all right (*looking at collar*) Antigarotte, they call this, what a misnomer – It has been garotting me, until my jugular, was as thick as my fingers! One must take precautions against surprise … I won't stay here alone – (*life preserver falls from sleeve*). There it goes again … my toe destroyer.

The reliance on weird anti-garotte devices was often portrayed as unmanly, weak and effeminate. The aim of this portrayal was to down-grade the activities of the men of blood who believed in using violent conflict to resolve social tension on the streets. The images employed to lampoon such fearful victims recall the depictions of women wearing defensive armour – copper bottoms – to prevent themselves from being lacerated by the London Monster, as Jan Bondeson's book on the eighteenth-century attacker shows. In 1856 *Punch* presented a humorous cartoon of a 'Mr Tremble' who wears an oversized crinoline to protect him from garotters. He is pursued by two garotters, one who sports what appears to be a life-preserver, while the other tries to strangle Mr Tremble with a piece of cloth. The caption reads: 'Mr Tremble borrows a hint from his wife's crinoline, and invents what he calls his "Patent Anti-Garotte Overcoat", which places him completely out of Harm's Reach in his walk home from the City.'[11] Mr Tremble, as his name indicates, has lost his senses and opted for a more passive form of non-physical self-defence. As he is protected by the feminizing crinoline, he has no use for the gentleman's umbrella that he carries over his shoulder!

Punch commented that in view of the garotting panic, 'gentlemen should moderate their attire' and that 'great-coats should be made a la porcupine [...] with spring daggers at the elbows and sharp spikes all up the back', the result being that 'tailors will turn armourers, and sword-makers and gunsmiths'. The magazine showed in jest how the sombre suit and the knight's armour could be combined in 'Protection of Pedestrians' of 1863. It is a picture of a pedestrian, best described as a 'shabby genteel', posing with an array of weapons with spikes attached to his arms and knees, and spurs attached to the backs of his boots. He holds a 'morning star' in his hand and there is a sword protruding out of his pocket. Around his neck he is wearing what appears to be a 'gorgette'. This latter item of attire, found in many portraits of seventeenth-century nobility, served as a way of protecting vulnerable parts of the body and was a statement of power. The cartoon boasts the inscription: 'To Garotters: "Cave Tomkins": *loq*. Let 'em try it on again, that's all.' Tomkins was the generic term for 'everyman' during this time, while an example of the phrase 'cave canum', accompanied by a mosaic of a dog to ward off burglars, can still be seen at the ruins at Pompeii today. The inscription can be interpreted as: 'Garotter: Beware of the Everyman.' Tomkins looks challengingly at the viewer, but he is over-armed to the point of absurdity and cannot be taken seriously, nor can his articles of knightly combat which, if worn individually, may have looked more intimidating.

Intended as a flamboyant homage to the glories of the medieval world, the rain-sodden Eglinton Tournament lost its lustre and inspired a general disdain for showy interpretations of the past which could not be adapted to suit the new value system of the middle classes.[12] As Girouard has observed, 'chivalry in its most fancy-dress form was still much in evidence all through the 1840s',[13] but it was mocked. The threat of violence in the 1850s and 1860s offered the Victorian gentleman an opportunity to become, using Kestner's words, an 'armoured male' and to re-enact fantasies of medieval chivalry on the labyrinthine streets of the metropolis. Tomkins is therefore representative of the way in which the medieval costume revival was taken to extremes – two decades after the 1840s. While designed with lower-class criminals in mind, the Security Against Violence Act (the Garotters' Act) 1863 followed the second Offences Against the Person Act 1861 and underlined the severity with which interpersonal violence – committed by civilians – was regarded.

Behind the humorous depictions of armoured gentlemen in the garotting farce and the satirical magazine *Punch* lay the need to characterize excessive violence as less than manly and antithetical to Britain's moral and national progress. At the same time, the concept of chivalry and the ideal of the gentleman were aspects of the Middle Ages that were reinterpreted with the expansion of Britain's middle class. The ideal of the gentleman was still heavily linked to the Middle Ages but, in contrast to the early-nineteenth-century Tory view, gentlemanliness was no longer synonymous with upper-class leisure, while knightliness became linked less with outward appearance and more with character. This is apparent in the way in which diligence and perseverance were promoted at Arnoldian public schools. By the 1850s men belonging to the professional and entrepreneurial classes who could call themselves gentlemen by attaining prosperity were sufficiently numerous to influence cultural changes. Gentlemanliness therefore became an ideal to strive towards through hard work, self-help and a commitment to show fairness to all. This shift in thinking slowly filtered into attitudes on what constituted appropriate self-defence and, as we have seen, Victorian street armour was still heavily advertised in the press and in fiction, albeit with diminishing appeal.

Urban heroes?

In *All the Year Round* in 1868, Dickens describes observing 'shirking fellows' at street corners and communicates his grudge against street ruffians as well as his displeasure at the foul language they utter. In his mind, the police were unable to do anything concrete to alleviate the problem and he concluded that 'the mass of the English people are their own trustworthy Police'.[14] In 1869, the year in which *Phineas Finn* was published as a novel, Dickens expands on his anti-garotting stance and relates to readers of *All the Year Round* his fantasies of personally tackling aggressive criminality on the streets of East London. Dickens was an admirer of the police force. When the Detective Department was formed in 1842 he often joined officers on their nightly duties in the less salubrious areas of the metropolis. 'On an Amateur Beat' explores his daydream of being a police officer and rising to the challenge of a physical confrontation with criminals:

> It is one of my fancies, that even my idlest walk must always have its appointed destination. [...] The other day, finding myself under this kind of obligation to proceed to Limehouse, I started punctually at noon. [...]
>
> It is my habit to regard my walk as my beat, and myself as a higher sort of police-constable doing duty on the same. There is many a ruffian in the streets whom I mentally collar and clear out of them, who would see mighty little of London, I can tell him, if I could deal with him physically.
>
> Issuing forth upon this very beat, and following with my eyes three hulking garrotters on their way home [...] I went on duty [...].[15]

From the eagerness with which Dickens 'eyes' the garotters and scans his environment for criminal activity, the reader is given the impression that had he been younger, he would have welcomed the opportunity to exert his physical prowess in making a citizen's arrest. Dickens's *flâneuring* pursuits offer him the opportunity to experience a sense of vulnerability in a more interactive way than is offered in the act of reading about attack and defence. As Elaine Freedgood has argued of mid-Victorian hot air ballooning, 'intense feelings of safety were experienced in an obviously dangerous circumstance'.[16] Dickens traverses all the roads on his urban excursion and does not 'leav[e] a part of it unachieved'.[17] The above extract suggests that his imagination lends him a sense of security in his hazardous quest to expiate the indulgences of comfortable bourgeois domesticity. Furthermore, both the garotting scene in *Phineas Finn* and Dickens's account are forays into urban fantasies of the suppression of violence and the punishing of 'salauds' (see below) and constitute attempts to claim the urban street for the middle-class pedestrian. Dickens portrays himself as a man of imagination, a *flâneur*, and also a would-be man of action.

The garotting farces are curiously silent on the subject of masculine gallantry – images of men behaving madly provoked more merriment than valiant heroes who used their own strength and pluck to fend off attackers. However, there were a small number of heroic pedestrians displayed in the press. Typical journalistic garotte attacks featuring victorious gentlemen correspond with a formula identified by Roland Barthes in 'The World of Wrestling' (1952). Barthes argues that, unlike boxing, wrestling is not a form of sport but a dramatic spectacle that has been scripted beforehand. Before a match even takes place, the audience can readily identify the hero and his evil adversary by appearance alone. The hero is slim and the villain, whom Barthes calls the 'salaud', is ungainly and obese. Barthes tells us that we ultimately expect the ugly wrestler to play as 'ugly' as he looks (that is, we know he will use underhand means), while the perfectly toned fighter will play fairly and suffer at the hands of the salaud, but will eventually turn out to be the winner. In the case of the garotte accounts, the garotter becomes the salaud, embodying a catalogue of mental and physical afflictions, while the gentleman represents the triumph of *mens sana in corpore sano*. The hero suffers but wins in the end. Barthes says that 'what is thus displayed for the public is the great spectacle of Suffering, Defeat, and Justice' and that 'wrestling presents man's suffering with all the amplification of tragic masks'.

In 1856, when a barrister, de Comerford Clarkson, is garotted, he still manages to attack one of the men with his fists, causing both to run away, and pursues the men. Although his attackers threaten him with stones and firearms, Clarkson, 'by the aid of a policeman', successfully 'captures' one of them, according to the *Illustrated London News*.[18] Once cornered, the captured garotter insists that he was not garotting but rather helping Clarkson. Garotters are therefore shown up as sly salauds, throwing into relief Clarkson's gallantry and honesty. Clarkson not only defends himself but plays a significant part in the arrest of these criminals, while the policeman is cast as a mere 'aid' or helper. The judge described Clarkson as 'a man of firm nerve' and even points out that 'his conduct under the circumstances in which he was placed reflected upon him the highest credit'. The Recorder at the court 'took the greatest pleasure in expressing his approbation of the courage and energy Mr Clarkson had displayed in pursuing and capturing so daring an offender as the prisoner, and that the public generally were much indebted to him for it'. Clarkson is represented not only as a model citizen, but also as the embodiment of British middle-class physical prowess. His body is therefore used to uphold the principles of the law, recalling the way in which Tom Brown uses his body as a force for protecting Arthur and the values he embodies. His hardy bravery is in contrast to Mr Whiffles's flabby vanity in the farce *The Garotters* (1873), where he is terrified of being 'garotted', 'savagely murdered' and 'cut off in the very blossoms of [his] beauty'.[19]

One of the most dramatic accounts in the representation of self-defence without weapons that pre-dates Hughes's fiction is the report of the attack on Lieutenant Bent in *The Times* in February 1857:

> On passing near the Sun-pier, he was suddenly seized by the throat from behind, and at the same instant two other men [...] appeared in front of him and commenced rifling his pockets. Although, from the manner in which he was seized and held, he was almost powerless, yet, being an athletic man, Lieutenant Bent made a determined resistance and struggled with his assailants, who, however, knocked him down, and inflicted several kicks about his head and body, one of the kicks severely injuring his eye [...] The thieves were making off, when the prosecutor regained his feet and another struggle ensued between them, but Lieutenant Bent succeeded in closing with Toole [the garotter], whom he secured, and held until assistance arrived.

As Simpson argues, 'heroism is not achieved by demonstration of ability, but by the exhibition of calm in the face of the possibly unmanageable'.[20] In the above cases, Clarkson and Lieutenant Bent exhibit not only coolness but also the ability to defend themselves without weapons.

Personal protection could test one's creative powers. In a letter to the *The Times* in January 1857, the author, named 'Self Defence', advises the reader to throw back the right leg and to entwine the limb around that of the attacker:

> By throwing the entire weight of your body towards him, no effort of his can save him from going down and you uppermost. The charm once broken, the game is your own [...] you can give the scoundrel 'a one, two for his nob' by way of refresher. This is the only defence against sudden attack to be relied upon.

Here 'Self Defence' promotes his (this is presumably a male writer) brand of personal protection. The type of defensive gesture employed recalls that used by Tom Brown against Flashman: 'Tom grasped his waist, and, remembering the old throw he had learned in the Vale from Harry Winburn, crooked his leg inside Flashman's, and threw his whole weight forward [...] then over they went on to the floor.' A key highlight is the way in which the gentleman is able to give the garotter a 'one, two for his nob'. He punishes his attacker for attempting to use methods of torture (namely garotting) usually practised on criminals. Therefore, this reader's suggestions demonstrate the way in which self-defence offers a return to the moral order.

A further example from *The Times* that month suggests a more enterprising form of unarmed retaliation to the garotte attack, the 'flying mare': 'Seize the arm placed around your neck with both hands, pull it forward, then quickly bend your face down towards your toes, and you will be astonished with what ease you throw your adversary over your head.'[21] This advice is intended for 'active m[en] with good nerve'.

One particularly apposite textual and visual source incorporates the competitive struggle between the 'reasonable man' and the 'man of blood'. *Punch* magazine's 'The Song of the Garotter' of 1862 combines both responses to garotting. The image described in the following poem was quoted twice in *Punch* and is worth examining in more detail:

Last night in walking home a skulking vagabond addressed me,
Says he, 'Pray, what's o'clock?' and, not intending any pun,
Full in his ugly face I let out my left, and floored him,
Observing as I did so, 'My dear friend, it's just struck one!'

So, ruffians all, take warning now, and keep respectful distance,
Or a bullet or a bowie-knife clean through your ribs I'll send;
Well armed, we'll straightaway shoot or stab the rascal who attacks us,
If SIR GEORGE GREY won't protect us, why, ourselves we must defend.[22]

In this poem, the 'man of blood' appears to have the last word: it is acceptable, even imperative, that the citizen respond to garotters using violence. However, it is the first stanza which really 'packs the punch'. Here the gentleman not only defends himself but also engages in physical and verbal rodomontade in a manner not dissimilar to modern superheroes in Hollywood action films in which a strike is accompanied by a humorous verbal retort. The watch – an object of desire for the garotter – is now used as a linguistic form of self-defence: the watch is not handed over, but the time is given with a verbal retort. In an illustration in the same edition of *Punch* entitled 'A Practical Application of an Old Pantomime Joke', the gentleman defends himself assertively, perhaps even overzealously. However, the image shows that he has indeed reacted gallantly to an assault in which he has been outnumbered: the gentleman has already defeated the accomplice who kneels on the ground behind him. Indeed, this example is a strong visual and literary articulation of manly self-defence and gentlemanly self-expression. However, the image, like the poem, also functions as a spoof.

While the use of weaponry was still widely advocated, the garotting panics signalled a growing acceptance of working within the limits of the civilising offensive, of an adoption of a violence-averse perspective. This is suggested by the manner in which overarming was presented as a form of hysteria. Kestner's 'armoured male' was becoming less and less a symbol of masculinity for the Victorian press during the panics, as the civilian who hid behind his armour in fear of violent robbery was perceived as less than manly. The garotting plays employ sensation and melodrama to entertain audiences, but they nonetheless also epitomize more serious preoccupations that were manifest in the press in the mid-Victorian era, namely the concerns surrounding the physical ability of the bourgeois male to defend his position in society and represent his class. Both the body and personal property were assaulted using a form of torture applied by offenders whose crimes were linked to the worst excesses of the Orient. Therefore, the onus was on the individual to protect himself physically from what appeared to be an all-encompassing attack on the social edifice.

The plays over-inflate popular anxieties to comic effect; however, with the appearance of the malevolent Bottles on stage, they instruct audiences to think that these criminals did exist and that crime panics should be taken seriously. They highlight the problems incurred by responding to crime using violence, although they offer the audience very few examples of 'civilized' and gallant behaviour. Instead, literary and journalistic explorations of the garotte attack negotiated the gap between the physical and spiritual. There is much scholarship which deals with the subject of bourgeois self-restraint, but, by contrast, the self-defence scenario, real or imagined, offered the middle-class man an exciting avenue for physical self-expression. In defending himself 'scientifically' and performing the useful duty of the citizen's arrest, the gentleman could boldly exclaim in a theatrical tone that he had 'just struck one' when faced with two or more brutish, un-British garotters. Moreover, the garotting panics highlighted the need for middle-class men to adhere to the civilizing offensive and explore modes of flamboyant self-defence in order to emphasize their mental, physical and imaginative advantage over lower-class criminals.

Part II
Anthony Trollope: Aggression Punished and Rewarded: 1867–87

4
Threats from Above and Below

Fighting for the franchise

Phineas Finn was first serialized from 1867 to 1869 in *Saint Paul's Magazine*, a publication which reflected the male-orientated interests of City professionals and was edited by Anthony Trollope himself.[1] It then appeared as a novel in 1869. *Phineas Finn* is the second in the 'Palliser' series which comprises six intertwined, political novels. As some of the themes in *Phineas Finn* are reflected in the other novels in this series, I will refer to them throughout the course of the following two chapters. Straddling the mid- to late-Victorian era, the series runs over two decades and includes the following works: *Can You Forgive Her?* (1865), *Phineas Finn* (1869), *The Eustace Diamonds* (1873), *Phineas Redux* (1874), *The Prime Minister* (1876) and, lastly, *The Duke's Children* (1880), which was published two years before Trollope's death. During his lifetime, Trollope did not devise this description for the novels. Between 1893 and 1928 Dodd, Mead and Company published the six novels under the title 'The Parliamentary Novels', but it was only in the twentieth century that the Trollopian Michael Sadleir suggested the term 'Palliser Novels'. This description was based on the fact that characters recur throughout these novels, most notably the Chancellor of the Exchequer, Plantagenet Palliser and his spirited wife, Lady Glencora. Reading the Palliser novels in order, the reader forms a long acquaintance with the Pallisers and Finn, whose lives become entangled with other incidental characters in this vast soap-operatic *roman à clef*. As Doyle later wrote in his memoirs, Trollope had 'the whole Victorian civilization dissected and preserved'.[2]

In the 1860s Trollope was at height of his fame, commanding thousands of pounds for his novels. Clearly, he had caught the public's attention, reflecting the current mood back to them in the form of fiction. *Phineas Finn* was one of his most financially successful novels in the Palliser series. This novel, together with *Phineas Redux*, offered not only escapist fiction in the form of society gossip but, like a newspaper editorial, also boasted personal commentary on key events of the day. Trollope intended *Phineas Finn* and *Phineas Redux* to be read as one novel. *Phineas Finn* is set in the years immediately preceding and including the passing of the Representation of the People Act 1867 (known today simply as the 1867 Reform Act). Against this giddy backdrop of significant historical events, we follow the fortunes of a young Irish parliamentarian as he navigates his way through the political world and has his resolve tested by the ways of English high society.

In his early twenties, Finn is offered a seat as Member of Parliament for the Irish borough of Loughshane, County Galway. Once in London, he wins the affection of the politically minded daughter of the Earl of Brentford, Lady Laura Standish, and her friend, Violet Effingham, who is an orphan and an heiress. Lady Laura reluctantly turns down Finn's marriage proposal because she is obliged to marry the wealthy but dour MP Robert Kennedy in order to help pay off the debts of her brother, the bombastic Lord Oswald Chiltern. Finn's fate is linked with Kennedy and Chiltern both in this novel and in *Phineas Redux,* and we see how Finn's private, physical response to his opponents' violent actions affects his social standing and political career. Unsuccessful in his bid to become Lady Laura's husband, Finn then proposes to Violet, Chiltern's own childhood sweetheart. This results in a duel between Finn and Chiltern which is of no benefit to the former as it is Chiltern who wins Violet's hand. Despite Kennedy's jealousy of the friendship between Lady Laura and Finn, a temporary bond is forged between Kennedy and Finn when Finn rescues him from garotters. Finn's pro-Roman Catholic opinions on church disestablishment and Irish tenancy rights do not accord with the views of his party and he becomes disillusioned with the political process. A wealthy, foreign widow, Madame Goesler, offers him marriage but he declines, retires from parliamentary duties and marries the simple Irish girl to whom he had originally and capriciously offered his hand at the start of the novel.

'What is a gentleman?' This question was a leitmotif in nineteenth-century fiction and, just as masculinity was a contested term, notions of gentlemanliness changed over time. As Waters's book argues, the gentleman was, by the 1850s, no longer embodied in the land-owning man of leisure.[3] Now, it appeared, a man could rise in rank with the right kind of education and social manners. Diligence and perseverance became trademarks of the middle-class gentleman, qualities which were taught at the public schools where the middle classes sent their sons to learn Greek and Latin, languages with which a society gentleman (like Finn, the son of a doctor) was expected to be fully conversant. By building relationships between pupils away from home, boys would become diplomatic, self-reliant and confident. Rigorous exercise and a frugal lifestyle would encourage physical hardiness, stamina and self-control, qualities which were grouped under the umbrella term 'character', a quality considered essential for work in the public and imperial spheres. One sees some of these qualities in the classically educated Trollope (a specialist in Cicero), a hard worker who combined novel writing with his career at the Post Office.

In 1862 the eminent judge, barrister and thinker James Fitzjames Stephen told *Cornhill Magazine*: 'When we speak of a gentleman we do not mean either a good man, or a wise man, but a man socially pleasant, and we consider his goodness and wisdom, his moral and intellectual qualities as relevant to his claims to be considered a gentleman only in so far as they contribute to his social pleasantness.'[4] Trollope would have had the opportunity to debate his views on the gentleman, being personally acquainted with Stephen. In response, Trollope put forward Finn as an ideal of gentlemanliness: 'Nature had been very good to him, making him comely inside and out – and with this comeliness he had crept into popularity.' So, Finn has not only the innate goodness that makes him trustworthy but also the social graces which are attractive in society. This points to the perceived moral dimensions which it was considered a gentleman ought to possess. Arguably, in *Great Expectations,* while Dickens's Pip becomes a gentleman through tailoring, education and the opportunities that money can buy, his guardian, Joe Gargery, represents what was then called one of 'nature's gentlemen' by virtue of his caring and good nature. The concept of a gentleman as a well-finished object of value permeated literature in many forms throughout the nineteenth century. As Samuel Smiles told readers of *Character* (1871): 'Most men are like so many gems in the rough, which need polishing by contact with other and better natures, to bring out their full beauty and lustre.'[5] As the novel shows, Finn not only benefits from contact with his social betters but he is also buffeted about by characters who are not always his moral superiors. As this shows, polished objects can easily tarnished if they are not maintained.

It might have been challenging to define gentlemanliness but it was clear what did not constitute gentlemanly behaviour. As the *Saturday Review* remarked in 1868 of the British public currently absorbed in the debates on Irish church disestablishment and electoral reform, 'a very considerable portion must be more interested in the protection of their own persons and properties than in any question of general politics'.[6] Trollope wrote *Phineas Finn* between November 1866 and May 1867, heady times in which meetings of politically agitated crowds became a frequent sight. The Hyde Park 'riot' of July 1866 was particularly notorious and shades of the occurrences that day form a backdrop to Trollope's discussion of politically motivated violence turned personal and also to the link between the appropriate articulation of aggression and the fitness to vote. The riot was initially planned as a peaceful meeting of the Reform League, an organization founded a year earlier to campaign for the working-class vote and presided over by a middle-class lawyer, Edmund Beales. The League was spurred into action by the plight of the poor whose lives had been blighted by food shortages and were angered by Liberal Robert Lowe's anti-working-class speeches to the House of Commons. The 65,000-strong Reform League had already held meetings in Trafalgar Square; however, Commissioner Sir Richard Mayne and the new Conservative Home Secretary, Spencer Walpole, feared trouble and banned a gathering the League scheduled in Hyde Park for the evening of 23 July 1866. The papers heavily criticized them for this action, particularly in the light of what happened next.

On seeing that the park was closed to them, Beales and his supporters headed towards Trafalgar Square to hear a speech given by the radical John Bright, who was, incidentally, also the inspiration for Trollope's firebrand Mr Turnbull in *Phineas Finn*. Meanwhile, an excited throng of 100,000–200,000 became increasingly agitated by being barred from Hyde Park and flouted the Home Office ban by tearing up the iron railings. The crowds then rushed through clubland, audaciously smashing windows at the Athenaeum Club and damaging property surrounding the park. In *Phineas Finn*, the setting up of a petition for the secret ballot produces similar acts of wrecking with rapacious attacks on personal property: 'The windows also of certain obnoxious members of Parliament were broken, when those obnoxious members lived within reach. One gentleman who unfortunately held a house in Richmond Terrace, and who was said to have said that the ballot was the resort of cowards, fared very badly;–for his windows were not only broken, but his furniture and mirrors were destroyed by the stones that were thrown.' Matthew Arnold was unimpressed by the proceedings in Hyde Park and his *Culture and Anarchy* (1869) warned against the rowdy Englishman who asserted 'his right to march where he likes, meet where he likes, enter where he likes [...] threaten as he likes, smash as he likes'. The

3,200 police officers that Mayne led were clearly outnumbered in what *Reynolds's Newspaper* called the 'battle of Hyde Park'. Fearing he had lost control, Mayne drafted in the Redcoats, an unprecedented measure since the formation of the Metropolitan Police. It was widely argued, particularly in the *Pall Mall Gazette*, that this action incited further disruption. While Beales's orderly sympathizers could be disassociated from the rowdy crowd, the image of mob violence came to be associated with working-class agitation for the vote. Crowds brandished various weapons including knives, cudgels and even the railings which they had torn down. The press published lists of injured officers – 28 officers were permanently disabled – and Mayne was himself struck hard by a stone while even Beales himself suffered, being robbed of his gold watch and chain. This was, to many eyes, an example of the 'lawless mischievous rabble' and 'scum of all nations' imposing its will over the law of government.

Trollope communicated his own views on violence in an article on the garotting panics, 'The Uncontrolled Ruffianism of London as Measured by the Rule of Thumb', which appeared in *Saint Paul's Magazine* in the same year in which *Phineas Finn* was serialized. As *Saint Paul's Magazine* catered for the interests of professional males working in London, Trollope's treatment of the theme associated with urban violence was specifically intended for those to whom political matters and the threat of robbery may have been considered likely. In the piece, Trollope sought to deflate fears over the perception of rising crime rates, but he also spent much space discussing the various manifestations of violence. For him, political violence, while as dangerous as ordinary crime, was cloaked in high-minded ideals and was therefore harder to criticize: 'It seems to us that that which is non-political is more easily handled, is more manifestly made odious to the eyes of the multitude, is more quickly made to appear as a thing clearly damnable and injurious to all concerned in it, than that which strives to make itself respectable with the excuse of politics.' For instance, as some papers suggested at the time, the demonstrators who tore into the park were only exercising their right to be able to access a public park.

The Times was unconvinced by lofty principles and readily suggested the connections between political skirmishes, public violence and street crime. The paper featured some shocking accounts of what had befallen genteel pedestrians and residents who found themselves in close proximity to the events unfolding in London's great park on that tumultuous night. One man was mugged while another was chased by groups of 300 pursuers armed with stones. A contributor protected himself as best he could with a loaded stick, while another was pelted with bludgeons and his female companion was 'subjected to the grossest possible insult at the hands of these cowardly ruffians'. It was alleged that garotters, crowds and street rowdies had a viciously harmonious working relationship. As the *Saturday Review* opined: 'We hardly think that the shopkeepers would feel very much wronged, or the peaceable folk very much grieved, if for the future the roughs were not permitted to reign unmolested for a whole day, and to range street and park at will, and to ply, with scarcely an attempt at interference, their profitable trade of larceny and garotting [...] Whenever and wherever there is a crowd, there is now an organized assault on property and person; that is, wherever there is a London crowd, robbery reigns triumphant.' As *The Times* warned: 'If crowds are to have their own way other people who do not belong to them must suffer.' In *Phineas Finn*, Mr Turnbull, who readers guessed was based on Mr Bright, warned of public demonstrations following the debate on parliamentary reform. Trollope's readers would have known what he meant by this and it seems that, through Turnbull, Trollope intended to evoke images of the Hyde Park fiasco in the minds of his readers.

The antithesis of the political rioter was the legitimate citizen who was qualified to vote. What distinguished the reform debates of the 1860s from those of the 1830s was the focus on individuality as opposed to the masses, as Pamela Gilbert's book demonstrates.[7] The fit citizen was not a man of the crowd. As Gilbert tells us, the ideal voter possessed sufficient physical and therefore mental space to form his own thoughts. Being literate, he had the potential for bettering himself and rising in society, and the vote he cast was influenced not by obligations towards his class, but was the result of his own convictions. However, what needs to be emphasized is self-sufficiency, a positive trait expressed in the act of self-defence or the citizen's arrest. As we saw in the previous chapter, the garotter attempted to rob the individual of those very qualities which made him 'fit' to vote. During an attack, the prey's personal space was eroded, his body and mind were threatened and his social status was devalued by the loss of his possessions. Moreover, the tussle between the lone, respectable pedestrian and the Hyde Park demonstrators is symbolic of the differentiation of the individual from the pack or horde of criminals.

We must add another point to Gilbert's list: during a time of political and social transition, citizenship was to be characterized by gentlemanly conduct, the avoidance of violence wherever possible and the ability to separate political differences from personal hostilities. As Peter

Gay has said in his classic survey of aggression in nineteenth-century European culture, *The Cultivation of Hatred* (1993), aggressive and assertive acts 'range across a broad spectrum of verbal and physical expression, from confident self-advertisement to permissible mayhem, from sly malice to sadistic torture'.[8] There are a multiplicity of violent acts in the Palliser series which makes it apparent that elevated social class did not automatically result in better behaviour. It is certainly surprising that more has not been written about Trollope's approach to the problem of bellicosity in all its nuances. While Trollope declares his admiration of physical bravery in the face of violence, he condemns gratuitous aggression, particularly violence perpetrated against women. In *Phineas Redux* Trollope points out that a duke could be just as guilty of violence towards his spouse as a collier. In *Can You Forgive Her?* he considered the effect of violence on women: 'What woman can bear a blow from a man, and afterwards return to him with love? [...] A woman may forgive deceit, treachery, desertion, – even the preference given to a rival. She may forgive them and forget them; but I do not think that a woman can forget a blow.' Public awareness around male violence towards women was increased in the period in which *Phineas Finn* and *Phineas Redux* were published. In 1868, the year of *Phineas Finn*'s serialization, Dickens incorporated the Sikes and Nancy murder scene in his readings, while in the year after the serialization of *Phineas Redux*, a number of editorials lobbied the police and the courts, raising the public's consciousness against domestic violence. This resulted in a rise in prosecutions and stiffer punishments.[9]

Whilst possessing an eye for politics, Trollope added a good measure of crime and aggression to spice up his novels. In fact, he showed that violence could be part and parcel of political life. Trollope's parliamentary candidates risk being pelted with eggs, verbal threats are issued, heirs and academics alike come to blows and the lure of the pistol duel is a constant theme throughout the series. Lower-class crime is also a threat. Robert Kennedy in *Phineas Finn* and Everett Wharton in *The Prime Minister* are threatened by the hand of the garotter, while the duplicitous adventuress Lizzie Eustace, Trollope's version of Thackeray's Becky Sharpe, is robbed of her diamonds, instigating an extensive search in *The Eustace Diamonds*. With these various crimes taking place, Trollope's police officers are given the exhausting tasks of controlling crowds, apprehending garotters and capturing thieves, but it is the pedestrian's encounter with crime which is the focus in the Palliser series.

The duel

> 'Will you fight me?'
> 'Fight a duel with you, – with pistols? Certainly not.'
> (Trollope, *Can You Forgive Her?*)

As Samuel Johnson maintained in a debate with Boswell: 'Now, Sir, it is never unlawful to fight in self-defence. He, then, who fights a duel, does not fight from passion against his antagonist, but out of self-defence; to avert the stigma of the world, and to prevent himself from being driven out of society.'[10] So, the duel was then considered a legitimate form of personal protection, perhaps not in response to an attack on one's body but in response to an assault on one's character. It is well known that duelling had largely ceased by the 1850s and yet, almost a century after Johnson's statement, the duel had not, as we generally expect, completely faded as a shadowy influence on the relationships between men in Britain. At the end of Volume 1 of *Phineas Finn*, Chiltern challenges Finn to a duel. Finn's reluctance to duel is based on his knowledge that 'few Englishmen fight duels in these days' and that 'they who do so are always reckoned to be fools'. Yet he feels bound to accept Chiltern's challenge to fight. It is certainly curious that Trollope, who intended his novels to reflect the times, should choose such a mode of settling disputes between his characters.

The duel is generally characterized by its formulaic quality and also by the antagonistic feelings of its participants to one another. Historians have traced the first duels back to sixth-century Burgundy in which the judicial duel, or trial by combat, was established and quickly spread throughout Europe. Around three centuries later, the duel of chivalry appeared on the scene. It was an ostentatious feud fought between two disputing knights on horseback in the presence of a large crowd. These two types of duel were replaced with the duel of honour, the earliest of which was purported to have taken place in Britain in the early seventeenth century. Imported from France, the duel of honour was, in effect, a more humane solution to the problematic increase of murderous attacks committed by gangs, termed 'killing affrays', which had bedevilled fifteenth- and sixteenth-century society. The duel was a means of regulating affairs between men of honour and offered a more civilized approach to dealing with the ill-feeling caused when a man was given the lie (that is, he was accused of being a liar), his property was coveted or a lady under his protection was insulted. Unlike the duel of chivalry, it was a private dispute and unlike the judicial duel, it was not legally sanctioned, all parties to the duel being liable to arrest and imprisonment.

Under the duel of honour, a potential duellist was faced with a selection of codes of duelling which advised him on matters such as organizing 'seconds' (the duellists' assistants) and choosing weapons. The most famous of these codes was the Clonmel Code, which was formalized in Ireland at the Clonmel Summer Assizes in 1777 and which mirrored those later protocols adopted on the Continent and in England, formulas to which Lord Chiltern himself would have adhered. Under this convention, a man who desired to retain his social standing as a gentleman was expected to accept the challenge. A man who did not was called a coward. Also, as Donna T. Andrew says, 'the willingness to fight a duel, as well as the recognition of being a person who was "challengeable" defined, in great part, what it meant to be a gentleman'.[11] While Chiltern's challenge and questioning of his behaviour causes Finn much consternation, this issuing of a life-threatening test is also a compliment to his friend, demonstrating that Chiltern considers Finn a worthy contender. As far as the procedure was concerned, the 'seconds' would initially attempt to resolve the dispute. Failing this, they were then responsible for organizing the duel as well as providing the surgeons and loading both weapons, ascertaining that they functioned equally well. It was customary for duellists to stand back-to-back and take, on average, six paces away from their opponent. They would then turn and wait for the signal to fire which was the drop of a handkerchief. The purpose of duelling was not necessarily to kill the opponent. During the heyday of the duelling pistol from the 1770s to the 1850s, pistol shots were exchanged until 'satisfaction' or grievous injury were achieved. In Finn's case, he receives a shot to the shoulder and, as Chiltern is satisfied, the duel is ended. It was no ignominy to be wounded and honour could equally be bestowed on the duellist who walked away from the confrontation or on the participant who emerged with scars. If one of the duellists was wounded or killed, all those who were party to the duel quickly vanished from the scene of the crime; duelling was illegal and a man could be arrested for taking part.

While the duel and the court were both adversarial in nature, the duel was a private method of resolving quarrels and was at odds with the rule of law, in which the state was responsible for meting out punishments. Whilst different in nature and execution, the duel had a feature in common with the citizen's arrest during the mid-Victorian era: it allowed the individual not only to defend himself but to punish the offender until he had achieved satisfaction. Despite its illegality, duelling was not as popular as in the eighteenth century but still saw a slight increase in the last decades of the eighteenth century and early years of the 1800s up until the 1840s, particularly with middle-class officers who felt bound to accept the challenges issued by the higher ranks to which they aspired. As Antony Simpson has shown, there were 840 duels in Britain or abroad, involving Britons, from 1828 to 1850.[12] This was despite the constraining influence of a civil society which had turned away in horror at the excessively violent deeds committed in the French Revolution, in a country in which the code of honour still prevailed. There were questions as to why duellists often received a lighter sentence than common thieves who were executed for their crimes. If duelling represented a destructive threat to the progress of peace, then many commentators, including judges, clerics, Evangelicals, thinkers (such as Jeremy Bentham) and even some duellists themselves believed that the practice should be ridiculed. It was felt that its participants should be shamed into desisting from taking up the pistols or that attitudes should be changed so that a man could decline to duel without cost to his honour.

As Robin Gilmour points out, in Walter Scott's day there was some confusion as to how a man should respond to a challenge to a duel, but by Trollope's time this issue had become more clear-cut.[13] By 1869 one correspondent to *The Times* observed that duelling was as anachronistic as 'port wine and drinking songs' and it had never truly been a British habit but an influence from France. One politician who was looking back from the vantage point of 1864, five years before the publication of *Phineas Finn*, remarked that if a man failed to pick up the duellist's gauntlet in 1841 he was branded a coward; ten years later, if that same man took part in a duel, he would have been considered a fool.[14] If Finn, a middle-class man, was called on to duel with Chiltern, a lord, he would at this time have been bound to accept the challenge if he wished to rise in society. Some key events served to change public opinion. The Mirfin–Eliot duel was fought in 1838 over an altercation at the Epsom Races in which Eliot's carriage collided with Mirfin's vehicle, causing Mirfin to be injured. After exchanging blows, Mirfin demanded satisfaction. The duel ended in Mirfin's death and Eliot's seconds were successfully prosecuted for murder and imprisoned for a year. This case is interesting in a number of ways. It was the first successful murder prosecution of either seconds or duellists in the Old Bailey since the mid-eighteenth century.[15] That Mirfin and Eliot were men of trade shows that duelling was not restricted to the aristocracy,[16] a fact which may have helped to vulgarize the duel in the minds of the upper classes.

Moreover, it was a lesson to other prospective duellists that the eye of the law was now more precisely trained upon them. Probably one of the most ill-famed pair of duellists were the brothers-in-law Lieutenant-Colonel David Fawcett and Lieutenant Alexander Munro who duelled in Camden Town in 1843. Fawcett was killed. The disgust at Munro's crime was such that the jury told Mr Baron Rolfe that it was unnecessary to sum up the trial and 'instantly' found the prisoner guilty. Munro was jailed for a year. This much-publicized event roused public indignation to the extent that an Anti-Duelling Association was formed and further hastened the demise of the duel.

According to the *Contemporary Review* of 1868, the days of duelling were 'rough and unfeeling days when the family could not quite count on where the father or brother of last night's party might be at breakfast-time'.[17] The Offences Against the Person Act 1837 helped to provide a context against which duelling could be further suppressed. In 1843 Queen Victoria gave her support to the London Association for the Suppression of Duelling which was formed in the autumn of that year, its members being derived from the army, navy, nobility and parliament. Self-sacrifice in war and the defence of the Empire were considered valorous; however, a man's disregard for his own life in the duel was depicted as antithetical to the civilizing process and was increasingly frowned upon by the public and the state. Victoria addressed the House of Commons in 1844, expressing her support for any measure which would ensure that 'the barbarous practice of duelling should be as much as possible discouraged'. In that year the War Office announced that any officer who took part in or was involved in a duel was liable to be court-martialled and, if the court saw fit, cashiered and punished as the court deemed appropriate. A further policy was added that any military man who was killed in a duel forfeited his wife's right to his pension after his death. Under this initiative, an officer was now able to decline a challenge, without shame, on the grounds that he was manfully protecting the interests of his family.[18] At the same time, cultural pressures served to discourage duelling. Turning one's wife into a widow and exposing one's family to destitution for selfish reasons was antithetical to the family values so espoused by Queen Victoria and Prince Albert. In *Men of Blood*, a book mainly about men's crimes against women, Wiener classifies duelling as a violent act committed by men on men. However, critics of the duel used the image of men's violence against women to condemn the practice. As *The Times* reported of Munro's trial, for Baron Rolfe, the crime of duelling was 'nearly as bad as those charges of the most dreadful character against the other sex.'

John E. Archer points out that although duelling 'had effectively disappeared by 1850', it persisted, despite being mocked by press, public and polite society.[19] The last recorded duel took place in 1852, although it was a contest not between Britons but between two Frenchmen, an event which attracted international notoriety and further hastened the demise of duelling. The cessation of duelling did not mean that interest in the practice had completely died out by the 1860s. It still continued in the Deep South of the USA and in Europe, notably in German universities, where it was referred to as the 'Mensur', in which participants fought to obtain scars which they wore with pride as a demonstration of their obliviousness to pain and fear. Jerome K. Jerome's depiction of the Mensur horrifies the reader through its grotesque and chilling imagery: 'Now and then you see a man's teeth laid bare almost to the ear, so that for the rest of the duel he appears to be grinning at one half of the spectators, his other side remaining serious; and sometimes a man's nose gets slit, which gives to him as he fights a singularly supercilious air.'[20] A significant number of periodical writers on duelling appeared in the periodical press, many of them prefacing their articles with a sigh of relief that it was no longer practised in England, but looking askance with curiosity to the Continent. For instance, as *Chambers's Journal* remarked in 1867: 'A formal challenge to fight a duel is so complete an anachronism in the England of the present day, that when we hear of one, we are apt, in our laughter, to forget that only a quarter of a century ago "hostile meetings" were still an institution with us.'[21] With this statement, the author then proceeds to lift the lid on contemporary French duelling, deciphering the jargon and describing with relish the weapons used, from the sabre to the pistol. With equal interest, a book review in the Broad Church periodical, the *Contemporary Review*, set the scene of the duel:

> What a study to watch the demeanour of the combatants in those anxious movements when they step towards each other at the end of their 'paces' and await the signal; or in those more awful moments after the explosion, when all artificial restraints are over, then the dying man breathes his generous forgiveness and the as generous survivor passionately wishes himself in the place of the fallen! Or when both survive, what lasting friendships will sometimes result from that strange acquaintance! Such are some of the 'romances'.[22]

The *Contemporary Review* was founded in 1866 by Alexander Strahan who had enjoyed success with his evangelical publication *Good Words*.

While religious influence played a part in discouraging duelling, it is interesting to observe that in this religious paper the duel is not viewed with repugnance but interest, with curiosity as to what motivated the duellists, coupled with a fascination with the protocol of the duel itself.

Quite possibly sensitive to this lingering, wistful obsession with the thrill of duelling, Trollope included his own romance of the pistol. According to Glendinning, Trollope's depiction of duelling betrays a nostalgic yearning for the days of the outmoded code of honour.[23] There are indeed romantic aspects to Trollope's Palliser plot. True to the words of the *Contemporary Review*, Chiltern and Finn maintain their friendship after Chiltern shoots him in the shoulder. Chiltern's regard for his Finn is evident by the support he gives to him during his trial in *Phineas Redux*. When Trollope's young men are insulted, they are forced to check themselves, to remember that 'fighting' (a euphemism for duelling) was no longer *de rigeur*. (The word 'fight' is used in numerous occasions in this way, for instance, in *The Eustace Diamonds,* when Frank Greystock admits: 'Men don't fight each other now-a-days;—not often, at least.') There is in these occurrences a sense that their romantic, belligerent duelling urges have been tempered by changes in convention. Therefore, Trollope could express what he may have observed – a yearning fascination among young men towards duelling – framing it as an anti-duelling statement which chimed with the values of the day.

One individual who resists such cultural change is Chiltern. Chiltern accuses Finn of betraying their friendship by continuing his pursuit of Violet. Chiltern is not dissuaded by her repeated rejections of the hot-headed lord and, as he regards Violet as his property, he resents Finn's competition. In short, for Chiltern, Finn has been dishonest. 'Giving the lie' was still, judging by Trollope's works, one of the worst offences that could be hurled at a gentleman. Accusations of deceit were often incitements to a duel. To be accused of falsehood was more than a mere insult – it was a direct attack on one's character, especially as honesty was the hallmark of gentlemanliness. The threat of being called a liar causes much anger and consternation to Trollope's male characters in this and other novels. For instance, Finn's close friend Laurence Fitzgibbon skilfully conceals his knowledge of the duel from curious interrogators and endeavours to cover up the affair but, as Trollope tells us, if Fitzgibbon were accused of falsehood 'he would have considered himself to be not only insulted, but injured too'. When Lord Fawn (another of Violet Effingham's admirers) questions the gentlemanly character of Frank Greystock in *The Eustace Diamonds*, he is affronted when he is merely told by Greystock's lover that his assertion is 'not true'. In *Can You Forgive Her?* the bullish and paranoid George Vavasor confronts the even-tempered John Grey with a catalogue of typical insults and touts a pistol at his rival: 'You are a coward, and a liar, and a blackguard. [...] I have come here with arms, and I do not intend to leave this room without using them, unless you will promise to give me the meeting that I have proposed.' Vavasor craves a duel, but Grey's calm stance merely shows up the vulgarity of such a proposal.

It is intriguing that during the 1860s, a decade after the 1852 duel, Trollope feels that he must emphasize that Finn's initial misgivings about the duel are not motivated by cowardice. Furthermore, Trollope makes it clear that it is not a fear of pain which discourages his hero from taking up arms. He tells us that 'Phineas was afraid of no violence, personal to himself; but he was afraid of, – of what I may, perhaps, best call, "a row" ... If there were to be blows he, too, must strike; – and he was very averse to strike Lady Laura's brother, Lord Brentford's son, Violet Effingham's friend. If need be, however, he would strike.' When he argues with Chiltern, Trollope writes that Finn was 'afraid of no violence, personal to himself; but he was afraid of [...] "a row"' as 'tumbling over the chairs and tables with his late friend and present enemy [...] would be most unpleasant to him'. Trollope's accentuation of his eponymous protagonist's heroism accords warmly with Thomas Hughes's advice to his young readers in *Tom Brown's Schooldays*, which states that if they must decline a fight it should be out of principle not out of fear for receiving 'a licking' or 'because [they] fear God, for that's neither Christian nor honest'.[24] Trollope tells the reader that his protagonist qualifies for the title of gentleman in that he is averse to unnecessary violence out of principle and not because it is a threat to his personal comfort. So, while Trollope's longing for the *strum und drang* of duelling days is manifest in his including such a scene in his novel, he also uses the duelling episode to make the point that a man's bravery does not need weapons for its articulation.

The dreaded duel adds a deliciously gloomy twist to the novel. Finn cannot enjoy his popularity and the company of his new friends knowing that there was a 'nightmare on his breast', the return of the spectre of 'customary' violence. However, the duel between Chiltern and Finn is an embarrassing affair. Trollope refrains from glorifying the duel and does not provide us with a lavish description of the event. His account differs in style from Jerome K. Jerome's later *Three Men on the Bummel*. Jerome intends to shock the reader into the realization that 'underneath our starched shirts there lurks the savage, with all his savage instincts untouched'.[25] By contrast, in his campaign against duelling, Trollope emphasizes the embarrassing nature of the incident. The men and their seconds meet on the Blankenberg sands, Finn is shot in the shoulder and the seconds disallow another round. The parties then leave separately for England. Trollope discusses both the prelude and the aftermath of the duel, but his description of the duel itself is surprisingly fleeting. The shameful nature of the affair is conveyed by the way in which the parties meet 'quite unobserved amidst the sand-heaps'. Trollope then writes that 'Phineas made his way through Blankenberg after such a fashion that no one there knew what had occurred' and 'not a living soul, except the five concerned, was at that time aware that a duel had been fought among the sand-hills'. As Mark Turner has said in his study on Trollope and periodical culture, the duel constitutes 'a male secret' and a 'male rite of passage',[26] but Trollope's treatment of the episode shows it to be far from gloriously manly.

We are told that Finn acts gallantly under the circumstances. In the duel there were no winners or losers and therefore it was not skill that was tested in the duel but bravery and coolness in the face of death. Yet, as the mid-Victorian era approached, the duels became less deadly, with deaths being the exception. For instance, by the 1830s, duellists replaced pellets with powder, which served to render the duel a performance rather than a life-and-death struggle. Knowing that Chiltern is intent on shooting with real ammunition, Finn's jibe at the code of honour is to shoot gallantly away from Chiltern, protecting Lady Laura's brother from his own folly. In the process, he takes a shot himself. Trollope tells us that for Finn, 'come what might, he would not aim at his adversary'. Finn prefers to suffer physical pain than cause injury even to an aggressor. Shooting away from Chiltern requires more effort than one would assume: 'Phineas felt very certain that he would not hit Chiltern in an awkward place, although he was by no means sure of his hand.'

In *Phineas Finn* Trollope demonstrates the manner in which the middle-class male should respond to violence from his social superiors. He shows that around two decades after the criminalization of duelling, there were lingering doubts as to the appropriate response to an insult. The men fight for the hand of Violet Effingham, but duelling, despite some residues of notions of the 'romantic', was considered less than chivalrous. Self-sacrifice in war and the defence of the Empire were considered valiant; however, a man's disregard for his own life in the duel was depicted as antithetical to the civilizing process. To add further ignominy, the duel gives Finn much petty aggravation when he is dogged by the parasitic newspaper editor Quintus Slide, who threatens his reputation among the voters by exposing him for taking up the pistols, thus indicating just how private acts of violence could mar a politician's career.

The duel between Finn and Chiltern is more than a confrontational episode between two men – it is representative of the novel's wider treatment of the competing identities of these characters. Trollope does not concentrate his exploration of gentlemanliness through one character but rather uses the tension created between his eponymous hero and his peers to put forward his views.

5
Lord Chiltern and Mr Kennedy

Thrill of the chase: masculinities at play

One can readily imagine the satisfaction of the reviewer of the *Spectator* when he or she cast their eyes over the pages of *Phineas Finn*. 'Kennedy is as perfectly sketched as Chiltern', the review exclaimed.[1] Polar opposites in character, the lord and laird certainly invite comparison, particularly so in reference to the novel's main figure, Phineas Finn.

In his treatment of Chiltern, Trollope plays with the reader's expectations. At the outset we are instructed to view Chiltern as a man of blood. When Finn first meets Chiltern, he is taken aback by his gruff nature and Trollope says that 'there was something in the countenance of the man which struck [Finn] almost with dread – something approaching ferocity'. He has red hair and a ruddy complexion, attributes which in literature generally betokened a lascivious and intemperate nature. Trollope writes in *Phineas Redux* that Chiltern had 'two expressions', namely 'one eloquent of good humour, in which the reader of countenances would find some promise of coming frolic' and another contrasting mood which was 'replete with anger, something to the extent almost of savagery'. To those who are in his care, his nature is unnervingly unpredictable. Even Violet herself is too disconcerted by his aggressive nature to accept his hand in marriage: 'It looked as though he would not hesitate to wring his wife's neck round, if ever he should be brought to threaten to do so.' To the reviewer of the *Spectator*, Chiltern is 'the savage and untameable element left in the English aristocracy'.[2]

Trollope tells us that the young man must exercise more self-control. His irascible nature spills out into acts of aggression and he often finds himself involved in physical confrontations. As Antony Simpson has argued, the brawl and duel offered opportunities for the upper and lower classes to exhibit heroism.[3] While Chiltern immerses himself in both these scenarios (the duel *and* the brawl), he does not appear heroic. We are told that Chiltern, a good scholar, nevertheless almost strangles a college officer whilst inebriated and is subsequently expelled from Oxford. He also 'f[alls] through his violence into some terrible misfortune at Paris, [and is] brought before a public judge', resulting in his notoriety in the two cities. The lord publicly disgraces himself through his actions, causing the public to be wary of him. As Trollope notes: 'The man well spoken of may steal a horse, while he who is of evil repute may not look over a hedge.' Chiltern's bad reputation influences the way in which the public react when he does legitimately defend himself against a ruffian at Newmarket. Rumours are spread that Chiltern 'had really killed him with his fists' in a fit of delirium tremens, although Trollope tells us that he was indeed sober at the time. As the garotting farces have shown, a lack of manliness was denoted through madness, physical violence and delirium tremens. This is therefore not the most favourable impression of his character.

However, his bipolar nature has its positive attributes and his model of masculinity has much to offer. Chiltern is, to borrow Philip Mason's description, a 'gentleman sportsman'.[4] He has huge reserves of physical energy. In fact, through Chiltern, Trollope makes an important statement on violence, showing that violence is not always the result of wickedness but can stem from frustration and lack of purpose. However, Trollope does explore the parameters of physical action and indicates the necessity both of cultivating and then harnessing physical strength. Chiltern has the makings of a good leader. What Trollope admires in him is his passion. In fact, Chiltern displays such furious levels of physical and emotional energy that he is described as being a 'wild beast' and 'griffin'. However, we learn that unlike the man of blood, Chiltern's nature is underscored by passionate feeling, in particular, his love for his childhood sweetheart, Violet Effingham. When he learns that a man (namely Finn) has offered his hand to Violet, to whom Chiltern has already offered his hand, he fears he will 'go and quarrel with the man, and kick him, – or get kicked', turning 'all the world' against him and as a result be called 'a wild beast'. The *Spectator* observed his behaviour with interest, concluding that Chiltern's 'individual character breaks through all ordinary restrictions to express itself'.[5] Throughout the latter half of *Finn*, the reader warms to Chiltern and in *Phineas Redux* Trollope often describes him as being gentle. Through his passionate nature he dominates those around him, but he is not an unfeeling brute. When Violet turns down his marriage proposals, her reaction distresses him, but Chiltern is not boorish and knows not to press her, adding that 'there is something to me unmanly in a man's persecuting a girl'. Thus, here he has the energy of a wild animal but the intuitive sense of a gentleman.

Chiltern's aggressive impulses are tamed by his marriage to Violet, although his participation in sport also allows him not only to gain self-control but to master his finer senses. Paradoxically, it is through Chiltern that Trollope highlights the virtues of bourgeois industriousness. Chiltern has no aptitude for professional life or for politics. His forte is sport and he experiences less bodily and mental frustration when employed in a physical task. As Dowling notes, Trollope valued productivity and energetic drive and, with these qualities in mind, likened his occupation as a writer to the actions of the man who, like Chiltern, rode to hounds: 'Trollope's enjoyment of the sport clearly involves the release of an explosive energy within established rules. The traditions of the hunt, those "accessories of the field" that Trollope knows so well, directs what is, in effect, a wild and chaotic chase. Riding to hounds is used [...] as a metaphor for the writing of novels.' As Trollope recounts in his autobiography: 'With nothing settled in my brain as to the final development of events, with no capability of settling anything, but with a most distinct conception of some character or characters, I have rushed at the work as a rider rushes at a fence which he does not see.'[6] So, Trollope aligns middle-class creativity in the form of novel-writing with upper-class sporting pursuits.

Through Chiltern, Trollope emphasizes what he calls in 'Uncontrolled Ruffianism' 'proper manly vigour'. His treatment of Chiltern is a reaction to contemporary scepticism on the dangers of physical development. The publication of *Phineas Finn* coincided with what Mike Huggins has termed the bourgeois 'sporting revolution',[7] when the middle classes sought to control sports which were once popular such as athletics and rowing. Wilkie Collins was suspicious of this new middle-class culture of the body and advances intellectualism as a key definition of the gentleman in his novel *Man and Wife* (1870). For Karen Volland Waters, Collins's brutish muscleman, Geoffrey Delamayn, is 'Tom Brown, all grown up and run amuck'.[8] As Collins writes:

> A man will go all the better to his books for his healthy physical exercise. And I say that again – provided the physical exercise be restrained within fit limits. But when public feeling enters into

the question, and directly exalts the bodily exercises above the books – then I say public feeling is in a dangerous extreme. The bodily exercises [...] will [...] slowly and surely end in leaving him, to all good moral and mental purpose, certainly an uncultivated, and possibly a dangerous man.[9]

The son of a lawyer, Delamayn is simultaneously a bourgeois 'model of manly beauty' and 'one of the fundamental follies of humanity'.[10] He is a lauded boat-rower for Oxford, but his poor knowledge of English culture – he mistakes a conversational reference to the poet John Dryden to be an allusion to a fellow university student of his, Tom Dryden – suggests that he is an academic underachiever. His physical strength has rendered him a brute and a bully. He exploits the affections of Anne Sylvester who becomes pregnant with his child and invents elaborate plots to shirk his duty to marry her, engineering her marriage to his already-betrothed friend Arnold Brinkworth. As Waters argues, Delamayn is counterposed with Sir Patrick Lundie, who is his opposite: Lundie is an older man, an intellectual with a club-foot whose knowledge of Scottish law ultimately unravels Delamayn's schemes.[11] The novel's physician argues that 'the violent bodily exercises' have not 'damaged [his] muscular power' but have exerted a detrimental effect on his 'vital power'.[12] According to an 1863 edition of *St James's Magazine*, the fashion for vigorous exercise and the new craze in anti-garotte boxing could be injurious to health: 'So far from agreeing with the advocates of severe physical training, we believe that it tends to ultimate debility of the muscular system, and all the organs of vitality.'[13]

If Delamayn represented the worst excesses of the athletic revolution, then his example was vigorously tackled by counter-examples. Dickens's lighthearted sending up of the amateur boxer Minor Canon the Reverend Septimus Chrisparkle in his unfinished novel *The Mystery of Edwin Drood* (1870) could not be more different from Collins's sceptical treatment of the sports-obsessed Delamayn. The avidity with which Minor Canon the Reverend Septimus Chrisparkle takes to his morning boxing routine attracts concern from his aunt who fears that this habit will ruin his health. This is not so, reassures Dickens, when he refers to the Muscular Christian's fresh-faced and healthy complexion: 'His radiant features teemed with innocence, and soft-hearted benevolence beamed from his boxing gloves.'

Phineas Redux was written during the serialization of *Man and Wife* and can be considered a response to fears of the over-exercised male. In contrast to Delamayn, Chiltern is depicted as a robust and enthusiastic aficionado of manly sports, whose intensive use of physical culture is represented as curative:

> He found his friend standing in the middle of the room, without coat and waistcoat, with a pair of dumb-bells in his hands. 'When there's no hunting I'm driven to this kind of thing,' said Lord Chiltern.
>
> 'I suppose it's good exercise,' said Phineas.
>
> 'And it gives me something to do [...] I've no occupation for my days whatever.'

His only problem is how to curb his wild energy. In *Phineas Finn* Trollope's hero is invited to ride to hounds with one of Chiltern's horses, Bonebreaker. While Finn successfully controls his animal, Chiltern is 'wild with rage against the beast' and subsequently suffers an accident, breaking his collar-bone and three ribs. Chiltern's selfishness results in the death of his horse: 'The horse did not move – and never did move again.' The animal is killed, a fact which Trollope euphemistically refers to by the slang term 'gruelled'. Trollope wishes to highlight Chiltern's selfish aggression in forcing the horse over the brook. However, his reluctance to use stronger terms in describing the death suggests that he intends to castigate Chiltern's selfish action but not to paint him in such negative tones that the reader loses sympathy for him. (Indeed, not all readers at this time would have sympathized with the hunt. One famous example of an anti-hunt novel is Anne Brontë's *The Tenant of Wildfell Hall*, which had portrayed foxhunting and cruelty to animals and women as mutually reinforcing habits.) Finn arrives first on the scene and offers Chiltern assistance. The latter confesses his admiration for Finn's riding skills and offers him the use of the ominously named Bonebreaker in the future, declaring that 'Irish fellows always ride' with success. Finn shows aptitude not only for the intellectual rigours of politics but has the makings of a good rider and so, in this way, Trollope attempts to combine the intellectual and physical aspects of gentlemanliness. Furthermore, Finn takes a cue from Chiltern and manfully and vivaciously tames a wild horse. In doing so, he helps his friend to his feet, rescuing him from his own follies.

Chiltern's fiery energy does not harm him. We can see that in his nocturnal wanderings around town, he does not have need of a weapon; he is physically strong enough to defend himself from attack, as is the case when he was assaulted at Newmarket. By taking part in the sport of foxhunting, Chiltern is able to gain the respect of his peers. Trollope was a keen supporter of foxhunting and hunted until 1878. In 1862 *Punch* produced a letter written by a City man to his friend, who is 'of good biceps', inviting his colleague to participate in the pursuit of 'garotter hunting' in the foggy streets of London. The chase is described in the manner of a foxhunt, the garotter being the 'game'. The aim is to entice the garotter, 'rush in and give the brute a thundering good thrashing, and then pass him over to the hands of the police'.[14] The article obviously mocks the over-violent response that some citizens had towards street attackers, but it also draws attention to the way in which street crime was seen as a sport and test for the gentleman. While the middle-class professional should not imitate Chiltern's overly aggressive impulses, the young peer's mastery over street criminals as well as animals is considered exemplary.

A measure of Chiltern's physical confidence is needed in order to prevent the middle-class man from becoming a victim like Dickens's Mr Goodman. While Trollope condemned the use of gentlemanly street weapons, he would have admired Chiltern in his role as Master of the Hounds, preserver and taker of life. He should be 'an irrational, cut and thrust, unscrupulous, but yet distinctly honest man; one who can be tyrannical, but will tyrannize only over the evil spirits'. His desire to save the fox and then to kill the animal should be 'intense and passionate'. Trollope tells us that a Master of Hounds should be 'somewhat feared by the men who ride with him'. Of the two of Chiltern's pursuits, the bloody pursuit of duelling had been virtually stamped out while foxhunting continued.

By contrast, Trollope considers foxhunting to promote self-control and moral fortitude. For him, a male participant in hunting, the sport is a way of *stemming* belligerence and he praises Chiltern's skill at foxhunting, showing how the sport allows him to channel his boisterous energy and aggression. Foxhunting civilizes Chiltern, transforming him from the 'wild beast' he describes himself as into 'an irrational, cut and thrust, unscrupulous, but yet distinctly honest man; one who can be tyrannical, but will tyrannize only over evil spirits; a man capable of intense cruelty to those alongside of him, but who will know whether his victim does in truth deserve scalping before he draws his knife'.[15] He may have animalistic fury but this dark aspect to his nature is tempered by his humanity and sense of justice, positive qualities lacking in those who ride to hounds in *The Tenant of Wildfell Hall*. Chiltern might, as the *Spectator* suggested, represent the last vestiges of English aristocratic savagery, and Finn's middle-class manliness was on the ascendency, but

Trollope was sympathetic to both, suggesting that a man of measured temperament needed to possess the best qualities of both the lord and the young parliamentarian to get ahead in the world.

Streetwise hero saves government minister

'After a somewhat prolonged and minute inquiry, we have been unable to meet with any one who has been garrotted [...] We ourselves have never had our pockets picked!'[16] This statement appeared in 'Uncontrolled Ruffianism', which was published in the January issue of *Saint Paul's Magazine*; four months later, Trollope had Mr Kennedy garotted. What can we make of this contradiction?

While an intense character, Kennedy is arguably one of the least dynamic of all the men in the Palliser series. He is an example of self-restraint taken to extremes. He is 'not unlike a gentleman in his usual demeanour', but is nevertheless 'a plain, unattractive man, with nothing in his personal appearance to call for remark'. He is too cold and stiff to be pitied when fortune turns sour for him. From the outset, the parliamentarian is portrayed as an arrogant man of extreme inaction who is 'afflicted with some difficulty in speaking' and whose eyes remain still even while he watches monkeys at the Zoological Gardens. Unsurprisingly, Kennedy hardly gives speeches. He is sternly religious but does not observe the so-called Protestant work ethic. Trollope tells us that he inherits his father's company which is run by servants who understand the business well enough so that he has never had to work. We know through Trollope's other characters that the author values industry and Smilesian self-help. Mr Low, Finn's lawyer-mentor, tells Finn that he can 'live upon what [he] earn[s], like a gentleman, and can already afford to be indifferent to work that [he] dislike[s]'. Gentlemanliness is thus defined as productivity and the freedom to choose the mode of work in which one is to be employed. Trollope is more sympathetic towards the jobless Chiltern who, despite his eccentricity and wild behaviour, finds an outlet for his skills and is subsequently awarded with a happy marriage while Kennedy is made to descend into insanity. Given Kennedy's bitterly straight-laced nature, it was, as the *Spectator* mused, 'a great idea, in itself, to conceive an attempt made to garotte such a man as this'.

Trollope based the scene on the real-life mugging of a Member of Parliament, an event which sparked the second garotting panic of 1862.[17] As the attack was perpetrated on a well-known individual, this incident was the apotheosis of the garotte assault on British values.

Trollope's aim was not to discuss the Pilkington assault but rather to use the news story as a basis for his own arguments. In July 1862 the MP for Blackburn, Hugh Pilkington, walked from the House of Commons towards the Reform Club when he was attacked by two men. Another MP, Mr Kershaw, followed him at some distance but helplessly watched as Pilkington was struck on the head and knocked to the ground. According to *The Times*, Pilkington lost consciousness whilst crossing Pall Mall. When he regained consciousness, his umbrella and even his hat were intact but his watch and purse were missing. His undergarments were 'saturated in blood' and he says that 'from the pain round the top of the neck and immediately under the chin' his doctor drew the conclusion that the attack 'was an attempt at garotting'. Papers disagreed on the details, which left room for interpretation. The *Daily News* describes Pilkington's attack in greater detail and refers to his fumbling steps along the Guards Memorial and the way in which he was able to find his way despite 'partial insensibility'.[18] He also could not remember feeling the blow or seeing the assailant. The paper describes the injuries to his jawbone and the 'very suspicious mark round the throat'[19] recognized by his doctor. However, the accounts differ in that the *Daily News* asserts that no one witnessed the attack, a statement clearly at odds with the account in *The Times*. One piece of evidence missing in *The Times* and reported in the *Daily News* is the garotte attack on another man. Mr Hawkins, son of a gentleman connected with the British Museum, was assaulted between St James's Street and Bond Street on the same night. Hawkins's notion of the attack was 'confused' and the assault was not witnessed by the policeman who arrived on the scene after the attack has been carried out.[20]

The best-known modern interpretation of the garotting scene in *Phineas Finn* is surely the BBC adaptation *The Pallisers* (1974), a classic British drama produced at the same time as ITV's highly successful series *Upstairs Downstairs* (1971–5). The garotting scene as presented in the drama is, in fact, considerably at odds with the original version in Trollope's novel. In the television episode, Kennedy quarrels with Finn over Lady Laura and turns into a side street, watched closely by two suspicious-looking men. Moments later, Finn is alerted by Kennedy's screams and runs to his aid. Finn is involved in an affray with the two attackers and punches them, causing them to run away.

In comparison with Pilkington's confusing ordeal, we are given a substantial amount of information about the attack in *Phineas Finn*. The differences between the press depiction of the attack and Trollope's version serve to de-emphasize gung-ho responses to street crime and to show a hero fearlessly responding to violence using the minimum of force. As in the adaptation, relations between Finn and Kennedy are strained, yet, when Finn leaves his colleague, he feels uneasy for his safety. Finn's colleague appears to be stalked by two men whom Finn suspects of harbouring malicious intentions, so he takes a different turning in the road so that he can watch to see if Kennedy emerges from the street down which he has walked:

> But Mr Kennedy did not reach the corner. When he was within two doors of it, one of the men had followed him up quickly and thrown something round his throat from behind him. Phineas understood well now that his friend was in the act of being garrotted and that his instant assistance was needed. He rushed forward, and as the second ruffian had been close upon the footsteps of the first, there was almost instantaneously a concourse of the four men.

Trollope embellishes this scene with elements of sensation. Finn sees Kennedy and also a 'dark glimmering of the slight uncertain moonlight' against which two garotters stand. Trollope's theatrical description is inspired by the striking images used in *Punch* magazine's 'The Song of the Garotter', in which a garotter threatens to perform an assault on a moonlit night.[21] In 1854 an elderly garotte victim described himself as watching 'by the light of a distant gas lamp [...] four hands over him, feeling about him for his property'.[22] Therefore, while Juliet McMaster argues that Trollope tends to avoid melodrama,[23] he is nevertheless highly influenced by dramatic images employed in contemporary journalism. Kennedy's pursuer is identifiable as Holland's 'nasty man' who creeps up behind his victim before garotting him. The 'something' that is thrown over Kennedy's neck is either a noose or handkerchief.

Importantly, as Trollope tells us, 'there was no fight'. In saving Kennedy, Finn did not use a weapon, nor did he perform a fantastic feat of boxing. His presence scares off one of the attackers, but he catches the other and holds on 'gallantly' to his collar, handling him as Chiltern would a fox. This is curious given that *Phineas Finn* appeared during a time when boxing was hotly discussed as a means of street defence.

In *Tom Brown's Schooldays* Thomas Hughes had advised his young readers to learn how to fight: 'The world might be a better world without fighting ... but it wouldn't be our world; and therefore I am dead against crying peace when there is no peace, and isn't meant to be. I am as sorry as any man to see folk fighting the wrong people and the wrong things, but I'd a deal sooner see them doing that, than that they should have no fight in them.'[24] The etiquette manual *Habits of Good Society*, published just after Hughes's novel, recommends gentlemen to acquire skills in boxing in order to strike down a man 'gracefully':

> Never assail an offender with words, nor when you strike him, use such expressions as, 'Take that,' &c. There are cases in society when it is quite incumbent on you to knock an offender down, if you *can*, whether you feel angry or not, so that, if to do so is not precisely good manners, to omit it is sometimes very bad manners; and to box, and that well, is therefore an important accomplishment, particularly for little men.[25]

So, to utter aggressive intentions was hardly civilized behaviour but vulgar, a sign of ill-breeding. Trollope understood the importance of being able to defend oneself and one's reputation verbally and physically. As he tells readers in his autobiography, fighting gave him the opportunity to gain kudos at school. His pride in winning a contest is barely concealed: 'I was driven to rebellion, and there came a great fight, — at the end of which my opponent had to be taken home for a while. [...] I trust that some schoolfellow of those days may still be left alive who will be able to say that, in claiming this solitary glory of my schooldays, I am not making a false boast.'[26]

For Trollope, vigorous parliamentary political debate is constructive, and he particularly admires the way in which his parliamentary heroes exude charisma. As Mason argues, Plantagenet Palliser is Trollope's vision of the gentleman. Yet, despite being hard-working, principled and clever, he lacks vivacity.[27] The MP for Silverbridge, John Grey, is handsome and good but, through the iron self-control he has over his feelings, he almost loses his wife-to-be who assumes he has no emotions. Too much self-composure was not beneficial. A little drama was what his heroes needed. Trollope underlines this point by depicting great debates as boxing matches and fair fights. Demonstrating his enthusiasm for physical sports, he describes the healthy political debate between Mildmay (based on Russell) and Daubeny (thinly disguised as Benjamin Disraeli) as 'two champions of the ring', lunging at each other, 'striking as though each blow should carry death if it were but possible!'.

The physical boxing match stimulates the muscle while the intellectual debate expands the mind's horizons and tests one's courage. There are awards for a healthy expression of intellectual bravado in that 'if a man can hit hard enough he is sure to be taken into the elysium of the Treasury bench'. Trollope's description of the gallantry of professional men recalls Samuel Smiles's observation in *Self-Help* that 'the lawyer in full practice and the parliamentary leader in full work are called upon to display power of physical endurance and activity even more extraordinary than those of the intellect'.[28] Trollope's treatment of professional work and physical exercise highlights the interconnectedness of mind and body in defining British masculinity. The parliamentarian's physical stamina is put to the test in heated debates, while the lawyer must possess the physique to enable him to continuously climb 'close and heated courts'. Therefore, if one were to subscribe to Smiles's viewpoint, then Trollope's use of gladiatorial imagery is apposite: the combatant politicians are stretched both physically and mentally in their vocations. His depiction of parliamentary debate also challenges Antony Simpson's assertion of the mid-Victorian era that 'instantaneous heroism is not a concept that exists in middle-class thought'.

One writer commented in 1844 that 'if affairs of honour were settled by fists [...] instead of by pistols, or by any other method short of murdering one another, the public would not be offended'.[29] Pierce Egan, the celebrated author of *Life in London* (1821), wrote in 1851 that 'humanity is shocked' by duelling and argues that boxing is 'at any time preferable to duelling not only because it is the safest mode of settling a quarrel, but either of the antagonists has the advantage of crying out "enough", and yet preserve all the true spirit and principles of honour'.[30] In 1868 the *Saturday Review* argued in a pro-boxing article entitled 'Our Police' that 'individual energy and self-reliance will ultimately be called into play by the absence of all extrinsic helps to the preservation of order'.[31] Yet this 'art of self-defence' was not unanimously regarded in the same light by all commentators. *Habits of Good Society* thought that to hit out was a class-conscious act:

> The 'compleat gentleman' should be able to use his fists. Low as this art is, and contemptible as are those who make a profession of it, it is nevertheless of importance to a man of every class [...] The fist has expelled the sword and pistol [...] Two gentlemen never fight; the art of boxing is only brought into use in punishing a stronger and more impudent man of a class beneath your own.[32]

As this quote suggests, boxing was widely considered an uncouth pastime. Despite this book's claim for boxing to be a classless art, the press was divided on the appropriateness of it for middle-class men. As we know, *St James's Magazine* doubted the longevity of the bodybuilder who over-exerted himself and argued that it was dangerous to emulate him.[33] Such thinking was in keeping with Collins's depiction of Delamayn.

Prior to the late 1860s, boxing had been governed by Broughton's Rules in the 1840s and the Old London Prize Ring. In 1866 the Pugilists' Benevolent Association adopted new guidelines which were formally published a year later and have become known as the Queensberry Rules, after the Association's enthusiastic supporter, the eighth Marquess of Queensberry, John Sholto Douglas. These rules advised which kinds of blows were permissible, restricted the match to around 20 rounds of three minutes each, stipulated that gloves be worn (they had usually only been worn during training) and created imperative weight catego- ries to which each boxer was assigned. The impact of the new rules was not immediate. As Wood says, despite the Queensberry reforms, some boxing rings were still governed by the old London Prize Ring rules and it was not until the 1880s and 1890s that the Queensberry reforms came to prominence.[34] This is apparent by the way in which some journalists felt that the prize ring was too violent and not the kind of ideal on which middle-class manliness should be forged.

However, there was a concern over boxing, because on the one hand it threatened to deplete a man of his vital energy but, more significantly, on the other hand the prize ring was considered a morally brutalizing arena. 'There is nothing manly in prize-fighting', stated John Brookes in *Manliness: Hints to Young Men* (1859).[35] Various sources concurred.

While the hysterically over-armed pedestrian provided fodder for the playwright's satirical pen, the image of the civilian who was overly boisterous with his fists also attracted scepticism. This trend is summed up in observations in the *London Review*. The 1862 article 'Pugilism in High Quarters' lamented that: 'Pacific Englishmen go about with bloody thoughts in their minds, and a perfect armoury of defensive weapons beneath their great coats.'[36] For the genteel social classes, it was consid- ered vulgar to experiment in boxing, a pursuit which had been 'relegated from the round of civilized life by every one, except the lowest class of public-house keepers and a few fashionable debauchees'.[37] *St James's Magazine* announced a year later that 'muscular Christianity is in vogue' but equally expressed scathing scepticism for its efficacy in despatching with street ruffians. The magazine asserted that 'many foolish youths and inexperienced fathers have been absurd enough to imagine that by putting on the gloves and assuming a few fantastic attitudes they would be competent to accomplish what the Champion of England himself would not venture to attempt – namely, floor half a dozen garotting footpads at a time, who may chance to spring out upon him with a view to ease him of his superfluous cash, his watch, or his gold chain'.[38] As the *Pall Mall Gazette* said in 1866 in 'Prize-Fighting': 'The link between prize fighting and manly bravery is imaginary. The enormous majority of the bravest men in the world, officers and privates alike, in the army and the navy, in England and in foreign countries, never took part in such displays either as spectators, or as principals, or as abettors.' A link between prize fighting and crime seemed obvious to the magazine: 'The promoting of the prize-fighting system, in every one of its forms, is not only a gross and pernicious barbarism, but is one of the many prolific causes of the crimes and vices of the lawless hordes which thrive in the lowest ranks of English society.'[39] This statement closely followed the Hyde Park Riots and so associated boxing with the criminals, the 'lawless hordes'. It was also not morally edifying even to watch a prize fight: 'But no one who has any acquaintance with the phenomena of English crime can entertain any doubt that wherever prize fighting in any of its forms exists as a local popular amusement or trade, its effects are to the last degree demoralizing upon all who come within its influence.'[40]

Halperin has argued that Finn is 'one of the few conventional Victorian heroes', namely that he is 'consistently passive, one to whom things happen'.[41] This statement needs further examination. Trollope's account of the attack on Robert Kennedy MP can be read in relation to W.H. Holland's journalistic writing on street violence as well as his suggestions put forward in *Good Words*. The attack also conforms to the description of the typical garotting given by Holland in his *Cornhill Magazine* article 'Science of Garotting and Housebreaking'. Trollope's novel *The Small House at Allington* (1864) was serialized in *Cornhill Magazine* from 1862 to 1864[42] at the same time as the appearance of Holland's article. Due to his close relationship with the periodical, Trollope would have been aware of Holland's depiction of the threat to masculinity posed by street violence. Holland contributed a further article on self-defence to *Good Words* in 1866, when the evangelical magazine had become the most popular of monthlies, surpassing *Cornhill Magazine* in its sales figures in 1864.[43] Turner's discussion of Trollope's letters on *Good Words* suggests that at least in 1863 Trollope was aware of the nature of the periodical and its contents. Holland advocated passivity, writing that 'a solitary individual in the hands of garotters has only one chance, and that is to be quiet' as 'resistance only brings severe physical punishment to the helpless victim, who, being in their hands, is entirely at their mercy'.[44] Even screaming, which some sources advised, was less passive. Holland's argument that the solitary victim of an assault should remain passive may have been more practical in a real-life scenario in which an individual is pitted against two or more attackers, but his advice runs counter to the idealized retaliation recommended in nineteenth-century papers: even the non-athletic were advised to counter a garotting by 'keep[ing] the chin down and kick[ing] the assailant's shins'.[45] Finn does very little but what he does do is effective. Like Pilkington, Kennedy has bruises round his neck but, thanks to Finn, he escapes having only lost a cravat. Trollope's fictionalized garotting is influenced by Holland's account of a typical garotting; however, Trollope recommends a much more engaged response to violent crime than Holland's article in *Good Words*. Trollope was not averse to fighting but here he shows that a man does not need to exhibit his masculinity by acting against criminals with bravado.

Trollope's description of the citizen's arrest by Finn recalls the heroic manner in which de Comerford Clarkson and Lieutenant Bent defend themselves during an attack by pursuing and holding on to the attackers until they can be apprehended. The garotting scene in *Phineas Finn* accentuates the positive impact of resourcefulness and instinct in response to interpersonal violence. The press often depicted policemen as ineffective 'snoozing Blues', arriving on the scene too late and spending their beats raiding larders for pies. Trollope does not portray the police officer who arrives on the scene in such a manner, but rather emphasizes that it is Finn and not the policeman who has been effective in catching the criminal. Finn's assertive actions contrast with Mr Kershaw's passive observations of Pilkington being garotted. Finn is in fact a *deus ex machina*. According to the police officer, Finn's performance was 'uncommon neat'. Finn does his duty as a gentleman by saving Kennedy and instantly earns himself wide acclaim: 'All the world knew that Mr Kennedy, the new Cabinet Minister, had been garrotted, or half garrotted, and that that child of fortune, Phineas Finn, had dropped upon the scene out of heaven at the exact moment of time, and had taken the two garrotters prisoners, and saved the Cabinet Minister's neck and valuables – if not his life.' Even the illustrious Duke of Omnium 'express[es] a desire to be introduced' to Finn and says 'something about the garrotters' to him when they meet.

While Kennedy is the archetypal garotte victim, Finn represents Trollope's version of the brave civilian and the garotte scenario offers Finn, an outsider, an opportunity to assert his presence in London society. Trollope's garotte scenario extolls the bourgeois body and its relationship to national identity. Finn does not like or admire Kennedy but he does protect the parliamentarian from being attacked by 'street Bedouins' whose crime constitutes an attack on British civil liberties. By protecting Kennedy, Finn guards what is 'of good report', namely British institutions, the key symbol of which is government itself. In 1869 Trollope's readers would have been aware of the political significance of the Irish Finn defending the Scottish Kennedy in an attack which takes place in London. Under the 1867 Reform Act, large numbers of Irish men living in England and Wales were given the vote, a development which 'solidif[ied] the particular colonial relationship between those who were classified as Anglo-Saxon and Celt'.[46] Thus, the self-defence scenario in *Phineas Finn* is more than a citizen's arrest and suggests that, to Trollope, those who support the ideal of British gentlemanly unity deserve to be counted.

If the metatextualism of the typical garotte attack represented in the press was that of sexual threat, then the garotting episode in *Phineas Finn* allows Finn to assert his virility by defending the impotent Kennedy from a form of violation. Finn's parliamentary speech preceding the garotte attack is frenetic, imprecise and punctuated by forgetfulness. By contrast, Finn's heroism during the garotte attack raises him to a godly figure, descending 'from heaven' at the right moment.

Indeed, the codes of behaviour that were extolled under the civilizing offensive find their way into the self-defence scenarios of Trollope and Doyle, and these scenarios suggest that the gentleman could be 'at the same time retiring and vigorously assertive, feminine and masculine'.[47] Finn's protection of Kennedy is exemplary and he employs what Trollope terms in 'Uncontrolled Ruffianism' as 'proper manly vigour' and gentlemanly restraint. Finn is a character who is to be admired by readers: 'He was a man of strong opinions, who could yet be submissive [...] he was pleasant to other men – not combative, not self-asserting beyond the point at which self-assertion ceases to be a necessity of manliness.' The garotte scenario constitutes the display of Finn's best qualities. By rescuing a parliamentarian, the young middle-class man affirms his masculinity by exercising traits, such as intuition and reticence, normally classed as belonging more to the female sex. Juliet McMaster has perceived the way in which Finn's character has feminine qualities, exercising power in a feminine way, thereby gaining the favour of influential women such as Lady Laura, adding that 'this is the kind of power usually wielded by women in Trollope's novels, and it is appropriate that there should eventually be a debate in *Phineas Redux* on whether or not Phineas is "womanly"'.[48] Gay writes that 'many thoughtful Victorians in

Hughes's day came to suspect the automatic association of manliness with activity and womanliness with passivity'.[49] As Glendinning points out, Trollope 'explored ambivalence and ambiguity', in which his women had manly qualities and his men were like women.[50] Combining his feminine and masculine traits, Finn's perfectly timed reaction to the assault ensures that Kennedy emerges with his memory of the incident intact. Finn shows due caution in approaching the garotters, but when he does confront them, he demonstrates pluck; he has 'fight' in him.

As his gladiatorial combat scene demonstrates, for Trollope, verbal and physical self-expression reinforce each other as methods for asserting manliness. One must be able to speak up and act when appropriate and necessary. As Turner points out, Finn's first attempt at parliamentary debate (prior to the garotte attack) descends into a panic attack as Finn's spirit slackens. As Turner has argued, Kennedy's excessive passivity is suggestive of impotence.[51] This is underscored by the garotte attack in which Kennedy cannot even remark on his own physical condition: 'Kennedy was now leaning against the railings, and hitherto had been unable to declare whether he was really injured or not.' Kennedy is in shock and it takes him a while to be able to speak. The *Spectator* reviewer particularly enjoyed reading of Kennedy 'sitting for two or three days at home as stiff as a poker, and never speaking above a whisper, – absorbed in the shock to his throat and his self-importance, and in the danger to his life which he had so narrowly escaped'.[52]

Finn protects his status as *flâneur* by knowing how to defend himself and his colleague. In 'Uncontrolled Ruffianism' Trollope is of the opinion that 'surely it would not be necessary for everybody to stay at home o'nights, or to walk always in the middle of the street, to avoid a danger that was so minutely infinitesimal'.[53] As far as he was concerned, a man should be able to walk around the city without fear, to saunter unarmed, ruminating. That is what he told readers of 'Uncontrolled Ruffianism'. However, as his novels show, a man should maintain guard. As part of the idea that knowledge constituted self-defence, in effect Trollope's advice to his male readers is that certain areas are at certain times out of bounds to even the most experienced of *flâneurs*. He therefore maps out the geography of risk. It is clear that he despises fear in men but, in *The Prime Minister*, he adjusts his views slightly and tells readers that he does admire caution. In this novel, Ferdinand Lopez, an entrepreneur of mysterious, foreign origin, quarrels with his friend, Everett Wharton, over a parliamentary seat whilst walking in St James's Park at midnight, the scene of garottings reported in the press during the garotting outbreaks. Lopez is very uneasy about entering the gloomy park: 'Now, certainly, among the faults which might be justly attributed to Lopez, personal cowardice could not be reckoned. On this evening he had twice spoken of being afraid, but the fear had simply been that which ordinary caution indicates.' His apprehensions are realized when the drunken Wharton is set upon by thieves who tackle him to the ground, press on his windpipe and strangle him with his own necktie. Here Trollope swaps his narrative tone for a scientific voice: 'It is a treatment which, after a few seconds of vigorous practice, is apt to leave the patient for a while disconcerted and unwilling to speak.' His tone recalls the factual articles written by Holland.

The theme of mental coolness recurs too. While Finn steps in calmly to deal with Kennedy's attackers, Lopez launches into his defence, 'hardly knowing how he was acting'. He is injured and loses his hat, a fact which is mentioned with great frequency in the following pages and is an evil omen: Lopez eventually commits suicide by throwing himself in front of a high-speed train at the Tenway Junction, that great terminus of lives and luggage. For Trollope, crime by strangulation was still a hot topic, a 'treatment' to be studied academically and also to be included as a sensational device in novels ten years after he was penning the attack on Kennedy. While Trollope deeply admires physical and mental heroism and the ability to fight, he would rather that his readers do not actively seek confrontation with the criminal element or walk heavily armed with angry intentions. His ideal civilian should exercise his judgement, not his right to bear weapons.

6
Phineas Redux

Phineas returned: not quite back in the saddle?

As Halperin argues, *Phineas Redux* 'reads well even without *Phineas Finn* in mind'.[1] This is correct; however, the novel also functions as the double of *Phineas Finn*, mirroring its plot in darker shades. In this sequel we see a change in Finn's manner. His initiation into violent and outmoded methods of conflict resolution such as duelling leads to a change of character. While Finn remains tenaciously moral in his political convictions, his aggressive actions almost result in the loss of his right to participate in the political world.

As popular as its predecessor, *Phineas Redux* was written in 1870–1 and focuses on period 1868–71.[2] The novel begins inauspiciously with the death of Phineas's wife and father. Frank Holl's illustrations sensitively depict a grieving Finn. He provided illustrations for *Redux* when the novel appeared in serialized form in the *Graphic* between 19 July 1873 and 10 January 1874. However, in the novel, Trollope's hero does not appear to be deeply affected by the losses, which indicates a change in the protagonist's character. Coaxed to London by old friends, Finn resumes life in public duty, aspiring to become a Member of Parliament, albeit for the sooty constituency of Tankerville. However, for the first time, he finds that he has to fight for a seat. He loses on the issue of the separation of the church and state but eventually gains the seat when the successful candidate is accused of bribing the constituents. This event mirrors an occurrence in Trollope's own life. In 1868 he stood as candidate for the Yorkshire borough of Beverley. It was an ignominious affair. Mud-spattered, he lectured to an uninterested audience who cared little for the writer's voice. He was shocked by the level of skulduggery he encountered and was unwilling to put aside his principles to charm the voters. As it turned out, Trollope landed at the bottom of the poll, an experience which ended his ambitions to enter Pugin's majestic Houses of Parliament.

Finn learns from Quintus Slide, the hypocritical editor of the once radical but now conservative newspaper *The People's Banner*, that Kennedy threatens to have a letter published in which he demands Lady Laura to return to him, naming Finn as her lover. Outraged, Finn confronts Kennedy, who attacks him with a revolver. Rather than using comedy to criticize the use of weaponry, as was the case with the garotting plays, Trollope includes his warning in a more serious fashion within a grim plot in the second half of *Phineas Redux*. After a dispute at a London club, Finn is suspected of murdering his political enemy, Mr Bonteen. A trial ensues but Finn is acquitted in the light of evidence brought forward by Madame Max Goesler, still his admirer. Finn attempts to return to parliamentary duties but disillusionment consumes him. At the end of the novel he turns to Madame Goesler and finally accepts her as his wife. He makes a comeback and plays a key role as friend to Plantagenet Palliser in the subsequent novel; however, Trollope shows his wrathful response to Bonteen's jibes could have resulted in his own demise.

Occurring at roughly the same points in both novels, the hunting scenes reflect changes in Finn's character, reflecting his successes and failures. Before he goes hunting, he is struck by the realization 'that he [has] reached a time of life in which it [is] no longer comfortable for him to live as a poor man with men who [are] rich'. Finn 'might have been rich, and have had horses at command, had he chosen to sacrifice himself for money'. A middle-class man in the illustrious society of dukes, parliamentarians and ladies, Finn's sense of financial inferiority preys more on his mind in this novel. His sorrowful disposition regarding his financial disadvantage is a reflection of Anthony Trollope's days in Harrow, when Trollope found himself seated next to 'the sons of big tradesmen who made their ten thousand a year'.[3] A man could, in theory, rise up the ranks with education but, as Trollope shows, the middle-class man such as Finn still had to earn his place in society. Finn's feelings of inadequacy are exacerbated by the way in which his horse, Dandolo, is unable, unlike the other horses, to jump over an obstacle. Dandolo stalls, causing Finn to fly over the head of the animal into a ditch. Finn strikes Dandolo 'severely over the shoulders' with a whip and, 'gnashing his teeth', curses 'the infernal brute'. Finn's behaviour is profoundly out of character; he is 'raging, fuming, out of breath, miserably unhappy, shaking his reins, plying his whip, rattling himself about in the saddle, and banging his legs against the horse's sides'. Madame Goesler attempts to console him but he barely notices her. His temper resembles Oswald Chiltern's worst excesses. Here it is Finn and not Chiltern who is 'wild with rage against the beast'. This is comparable to the way in which, in *Phineas Redux*, Tom Spooner, an elderly landowner, vents his frustration on his horse when Adelaide Palliser spurns his advances: '"She's the d—t vixen that ever had a tongue in her head," said Tom Spooner, lifting his whip and striking the poor off-horse in his agony.'

Finn is not intentionally cruel to his horse. He whips and digs his spurs into the creature in order to encourage it to take the fence. However, the contrast of Finn's behaviour to his 'comely' nature is alarming. Trollope may not have intended this as a reference to Victorian melodrama, but the image of the gentleman whipping his horse was used by various writers to indicate evil or cruelty. In *Great Expectations* Drummel mounts his horse in 'his blundering brutal manner, calling for a light for the cigar in his mouth'.[4] Judith Walkowitz writes that in her campaigns for the repeal of the Contagious Diseases Acts, Josephine Butler reworked images from melodrama, incorporating the villainous horse-whipper who was also a woman-beater.[5] In *Man and Wife* Delamayn announces that: 'The grand secret in dealing with a woman, is to take her as you take a cat, by the scruff of the neck.'[6] When cruelty to animals and violence towards women were seen as a mutually reinforcing habits, Finn's simultaneous beating of the horse and lack of attention to Madame Goesler highlight this selfish and most unattractive new streak in his nature.

Frustration and feelings of inadequacy, as Trollope shows, are major causes of male violence. Also positioned at the same points in both novels are Finn's two main encounters with Kennedy, the garotte attack and the meeting in a London hotel. In this latter scene in *Phineas Redux* we see the image of masculine insanity coupled with the use of weapons. In *Phineas Redux* Finn learns that Kennedy means to publish a letter requesting his wife Laura to return to him and names Finn as her lover. Finn confronts Kennedy at his hotel, telling him that he will not submit to Kennedy's threat of publication. Incensed, Kennedy threatens Finn with a firearm and Trollope writes that 'the pistol in a moment was at [Finn's] head, and the madman pulled at the trigger'. However, Kennedy's lack of manual dexterity offers Finn a lucky escape: 'The mechanism of the instrument required that some bolt should be loosed before the hammer would fall upon the nipple and the unhandy wretch for an instant fumbled over the work so that Phineas, still facing his enemy, had time to leap backwards towards the door.' Fortunately for

Finn, Kennedy misses his aim. By aiming at Finn, Kennedy commits an assault, defined in *Archbold's* as 'an attempt to commit a forcible crime against the person of another' using 'a cane, stick or fist, although party misses his aim'.[7] Trollope indicates Kennedy's total lack of control over himself and his emotions: 'It was clear to Phineas that the man was so mad as to be not even aware of the act he had perpetrated.'

In her study on guns and violence in English history, Joyce Lee Malcolm quotes the work of James Paterson, a lawyer whose book appeared in 1877, only a few years after *Phineas Redux*. In it he argues that 'the right of each to carry arms [...] and these the best and the sharpest [...] for his own protection in case of extremity, is a right of nature indelible and irrepressible, and the more it is sought to be repressed, the more it will recur'.[8] Malcolm concludes that 'criminals could expect people to be armed and prepared to use force to protect themselves and their property'.[9] However, she has not observed that Paterson later campaigns against the 'right' of civilians to be armed. Rather, Paterson argues for the passing of more impartial laws which would signal 'an end to the barbaric habit of clothing oneself in triple coats of mail, and to girding on daggers and loaded arms' and promote a situation in which 'each individual, inspired with his confidence, ceases thereafter to think of anything beyond more peaceful weapons'.[10] Taking Paterson's observations, it may have been legal to carry loaded weapons, but for a growing number of critics, the most desirable condition was that in which citizens could traverse the streets minimally armed or completely unarmed. The firearm is not a source for good in either *Phineas Finn* or its sequel but is a desperate resort to settling disputes when gentlemanly social tact and diplomacy break down. The pistol also gained notoriety as a weapon of assassination. *Phineas Finn* was serialized only two years after the assassination of Abraham Lincoln by John Wilkes Booth in 1865. Contemporary papers described him as Britain's 'best friend', the loss of whom was 'unspeakably great'.[11] After describing the murder of the President in detail,[12] *The Times* quoted the words of an American in London: 'The ball that penetrated his brain was addressed to the heart of each and every one of us.'[13] In 1872 a 'demented youth', Arthur O'Connor, a young City clerk, threatened Queen Victoria with what turned out to be an unloaded pistol. It was described in the press as a 'silly' attack. Therefore, when misused, the pistol was associated not with the defence against evil but the loss of something treasured and a sign of mental instability.

When Trollope's heroes are forced to look down the barrel of a gun, their gallant natures are tested and such confrontations further allow

Trollope to elaborate on what he believes to be the best reaction to a physical threat. The scene also says much about Finn's attitude towards attack. Frank Holl's illustration from the *Graphic* of 6 September 1873 shows Finn shielding his face from the bullet while Kennedy looks wizened and frantic. More famous is perhaps Bradley Headstone's campaign of hatred against Eugene Wrayburn in *Our Mutual Friend* (1865), published in the same year as *The Eustace Diamonds*. Yet Trollope with equal engagement portrays the dangerous unravelling of masculine composure with painstaking detail in the unhinging of George Vavasor, which culminates in his murderous assault on John Grey in *Can You Forgive Her?* A parallel with *Phineas Redux* occurs in *Can You Forgive Her?*, in which the irascible George Vavasor (neither Kennedy nor Vavasor know how to use their weapons) visits Grey in his chambers and threatens to shoot him if he rings for assistance. Grey proceeds to reach for the cord. As far as Trollope is concerned, Grey is to be commended for his cool head. The bullet passes his head but Grey is not shaken and does not tell anyone of the matter just after it has happened. Finn is not injured in the altercation with Kennedy but nonetheless emerges considerably shaken.

Before the duel, Finn is 'afraid of no violence, personal to himself'. However, his impressions after the attack demonstrate a horror of interpersonal threat: 'He had once stood up to be fired at in a duel, and had been struck by the ball. But nothing in that encounter had made him feel sick and faint through every muscle as he felt just now.' He tries to remedy his panic with alcohol. It will be demonstrated below that Trollope argues that this new fear of violence accompanies Finn's readiness to perpetrate aggressive acts on others. As an added gesture, intended more as an insult rather than an assault, Kennedy sees Finn's hat lying on the floor of his room and throws the article down the stairs of the hotel. Finn's hat is so important that the trembling Finn considers risking his life in retrieving it from Kennedy's grasp. By then it is too late to recover his presence of mind.

The murderous life-preserver

Some who take delight in wandering about through strange lands, among lions might look upon the proposed state of constant preparation under arms as one of pleasurable excitement but for us who are accustomed to regard the security of our pockets and persons as an affair of the police, – to us, such suggestions are more terrible than the evils supposed to be general.[14]

In 'Uncontrolled Ruffianism' Trollope advises against viewing the city as a playground for the gun-toting and knuckleduster-wielding urban explorer. As *Phineas Redux* shows, weapons can haunt their owner.

Trollope did not profess to believe that people were wholly good or completely evil. Rather, in *The Eustace Diamonds*, he says that a man's character could change:

> There are human beings who, though of necessity single in body, are dual in character;—in whose breasts not only is evil always fighting against good,—but to whom evil is sometimes horribly, hideously evil, but is sometimes also not hideous at all. Of such men it may be said that Satan obtains an intermittent grasp, from which, when it is released, the rebound carries them high amidst virtuous resolutions and a thorough love of things good and noble.

As we see in *Phineas Redux*, various events can influence such a transformation. Notably, there is the brush with violence. The German Mensur was an act of initiation and the objective was not necessarily to win but to receive an injury, a souvenir that demonstrated to others that the duellist could bravely withstand pain. Finn receives a wound on the right shoulder. Turner argues that the duel is an affirmation of his love for Violet, gives him his own painful 'cherished scar' and makes him feel like a man.[15] When his shoulder aches, he remembers the duel with pride. This is not the first blemish to appear in the novels. In *Can You Forgive Her?*, the boy, George Vavasor, defends his family against burglars. The only weapon he uses is the burglar's stick which he manages to grasp and wield against the attacker. The burglar retaliates. Vavasor's action is brave but leaves him with a prominent scar across his face, a metonymic 'gaping hole' that changes in appearance to match his increasingly morose temperament.

While the wound constitutes a secret source of pride for Finn and a sign of his sexual coming of age, affirming his place in the world of men, his injury is at the same time also a signifier of his gradual corruption and decline. This is comparable to the wound Watson receives on the shoulder from a Jezail bullet. In his examination of the Sherlock Holmes stories, Joseph Kestner tells us that 'it is crucial to recognize that Watson returns from the Afghanistan campaign with a wounded body, a body therefore not capable of sustaining the penis/phallus equation of dominant masculinity'.[16] He is already demoralized by his lack of money and social status, and the pistol duel with Chiltern has punctured his moral code. This is apparent in his demeanour towards his rival,

Mr Bonteen, at the Universe Club. As Shirley Letwin argues, 'to remain aware of evil and ready to fight it without descending into vulgar suspicion and aggressiveness is the burden of discretion that a gentleman should have the strength to bear'.[17] Unfortunately, Finn falls short of this mark.

Bonteen, President of the Board of Trade, despises Finn. When at a London club, he overhears Bonteen accuse him of being Lady Laura's lover. Finn approaches Bonteen and demands an explanation. Trollope gives us a lengthy description of the impact that Finn's retaliation will have on himself and those around him, and says that 'when men could fight readily, an arrogant word or two between two known to be hostile to each other was only an invitation to a duel'. Again, this is a reference to the confusion caused in the wake of the demise of duelling. To underscore Finn's change of attitude, Trollope has his hero remark that 'there are times in which one is driven to regret that there has come an end to duelling, and there is left to one no immediate means of resenting an injury'. Quarrellers, let alone duellists, are unwelcome in the club environment. Thus, in the more 'civilized' society of the late 1860s even a mere verbal dispute could give cause for apprehension. In *Phineas Finn*, Finn is reluctant to strike out against Chiltern and fears a 'row'. However, in this scene he is attracted to confrontation. Finn does not merely argue with Bonteen; he also expresses a willingness to duel. In a conversation with his old friend Laurence Fitzgibbon, Finn tells him that Bonteen 'hasn't spirit enough to go out with [him]' to duel and even expresses his readiness to 'shoot' him.

Disappointingly, Trollope does not offer suggestions on how best to tackle personal insult, but he most certainly discusses at length one mode of retaliation which he considers wholly inappropriate. Finn casts a shadow over his own reputation by threatening to strike out against his enemy. When Bonteen exits the Universe Club, he acknowledges Finn's friends but brazenly ignores him. Finn's response to the cut is wrathful: 'With a laugh, he took a life-preserver out of his pocket, and made an action with it as though he were striking some enemy over the head.' This small gesture may appear insignificant; however, it is classified as an assault. *Snowden's Magistrates Assistant, and Police Officers and Constables' Guide* of 1859 writes: 'To lift up the hand in a threatening manner, so as to exhibit an intention coupled with an ability to do harm, is an assault, though no blow be struck, for it is an attempt to or offer to do violence.'[18] Once the defender of justice, Finn is now the aggressor because his gesticulation with a life-preserver is not equal to Bonteen's treatment of him which, though insulting, is not threatening. Finn's assault is his first act of physical aggression to stem from premeditated and gratuitous malice, and is distinguished from any previous acts of violence. We saw a precursor of this behaviour when he actually struck Dandolo, but this violent response to the horse's obstreperous nature does serve a positive purpose, in that Finn is attempting to encourage the horse to resume its course. His gesticulation has catastrophic consequences for his reputation: he learns from his friends the next morning that Bonteen has been murdered.

Trollope's account of strong enmity between two men recalls Dickens's treatment of the intense rivalry between Headstone and Wrayburn in *Our Mutual Friend*. In this regard, Dickens's schoolmaster Headstone provides a useful analogue to Finn. Headstone is plagued by feelings of inadequacy, especially before his social superior Eugene Wrayburn. As Headstone's rage towards Wrayburn increases, he stalks the lawyer and hatches plans for his death. An eerie description of Headstone's pursuit of Wrayburn suggests that violent intentions lead to the death of the enraged perpetrator of violent acts: 'The haggard head floated up the dark staircase, and softly descended nearer to the floor outside the outer door of the chambers.'[19] It appears that Headstone is hatless, an impression suggested by his dishevelled appearance. In this warning, Dickens argues that Headstone's very fury renders him a disembodied ghoulish apparition as he traverses the darkness 'like a haggard head suspended in the air: so completely did the force of his expression cancel his figure'.[20] The schoolmaster has relinquished his lower-middle-class respectability and is a man now only fit for the gallows or a demise by other means, as his name, bearing deathly connotations, suggests. The theme of the hat and the injured head is elaborated in Trollope's account of Bonteen's death. Bonteen is a coarse individual, a 'devil' who 'flushed with much wine' is prone to arrogance. Bonteen has his just deserts for his 'devilish' behaviour when he is himself murdered. The dislodging of his hat literally facilitates the death of its owner but its fall is also an inauspicious symbol of Bonteen's capitulation.

Knobsticks, also known as knobkerries, have a supple shaft and are topped on either one or both ends with a lead ball around which string is woven. They are roughly a foot long and can be carried easily under a coat. They formed part of the gentlemanly collection of street weapons. However, Trollope is fascinated with a related type of stick and has expressly chosen to give it a starring role in *Phineas Redux* – the life-preserver.

During the course of the second half of *Phineas Redux*, the life-preserver increasingly encroaches upon our attention and so it is worth discussing

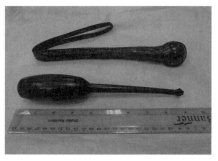

Figures 6.1 and 6.2   An assortment of life-preservers. These weapons are of a variety of weights and are comprised of materials including whalebone and lead.

the weapon and its significance. As Trollope says: 'There had been a run upon life preservers, in consequence of recommendations as to their use given by certain newspapers; – and it was found as impossible to trace one particular purchase as it would be that of a loaf of bread.' Contemporary sources do not suggest that the Victorian public ever confused the defensive stick with other 'life-preservers', namely life-jackets, floating apparatuses and fireguards which were also advertised in the press. 'Life-preservers' were probably relatively easy to obtain and the term 'life-preserver' appears to have been widely understood. The term 'life-preserver' is interchangeable with 'cosh' but not with trun-cheon or cudgel. The *OED* defines a cudgel as 'a short thick stick used as a weapon; a club'.

The critical approach to the over-use of weaponry for urban pro-tection is apparent in *Phineas Redux*, as well as in his journalistic writing. In 'Uncontrolled Ruffianism' Trollope argues that it would be unfortunate to 'be ever on our guard, to hurry along, looking over our shoulders to the right and to the left, mindful always of the cudgel in our hands'.[21] Thus, within this sentence Trollope links overarming with fear and suggests that this type of fearful retaliation is unmanly. In *The Prime Minister*, the hero of the novel and parliamentary candidate Arthur Fletcher follows the advice of a friend and arms himself with a big stick against the resentful Ferdinand Lopez who threatens to horsewhip his rival in love and politics. Trollope portrays Lopez as bordering on lunacy, but in the light of Trollope's words in 'Uncontrolled Ruffianism', Fletcher's actions are cowardly, relying as he does on a police officer as well as his own stick and friend for his protection.

An interesting comparison can be made between the life-preserver and the police truncheon. During the latter half of the nineteenth century, changes in the design of truncheons effectively made police weaponry less conspicuous. The original batons introduced when the Metropolitan Police was formed in 1829 were 20 inches long and were ornately and brightly decorated with the Garter Coat of Arms and the initials 'MP' in gold and red lettering. They were often painted by officers themselves. By the time of the first garotting panic, the size was reduced to 17 inches (43 cm) and officers who wished their weapons to be ornamented had to provide their own decorative designs. By the mid-1880s the truncheon case

Figure 6.3   Police truncheons.

was replaced by the truncheon pocket, sown into officer's trousers. The size of the baton was now 15 inches (38 cm) and decorative truncheons were disallowed.[22] This suggests that while the officer was entitled to uphold the law, the tough method with which he was sometimes required to enforce the law was to be made less readily apparent to a public which was beginning to question violent means.

The Victorian police officer's truncheon is a larger, thicker wooden instrument. By contrast, the life-preserver has a thinner handle, a distinctly weighted and bulbous end, and can be constructed of a variety of materials, including whalebone, cane and lead. Whilst very plain in appearance, life-preservers were sometimes finely crafted. They were even displayed alongside the Bramah and Chubb locks at the Crystal Palace in 1851. Unlike the typical knobstick, the weighted end was not covered with string, making the strike harder and more deadly. In the BBC's *The Pallisers*, Finn's weapon has a leaden ball attached to the handle with a supple shaft. It is one of the strangest life-preservers I have encountered so far in my research but, as Trollope himself shows, odd-looking variations on the theme of the defensive stick certainly abounded. As he reiterates in *Phineas Redux*, in the late 1860s 'there had been much garotting in the streets, and writers in the Press had advised those who walked about at night to go armed with sticks. Finn had himself been once engaged with garotters, – as has been told in a former chronicle, – and had since armed himself, thinking more probably of the thing which he had happened to see than men do who had only heard of it'. Finn carried 'some stick or bludgeon at night' and purchased a life-preserver after the attack. In any case, whether he owned one or not, it was not used in the attack on Kennedy. By juxtaposing his frequent accounts of weapons crazes with a description of Finn's misuse of his weapon, Trollope leaves us with the strong impression that armed self-defence can easily lead to the committing of offensive acts. When Finn is arrested on suspicion of murdering Bonteen, his possessions are rifled, his laundry searched, his private life and manliness questioned. His own life-preserver is subject to much inspection. For instance, even his own lawyer believes him to be guilty, while his mentor, Mr Low, inspects Finn's life-preserver for suspicious marks.

In the course of Finn's trial, a boy finds a discarded life-preserver in a garden near where Bonteen was murdered. Trollope relishes the opportunity to describe the weapon in detail:

> The instrument was submitted to the eyes and hands of persons experienced in such matters, and it was declared on all sides that the

thing was not of English manufacture. It was about a foot long, with a leathern thong to the handle, with something of a spring in the shaft, and with the oval loaded knot at the end cased with leathern thongs very minutely and skilfully cut. They who understood modern work in leather gave it as their opinion that the weapon had been made in Paris.

The Metropolitan Police Historical Collection keep a weapon very similar to the one described above. As it transpires, the jettisoned weapon once belonged to Joseph Emilius, a character readers had already met in the earlier novel *The Eustace Diamonds*. Trollope paints him as a shifty character with a shady past, a Christian clergyman who converted from Judaism, changing his religion and his name (from Yosef Mealyus to Joseph Emilius) in one stroke. Trollope's description of Emilius is uncomfortably tinged with no small measure of anti-Semitism: he was 'a renegade Jew', a 'greasy, fawning, pawing, creeping, black-browed rascal'. Learning that her new husband is a spendthrift and, she suspects, a bigamist, Lizzie Eustace appeals to her friend, the Minister for the Board of Trade, for assistance. Bonteen then delves into Emilius's past and his research confirms that the clergyman is indeed still married to a woman in Prague. Emilius is then prompted to murder Lizzie's defender

Figure 6.4   Joseph Emilius's weapon.

to avoid exposure. Comparing *The Eustace Diamonds* and *Phineas Finn*, it is apparent that Emilius is a foreign, roguish element whose murderous attack on a government minister mirrors the garotte attack on Kennedy which was itself perpetrated by criminals who were considered part of an alien, and subhuman, group.

In *Character* Smiles stressed the effects of the 'integrity of individual character' on the health of the state and its empire: 'In fine, stability of institutions must depend upon stability of character. Any number of depraved units cannot form a great nation. The people may seem to be highly civilised, and yet be ready to fall to pieces at the first touch of adversity.' States without gentlemanly 'character' may be 'rich, polite, and artistic; and yet hovering on the brink of ruin'.[23] There was a public fascination with fakery in its various guises, with the unravelling of unpolished and, by inference, deceitful men, of liars and imposters. Trollope preferred honesty. As he says in *Can You Forgive Her?*: 'For myself I like the open babbler the best. Babbling may be a weakness, but to my thinking mystery is a vice.' His grandest and most enduring vision of deceit is embodied in the character of Augustus Melmotte, the illustrious, foreign swindler who exploits the avarice of the English aristocracy for his own gain and eventually dramatically topples to his own demise in *The Way We Live Now* (1875). The novel was one of his bestselling creations. Emilius, a social imposter, made his appearance in Trollope's novel at around the same time as the Tichborne Case was finally laid to rest. This saga surfaced in the press in 1866, the year in which Trollope was writing *Phineas Finn*. When, in 1854, Roger Tichborne, a well-to-do young man from Hampshire, was lost at sea, his distraught mother sent advertisements across the globe to appeal for him to contact her. Her plea was answered by Arthur Orton, an Australian butcher, who claimed he was the Tichborne heir. The drowned man's mother believed Orton to be her son despite the fact that the real Roger Tichborne had been good-looking, slim and well-spoken, and Orton was his opposite. It was readily apparent that the 'polish' he had attempted to apply was tarnished. Arthur Orton had given himself away through noticeable deficiencies in his education and his lack of refinement. He had tried fraudulently to acquire the status of gentleman and his misfit character made him stand out in ways of which he was clearly unaware.

Emilius's murder weapon, despite its name, is not used for self-defence but has its reputation blackened by being involved in a murder. It is a weapon also associated with shifty characters and brought misfortune on his hero. Contemporary journalism and reports of attacks from the nineteenth century tell us that the life-preserver was used predominantly by burglars. It formed part of their kit, along with the skeleton key, lantern and crowbar. For instance, in an article in *Cornhill Magazine*, based on interviews conducted with criminals, the writer tells us that 'pistols are seldom carried by them; the weapon is generally a "neddy" or life-preserver'.[24] In Taylor's *The Ticket-of-Leave Man*, we learn that the colleague of Hawkshaw, the play's detective, had been murdered by the villain, Dalton, with a life-preserver: 'He was never his own man afterwards. He left the force on a pension, but he grew a sort of paralized – lost the use of his limbs first, and then got queer in the head.'[25] It is a weapon which Dalton uses on numerous occasions during the play.

A way of understanding social unrest is by housing paraphernalia associated with turbulent times within museum walls, to be observed and studied. Notable examples are Berlin's Checkpoint Charlie Museum and the Central Museum of the Revolution in Moscow. It is often said that the Victorian era heralded the start of museum culture, seeing the inauguration of great collections such as the Victoria and Albert Museum and the Natural History Museum, which sprang up in the wake of the Great Exhibition. But when it came to studying the darker aspects of civilization, the Scotland Yard Crime Museum was symbolic of the desire to collect the guilty emissaries of the violent mind. The Prisoners' Property Act 1869 permitted the police to keep objects belonging to criminals to be used for police teaching. In the year after *Phineas Redux* appeared as a novel, the museum was unofficially opened at Great Scotland Yard. It quickly became known as the 'Black Museum'. As a journalist from the *Observer* said in 1877: 'The building is, indeed, as it is called, a *Black Museum*, for it is associated with whatever is darkest in human nature and human destiny.'[26] A grim iron-barred, repository, the museum contained the bloodstained clothing of murder victims, knives, life-preservers, daggers, pikes and even the coat worn by the Tichborne Claimant during his trial. Nowadays, the collection is referred to as the Crime Museum. Had the murder case in *Phineas Redux* really occurred, Emilius's life-preserver would certainly have taken its place in the collection.

Leaps in the dark

Crawford Wilson's *The Antigarotte* (1863) had delighted audiences with its comic interpretation of the consequences of wearing of urban armour. By contrast, *Phineas Redux* took a sterner approach, showing how the main protagonist's reliance on weapons posed a greater threat to him than a toe injury. Trollope builds on the work of weapon-sceptical farce writers by dramatically increasing the stakes for those who wish to use street armour. Finn's life is imperilled and his mental hardiness erodes. Frank Holl's illustration in the November 1873 edition of the *Graphic* shows a listless, imprisoned Finn, slumped in his chair. His scrape with the legal system – a trial which lasts several weeks – changes him, and the varnish on his character begins to fade. The 'uprightness, the manly beauty' and 'the outward grace of his demeanour' shiver into sickliness and self-pity. As the *Spectator's* review of *Phineas Redux* commented: 'We see how morbidly susceptible he is to the attacks on him which result in his exclusion from office. We are perfectly aware that it is this sensitive element in him which both endears him to women, and, to some extent makes him fail in which we should call the manlier side of life.' [27] As Finn says himself: 'I am womanly [...] I can't alter my nature.' While his womanly characteristics aided him in defending Kennedy from street ruffians, Trollope shows that the over-cultivation of feminine sensibilities can be detrimental.

Sitting forlornly in his jail cell, Finn realises that his life hangs in the balance, with two incriminating objects implying his guilt: a grey coat and a life-preserver. On the night of Bonteen's murder, Lord Fawn observes a man darting away in a grey coat and, on the basis of witnessing the quarrel, deduces that the owner who is flitting away is Finn. Finn's coat is identical, which leads the befuddled Fawn to mistake him for the killer. Given the length of the trial, the reader has the impression that the investigation surrounding these two items gives Trollope a perfect opportunity to cross-examine his protagonist's nature and to make further comments on crime and aggression.

As Glendinning argues, the scenes of violence in Trollope's work reflect a violent aspect of his character.[28] Perhaps it is fairer to say that Trollope was intrigued by what precipitated the violent turn in human nature, and he was also interested in recording the manifestations of the public interest in crime. In the murder trial of Finn, his lawyer, Chaffenbrass, interrogates a novelist who witnesses the clash between Bonteen and Finn at the Universe Club. Chaffenbrass cites examples of premeditated murders from literature through the ages, including *Hamlet*, *Macbeth*, Scott's *Kenilworth* (1821) and Bulwer Lytton's *Eugene Aram* (1832). Thus, Trollope places his own novel as one in the history of novels by well-known writers of which violent acts and the motivations behind them form a key part of the plot. As Trollope shows here, novels offer violence as entertainment while the courts are a stage on which 'those bewigged ones' act out or 'perform' their lengthy 'parts'. The Old Bailey is the scene of action in the second half of *Phineas Redux* and is filled with all manner of social classes, from the Prime Minister to members of the public, indicating that the attraction of a sensational crime story is universal. The public will do anything to grab hold of a good story, as Trollope indicates with his description of the trials an individual must go through before being able to witness a trial themselves. He discusses the incommodious business of fighting for and retaining a seat or merely just a place in the crowd, tucking in one's elbows and suppressing a sneeze, concluding that it is perhaps more comfortable to read the report in *The Times* in the comfort of one's own home.

The scenario in which Finn finds himself was paralleled in Fergus Hume's bestselling 1887 novel *The Mystery of a Hansom Cab*, which begins with a newspaper report of a murder. In *Sherlock's Men* Joseph Kestner writes that although initially published in Australia, *The Mystery of a Hansom Cab* 'soon achieved enormous publicity when it was published in England in 1887, to become the best-selling detective novel of the century'.[29] Though innocent, Brian Fitzgerald, who like Finn is an Irishman, is put on trial for his life for committing the murder of Oliver Whyte in the back of a hansom cab. Fitzgerald is arrested on the basis that he had worn the same coat as the killer, who was seen exiting the cab on the night of the murder. Furthermore, he had also vowed to 'kill' White in the open street if he married the woman Fitzgerald intended to marry. Mr Gorby, the detective, believes from this unguarded outburst that Fitzgerald was the murderer.

Like Finn, Fitzgerald is released in the light of evidence and by the efforts of his lover. Finn is rescued by Madame Goesler's detective work, which helps to pin the guilt on Joseph Emilius. Madame Goesler's shrewd nature and assiduous pursuit of the truth should earn her at least a footnote in the annals of detective fiction, alongside Violet Strange and Richard Marsh's lip-reader Judith Lee. She uses any means at her disposal, interrogating and bribing Emilius's landlady. She even journeys to Prague to seek out the locksmith who Emilius instructed to create a copy of the key for him (this copy allowed him to sneak out at night to commit the murder). However, the weariness, mental anguish and disillusionment suffered by Finn and Fitzgerald are painstakingly depicted in *Phineas Redux* and *The Mystery of a Hansom Cab*. They resent being the subject of gossip and morbid fascination. As a result of his ordeal, Finn is 'low in heart, disgusted with the world, and sick of humanity', no longer 'fit for use', while Fitzgerald goes from being 'gay and bright' to 'ill and worried'.[30] The public reaction to Finn's trial in *Phineas Redux* is particularly telling. Most of the Members of Parliament and even some of Finn's closest friends believe him to be guilty of the murder. This fate also befalls Fitzgerald. In *Phineas Finn*, Chiltern damages his own reputation through brawling, with the result that his act of self-defence at Newmarket is viewed with suspicion. Correspondingly, in *Phineas Redux* it is Finn's aggressive gesture with the life-preserver which problematizes his alibis in court. His defence of Kennedy is rendered insignificant. Both novels underline the prescript that unnecessary displays of murderous wrath, however much disconnected from a *real* intent to murder, could nevertheless result in trial at the dock.

Finn and Fitzgerald are rescued from the gallows by women. Once a 'gentleman' and saviour of Kennedy, Finn's masculinity is now presented in the light of this hero-saviour role reversal as pale and shrunken. Both Finn and Fitzgerald are eventually redeemed – they marry their rescuers – but the trauma they suffer stays with them. Once a young rising star in politics during the period when Disraeli was busying himself with electoral reform, Finn now takes his own 'leap' into the dark. Re-enacting the actions of the murderer, he dons the grey coat with which he had been mistaken for Emilius and, shaking, he walks to the murder spot. His is a furtive fancy; he risks being seen by his colleagues at the nearby club and while this risk causes him unease, he also derives pleasure from the danger: 'But he walked fast, and went on till he came to the spot at which the steps descend from the street into the passage, – the very spot at which the murder had been committed. He looked down it with an awful dread, and stood there as though he were fascinated, thinking of all the details which he had heard throughout the trial.' In this strange catharsis, Finn crosses the threshold between innocence and guilt, between himself and the man of blood. In order to understand the events that occurred, he steps down into the sombre recesses of the killer's mind as the man waited in the passage, weapon in hand, for his victim to approach. The passageway in which Finn now stands is, as Trollope says, 'a spot to which an honest man at night would hardly trust himself with honest purposes'. It is a lonely alleyway in which it is 'best to step aside and let the suspicious follower pass on'. We observe more of this role-playing with Sherlock Holmes, whose ability to mimic the inhabitants of the criminal underworld allows him to come closer to solving crime.

In *The Mystery of a Hansom Cab*, Fitzgerald and Madge exit the novel bound for a new life in England, while Finn and Madame Goesler disappear in Europe for a few months. As Moody has observed, 'Trollope justifies unheroic heroes and redefines worldly loss, defeat and individual withdrawals from social life and competition as misunderstood and understandable choices whose courage is underrated'.[31] Trollope does not condemn Finn's decision to turn away from the world of politics; however, at the close of *Redux,* Trollope tells us that Finn's redemption is incomplete without productive and, by inference, masculine work: 'Of Phineas every one says that of all living men he has been the most fortunate. The present writer will not think so unless he shall soon turn his hand to some useful task. Those who know him best say that he will go into office before long.' The 'useful task' to which Trollope alludes is intended as a moral corrective to Finn's earlier transgressions. Trollope admired the energetic bachelor, but at the end of the novel he feels that he must rein in his hero's boisterous energy. Finn's sexual flightiness, the source of his strife in both novels, is to be replaced with constructive and, quite possibly, creative and morally edifying 'gladiatorial' work in the field of politics. Looking back over the Palliser series, Trollope emphasized the importance of middle-class masculine charisma, physical showmanship and an appreciation of minimal violence, but was too shy to bestow these qualities on a single individual to any great measure.

Part III
Physical Flamboyance in the Holmes Canon: 1887–1914

7
Exotic Enemies

Obstructing the flow of violence

The Holmes canon is redolent of late-nineteenth-century preoccupations with acts of brutality committed not merely by lower-class street ruffians but by higher classes, mainly middle-class professionals. In 'ASB', Doyle warns that violence literally and metaphorically 'recoil[s] upon the violent' and explicitly links the violent man with the trope of degeneration. While he does not suggest methods by which ancestral retrogression can be prevented, Doyle shows that the curbing of violent acts figuratively protects society from the bloody effects of degeneration and disease.

Dr Grimesby Roylott is represented both as a profligate upper-class tyrant and also a middle-class professional turned evil. The descendant of squires, the Roylotts of Stoke Moran, who have squandered the family fortune, Roylott trains as a doctor and makes his living in Calcutta. However, he embodies the worst features of Wiener's 'empire man' and threatens, at least on a small scale, the management of the Empire. In India, Roylott responds hysterically to a number of burglaries in his house and he thrashes his servant to death. He narrowly escapes the death penalty for his crime and, once released from prison, returns to England a broken man. (We have, with *Phineas Redux* and *The Mystery of a Hansom Cab*, seen the psychological impact which a close encounter with the death penalty can have on a Victorian man.) On returning to England, he egregiously involves himself in brawls and perpetrates further acts of violence against local villagers. Roylott, the brawler, recalls the untamed Chiltern in *Phineas Finn,* but he lacks Chiltern's good nature. Furthermore, his violent acts are not outbursts of a restless character but emanate from a will to do harm.

Roylott's stepdaughter, Helen Stoner, cannot account for her sister's sudden hysteria and death during the night. She suspects Roylott and points out to Holmes that his hereditary 'violence of temper approaching to mania' might have some part to play. As Holmes surmises, it is Roylott's ancestral degeneration and a lack of self-control that render him violent, but ultimately it is his profession which allows him to have the know-how to perpetrate murder on the sly. Referring to the case of Dr William Palmer, the Rugeley doctor/serial killer who was arrested in 1856, Holmes notes that: 'When a doctor does go wrong he is the first of criminals. He has nerve and he has knowledge.' Doyle's readers were familiar with the figure of the evil professional and the idea that savagery and respectability could reside within the same mind was underscored by the Whitechapel murders. E.W. Hornung's popular tales, contemporary with Doyle's stories, feature the amateur burglar A.J. Raffles, who states that 'it is [his] conviction that Jack the Ripper was a really eminent public man whose speeches were very likely reported alongside his atrocities'.[1] The reports of the Whitechapel murders suggested the culprit was a respectable man: the *Illustrated Police News* of 8 December 1888 portrayed him as a medical doctor. The crimes were representative of the most extreme acts committed by educated men of blood. They constitute a background against which the more defensive deeds of Watson, also a middle-class doctor, and Holmes can be compared. Thus, as the story was published shortly after the East-End murders, 'ASB' is an indictment of male violence against women and an exposé of the man of blood.

Snakes in the grass

The trope of the poisonous snake in 'ASB' is a metaphor for the manner in which violent deeds were considered to inspire further aggression, ultimately leading to a decay of moral order. In the canon, the serpent represents the malevolent deeds of wealthy, educated yet unscrupulous middle-class men whose gentlemanly graces are indicative of the predatory snake that mockingly bows down to its prey. Like the serpent in the Bible, they are arch persuaders, tempting their victims to ruin. Roylott's weapon is a swamp adder while Professor Moriarty's 'face protrudes forward, and 'slowly oscillat[es] from side to side in a curiously reptilian fashion',[2] and the visage of blackmailer Charles Augustus Milverton recalls 'the serpents in the Zoo', which have 'deadly eyes and wicked, flattened faces'.[3] In 1892 an article in the *Strand* argued that the 'raffish' snake was a freakish contortion of nature, presenting an 'extravagance

in ribs and vertebrae; an eccentric, rakish and improper proceeding'.[4]
The accompanying drawing of a top-hatted 'raffish' snake presents a pictorial link between the author's negative appraisal of the ophidian and
the familiar figure of the gentleman-villain of stage melodrama. In Joseph
Conrad's *Heart of Darkness* (1902), a large river on the 'dark' patch of the
map tempts Marlowe to exploration: 'It fascinated me, as a snake would a
bird – a silly little bird.'[5] The ominous river beckons him to navigate into
the limits of self-restraint, where civilized behaviour and high principles
collapse into brutality. When Holmes encounters his own serpents, he
takes a journey into the treacherous recesses of the criminal mind.

The physiognomies of Roylott's and Moriarty's appearances indicate
their 'moral abjection', a term which Julia Kristeva defines as 'sinister,
scheming, and shady: a terror that dissembles, a hatred that smiles'.[6] For
Holmes, Moriarty's smiling and blinking mannerisms in 'AFP' veil latent
violence. In contrast to his snakelike enemies, Holmes is the familiar
'hound' which, in 'The Adventure of the Bruce Partington Plans' (1908),
'runs upon a breast-high scent'. He uses his knowledge of physiognomy
to sniff out villainy. While the bloodhounds and snakes are predatory animals, the former is characterized by faithfulness and the latter
by betrayal. Roylott's snake ultimately kills its owner, whereas the
Sherlockian bloodhound serves the cause of justice.

Roylott functions as a conduit for the transmission of societal *disease*. During the garotting panics, the spread of thuggee and garotting
was metaphorically linked to the spread of cholera. Here it is not the
Indian thug who poses a risk to the health of the body politic. Instead,
it is a higher-class English man of blood – bitten by the snake and cor-
rupted by violence – who carries the contagion of degeneration. Stoner's
description of her father's condition – a hereditary 'violence approaching
mania' – suggests his family bloodline is tainted with syphilis, a disease
which, as Elaine Showalter has argued, attracted as much concern as
the AIDS panic in the 1980s.[7] Henrik Ibsen openly treated the subject of
congenital syphilis in his 1882 play *Ghosts*, highlighting the injustice
of the way in which the 'sins of the father' were wrought on the innocent child. The play elicited over 500 articles in England a year later.[8]
Then, in 1893, Sarah Grand featured this concern in her bestselling and
disturbing triple-decker novel *The Heavenly Twins*, in which she had
her maidenly 'angel of the house' die of the disease after contracting it
from her infected husband. As Showalter notes, Doyle's story 'The Third
Generation', which appeared in 1894, two years after 'ASB', tackles this
theme in which a husband-to-be learns that he has inherited a 'hereditary taint' from his dandy grandfather.[9]

Roylott inherits a shrunken familial legacy and a concomitantly diminished virility. His inherited 'mania' has simultaneously turned him into a man of blood *and* emasculated him. As Catherine Wynne has argued, the swamp adder symbolizes his limp phallus.[10] When Roylott bends Holmes's firepoker to intimidate the detective, Holmes straightens the utensil, displaying his physical strength to Watson. This act underlines the detective's capacity to correct the deformity in Roylott's family tree. As Holmes tells Watson, the hunting crop is his favourite weapon and he prefers it to using a firearm. Used in riding, it is not, unlike some of weapons discussed in this book, deliberately designed to injure humans. Furthermore, as the leather end on the hunting crop is looped, it is considered to be less painful than a full horsewhip of the kind with which Arthur Fletcher is threatened in *The Prime Minister*, not to mention less formidable than the cat o' nine tails. However, as its appearance is whip-like, the hunting crop stands perhaps more as a symbol of chastisement.

The hunting crop with which Holmes beats the snake in 'ASB' hints at the whip used in nineteenth-century flogging. Angus McLaren points out that by the end of the nineteenth century, it was felt that 'unmanly behaviour', that is, non-heterosexual or criminal activity, should be punished by flogging.[11] Holmes's hunting crop claps down on the pistol-touting John Clay in 'The Adventure of the Red-Headed League' (1891), but 'A Case of Identity' constitutes an even more apt example of McLaren's observation. Holmes is incensed by James Windibank's shabby and devious treatment of his stepdaughter, whose money he covets. Windibank disguises himself as her lover and disappears on their wedding day, thus ensuring that the faithful and mystified Mary Sutherland will never look at another man and will leave the family home, taking her money with her. Angered that Windibank's action cannot be righted by legal means, Holmes tells him that if she had a brother, he should have avenged her by whipping the miscreant. Holmes then presents his hunting crop which is sufficient to induce Windibank to take to his heels, exposing his cowardly nature.

Wiener writes that the *fin-de-siècle* equivalents to the 'man of blood' and the 'ordinary reasonable man' are the 'imperial man' and the 'home Englishman' respectively.[12] The imperial man, he argues, espouses violence more readily. Joseph Kestner and Diana Barsham have shown how Sherlock Holmes embodies both Bohemian and English gentlemanly traits. For Barsham, 'Holmes is able to stand either side of the law whose principle of justice he embodies'.[13] He has dealings with the law and the lawless, and his support of domestic values requires him to travel, to interact with and to suppress imperial violence. This persuasively invites the conclusion that Holmes is neither fully 'imperial man' nor 'home Englishman'. Wiener notes that 'even the imperial masculine model, while more accepting of violence, increasingly limited its scope while ever more sharing the domestic model's exaltation of self-discipline as a core value'.[14] Clearly, Roylott is impervious to such influences. So, Holmes, the unconventional yet disciplined middle-class amateur, contrasts strongly with the figure of the evil stepfather of the Empire whose behaviour is repugnant not only to family values but also to bourgeois ideals of masculine self-control and the civilizing offensive. Holmes suppresses Roylott by beating the dangerous animal, which itself symbolizes Roylott, who constitutes an unruly emissary of Empire. Holmes's punitive and defensive deeds halt the spread of degeneration, regulate masculine aggression and protect the British body politic. In illustrating the ferocity of the imperial outsider, Doyle highlights the heroism of Holmes, who, despite his dabbling in things foreign, represents a true Briton, battling to unravel the skeins of degeneration.

'Deep, savage lines' and 'wicked-looking revolvers'

The link between the Holmes adventures and the social acceptability of gun ownership is generally accepted. The firearms historian Frederick Wilkinson shows that firearms were in abundance in the late-nineteenth century.[15] Peter Hitchens has recently argued that 'Sherlock Holmes frequently set out on his private missions with a revolver, as did his colleague, Dr Watson' and concludes that 'it is quite clear from the stories that the author expects his readers to think this is entirely normal and legal'.[16] Donald Rumbelow, an expert on the Whitechapel murders, concurs.[17] Containing numerous references to various firearms, the Holmes adventures would appear to reflect these views. Yet the addendum to the *Compendium of Canonical Weaponry* (1969) notes that Watson 'does not want to dwell on violence and other painful and offensive subjects' and that he 'would have been quite in accord with our anti-violence campaign', taking 'a less hydrophobial attitude towards gun legislation than certain rifle and gun associations'.[18] In fact, as I will show in this section, Watson expresses disapproval of firearms by providing detailed accounts of the weapons used by Holmes's enemies in 'AEH' and sensationally describes the damage wrought by adulterated firearms in 'VF'.

In January 1885 *The Times* reported 'an epidemic of revolvers', a new 'monstrous fashion', pointing out that firearms were not only used by the police force in extreme cases, but were also a must-have for gentlemen of Paris and London, who had their clothing altered to accommodate such weapons. As the paper announced: 'An epidemic of revolvers and the violences attendant on the habit of carrying them has been ravaging the United Kingdom.' The editorial offers a strong critique of this cultural climate, written during a time when displays of masculine violence were increasingly condemned. The paper campaigned against their use in view of the accidents caused by such weapons. Rudyard Kipling appears to have had this opinion. In his travels from Japan to America in 1889, he was asked by a Californian whether he 'understood' pistols. His response was unequivocal:

> 'N-no,' I stammered, 'of course not.'
> 'Do you think of carrying one?'
> 'Of course not. I don't want to kill myself.'[19]

In the same January edition *The Times* believed that children were particularly at risk and that rash individuals could pose a risk to the general public, with the effect that 'a slight panic might produce a fusillade in the quietest street'. Another example which suggests that the support for guns was not unanimous was the view taken by some politicians during the debates over the 1895 Pistols Bill. This Bill aimed to bestow on the police powers to search individuals suspected of possessing firearms and to restrict the purchase of cheap pistols by imposing a licence fee. Malcolm suggests that despite vociferous objections, the Bill was submitted to the House of Lords, where it floundered. Yet this point merely downplays the important and growing movement against the use of offensive weapons. One private member, the Marquess of Carmarthen, was influenced by press cuttings he had assiduously collected on firearms injuries which occurred with such frequency that they 'were to be counted by hundreds'. He was moved to introduce the Pistols Bill in 1895, telling the House that judges, coroners and juries were ardently sympathetic to his cause.[20] One can only ask oneself what his opinion would have been on the alternative non-violent firearms which were patented at this time. For instance, only a few years after the Pistols Bill was discussed, the new affordable sport magazine *Health and Strength* featured an advertisement for the 'liquid pistol' which, it claimed, had been patented in 1888. According to the advertisement, the liquid gun could 'protect bicyclists against vicious dogs and footpads; travellers against robbers and roughs; homes against thieves and tramps'. Hardly a weapon, this water pistol was a harmless distraction to assailants.[21]

The earlier Holmes adventures written in the 1890s do contain references to Holmes and the good doctor using firearms, but the examples are notably restrained. They shoot at very few living beings. Holmes targets the Andaman Islander, Tonga, in 'The Sign of Four' (1890); Watson shoots dead Jephro Rucastle's mastiff in 'The Adventure of the Copper Beeches' (1892) and the beast in 'The Hound of the Baskervilles' (1901–2; hereafter 'THB'), while in 'The Adventure of the Beryl Coronet' (1892) Holmes holds a pistol to Sir George Burnwell's head when he attempts to beat the detective with a life-preserver. In 'The Adventure of the Musgrave Ritual' (1893; hereafter 'AMR') Watson describes Holmes sitting 'in an arm-chair with his hair-trigger and a hundred Boxer cartridges', decorating the wall 'with a patriotic V. R. done in bullet-pocks'. Here Holmes, with a daring flourish, emblazons his support for his Queen with the firearm, the very weapon often employed to target the monarch. In 1882 Roderick MacLean fired at Queen Victoria on her arrival at Windsor Station. He was declared insane. In sharp contrast, Holmes's display of his skill with firearms is legal, patriotic, somewhat witty and, moreover, controlled. Arguably, the greatest enemy to look down the barrel of Holmes's gun is Moriarty and yet Holmes's use of the firearm is not heroic. During his colloquy with Holmes in 'AFP', Moriarty jibes that 'it is a dangerous habit to finger loaded firearms in the pocket of one's dressing-gown'. The detective is then driven to display his weapon, to show his cards as it were. Moriarty's critique of Holmes is of course hypocritical; his own henchmen are surreptitiously armed with all manner of firearms and bludgeons.

In the 'Return of Sherlock Holmes' series, the perniciousness of firearms becomes clearer. By way of illustration, in 'Adventure of the Dancing Men' (1903) Elsie Hilton Cubitt's American stalker, Abe Slaney, attempts to kidnap her. Slaney waves his gun to scare off her husband and let him escape, but he misinterprets the gesture and shoots at the intruder. In return, Slaney fires at her husband, wounding Elsie in the process and leaving her a widow. Both men might have survived had neither man carried a revolver. The carrying of firearms results in the death of the owner.

In the wake of the Boer War, Doyle enthusiastically supported the cause of military defence and campaigned in support of the creation of a rifle corps to defend Britain and British interests. Yet he was more cautious in recommending the use of firearms for civilian defence. In 'THB' Watson chases a man across the moor, mistaking him for a convict and remarking that: 'A lucky long shot of my revolver might have crippled him, but I had brought it only to defend myself if attacked, and not to shoot an unarmed man who was running away.' Watson's comments suggest that an understanding of what constitutes responsible self-defence is equated with manliness and self-control. At the same time, this incident highlights the dangers to which the carrying of a gun could lead, as the fleeing man was a convict but could have been Holmes, who was also out on the moor that night. From 1903 onwards, it appears that while Holmes and Watson are entitled to carry firearms, it is their reluctance to use them for shooting which gives them the moral right to carry such weapons. In 'AEH' Moran grabs Holmes by the throat with 'convulsive strength' in an attempt to murder him. Watson, armed with his regulation firearm, does not shoot at Moran; he merely pistol-whips the colonel, rendering him unconscious until he can be apprehended. Thus, Watson uses his gun not as a firearm but wields it as an everyday object which has not been designed to maim or kill.

Set against the context of debates over gun ownership and gun crimes, 'AEH' and 'VF' warn readers of the perils of firearms. In 'AEH' Holmes returns from exile, knowing himself to be a target of the late Professor Moriarty's henchman, Sebastian Moran, formerly Colonel of the Indian Army and a very accomplished shot. Holmes constructs a wax effigy of himself at 221b Baker Street and observes Moran's attempt to assassinate the bust he believes to be Holmes. As soon as he is able, Holmes returns to his lodgings and examines the effigy. His conclusions as to the weapon Moran used are startling.

Holmes's inspection of the damaged waxwork reveals that the expanding revolver bullet that had killed Ronald Adair was shot from an airgun. Holmes comments that 'there's a genius in that, for who would expect to find such a thing fired from an air-gun'.[22] The firearm used by Moran was manufactured by the blind German mechanic Von Herder, the scientist employed by Moriarty to build efficient killing machines. Like Roylott, Von Herder exemplifies the learned gentleman whose scientific expertise is put to evil use. However, Von Herder poses a greater threat to the British Empire, especially at a time when German military might was growing.

Von Herder's contraption causes Holmes an unusual level of apprehension. The firearm is a furtive and underhand method of killing, operating on an innocent force, air. As Holmes says, it is 'noiseless and of tremendous power'. Therefore, Von Herder's airgun is a technologically advanced weapon of quasi-science-fictional power and of an unusual capacity for stunning at a great distance. Stephen Farrell, a firearms specialist and Sherlockian, remarks of the airgun that 'any victim would appear to have been shot with a revolver, regardless of the range involved'.[23] The manufactured weapon was not only designed to murder with stealth but also to lead the police force to the wrong conclusions as to how the murder had been perpetrated. The murder of Ronald Adair echoes the horrific Whitechapel killings, which were perpetrated in silence by a murderer who escaped detection and whose *modus operandi* was hotly disputed. Watson's account of the discovery of the mutilated body of Adair near the beginning of 'AEH' recalls in part the description of the Whitechapel victim Mary Kelly:

> His head had been horribly mutilated by an expanding revolver bullet, but no weapon of any sort was to be found in the room [...] No one had heard a shot. And yet there was the dead man, and there the revolver bullet, which had mushroomed out, as soft-nosed bullets will, and so inflicted a wound which must have caused instantaneous death.[24]
>
> The face was slashed about, so that the features of the poor creature were beyond all recognition [...] A more horrible or sickening sight could not be imagined [...] There was no appearance of a struggle having taken place, and, although a careful search of the room was made, no knife or instrument of any kind was found.[25]

One of the bodies on the double murder committed by Jack the Ripper in October 1888 is described in the popular paper the *Star* as 'hacked and disfigured beyond discovery',[26] while Adair is 'horribly mutilated'. In both cases there is no trace of the weapons which have so savagely obliterated the victims' faces and erased their identities. The dum-dum shot is not only a ghastly injury but also constitutes a *ripping* open of the body, an attack on masculine corporeal integrity.

Doyle revisits the image of the mutilated male body in 'VF', which appeared at the beginning of 1914. Being set before Moriarty's death, 'VF' acts as a prequel to 'AFP'. On entering the manor of a John Douglas, Holmes and Watson encounter his supposed corpse: 'Lying across his chest was a curious weapon, a shot-gun with the barrel sawn off a foot in front of the triggers. It was clear that this had been fired at close range, and that he had received the whole charge in the face, blowing his head almost to pieces. The triggers had been wired together, so as to make the simultaneous discharge more destructive.' The alterations to the weapon suggest that the owner wanted to be assured of hitting his aim. At the same time, this American firearm is sawn off in order to fit into the trouser pocket of the assassin. It transpires that Douglas's murderer is an Irish-American Freemason from the 'Scowrer' society, which, according to Wynne, was based on the Molly Maguire phenomenon, a form of bellicose American-Irish trade unionism.[27] Furthermore, as Wynne points out, Moriarty's name is Irish and his network is modelled on Fenianism.[28]

Having been exposed by a journalist, the Scowrers track down their informant to England, where he lives as John Douglas. Douglas wrestles with his would-be assassin, who is armed with the deadly shotgun, and accidentally shoots dead his assailant, an act of justice which echoes the adage from 'ASB' of violence returning or 'recoiling' upon the aggressor. After swapping clothes with the dead man, Douglas makes an escape, although he later mysteriously drowns at sea. Therefore, in this story and in 'AEH', we see a Moriarty-led nexus of evil at work.

The reference to the airgun in 'AEH' is an extension of the racial dynamics employed by Doyle in his writings, explaining Britain's conduct during the Boer War. Airguns had fired small pellets and were used to kill vermin and game. These weapons were also used for target shooting and occasionally for defensive purposes by the military and civilians. Here, Von Herder's firearm is filled with soft-nosed 'dum-dum' bullets, crafted by pulling back the jacket from existing projectiles. This resulted in their expansion inside the body, causing a ghastly exit wound. As the bullet so dramatically felled the enemy to the ground, the dum-dum was therefore referred to as a 'manstopper'. This projectile was developed under the aegis of the Indian Army in a suburb of Calcutta (this is, incidentally, where Roylott lived) called Dum Dum and was first used in the Tirah Campaign in 1897–8. However, its use caused great controversy a year later at an international convention at The Hague, which encouraged a more humane conduct of war.[29] Unwilling to sign a declaration relating to restrictions on the use of dum-dums, the British government did disallow their employment in the Boer War. As Doyle stated in the *Daily News*: 'It is notorious [...] that the British, whose wars are usually against savages, had prepared large quantities of soft-nosed bullets [...] It is only just to say, however, that they were never intended to be used against white races, and that a War Office forbade their use in the South African War.'[30] So, as far as Doyle was concerned, to use dum-dums against the Boers was a travesty, but their use against native Africans was justified. A similar stance had incurred the wrath of a Russian delegate at The Hague in 1899 who 'resented' the 'distinction made between a savage and a civilized enemy'.[31] That the native African had not been offered the opportunity to sign the Hague Convention and thus prevent an enemy from using a dum-dum against him was obviously of little consequence to Doyle. As Paula Krebs notes, for Doyle 'black men became the locus of animal sexuality to be counterposed against the white man's controlled, civilized sexuality'.[32] Francis Galton had argued in *The Times* in 1873 that 'average negroes' did not possess 'intellect, self-reliance, and self-control'.[33] Therefore, as the native African fighter was too 'savage' to be reasoned with, the only option was to stop him in his tracks with excessive force.

In 'AEH' Doyle places the dum-dum in the hands of an ex-Colonel of the Indian Army, which was responsible for the manufacture of the dum-dum. Moran disregards the racially influenced guidelines behind its use and redirects such weapons for the purpose of killing white, British civilians, namely Holmes. The weapon he uses is the gun, perfected: it is powerful, devastating in its impact and silent. At that time, elaborate firearms appeared on the market, including the combination six-shot revolver, knife and knuckleduster from 1890, manufactured by the Belgian firm Dolne and now kept at the Royal Armouries, Leeds. It would have been purchased by wealthier middle-class customers, often whilst abroad in the two major manufacturing countries of combination weapons, France and Belgium.[34] Other bizarre devices available in Britain included the Frankenau combination pocket book and revolver and the knife pistol by a successful British knife company, Unwin and Rodgers. Catherine Dike's lavishly illustrated history of novelty, multifunctional walking-sticks, *Cane Curiosa: From Gun to Gadget* (1983), shows that gun-canes, swordsticks, life-preservers with projecting spikes and other multiplex weapons were readily available in the late-Victorian era. As she observes, with the rise of the middle classes, swords were restricted to military use, but a gentleman could possess various types of cane and swordstick.[35] Opened in 1857, the New Oxford Street emporium James Smith and Sons sold umbrellas to notables such as Gladstone and Lord Curzon, and stocked 'sword sticks' and 'dagger canes'. James Smith and Sons Umbrella Shop is still in business today, selling to customers worldwide and providing props for television dramas. It still retains its frontage, advertising its wares, alerting the curious passer-by of today to yesterday's approach to the problem of urban crime.

One form of violence which would have exacerbated a sense of unease was the Fenian dynamite attack on London in the 1880s. Bombs were deployed in numerous targets around the metropolis, including the Tower of London, Nelson's Column and at various train and underground stations. Explosions occurred at Scotland Yard and Tower Bridge, a government office in Whitehall and at the Tower of London. On one occasion a bomb thrown out of a carriage window injured 60 commuters. The bombers also left timed devices in luggage rooms at various stations in the metropolis. According to *The Times* in 1885, one unexploded device found in a portmanteau contained the following ingredients: 'Tin box containing an American clock, with a pistol attached to the back of the clock, a cake and three-quarters of Atlas powder [an American gunpowder which gained notoriety for being the explosive used by dynamiters]; ten detonators were stuck into the cakes which were in the tin, and one in front of the muzzle of the pistol.' A later article published in the *Strand* in 1894, entitled 'Dynamite and Dynamiters', features a photograph of the unexploded clockwork machine at Paddington station in which the pistol incorporated in the device is clearly visible, showing that a single firearm could, when wired up for detonation, slaughter countless numbers. The head of an organization specializing in assassinations, Moriarty is never depicted wielding a firearm and does not even utilize a weapon against Holmes in the final battle at Reichenbach in 'AFP'. However, he is the head of a vast web which poses a threat to every individual.

Moran and the leader of the Scowrers, Bodymaster Boss McGinty, are linked to the Moriarty nexus of evil through physiognomy and metonymy. Incidentally, Moran also shares the same ancestral name as Roylott, implying that Colonel Moran's blood is also tainted. By contrast, Holmes's embodies physical health. In 'VF' his knowledge of sport leads him to conclude that there is a missing dumb-bell which Douglas used to submerge his clothing on his escape: 'Consider an athlete with one dumb-bell. Picture to yourself the unilateral development – the imminent danger of a spinal curvature. Shocking, Watson; shocking!'

Roylott's weapon is a coiled, cold-blooded animal, while the sinister signature weapon of Moriarty's organization is the adulterated and twisted firearm. In 'AEH' Moran's firearm has 'a curiously misshapen butt', suggesting a cruel bent or twist to its owner's nature. This image harmonizes with the description of Moran's family tree which occurs in the same story: 'There are some trees […] which grow to a certain height, and then suddenly develop some unsightly eccentricity.' Moran represents a greater challenge to Holmes than the ordinary criminal. Holmes tells Watson that he 'cares nothing' for Moran's sentinel Parker, who is 'a garroter [*sic*] by trade'. Here, the low-life thug-garotter folk devil has been eclipsed by an even greater threat, the spectre of the violent, imperial double of the home gentleman. Moran's malevolence is indicated through his physiognomy and his sartorial choices. Watson comments that 'one could not look upon his cruel blue eyes, with their drooping, cynical lids, or upon the fierce, aggressive nose and the threatening, deep-lined brow, without reading Nature's plainest danger-signals'. Moran is a gentleman-villain who has 'the brow of a philosopher' and the 'jaw of a sensualist', which suggests he uses his intellect for barbarous purposes. Villainy is literally etched on his face, which is 'gaunt and swarthy, scored with deep, savage lines'. Moran's appearance resembles the wrinkled features of the malevolent villain in melodrama. Peter Brooks has argued that in melodrama 'evil is villainy; it is a swarthy, cape-enveloped man with a deep voice'.[36] Brooks's observation can be applied to an analysis of Moran's appearance. Watson perceives Moran's opera-hat, his 'gleaming' 'evening-dress shirt front', his 'shining' eyes and 'convulsed' features. As John Harvey notes, 'blackness is lightless so it can be merciless'.[37] Furthermore, as Harvey writes, there is a link between the height of imperial power and the donning of black.[38] Like Moran, McGinty in 'AVF' has a 'swarthy' complexion, 'strange dead black' eyes and possesses a 'wicked-looking revolver' to match his shady appearance. Both Moran and McGinty dominate the stories in which they appear. As Brooks argues of melodrama, 'for the greater part of the play, evil appears to reign triumphant, controlling the structure of events'.[39] McGinty is a brutal leader and Moran is a combination of the familiar stage villain, a scientist and empire man with a tendency to brutality, an expert shot with an expertly crafted gun. His defeat is signalled by the relegation of Von Herder's airgun to the Black Museum at the end of the adventure. The contents of this museum were featured in 'Another Chamber of Horrors: The Police Museum of Scotland Yard' in the anti-Afrikaan magazine *Black and White Budget* in 1901 alongside articles on the Boer War. Doyle's name appears on the visitor's list for the Black Museum in 1892 and he would therefore have been made aware of the extent of the size of the Museum's collection of seized firearms.[40]

In her classic Ripper-inspired novel *The Lodger* (1913), Marie Belloc Lowndes takes further Doyle's personification of weapons when she embellishes her characters' trip to the Black Museum with a touch of the macabre. The guardian of the collection notes the horrified reaction of one visitor to the items on display: 'He said that each of these things, with the exception of the casts [death masks of executed criminals], mind you – queer to say, he left them out – exuded evil, that was the word he used! Exuded – squeezed out it means. He said that being here made him feel very bad.'[41] Here the weapons and accessories used by criminals are still warm with the malevolence with which they were employed. There is the suspicion that, by virtue of their close symbolic association with their owners, McGinty's 'wicked-looking revolver' and Moran's twisted airgun are imbued with sinister life-forces of their own. When Moran's airgun is relegated to the Black Museum, the inter-personal, international and, by inference, sexual threat posed by him is curtailed. But, as Lowndes's fanciful extract suggests, his weapon's power to do evil is only stymied as long as it remains behind bars.

8
Urban Knights in the London Streets

'A straight left'

In the opening article to his new publication of 1898, *Sandow's Magazine*, the German bodybuilder Eugen Sandow linked physical and mental self-sufficiency with racial regeneration. He argued in 1898 that the aim of physical culture was to 'raise the average standard of the race as a whole' and to 'undo the evil which civilization has been responsible for, in making man regard his body lightly'.[1] An advertisement in *Health and Strength* in 1900 for a muscle-building apparatus, Macfadden's Health and Strength Developer, was prefaced with the statement: 'Weakness is a crime – don't be a criminal.' Furthermore, in 'Health is a Duty' of that same year it was argued for individuals who neglected their health that 'the evil consequences inflicted upon their dependents, and on future generations, are often as great as those caused by crime, yet they do not think themselves in any degree criminal'.[2] Dr Roylott and the round-shouldered Moriarty and his criminal network embody what Daniel Pick argues was a uniquely British perception of degeneration, namely that 'a relative deterioration in the body of the city population' could herald the 'disintegrative effects upon the nation and empire'.[3] Therefore, for Sandow and his contemporaries, heroic acts of self-defence were not only desirable: to build up one's muscles and exercise one's virtue in protecting oneself and others helped to guard the race from physical retrogression.

Sandow gave lessons in muscular development to Doyle who was himself a prolific sportsman, arguably one of England's greatest sportsmen at that time. The *Strand* described Doyle as 'brown and bronzed',[4] recalling the image of Thomas Hughes's brawny, suntanned hero Tom

Brown, another perfect specimen of British fitness. Doyle was an all-round sportsman and his pursuits included skiing, cricket, billiards and football, but it is probably his passion for boxing that is best remembered. For Sandow, physical culture constituted a moral dimension, inspiring qualities such as willpower and a forbearance of aggression. His physical culture hero was 'gentle, and only uses his powers against his fellow-men when called upon to do so in the defence of the oppressed and helpless', while the bully and tyrant are generally physical 'weakling[s]'.

In his memoir Doyle was explicit in his admiration of the prize ring, being as it were 'an excellent thing from a national point of view – exactly as glove-fighting is now'. Expressive of his passion for the old forms of fist-fighting was his novel *Rodney Stone* (1896), which contained lengthy descriptions of fights which drew together aristocratic patrons and working-class pugilists. But Doyle also had much to say about the middle-class man, demonstrating that he should be able to prove himself and his social status using his brains and body alone. When he was a young doctor, he joined a whaling ship and boxed a round with the steward. His competitor was most impressed by Doyle's ability and was convinced that he was 'the best sur-r-r-geon we've had' as he had given the steward a black eye. Doyle concluded that: 'It struck me as a singular test of my medical ability, but I daresay it did no harm.'[5] Doyle wrote in his autobiography that he had 'always been keen upon the noble old English sport of boxing' and modestly described himself as 'a fair average amateur',[6] although eventually his knowledge of the art was so highly esteemed that he was invited to referee the World Heavyweight Boxing Championship match between Jim Jeffries and Jack Johnson in 1910.[7]

Holmes's boxing skills are often referred to throughout the canon. In 'A Study in Scarlet' (1887) Watson notes that Holmes is an 'expert singlestick player, boxer, and swordsman'.[8] The detective's talents unlock the door to Pondicherry Lodge when, in 'The Sign of Four', Holmes reminds the porter who guards the door that he had fought him at a boxing club:

> 'Not Mr. Sherlock Holmes!' roared the prize-fighter. 'God's truth! how could I have mistook you? If instead o' standin' there so quiet you-had just stepped up and given me that cross-hit of yours under the jaw, I'd ha' known you without a question. Ah, you're one that has wasted your gifts, you have! You might have aimed high, if you had joined the fancy.'

Watson lavishes even more praise on his friend's skills in the later story 'The Adventure of the Yellow Face' when he says that Holmes was 'undoubtedly one of the finest boxers of his weight'. We also see Holmes in action in 'ASC' when he demonstrates his proficiency despite having a physically strong adversary with which to contend:

> You are aware that I have some proficiency in the good old British sport of boxing. Occasionally it is of service. To-day, for example, I should have come to very ignominious grief without it … [Jack Woodley] had a fine flow of language, and his adjectives were very vigorous […] He ended a string of abuse by a vicious backhander which I failed to entirely avoid. The next few minutes were delicious. It was a straight left against a slogging ruffian. I emerged as you see me.

The above scene recalls the wrestling match between the Barthesian salaud and the hero. Woodley is a 'brutal, heavy-faced, red-moustached young man' who attempts to force Violet Smith to marry him. Woodley – who is clearly a man of blood – catches Holmes off-guard in an underhand move. While Woodley's back-handed hit is acceptable in a boxing match, such a manoeuvre is not permitted without the use of gloves.[9] Swearing, as James Fitzjames Stephen had pointed out in his 1862 *Cornhill Magazine* piece on the subject of the gentleman, was distinctly ungentlemanly. Doyle had envisioned a salaudian contest in *The Stark Munro Letters* (1895), a novel which describes the friendship between two medical graduates, Stark Munro and Cullingworth, who intend to go into practice together. As Douglas Kerr has observed, in their sparring matches, Stark Munro, a trained amateur, keeps his head while his opponent loses his temper, demanding that the fight be continued without gloves. It becomes apparent that Cullingworth's brutish and heated fighting style is matched by his questionable practices in his professional life.[10]

Similarly, in the affray in 'ASC' Holmes emerges victorious, bearing only a cut lip, while Woodley is transported away from the scene. Sidney Paget's illustration of the fighters shows Holmes masterfully defending himself, averting Woodley's punches. Woodley may be a burly ruffian but Holmes exploits Woodley's lack of finesse and overcomes him. The hat also acts as a symbol. In Paget's visual interpretation of the struggle between Moriarty and Holmes in 'AFP', the tumbling hat (belonging either to Holmes or his nemesis) is metonymic of destruction. In 'ASC' Holmes, unlike his adversary, still wears his deerstalker, which suggests that he has kept his cool; Woodley's headgear has fallen to the ground.

'ASC' expresses Holmes's growing unease with firearms usage. The 'hero' of the story, Bob Carruthers, shoots at Woodley in order to defend Violet Smith against Woodley and the defrocked clergyman Williamson. When Williamson exhibits his own revolver, Holmes is forced to produce a firearm to frustrate Williamson's intended act of violence. Holmes orders the firearm to be taken from Williamson but also expresses his displeasure at Carruthers's use of firearms: '"Enough of this," said my friend, coldly. "Drop that pistol! Watson, pick it up! Hold it to his head! Thank you. You, Carruthers, give me that revolver. We'll have no more violence."' Holmes's annoyance at having to use a revolver to settle a dispute can be contrasted with his excitement in practising his boxing skills whilst confronting Woodley in hand-to-hand combat earlier in the story. Holmes emphasizes his displeasure to Carruthers when he informs him that he 'would have done better to keep [his] pistol in [his] pocket'.[11] Thus, in this story Doyle equates the use of the firearm with the loss of self-control and extols the glory of hand-to-hand combat.

The adventure of the mystery of 'Bar[t]itsu'

In 1901 the *Black and White Budget* discovered a new gentleman's urban retreat – the Bartitsu Club. If Doyle's 'THB' was intended to inspire a wave of patriotism after a dip in national confidence during the Boer War,[12] then the emerging martial art of Bartitsu, appearing in middle-class magazines during the conflict, was the encapsulation of British civilian gallantry.[13] Yet Bartitsu would have slid into obscurity had it not been for its curious appearance in the Holmes canon.

Conducted in secret, the final showdown of the 'duel' between Holmes and Moriarty is in no way similar to the pistol duel between Mirfin and Eliot or Fawcett and Munro – it is a wrestling match between two Victorian masterminds. When Holmes returns to London in 'AEH' he tells Watson that he and Moriarty went to battle at the Reichenbach Falls unarmed. Holmes managed to 'slip through' Moriarty's grip as he possessed 'some knowledge' of 'baritsu, or the Japanese system of wrestling', adding that the art had on occasion been useful to him. In a world where weaponry was commonplace and advertised on shop fronts, Holmes went to his final battle equipped only with his command of what appears to be an obscure form of martial art. It served him well. Moriarty lost his footing, screaming as he plunged from a great height to his death.

Despite the popularity of Holmes and the abundance of works on Doyle and his creation, references are seldom made to Bartitsu. However, a very small number of martial arts experts who are also

Holmes enthusiasts have turned the magnifying glass on this topic. In 1996 the Sherlockians Yuichi Hirayama and John Hall posited that baritsu was either 'bujustu' (an umbrella term for the skills acquired by the Samurai to be used in war, including riding, single-stick fighting and building castles), Bartitsu or jujitsu (a Japanese martial art which we will examine in further detail below). They favoured jujitsu on the basis that Bartitsu had not yet appeared on the scene by the time Holmes had to grapple with Moriarty in 'AFP', which was set in early 1890s.[14] In response a year later, Richard Bowen (1926–2005), the late Vice-President of the London Judo Budokwai, strongly promoted the theory that the mysterious sport 'baritsu' was 'Bartitsu', founded in the 1890s by an Anglo-Scottish engineer, Edward William Barton-Wright (1860–1951).[15] It has been generally suggested that Doyle's misspelling most likely originated from an article from *The Times* of 1901, which was printed as Doyle was penning 'AEH' and describes the Japanese assistants who were 'engaged to act as instructors at Mr Barton-Wright's school of physical culture in Shaftesbury Avenue, where the "Baritsu" system of self-defence [was] taught'. Doyle might have merely included the martial art in his adventure as an interesting puzzle he set future readers to work out for themselves. While he mentions boxing in his memoir and describes the inspirations behind his scene at the Reichenbach Falls, he does not cast any light on baritsu itself. He may not have known much about it. Indeed, there were some sports, such as horseracing, which did not interest him. Yet it is baritsu and not boxing which enables the detective to escape from the clutches of Moriarty. Perhaps this inclusion in the text is a testament to Doyle's opinion (possibly one that he may have changed) that the martial art should be better known.

The Bartitsu Club left a rich legacy, attracting the attention of the Prince of Wales and, on a darker note, Sir Cosmo Duff Gordon who, together with his wife, would later become notorious for escaping the Titanic disaster in a half-empty lifeboat. Unfortunately, its own fame was short-lived. By the time Doyle's 'baritsu' appeared in 'AEH' in 1903, the Bartitsu Club was a fragment of history. Barton-Wright's exorbitant fees appear to have played a role in the Club's demise. In 1907 it became the Bartitsu Light Cure Institute. His dabbling in electrotherapy sparked costly law suits from burnt patients and complaints from a rather disgruntled Medical Council, claiming he had infringed regulations.[16] The inventor of Bartitsu found himself on hard times. Eventually his name slid into insignificance and in 1951 he was buried in a pauper's grave in Kingston-Upon-Thames.

Since Bowen's 1997 article, interest in Bartitsu has been flourishing and performances are now given at the Royal Armouries, Leeds. Renowned for his work as the Cultural Fighting Styles Designer in *The Lord of the Rings* films (2001–3), Tony Wolf is a practitioner of an extraordinarily wide variety of forms of combat, from Western to Polynesian styles, and gives Bartitsu masterclasses across the globe. As he emphasizes, Barton-Wright's mixing of martial arts of East and West – Bartitsu is a synthesis of British boxing, French *la savate* (kickboxing) and Japanese jujitsu (translated as 'the art of yielding') – predated Bruce Lee's mixed martial art Jeet Kune Do by 70 years.[17] Considered from a cultural and literary angle, a nexus of periodicals communicated modes of rational masculine self-presentation to cater for a growing interest in self-defence. Furthermore, the marketing of Bartitsu also tells us much about the emergence of a knowledge of self-defence as a consumer item.

The change in attitude towards the use of firearms in settling disputes was foreseen, albeit humorously, in a *Punch* cartoon of 1885 entitled 'An Honourable Adjustment', featuring two images of men fighting. The first describes the 'old style' of combat: the pistol duel conducted on the edge of a wood in the presence only of two seconds and a surgeon, with the duellists recoiling from the noise. The 'new style' shows rather lavishly dressed moustachioed gentlemen wearing gaiters and boxing in the ring, watched not by a rowdy rabble but by a considerable group of equally genteel ladies and gentlemen sitting in the park. Does this suggest that boxing, as practised by gentlemen, has become an official spectator sport, part of pleasurable genteel entertainment? While gentlemen did box – and Doyle and Holmes are clear examples of such amateurs – it was the working-class man who excelled in this field. Indeed, in his survey of late-Victorian boxing, Stan Shipley has observed that while many boxing managers were middle class, university graduates and army officers were not national champions and that the middle class did not appear to 'shine as exemplars of physical courage and endurance'.[18]

Barton-Wright tapped into the need for a bourgeois form of self-defence, something which he could promote as being British and yet was also exotic and refined. Like Doyle, Barton-Wright was a brainworker with a keen interest in probing the limits of his imagination, his mind and his physical capabilities. From its very origins, Bartitsu was the product of one professional's indefatigable energy. Barton-Wright invented the martial art while he was working as an engineer in Japan in the 1880s. As the sports journalist Mary Nugent said of Barton-Wright: 'He explains that his study of wrestling, first seriously undertaken in Japan, was the result of his not drinking; men drink and lie about on club verandahs a great deal in the East, he didn't happen to find amusement in that.'[19] His teacher was Jigoro Kano who, in the same decade, reformed older forms of Japanese armoured and unarmoured forms of jujitsu, thus inventing a new combat sport, Kodokan judo.

The first known promotion of Bartitsu appeared in 1899 in the form of two lengthy and generously illustrated articles in two parts in March and April, both entitled 'The New Art of Self-Defence: How a Man may Defend Himself against every Form of Attack' (henceforth 'New Art'). In these pieces, Barton-Wright exploits the presentational style of *Pearson's Magazine*. This highly popular publication for the middling classes on both sides of the Atlantic featured articles on extraordinary topics such as the discovery of canali or 'channels' on Mars and H.G. Wells's apocalyptic adventure *The War of the Worlds* (1897). This format was so successful that Bartitsu began to be noticed by editors of other magazines. Awareness of Barton-Wright's new form of self-defence spread quickly. Bartitsu first appeared in a plethora of periodicals and papers, including *Pearson's Magazine*, the *Daily News*, *Black and White Budget* and *Health and Strength,* and was subsequently incorporated into 'AEH' in the *Strand*. Sidney Paget's oldest brother, Henry Marriott Paget, produced illustrations of a performance of Bartitsu which appeared in the *Graphic* in March 1899. Barton-Wright's 'New Art' was also reprinted and adapted for overseas use, appearing, for instance, in the *Chicago Daily Tribune* on 2 April 1899.

Bartitsu, it was boldly claimed by its inventor, could be employed 'against every possible form of attack, whether armed or otherwise',[20] although it must be pointed out that none of the manoeuvres presented by Barton-Wright in his monographs are employed against assailants armed with knives, pistols and other weapons. Interested readers, he advised tantalizingly, should apply to him personally for instruction in this matter.[21] He argued that his art was an unarmed or barely-armed measured response to assault: Bartitsu was useful when 'pass[ing] through a locality late at night where there is a likelihood of such an attack' and when one does not 'wish to run the risk of bringing [one-self] within the law by relying upon a revolver'.[22] As an alternative to firearms, Barton-Wright's art is the antidote to the 'epidemic of revolvers'. This defensive approach to aggression is in harmony with Holmes's advice in 'ASC', when he warns Carruthers of the legal penalties of using firearms.

Barton-Wright shows that he complements the principles of self-defence enshrined in *Archbold's*, namely that one should not use an inappropriate level of corporeal force in relation to an assault: 'It must be borne in mind that you are not seeking a quarrel or attacking, but simply defending yourself.'[23] As the *Black and White Budget* commented in 1900: 'Bartitsu has been devised with a view to impart to peacefully disposed men the science of defending themselves against ruffians.' The first piece of advice Barton-Wright gives is to walk in the middle of the road, which we have seen H.W. Holland advise. In *The Mystery of a Hansom Cab*, Hume's lawyer and detective traverse the Melbourne slums and walk 'for safety' in the middle of an alleyway 'so that no one c[an] spring upon them unaware'.[24] However, the 'peacefully disposed' man that Barton-Wright has in mind does not directly equate to Wiener's 'much more pacific Englishman' or the ideal of masculinity espoused by Holland. Rather, Barton-Wright invites the reader to enact such scenarios through the aid of verbal and pictorial demonstration.

Barton-Wright's article was timely. The 'Hooligan' made his appearance in the British press in the wake of the 1898 August Bank Holiday, one year before *Pearson's Magazine* hosted Barton-Wright's articles. According to the *Pall Mall Gazette*, the principal aim of Bartitsu's promoters was 'to provide a means whereby the higher classes of society may protect themselves from the attacks of hooligans and their like all over the world'.[25] As Geoffrey Pearson shows, these urban gangs were a new form of folk devil, descendants of the mid-Victorian-era garotter. While they were armed with clubs, knuckles, iron bars and leather belts, Pearson doubts that they carried firearms.[26] Nevertheless, the press did represent the hooligan as a threatening presence: 'When he attacks a man he frequently does so for the mere sake of injuring him. The police, of course are too often the victims of these desperados.'[27] Thus, such weapons were missiles against which Bartitsu could be usefully employed. If we accept Geoffrey Pearson's argument on hooligans and pistols, then it is likely that the hooligan scares contributed to the burgeoning culture of 'British' self-defence which avoided the belligerent and unmanly act of employing a firearm against an opponent equipped only with basic weapons. A considerable collection of articles appeared referring to 'hooligans'. If, as Wood has argued, barbarism threw civilization into relief, then perhaps the scares promoted the growth of a burgeoning culture of 'British' self-defence which avoided the aggressive and increasingly unmanly action of using a firearm against a ruffianly lower-class opponent equipped only with basic weapons. The public may have been influenced to consider their own vulnerability, but Barton-Wright's method of self-defence offered readers of *Pearson's Magazine* the means with which to assert themselves with bravado in the face of the rascally violence against which the police officer might have struggled.

Barton-Wright follows a literary tradition when he presents his martial art as a British form of self-defence. Pierce Egan's well-known self-defence manual was supplemented with a word on the 'Englishness' of physical heroism, arguing that 'Englishmen need no other weapons in personal contests than those which nature has so amply supplied them with'.[28] In 1910 the former lightweight boxing champion Andrew J. Newton said in his manual *Boxing* that 'the native of Southern Europe flies to his knife', whereas the 'Britisher [...] is handy with his fists in an emergency'. Elsewhere it was maintained that the 'Italian, Greek, Portuguese, or South American' 'give preference to the knife' while the Englishman extols boxing.[29] For Barton-Wright, British boxers 'scorn taking advantages of another man when he is down', while a foreigner might 'use a chair, or a beer bottle, or a knife' or, 'when a weapon is available', he might employ 'underhanded means'.[30] The views of these articles reappear in a later self-defence manual of 1914, where it is argued that Britons 'live in a country where knife and revolver are not much in evidence'.[31] This statement about the low number of firearms and edged weapons can be read as an attempt to extol British virtues and is not necessarily representative of reality. The knife is a weapon of the Other. Barton-Wright's view that English practitioners of Bartitsu are principled men is reflected in the Holmes canon, where Holmes never uses a knife, although his enemies, whether foreign or British, do so at times.

As the distinguished comedian Dan Leno quipped in *Sandow's Magazine* in 1900: 'Man is built wrong ... If someone is coming up behind you, how are you to see him? You can't. Why? Because you want a pair of eyes in the back of your head.'[32] Barton-Wright did not solve this deficiency in the construction of the human body but he did show how other weaknesses, of size and power, could be subverted to useful effect. His art is based on the principles of jujitsu, namely that the weight and strength of the enemy are to be used against him. It is possible to divine from Barton-Wright's description of Bartitsu just how Holmes might circumvented Moriarty's physical force and unbalanced him at the Reichenbach Falls: '(1) to disturb the equilibrium of your assailant; (2) to surprise him before he has time to regain his balance and use his strength; (3) if necessary to subject the joints of any part of his body, whether neck, shoulder, elbow, wrist, back, knee, ankle, etc. to strain which they are anatomically and mechanically unable to resist.'[33] Premised on deflecting the power of the assailant to their own disadvantage, jujitsu and Bartitsu represent the epitome of reasonable defence. The habiliments worn during the garotting panics could be shed and the body itself could be a shield: 'A trained exponent, through practice, makes his throat so strong that it is quite impossible to throttle him, and he is, therefore, quite safe against garrotting.'[34] Garotters beware.

Percy Longhurst had a few words to say on this. Longhurst was the British featherweight wrestling champion and secretary of the National Amateur Wrestling Association. After seeing a performance of jujitsu, he took up the martial art himself: 'Remember, too, that if the initial success be with you it is a double advantage on account of the moral effect.' In 'ASB' Holmes is the defender of moral values and physically tackles the serpent-nemesis Moriarty; in 'AEH' the detective battles with the snake-like Moriarty and is victorious through his use of Bartitsu. *Sandow's Magazine* and particularly *Health and Strength* draw on images from the Roman amphitheatre and depict men tackling wild animals. Thus, physical culture offered the spectator the opportunity to engage in gladiatorial fantasies. A photograph of Frederick Lord Leighton's sculpture *Athlete Wrestling with a Python* was reprinted in *Sandow's Magazine* in 1899[35] and the *Strand* in 1902,[36] and subsequently appeared in *Health and Strength* in 1907.[37] The photograph of Leighton's statue visually encapsulates Holmes and Moriarty's struggle at the Reichenbach Falls, but it is Holmes who overpowers the snake. Barton-Wright told readers of *Pearson's Magazine* that his martial art was potentially 'very terrible in the hands of a quick and confident exponent' and perfectly adapted for those who find themselves 'confronted suddenly in an unexpected way'.[38] In contrast to Moriarty, Holmes controls his physical activity through the use of a rational technique, whereas Moriarty lunges forwards, representing a 'desperate savage'.

As Doyle writes in his autobiography: 'An exhibition of hardihood without brutality, of good-humoured courage without savagery, of skill without trickery, is, I think, the highest which sport can give.'[39] Yet Barton-Wright (not to mention Holmes) is very much concerned with performance and trickery. Both in his professional life and in his amateur pursuits, a gentleman was not supposed to be seen to be trying too hard. Barton-Wright was clearly a showman. He toured the country with his assistants, putting on performances for the general public. The Prince of Wales requested a performance but Barton-Wright had to decline, having allegedly sustained an injury whilst fighting ruffians. His injuries are like cherished scars in which his weakness highlights his physical prowess and daring. At the athletic Bath Club in 1899 he demonstrated how to fell an opponent to the ground despite having apparently sprained a knee. His 'How to Pose as a Strong Man' of 1899 (also published in

Pearson's Magazine) is aimed at men of average strength. He demonstrates 'how to lift a chair with four men packed upon it' and shows 'how to stand on one foot and to defy anyone to upset your balance by a slow, straight push'.[40] Bartitsu could be learned thoroughly in class or a rudimentary knowledge could be acquired by reading and private practice. Barton-Wright's tricks proposed to convey a sense of strength and physical brilliance on the would-be Bartitsuka. The self-defence scenario inspired the ability to improvise in an unscripted and perilous situation, and also evoked a physical reaction that looked visually striking and effortless.

For Barton-Wright, one defensive blow could 'with an ordinary malacca [*sic*] cane [...] sever a man's jugular vein through the collar of his overcoat'.[41] He emphasizes that his sport gives the Bartitsuka the power to injure and says that 'if a policeman is holding a prisoner in a certain position, it is not necessary to break the man's arm to show his power [...] So in these methods of self-defence when your opponent is once at your mercy he will cry "Hold!" long before you could seriously injure him'.[42] Moreover, once an assailant has been defeated, he is 'then at the mercy of the man he has attacked, who can choose any part of his body on which to administer punishment'.[43] Considered against the advice of *Archbold's*, such an act extends beyond the use of reasonable force. However, as Wolf points out, some form of physical retaliation is necessary in self-defence to keep the assailant from attacking again. Nevertheless, the attraction of Bartitsu is the exhilarating feeling of self-confidence and the power to do injury but the 'manly' self-control to prevent committing such an action. Barton-Wright frames his martial art within the confines of what is legally permitted and increasingly culturally endorsed as constituting appropriate masculine assertiveness. Indeed, in a manoeuvre to counter a knife attack, he recommends the use of a mere coat to stun the assailant.[44] Modern examples that take their cue from nineteenth-century works of fiction also allow us to draw parallels between then and now. One example is the highly popular British television mystery series *Jonathan Creek*. It is a modern twist on the Sherlock Holmes series with Dr Watson and Holmes respectively replaced by a female crime writer and a cerebral magician's assistant with remarkable powers of reasoning who often assists the police in dealing with tricky puzzles. In the episode 'The Three Gamblers' (2000) the duffle-coated eponymous hero, played by the comedian Alan Davies flicks a playing card at an armed assailant, knocking the gun out of his hand. It is a humorous scene, in which, Creek, an unlikely-looking cavalier, saves the day, but one which also chimes with modern-day notions of reasonable force as well as with the idea of using one's intellect as a defensive weapon. As regards Richard Sennett's conception of the urban 'attack-and-defense' response, hand-to-hand methods of brilliant improvisation devised by Barton-Wright set up walls between the attacker and the civilian using the minimum amount of force.

Exploring the 'criminal jungle'

'Up, citizens, then, and do your own police work!' decried the *Star* in the autumn of terror in 1888.[45] The Whitechapel fiend had struck again. Led by George Lusk, the Whitechapel Vigilance Association was one of the best-known anti-Ripper initiatives run by civilians, who were local men. Toynbee Hall also reacted. Founded in 1884, Toynbee Hall was populated by 'young university men of strong convictions'[46] offering their services to build a sense of community for London's East End. This settlement was portrayed as an island surrounded by crime and destitution: 'Is there not Toynbee Hall in the very midst of the murder quarter, and do not its philanthropic young missionaries live close to all the squalor and filth of which we hear?'[47] The darker sides of the city could be cast in various ways. They were loci of anxiety, sore spots to be healed by philanthropy or mapped by investigative techniques or exotic sites for imperial adventure. As Joseph McLaughlin says of Conrad's *Heart of Darkness* (1899), the 'darker and more sinister the jungle is made to appear, the more exalted is the "intrepid explorer" who survives the experience'.[48] Some of these philanthropic volunteers became patrollers, assisting the police in tracking down the Ripper, working on long shifts in addition to their usual tasks. The best-known image of the Toynbee Hallers is the one printed in the *Illustrated London News* on 4 December 1888, in which the Hallers are presented as leisured *flâneurs*. Curiously, their personal appearance prefigures Paget's illustrations of Holmes and Watson. In 'The Sign of Four' Holmes and Watson are also described as being 'two knight-errants to the rescue'. The Hallers carry expressions of inquisitiveness which suggests that to them the search for the Ripper is a form of mental stimulation. The man in the deerstalker smiles and exudes aplomb, recalling Freedgood's observation that calm can be experienced in the most dangerous of situations. We do not know how they were armed, but crucially the *Illustrated London News* decided to signal their intrepid spirits by depicting them unarmed, with the main patroller carrying only a walking-stick. There is as yet no evidence to suggest that Jack the Ripper's crimes inspired a wave of self-defence scenarios in fiction beyond the media cultivation of myths, as well as suggestions by newspaper readers on how to catch the killer.[49] While the Ripper was represented as a 'man of blood', he (or indeed she) had no fixed identity and possible suspects changed all the time. It is likely that the Ripper's multiple personalities problematized attempts to set up narratives of defence as it was unclear against whom the writers should define their heroes.

Appearing just before the publication of Barton-Wright's first articles, Anthony Hope's *Rupert of Hentzau* (1898), the sequel to the bestselling *Prisoner of Zenda* (1894), features swordfights, the last of which ends in the vanquishing of the villain, Rupert. As Donna T. Andrew shows, the 1937 film adaptation of *The Prisoner of Zenda* was a twentieth-century fantasy of duelling and she charts the aversion of the middle classes to the sport.[50] Yet the novel itself participated in a cultural fascination with an illegal way of settling honour disputes which had only a few decades earlier been eradicated. In Marie Corelli's successful novel *The Sorrows of Satan*, the Devil, disguised as a foreign count, laments the demise of the sword duel:

> 'There is no real use in this flimsy blade [...]. In old times, if a man insulted you, or insulted a woman you admired, out flashed a shining point of tempered Toledo steel that could lunge – so!' and he threw himself into a fencing attitude of incomparable grace and ease [...] 'But now [...] men [rely] no more on themselves for protection, but content to go about yelling "Police! Police!" at the least threat of injury to their worthless persons.'[51]

He scours London for his saviour, anyone who will spurn him so that he may go to Heaven. The count tempts the novel's narrator with traditional means of upholding honour which, as Wiener says, 'were no longer considered manly by either state authorities or a growingly "respectable" public'.[52] However, as is apparent, the narrator is impressed by the count's performance. How then was it possible to defend oneself gallantly, with 'grace and ease', without recourse to violent weapons? A small number of Victorian men-at-arms appeared to have the answer.

'The Irish blackthorn ... if carefully selected, possesses all the strength of the oak, plus enormous toughness, and a pliability which makes it a truly charming weapon to work with.'[53] This handy hint appeared in *Broad-Sword and Single-Stick* (1890), which applies swordplay for civilian self-defence and elaborates on the use of canes, sticks and cudgels for personal protection. The principal writer who also authored most of the book, Sir Rowland George Allanson-Winn, had won the heavyweight and middleweight boxing championships for Trinity College, Cambridge, and was also a weapons enthusiast. *Broad-Sword and Single-Stick* condones the use of weapons and assesses their qualities, but at the same time represents fresh interpretation of the issue of personal protection. Allanson-Winn did not recommend life-preservers because the bulbous end of the weapon is not thick enough to guarantee hitting the adversary squarely on the head. He preferred cudgels and enthusiastically advocated the blackthorn cudgel as a weapon against housebreakers. A strong but supple wood, blackthorn is one of the woods out of which the Irish shillelagh is carved.

However, Doyle casts a shadow over the weapons mentioned in Allanson-Winn's book. In 'The Adventure of the Greek Interpreter' (1893; hereafter 'AGI') Mr Melas's kidnapper threatens the interpreter with a 'most formidable-looking bludgeon loaded with lead'. But it is Doyle's 'AAG' which makes a greater impact on the reader. In this story he examines the moral limits of personal protection and puts Allanson-Winn's favourite weapon in the wrong hands. Eustace Brackenstall, a veritable man of blood, keeps a blackthorn cudgel for use against burglars. A swarthy and vain domestic tyrant, Brackenstall also tortures household animals, verbally abuses his wife and uses the cudgel to beat her 'savagely'. Witnessing a beating, Captain Croker, Mary's fair-haired athletic defender, rushes to her aid. He plays the part of the chivalrous gentleman, ready to fight the perpetrator of cruelty towards women, children and animals. He inadvertently kills Brackenstall with a fire poker. Unlike the blackthorn cudgel, the fire poker is not designed for maiming. Even nowadays, it is lawful to employ such a tough and deadly household item for personal protection if used according to the dictates of 'reasonable force', but using a weapon such as a blackthorn cudgel which is kept for the protection against attackers is unlikely to constitute self-defence. As Croker tells Holmes, it was a 'fair fight' to the death and for the protection of Mary's life. So, Croker's physically vigorous defence of Brackenstall's wife is an act of knightly chivalry. The use of the fire poker as a method for self-defence contrasts favourably with the display of armoured hypermasculinity during the garotting outbreaks. Here Croker does not arrive on the scene pre-armed. Instead, his use of a fire poker reflects his mental prowess.

When it is apparent that Brackenstall has been killed by the impact of the fire poker, Croker and Mary Brackenstall attempt to disguise the incident as an act perpetrated by burglars. Feeling that the police might be on his trail, Croker visits Holmes and confides in him and Watson. A mock trial ensues in which Holmes and Watson are judge and jury.

As Holmes announces: 'I am not sure that in defence of your own life your action will not be pronounced legitimate.' The detective sympathetically acquits Croker and permits him to leave with a head start over the police officers in pursuit. As Holmes, the 'judge', is here a paragon of justice, his views of self-defence and the defence of others as expressed in 'AAG' are set up as guidelines.

Allanson-Winn's motivation behind writing *Broad-Sword and Single-Stick* was in fact to impart advice as to how everyday objects could be used to fend off attackers. *Broad-Sword and Single-Stick* advises against spring-dagger umbrellas and swordsticks which were in use in late-nineteenth-century Britain, as these devices might encourage an 'excitable' or 'hasty, hot-tempered individual' to draw blood.[54] However, a skilled swordsman could prepare himself 'at a moment's notice', grabbing 'any weapon chance may place in [his] hands: the leg of an old chair, the joint of a fishing rod, or the common or garden spade'.[55] Given large sections of the book are devoted to swordplay, *Broad-Sword and Single-Stick* would not have been well known outside of its immediate readership. However, Barton-Wright invited him to teach at the Bartitsu Club and so it is quite possible that Allanson-Winn's expertise, popularized by Barton-Wright, found its way into the parlours of the middle classes.

Barton-Wright does not tell his readers which canes to buy based on their striking merits, but he builds on Allanson-Winn's idea of using everyday objects and he teaches the average reader of *Pearson's Magazine* how best to manipulate the cane he already possesses. Lacking a hilt, the ordinary walking-stick could not be guided by the fingers as in fencing or single-stick play; the momentum of force now had to come from the wrist. We know from 'A Study in Scarlet' that Holmes is a proficient single-stick player. In 'The Adventure of the Illustrious Client' (hereafter 'AIC'), a story appearing much later in 1924, Doyle describes Holmes being attacked outside the Cafe Royal by two men wielding sticks. The second attacker overpowers him but, as he tells Watson, his single-stick skills allowed him to successfully fend off the first assailant. As he informs Watson: 'I'm a bit of a single-stick expert, as you know. I took most of them on my guard. It was the second man that was too much for me.' His statement to Watson suggests that more than two men may have been present and that, despite being outnumbered, Holmes largely escaped an assault on him which was intended to be murderous. Holmes might have adapted to Barton-Wright's new art, but a complete beginner could also acquire the skills with even more ease as the technique was different. The featherweight wrestling champion and jujitsuka (that is, a practitioner) Percy Longhurst told his readers that 'self-defence with an ordinary walking-stick or umbrella may be carried to a pitch undreamt of by the ordinary man; but it is not necessary to use the weapon with the skill of M. Vigny [of whom we will hear more later] to discomfort a chance assailant'.[56] A modern parallel of the art of transforming the everyday walking-stick into an ad hoc means of personal protection is Shihan Kevin Garwood's *Cane Work* courses in which people of all ages, including pensioners, learned how to defend themselves with their sticks.[57] As Trollope argued in 'Uncontrolled Ruffianism':

> We had been told that we ought to stir no whither after nightfall in the streets of London, without carrying with us, at the least, a huge knobstick wherewith to assail, on the instant, any garotter by whom we might be attacked – whereas it is our custom and our comfort to be accompanied by a somewhat soft and ancient umbrella, which we love well.[58]

He might have appreciated the opportunity to learn how to use what he had described as his beloved 'soft and ancient umbrella' for personal protection in place of a life-preserver.

Judith Walkowitz cites Barton-Wright's profusely illustrated two-part piece of 1901, 'Self-Defence with a Walking-Stick: The Different Methods of Defending Oneself with a Walking-Stick or Umbrella when Attacked under Unequal Conditions', as an example of the types of extraordinary subjects designed both to 'amuse' and 'instruct', in which *Pearson's Magazine* specialized.[59] Yet this instructional article has much to reveal about the interplay of fiction and ideals of masculine role play as a response to crime.

The newly fashionable, minimally aggressive forms of self-defence of the 1900s opened urban spaces and created avenues for the possibility of masculine self-expression along accepted cultural lines. In 'Walking in the City' (1974) Michel de Certeau relates urban walking to speech, arguing that the act of strolling is dictated by the structure of the city, but, as with language, boundaries can be negotiated, resulting in shifts in meaning and changes in direction. He writes: 'Charlie Chaplin multiplies the possibilities of his cane; he does other things with the same thing and he goes beyond the limits that the determinants of the object set on its utilization.'[60] So too did Barton-Wright and his peers.

Importantly, Barton-Wright's re-conceptualization of fencing and single-stick play catered to the interests of the readers of *Pearson's Magazine* and the *Strand* who may also have consumed men's fiction. Doyle was a proponent of New Chivalry, a concept which, as Mark Girouard points out, moved away from the worship of women and instead exalted the heroism of young men.[61] It is well known that 221b Baker Street is a homosocial environment where both Holmes and Watson, but Holmes in particular, distance themselves from the female sex. Bartitsu chimed with such lifestyle preferences. When Barton-Wright recommends the manoeuvre 'A Good Way of Conducting a Person out of the Room', the title 'room' alludes to a bachelor's 'room' or club.[62] The technique would have been particularly useful for expelling unwelcome intruders such as the poker-bender of 'ASB', Dr Roylott. His invention was overwhelmingly styled as a gallant martial art for urban explorers. It was a form of urban display to be enacted for men by men in a masculine environment outside of the domestic home, a manifestation of what John Tosh has famously termed the late-Victorian 'flight from domesticity'.[63] Indeed, Barton-Wright's articles are devoid of photographs of women. In an interview conducted in 1901 with the sports journalist Mary Nugent, he revealed that 'he found ladies a little – just a little – tiresome' as they 'expect to be taught for less because they are ladies' and 'think they will know things when they don't'. While the Bartitsu Club took in female pupils, the price of the classes and the fact that the school focused on teaching men may in reality have discouraged a number of female students from applying.

According to Barton-Wright, Bartitsu with a walking-stick (known as *la canne*) was not only a 'useful and practical accomplishment' but also 'a most exhilarating and graceful exercise'.[64] It is widely acknowledged that Holmes embodies the incompatible traits of sanguine calculation and intellectual ostentation. For instance, Douglas Kerr has insightfully built on James Eli Adams's observations on the dandyish aspects of Carlyle's ascetic thinker and argues that Sherlock Holmes too *exhibits* his cold rationalism.[65] Bartitsu is a physical manifestation of the rodomontade in which Holmes so frequently indulges. It is both to be studied and displayed. This is apparent during a performance of the art. Robert Temple and Keith Ducklin's performance of Bartitsu at the Royal Armouries showed that *la canne* is a controlled yet dynamic form of physical exposition. Strikes are 'given by swinging the body on the hips – and not merely by flips from the elbow'.[66] The weight rests on the knees in the same manner as in fencing, while the upper body is free to perform highly gestural striking actions. Barton-Wright's monographs are embellished with photographs of the Bartitsuka striking masterful poses. Bodily self-expression is rendered legitimate by virtue of the sport being a 'scientifically planned'[67] response to street violence.

Figure 8.1   'Guard by Distance'.

This shows that the shift away from the use of weaponry to everyday objects for self-defence opened avenues for the possibility of masculine self-expression along accepted legal lines, whilst allowing for the flirtation with older styles of combat, reinvented for a new generation.

Exhilarating masculine romances could be translated into narratives of urban vulnerability in which Barton-Wright invited the reader to enact scenes depicted in *Pearson's Magazine* in order to fight Rupert of Hentzau himself. The Swiss *maitre d'armes* Pierre Vigny was the actual inventor of *la canne* which Barton-Wright subsumed into his own repetoire. Vigny began to research defensive techniques with the walking-stick in the 1890s and ran a school of arms in Switzerland before collaborating with Barton-Wright and becoming an instructor at the Bartitsu Club. He subsequently inaugurated his own martial arts school in London in 1903, enthralling audiences with his vivacious performances. A dashing, self-confessed *flâneur*, he took 'nightly excursions into the roughest of the rough quarters of Paris, Lyons, Marseilles, Naples, Genoa' in order to test his defence skills against criminals who were prepared to 'commit a brutal assault for five francs, and a murder for twenty'.[68] It was claimed that he had also combated hooligans. Thus, Vigny's depiction of acts of

Figure 8.2   Self-defence with a hooked stick.

self-defence opened up possibilities for an engagement with masculine romance beyond the vicarious experience of the reading of the Holmes adventures, for a tussle with the urban heart of darkness, what Holmes calls the 'dark jungle of criminal London'. Vigny's blend of French and English martial arts is rendered appealing for the British market due to his stoicism and collectedness, two 'British' national traits, and, like Sherlock Holmes, Vigny's composure and self-assurance give him licence to experiment with eclectic and unusual tastes.

At times, Barton-Wright's presentational style betrays a preoccupation with the masculine psyche and pictorial representations of conflict between the man of blood and the assertive, physically flamboyant practitioner of the defensive arts. When Barton-Wright performs with his Japanese assistants, he sometimes plays the part of the darkly attired villain. When he demonstrates manoeuvres with fellow Englishmen, he plays the part of the gallant Bartitsuka while his enemies wear black. Readers could more readily distinguish between the hero and the attacker if they were presented in such stark colours, but such imagery also recalls the duel between Holmes and his shadowy, swarthy adversaries.

9
Foreign Friends

Sadakazu Uyenishi: 'jump into space'

A bronze statue of Sherlock Holmes stands outside Karuizawa Town, near Tokyo. It was built in 1988 by the Japan Sherlock Holmes Club, a successful society founded in 1977. Sherlock Holmes first appeared in Japan in 1894 in an edited version of 'The Man with the Twisted Lip', published in the political magazine *Nihon-jin*. Over a century later, the great detective is now the most widely recognized English figure in Japan, more famous, it is said, than even the Beatles.[1]

There is a considerable body of outstanding work on Doyle and Orientalism,[2] yet more research needs to be done on the cultural significance of Japanese objects in the canon. As Olive Checkland has observed, the British regarded Japan with a colonial eye, fetishizing Japanese objects in a bedazzled yet condescending manner.[3] After the Meiji Restoration in 1868, Japan became an increasingly important participant on the worldwide exhibition circuit, impressing visitors to exhibitions in Paris in 1867, Melbourne in 1875 and Glasgow in 1901. Japan and Britain soon found themselves forming a special relationship, comparing notes on economics, architecture, industry and design. British artists, notably Charles Rennie Mackintosh, were charmed by the bold lines and the interplay of light and space in Japanese art, untouched by Western influence for 200 years. His creations such as the Glasgow tearooms and the Glasgow School of Art still attract tourists from around the world.

Writers were also fascinated by the country. Kipling visited Japan in the 1880s and was astonished by the delicacy of Japanese design, its vulnerability a temptation for the unscrupulous individual or criminal:

> The books have long ago told you how a Japanese house is constructed, chiefly of sliding screens and paper partitions, and everybody knows the story of the burglar of Tokio who burgled with a pair of scissors for jimmy and centre-bit and stole the Consul's trousers ... But all the telling in print will never make you understand the exquisite finish of a tenement that you could kick in with your foot and pound to match-wood with your fists.[4]

As Harry Ricketts argues, for Kipling and Oscar Wilde, Japan was inextricably associated with objets d'art, encapsulated in Kipling's statement on visiting the country in the 1880s: 'And I was in Japan—the Japan of cabinets and joinery, gracious folk and fair manners.'[5]

British artists were virtually assured of a profit if they embellished their work with Japanese items.[6] Perhaps the appearance of emissaries of Japan in the canon can be read as an attempt to furnish the adventures with an air of Japonisme, reflecting trends in decorative arts. Besides Bartitsu there are a number of Japanese objects scattered throughout the collection of adventures: the Japanese cabinet ('The Adventure of the Gloria Scott', 1893); the Emperor Shomu and the Shoso-in, near Nara ('AIC', 1924); and the Japanese vase ('The Three Gables', 1926). Notably, in the early story 'AGI', the inanimate curiosity is observed out of the corner of the eye. The kidnapped Greek translator Mr Melas recounts catching 'glimpses of velvet chairs, a high white marble mantelpiece, and what seemed to be a suit of Japanese armour at one side of it'. Thus, the Japanese armour is taken out of its context, placed in an English surrounding and reduced to a static domestic ornament.

Surveying the canon, it is curious to see the way in which Japan and Japanese imagery start to emerge from the page in 'AEH' as they did in physical culture during this time. This is certainly true about 'baritsu', which leaps off the page. Had anyone heard of Japanese martial arts before Barton-Wright introduced them to Britain? As Hirayama and Hall note, there were exhibitions of Japanese wrestling at the Japanese Village which appeared from 1885 to 1886 at the same time as the *Mikado* hit the British stage. In 1892 the Secretary of the Japan Bank of Tokyo and pupil of Jigoro Kano, Tetsujiro Shidachi, gave a lecture to the London-based Japan Society (founded in 1891). The demonstration was reworked and appeared in the *Idler* in 1892 under the title 'Japanese Fighting (Self-Defence by Sleight of Body)', a volume in which Doyle was heavily featured.[7] Yet these performances and publications did not lead to a wider awareness of Japanese martial arts. By the time Barton-Wright gave his own lecture to the Japan Society in 1901, entitled 'Ju-Jitsu and Ju-Do', he had already set a trend.

If Japan warmly received Doyle's vision of dynamic manliness in the form of Sherlock Holmes, then it exported its own examples of masculinity to Britain. When Barton-Wright returned in Britain in the late 1890s, two Japanese assistants followed him. They were Sadakazu Uyenishi and Yukio Tani. As Connell has argued, relationships between men are influenced by shifting hegemonic masculine pecking orders in which the values of the dominant order of the time permeate cultural attitudes towards sexuality, gender, violence and race. While the numbers of men closely embodying the hegemonic ideal might be small, larger numbers benefit from the advantage that being a man and the possession of certain masculine values gives them over women. They reap what Connell calls the 'patriarchal dividend'.[8] Connell's observation recalls Barton-Wright's interview with Mary Nugent, in which he conveys his female students as both morally and intellectually the weaker sex, questioning their scruples and their knowledge of the art. This is a curious statement for a magazine such as *Health and Strength* which, while the publication catered to a mainly male market, also offered much material for female readers. One has the impression that Barton-Wright is winking at the male consumers of *Health and Strength*, attempting a rapport with them through a hegemonic masculine tone.

At the same time, Barton-Wright also attempts to place himself higher on the scale than Uyenishi, both literally and figuratively. Contemporary commentators habitually referred to his Japanese assistants as 'little Japs', a description he was also prone to using in his work as he paraded his assistants around the music hall scene. As Tony Wolf says, Barton-Wright was eclipsed by his Bartitsu protégés whose superior wrestling skills and foreign appearance caught the eye of the public. When the Bartitsu Club stopped functioning as a martial arts school, Barton-Wright's Japanese assistants opened their own dojos (schools), appeared in the popular press and became minor celebrities in their own right. Sadakazu Uyenishi particularly interests me from a historical and cultural perspective. Uyenishi promoted jujitsu to the British public but constructed an identity for himself that was both foreign and also situated within British culture. Surprisingly, his teaching also found its way into the workings of the British suffragette movement. It is worth examining *The Text-Book of Ju Jutsu as Practised in Japan* (1905; hereafter *Text-Book*), a self-instruction manual written by Uyenishi.

Uyenishi's publication was an integral work on jujitsu and inspired a surge in self-defence manuals in the subsequent year. Some books published in its wake include Percy Longhurst's *Jiu-Jitsu and Other Methods of Self-Defence* (1907), Yukio Tani and Taro Miyake's *The Game of Ju-Jitsu, for the Use of Schools and Colleges* (1906) as well as reprints of Uyenishi's *Text-Book*. Uyenishi's publication clearly demonstrates the possibilities for self-invention in the practice of Edwardian jujitsu. He was also the instructor to Emily Watts, one of the first female jujitsukas and author of *The Fine Art of Jujutsu* (1906). In this manner he directly influenced the development of women's self-defence training in Britain.

Uyenishi was a key practitioner of martial arts in London. After the closure of the Bartitsu Club, he set up his own School of Japanese Self-Defence at Piccadilly Circus in 1903. *Text-Book* underscores his reputation and influence but in a more subtle manner than that employed by Barton-Wright. In order to promote himself, Uyenishi allows the reader to infer that it is his work that has directly helped with the proliferation of Japanese martial arts in Britain:

> When I first arrived in this country the number of people who were acquainted with Ju-jutsu, or who had even heard of the science, might almost have been counted on one's fingers. But the past four years have worked many changes. All Britishers have at least *heard* of Ju-jutsu, while a vast and rapidly increasing number take a larger or smaller interest in the subject.

The 'past four years' to which Uyenishi alludes encompass the teaching conducted at the Barton-Wright school until 1902 and also the setting up of institutes by both Uyenishi and Yukio Tani in London. This observation of Uyenishi is expressive of his desire to be counted as an influential figure in the martial arts world. The growth in the number of jujitsu enthusiasts to which he refers is evident from a reading of *Health and Strength*. Alongside articles and interviews conducted with jujitsukas, Uyenishi and Tani's schools also appear frequently in the magazine's advertisements. In a 'Word Portrait' by the editor of *Health and Strength*, Uyenishi is described as the 'Ju-jutsu World's champion'. This compliment further solidifies his reputation in sports and amongst amateur sportsmen who consumed *Health and Strength*. The book was also a great success and was reprinted frequently from 1905 onwards until the 1950s.

The armour that Mr Melas sees out of the corner of his eye conjures up images of feudal Japan before Jigoro Kano's revision of traditional jujitsu into a modern sport, judo. As Tony Wolf suggests, there were elements of Kano's judo in the teachings of Japanese jujitsuka. While Uyenishi was a professional jujitsuka and a pioneer of judo in Britain, *Text-Book* is very much addressed to the British amateur: 'I have endeavoured to so express myself, that you will most of you be able to teach yourselves, and be fitted to combat on fairly equal terms, any but the most skilled and experienced opponents.' It was not imperative to purchase the uniform of the mat (known as the 'gi' – pronounced 'gee'): the only equipment needed is 'a stout jacket fastened by a sash' and 'any matting, provided it be thick enough, and not too rough'. The consumer is offered an array of physical and mental benefits, and jujitsu is 'second to none' as 'a means of developing rapidity of movement, and perfect balance'; it was a 'developer of strength and muscle of the right quality'; a 'magnificent sport, game, or exercise' and also promoter of 'mental, moral, and physical qualities which it calls into play'. Therefore, the amateur gentleman could learn the art of physical prowess with only minor adjustments to his existing lifestyle.

As McLaughlin argues, for Holmes the 'collapse of boundaries also becomes a source of pleasure'.[9] Holmes explores the East through commodities and travel. He owns a Persian slipper and has spoken with the Dalai Lama. He also, to Watson's chagrin, consumes cocaine as a tonic for boredom and restlessness. McLaughlin writes that 'the Holmes tales are precisely about two phenomena in late nineteenth-century London: the recognition of urban blight; and its connection to an awareness of the colonies as an invasive source of new and even more menacing dangers'. Just as sinister immigrants could threaten the body politic, foreign imports such as cocaine could, if taken indulgently, end in the physical annihilation of the consumer, as McLaughlin argues with reference to the character of Thaddeus Sholto in 'TSF'.[10] Sholto's addiction emasculates him and, as McLaughlin alleges, 'the effeminate Sholto is an echo of the decadent eighteenth-century aristocrat against whom middle-class Victorian heroes are structured'.[11] What of other Eastern influences? By being a form of self-defence which was also helpful, Bartitsu allowed the gentleman to indulge physically in Eastern pleasures, to fortify, not endanger, life and limb and to revitalize British masculinity.

Text-Book is a pictorial essay in raw physical energy. Uyenishi, a foreigner, skilfully positions himself within British culture. He tells readers that despite his 'knowledge of English being so small', the positive reception he has received in Britain has greatly assisted him in surmounting the language barrier. He expresses his intention to work for British interests, arguing that jujitsu is 'a matter of supreme and even National Importance' for Britain, presumably in the defence of the nation as well as the individual. This is in harmony with the comments made by Eustace Fry, a contributor in *Health and Strength*. As Uyenishi was involved with the magazine, it is likely he read this article. Fry zealously linked physical culture with national defence, predicting a 'titanic struggle [between] East and West' and recommending British readers to embrace Japan as a vital ally.[12] Fry argued that: 'Every Jap is an athlete of a high order. Even the women of Japan are not effeminate, while the men are men worthy of the name [...] So the Japs, in addition to their superior physical condition, are possessed of a weapon, that in hand-to-hand struggle, would give them an enormous advantage over Europeans.'[13] This perspective was complemented by the views of a British commentator on the Japan-British Exhibition regarding the similarities in the physiognomy and manner of the people of both islands, arguing that these 'constitute a good augury for the growth of sympathy between east and west'.[14]

The Japanese victory over Russian forces in the Russo-Japanese War of 1904–5 stunned the British press and gave further credibility to jujitsu, a small country fighting a larger one. Fry's article represents the most extreme rationale for an adoption of Japanese martial arts, but such textual sources suggest that the 'heart of darkness' represented by crime and violence within Britain could be combated with early-twentieth-century manly initiatives to explore the East through physical education. Admiral Togo of the Japanese fleet was hailed as an international star and photos of him appeared in the *Strand* at that time. As Hirayama and Hall suggest, his physical appearance was similar to that of Edward VII.[15]

In *Text-Book* Uyenishi cultivates an identity that is distinctly Japanese and yet sympathetic to British customs. He is referred to as a 'courteous, refined little gentleman, with gold-rimmed spectacles'.[16] Small stature is a negative trait in 'TSF'. Kestner argues that Jonathan Small's surname refers to his phallic deficiencies, an impression further underscored by the symbolic loss of his leg which denotes castration.[17] It is 'the idea of small' which Kestner argues 'pervad[es] the text' and is 'an element which complicates the conviction of male heroism in the tale'.[18] Furthermore, Thaddeus Sholto is also described as being a 'twitching' male of short stature. Therefore, small stature was symbolically linked to a loss of masculinity and a lack of physical heroism. But here Uyenishi is part of British culture, not an outsider like Tonga. He speaks the language and shapes culture. The inset photograph depicts him immaculately dressed in a suit with stiff collar. In this picture he embodies the image of the archetypal English gentleman, exhibiting an appreciation of English tailoring. At the same time, at the back of the book he is pictured at home in Osaka with his family wearing Japanese formal attire. His image of traditional Japan may also have been designed to satisfy the British reader's desire for cultural quaintness and newness. As one traveller to Japan had remarked: 'But the rare charm of Japanese life, so different from that of all other lands, is not to be found in its Europeanized circles.'[19] The inset photograph of Uyenishi and the image of him at home in Japan frame the pictures in which he is presented partially clothed and physically active. This visual contrast recalls the English public school tradition of the playing of rough-and-tumble sports such as rugby by young gentlemen who would otherwise be expected to don formal English wear at all other times. Therefore, in adopting the sartorial formalities associated with both cultures, Uyenishi invites the reader to consider the links between Japanese culture and that of middle-class Britain. By striking down prejudices, Uyenishi creates room to move through the throng of hegemonic masculine voices.

Professor S. K. Uyenishi.

Figure 9.1 Sadakazu Uyenishi: In Britain. From *The Text-Book of Ju Jutsu as Practised in Japan* (1905), frontispiece.

S. K. Uyenishi at Home in Osaka.

Figure 9.2   Sadakazu Uyenishi: At home. From *Text-Book*, pp. 102–3.

Text-Book is designed as a subtle response to Barton-Wright's textual treatment of Uyenishi. Importantly, Uyenishi revises the meaning of small stature in *Text-Book* and at the same time demonstrates his own virility through physical motion and close combat. Uyenishi's efforts thus suggest the potency of self-defence, both for the upholding of British social values and for the re-evaluation of common preconceptions of gender and masculinity. Uyenishi may be comparatively small in stature but is 'capable of overcoming the strongest man who can be brought against him'. In *Text-Book* he takes his own space in the printed medium to make this point for himself, using his own words and controlling the way his image is transmitted to the audience. The photographs of him tackling his opponents are sensual in nature and draw attention to his taut limbs and erect musculature. Regardless of whether he was familiar with Doyle's treatment of the small, non-white man in 'TSF', Uyenishi's *Text-Book* quite clearly challenges any misconceptions there may have been linking small stature with a lack of virility.

Importantly, Uyenishi uses photography as an educational tool, clearly demonstrating to his readers how the manoeuvres are executed.

At the same time, he uses the camera to explore the possibilities offered by jujitsu for the visual articulation of identity. He often explains manoeuvres in the form of a set of photographic stills which, when presented together, lend an air of cinematicity to his lessons. This presentation is most likely inspired by the work of the then recently-deceased Eadweard Muybridge, whose *The Human Figure in Motion* (1901) charted the body in action using photographic stills. Uyenishi appropriated Muybridge's approach not for scientific studies but as a teaching aid, thus endeavouring to make jujitsu as accessible as possible to readers who wished to teach themselves the Japanese art of personal protection. Moreover, by aligning his self-presentation with the style of Muybridge's photographic studies, Uyenishi emphasizes the physical dynamism of jujitsu in slow motion. In his exposition of the technique 'Jump into Space', he literally appears to be flying through the air in a super-human fashion. Such images confirm his statement

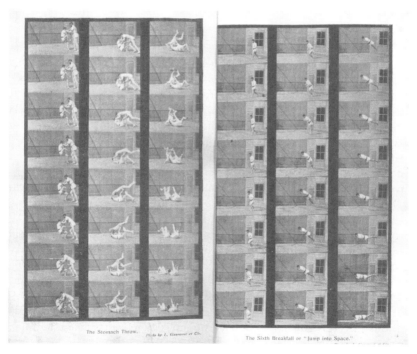

Figure 9.3 Uyenishi jumps into the ether. 'The Sixth Breakfall or 'Jump into Space'. From *Text-Book*, pp. 74–5.

that jujitsu 'is never monotonous or uninteresting either to performer or spectator'!

Together with Uyenishi's *Text-Book*, Doyle's use of Bartitsu publicized the utility of Japanese martial arts to the extent that Robert Baden-Powell's well-known *Scouting for Boys* (1908) included a number of references to jujitsu and Japanese culture: 'Unfortunately, chivalry with us has, to a large extent, been allowed to die out, whereas in Japan it is taught to the children.' The *Strand* magazine contained copious articles on the majesty of Japanese culture, pointing out the existence of Japanese equivalents of figures such as 'King Arthur'.[20] Toshio Yokoyama argues that British writers during the medieval revival of the 1850s expressed affinity with Japan by drawing parallels between Japanese and British culture, referring to 'Japanese knight-errantry'.[21] Thus, the *Strand* articles and Baden-Powell's book appeal to readers to look to non-Western influences to supplement existing constructions of British masculinity. It was claimed that Baden-Powell's sister became proficient in the art of self-defence with a parasol cane.[22]

Jujitsu, abroad and beyond

By 1908 Japanese martial arts were beginning to furnish playwrights with material. The farce *Ju-jutsu, or the Japanese Wrestler* expanded metropolitan interest in martial arts to Oxford, where the play was performed. It is now kept in the Lord Chamberlain's Manuscript Collection, alongside the garotting plays. In a similar manner to the garotting farces, *Ju-jutsu* argues that a hysterical reaction to interpersonal violence coupled with the incapacity to defend oneself is both weak and effeminate. In *Ju-jutsu,* the main protagonist is rendered a ridiculous figure (dressed in women's clothing) by his very inability to practise jujitsu. This play was certainly not the only text written after 'AEH' which explored the link between Japanese martial arts and British manliness. More influential works of fiction and fact demonstrated a keen awareness of the beneficial influence of Japan and jujitsu on British culture and the individual body respectively.

The Japan-British Exhibition of 1910, held at White City in West London, was the apex of Japan's participation in the worldwide exhibitions scene. This was an ambitious display of all things Japanese, presided over by the Japanese government, where visitors were tempted with horticultural halls, historical displays, recreated villages, lakes and gardens and state-of-the-art fairground rides. Attracting 8,350,000 visitors, it was a resounding success.[23] In an otherwise wide-ranging account of the Japan-British Exhibition, Olive Checkland omits to mention the Jujitsu Hall which, according to the exhibition historian Bill Tonkin, was a popular feature. Tonkin keeps an extraordinarily extensive collection of postcards, and the postcards dating from the Exhibition show sumo wrestling, fencing and jujitsu were demonstrated.[24] Visitors could purchase postcards of wrestlers in their gear as well as action stills. As the postcards show, this vision of Japanese martial arts was different from Uyenishi's, the former emphasizing the contrast to the appearance of the visitors and performers.

Brought to Britain by an engineer who marketed his brand of self-defence to the men of Britain, to customers who cultivated gentility, jujitsu grew in popularity and became a mechanism for personal reinvention. The empowering aspects of jujitsu were appropriated by various groups and it spread internationally. For instance, the Viennese were introduced to 'Yu-Yitsu' by Hans Köck in 1905, while Vigny opened a school in Geneva in 1912 and the New Zealand-born Florence Le Mar, 'The World's Famous Jujitsu Girl', toured the globe to display her skills. Of particular interest here is the martial arts scene in Paris at the turn of the century, aspects of which closely paralleled the British model.

Bartitsu was short-lived but it influenced a trend for jujitsu-qualified fictional heroes. Sherlock Holmes and A.J. Raffles, the genteel hobbyist housebreaker, inspired the creation of the hugely popular French gentleman-thief Arsène Lupin. Maurice Leblanc's Lupin stories were first serialized in the magazine *Je Sais Tout* in 1905. Lupin swiftly became a veritable French national icon and over the last 100 years Leblanc's creation has inspired countless interpretations in novels, in film and on stage.

Lupin is a highly capable jujitsu practitioner. In the 'The Mysterious Passenger' (1907) he defends himself using a manoeuvre, the 'carotid hook', against an assailant who has killed a women and children and who wields both a revolver and a knife. In 'The Escape of Arsene Lupin' (1909) Lupin's adversary, Inspector Ganimard, grasps him by the throat, but he retaliates confidently with jujitsu: 'The struggle was short. Arsène Lupin hardly made a movement in defence and Ganimard let go as promptly as he had attacked. His right arm hung numbed and lifeless by his side ... "If they taught you jiu-jitsu at the Quai des Orfèvres," said Lupin, "you would know that they call this movement udi-shi-ghi in Japanese." [...] "Another second and I should have broken your arm ..."'[25] If London was the home of Bartitsu, then Leblanc places Paris on the martial arts map by pinpointing an area with which his readers would have been familiar where the art is taught. In his highly informative article on literature on jujitsu in Paris during the

Belle Epoque, Aaron Freundschuh (whose eye is trained exclusively on France) points out that the 'Quai des Orfèvres' was the location of the National Police headquarters in Paris.[26] This begs the following question: if French officers were ostensibly so well-equipped, then how much martial arts training did London police officers receive?

Uyenishi notes that the British army had added the Japanese martial art to the repertoire of gymnastic exercises while a goodly number of 'tricks, locks, holds, and throws' of jujitsu already formed part of police training.[27] In *The History of Mr Polly* (1910) H.G. Wells's humorous description of his eponymous hero's predicament is suggestive: 'Mr. Polly was under restraint of little Clamp of the toyshop, who was holding his hands in a complex and uncomfortable manner that he afterwards explained to Wintershed was a combination of something romantic called "Ju-jitsu" and something else still more romantic called the "Police Grip".'[28] This is a subject which merits closer inspection, especially as it appears that Japanese martial arts, initially introduced to Britain by Barton-Wright for civilian use, were considered to be sufficiently effective as to be introduced in police training. In an article printed in the *Daily Mail* at the beginning of 2010, entitled 'The Non-PC Guide to Policing: How to Apprehend a Criminal, 1907-Style', Stephen Wright introduces images of jujitsu training kept at the City of London Police archives.[29] This suggests that there is much information to be mined in an area which has so far been sparsely covered.

Leblanc echoes the work of Doyle and also of the French self-defence instructor Émile André. André had introduced his book *L'Art de se Défendre dans la Rue* to France in the same year that Barton-Wright's own martial art appeared in *Pearson's Magazine*. As Freundschuh argues, André's text was aimed at what is colloquially referred to as the 'rubbernecker', the opposite of the bourgeois pedestrian.[30] However, while the bold line drawings and inexpensive design of André's *100 Façons de se Défendre dans la Rue Sans Armes* (1905) suggest that the book could be read by those of lesser means, the book was not expressly aimed at the lower-class Frenchman. André's illustrations depict the top-hatted Frenchman being garotted and threatened with a knife attack by flat-capped garotters, while others depict gentlemen defending themselves with *la savate*. Just as Holmes is both classless and yet embodies some 'middle-class' qualities such as hard work and the defence of family values, here the struggle against crime, André's illustrator's depiction of a street mugging, is an opportunity to exhibit class and national identity.

Holmes and Lupin defend women against the spectre of the man of blood. By the end of the Edwardian era, one woman in particular felt that she could do that job herself. At around this time, Edith Garrud entered the scene. When Uyenishi left London in 1909, Edith's husband, William Garrud, took over. He taught male pupils while she gave classes to women and children. Dramatically, a year later she had divorced William and opened the School of Ju-jutsu in Regent Street. Garrud was a plucky jujitsuka who trained the bodyguards of Women's Social and Political Union leader Emmeline Pankhurst, but also offered her London dojo as a refuge for suffragettes after their campaigns.[31]

From the 1850s to 1914, civilian self-defence had shifted from an approach virtually resembling an armed attack to a physically defensive, corporeal response, based not on visible bodily strength but on performance and trickery. From 1914, concerns of national security took priority over civilian protection. The contrast is most evident in *Health and Strength*. From the announcement of the start of the War, copious articles on self-defence were replaced with columns on fitness in preparation for military service. Now the walls that were built were between nations. As Greenfield, O'Connell and Reid argue, 'heroic models of masculinity so beloved of the pre-1914 middle classes had been greatly undermined by the realities of emasculating trench warfare'.[32] Nevertheless, in 1918 masculine physical culture received a boost with the founding of the London Budokwai, under Gunji Koizumi, an instructor who worked at Uyenishi's dojo in 1906. It was the first school of judo in Europe.

Notes

Introduction

1. R. Sindall, 'The London Garotting Panics of 1856 and 1862', *Social History*, 12 (1987), 351–9 (p. 351); and Shani D'Cruze, 'Introduction: Unguarded Passions: Violence, History and the Everyday', in Shani D'Cruze (ed.), *Everyday Violence in Britain, 1850–1950, Gender and Class* (Harlow: Longman/Pearson, 2000), pp. 1–19 (p. 1).
2. Clive Emsley, *Crime and Society in England, 1750–1900*, rev. edn (London: Longman/Pearson, 2005), p. 42.
3. See Jan Bondeson, *The London Monster: A Sanguinary Tale* (Cambridge: University of Pennsylvania Press/Da Capo Press, 2002), p. 44 and Jennifer Westwood, *The Lore of the Land: A Guide to England's Legends from Spring-Heeled Jack to the Witches of Warboys* (London: Penguin, 2005), p. 343.
4. Emsley, *Crime and Society*, p. 300.
5. Rob Sindall, *Street Violence in the Nineteenth-Century: Media Panic or Real Danger?* (Leicester University Press, 1990), p. 30.
6. Lynda Nead, *Victorian Babylon: People, Streets and Images in Nineteenth-Century London* (London: Yale University Press, 2000), p. 10.
7. Sindall, *Street Violence*, p. 7. By the 'central class', Sindall is referring to the middle classes.
8. Richard Sennett, *The Conscience of the Eye: The Design and Social Life of Cities* (London: Faber & Faber, 1991), p. xii.
9. Jerry White, *London in the Twentieth Century: A City and its People* (London: Vintage, 2008), p. 16.
10. William S. Gilbert, *London Characters and the Humorous Side of London Life* (c. 1871), http://www.victorianweb.org/books/mcdonnell/streets1.html, accessed 8 May 2010.
11. Sennett, *Conscience of the Eye*, p. xii.
12. Clive Emsley, *The English Police: A Political and Social History* (London: Longman/Pearson, 1996), p. 62.
13. John Carter Wood, 'A Useful Savagery: The Invention of Violence in Nineteenth-Century England', *Journal of Victorian Culture*, 9(1) (2004), 22–42 (p. 24).
14. Emsley, *Crime and Society*, p. 282.
15. See Wiener, *Men of Blood* and subsequent articles by Wiener on the subject (1997 and 2001).
16. Wiener, *Men of Blood*, p. 153.
17. Colin Greenwood, *Firearms Control: A Study of Armed Crime and Firearms Control in England and Wales* (London: Routledge & Kegan Paul, 1972), pp. 18–25; and Joyce Lee Malcolm, *Guns and Violence: The English Experience* (Cambridge, MA: Harvard University Press, 2002), p. 111.
18. Wood, 'A Useful Savagery', pp. 24 and 33.
19. Karen Volland Waters, *The Perfect Gentleman: Masculine Control in Victorian Men's Fiction, 1870–1901* (New York: Peter Lang, 1997), pp. 39–40.

20. Peter Gay, *The Cultivation of Hatred*, 'The Bourgeois Experience: Victoria to Freud'*, 5 vols (London: W.W. Norton & Company, 1993), vol. III, p. 115.

21. Jerome, *Three Men on the Bummel* (Bristol: J.W. Arrowsmith, 1900), p. 208, in Gay, *Cultivation of Hatred*, p. 12.

22. Norbert Elias, *The Civilizing Process: State Formation and Civilization*, trans. by Edmund Jephcott (Oxford: Blackwell, 1982), p. 229.

23. Jennifer Davis, 'The London Garotting Panic of 1862: A Moral Panic and the Creation of a Criminal Class in Mid-Victorian England', in V.A. Gatrell, Bruce Lenman and Geoffrey Parker (eds), *Crime and the Law: The Social History of Crime in Western Europe Since 1500* (London: Europa, 1980), pp. 190–213.

24. Geoffrey Pearson, *Hooligan: A History of Respectable Fears* (London: Macmillan, 1983).

25. See Sindall, 'Garotting 1856 and 1862' and his subsequent publication *Street Violence* (1990).

26. Pearson, *Hooligan*, p. 7.

27. Martin Wiener, *Reconstructing the Criminal: Culture, Law, and Policy in England, 1830–1914* (Cambridge University Press, 1990), p. 10.

28. Sindall, *Street Violence*, p. 24.

29. Eve Kosofsky Sedgwick, *Between Men: English Literature and Male Homosocial Desire* (New York: Columbia University Press, 1985), p. 164.

30. Waters, *Perfect Gentleman*, p. 39.

31. James Eli Adams, *Dandies and Desert Saints: Styles of Victorian Masculinity* (London: Cornell University Press, 1995), p. 195.

32. Christopher Breward, *The Hidden Consumer: Masculinities, Fashion and City Life 1860–1914* (Manchester University Press, 1999) and John Harvey, *Men in Black* (London: Reaktion Books, 1997).

33. Breward, *The Hidden Consumer*, pp. 258–9.

34. See Mike Huggins, *The Victorians and Sport* (London: Hambledon, 2004), p. 31.

35. Gay, *Cultivation of Hatred*, p. 110.

36. Antony E. Simpson, 'Dandelions on the Field of Honor: Duelling, the Middle Classes and the Law in Nineteenth-Century England', *Criminal Justice History*, 9 (1988), 99–155 (p. 108).

37. Wood, 'A Useful Savagery', p. 32.

38. E. Anthony Rotundo, 'Learning About Manhood: Gender Ideals and the Middle-Class Family in Nineteenth-Century America', in J.A. Mangan, and James Walvin (eds), *Manliness and Morality: Middle-Class Masculinity in Britain and America, 1800–1940* (Manchester University Press, 1987), pp. 35–51 (p. 40).

39. John Carter Wood, *Violence and Crime, Violence and Crime in Nineteenth-Century England: The Shadow of Our Refinement* (London: Routledge, 2004), pp. 33 and 140.

40. Judith Walkowitz, *City of Dreadful Delight: Narratives of Sexual Danger in Late-Victorian London* (London: Virago, 1992); Deborah Epstein-Nord, *Walking the Victorian Streets: Women, Representation, and the City* (London and Ithaca: Cornell University Press, 1995); and Nead, *Victorian Babylon*.

41. Deborah L. Parsons, *Streetwalking the Metropolis: Women, the City, and Modernity* (Oxford University Press, 2000).

42. Wiener, *Men of Blood*, p. 179.

43. Ian McEwan, *Saturday* (London: Jonathan Cape, 2005), pp. 81–99.

44. These include Richard Bowen, 'Further Lessons in Baritsu', *The Ritual Bi-Annual Review: The Northern Musgraves Sherlock Holmes Society*, 20 (1997), 22–26; Yuichi Hirayama and John Hall's, 'Some Knowledge of Baritsu: An Investigation of the Japanese System of Wrestling used by Sherlock Holmes', *Musgrave Monographs*, 7 (The Northern Musgraves, 1996), and Tony Wolf's, 'The Manly Arts of Self-Defence in Victorian and Edwardian England', in Tony Wolf (ed.), *The Bartitsu Compendium: History and Canonical Syllabus* (Raleigh, NC: Lulu.com, 2005), pp. 21–40.

45. Douglas M. Catron, '"Jiu-Jitsu" in Lawrence's "Gladiatorial"', *South Central Bulletin*, 43 (1983), 92–94 (p. 94).

46. Bill Brown, 'Thing Theory', *Critical Inquiry*, 28 (2001), 1–22.

47. Elaine Freedgood, *The Ideas in Things: Fugitive Meaning in the Victorian Novel* (University of Chicago Press, 2006), pp. 30–54.

48. David Trotter, 'Household Clearances in Victorian Fiction', *19: Interdisciplinary Studies in the Long Nineteenth Century*, 6 (2008) http://www.19.bbk.ac.uk/index.php/19/issue/view/69, accessed 8 May 2010, p. 11.

49. Wiener, *Men of Blood*, p. 1.

50. Gay, *Cultivation of Hatred*, p. 97.

1   Foreign Crimes Hit British Shores

1. C.J. Collins, *The Anti-Garotte* (1857), British Library, Lord Chamberlain's Manuscript Collection, L52964. p. 1. As the titles of the garotting plays to which I refer are so similar, I have included either dates or playwrights' names in every reference.

2. Clive Emsley, *Crime and Society*, p. 299.

3. 'What Better Measures Can Be Adopted to Prevent Crimes of Violence Against the Person?' (1867), quoted in Thomas Barwick Lloyd Baker, '*War with Crime': Being a Selection of Reprinted Papers on Crime, Reformatories, etc* (London: Longmans and Co., 1889), p. 24.

4. Davis, 'London Garotting Panic', p. 190.

5. Sindall, 'Garotting 1856 and 1862', p. 351.

6. Neil R. Storey, *The Grim Almanac of Jack the Ripper, London 1870–1900* (Stroud: Sutton, 2004), p. 37.

7. 'Burkins, the garotter [...] has confidentially informed his reverend instructor that to the melodramas at the Victoria must be ascribed his ruin.' George Augustus Sala, *Twice Round the Clock; or The House of the Day and Night in London* (London: George Robert Maxwell, 1878), p. 270. Mayhew's *London Labour and the London Poor* (1862) includes an interview with a garotter. See John Binney, 'Thieves' (1862) in Henry Mayhew, 'Those That Will Not Work', *London Labour and the London Poor*, Victor Neuburg (ed.), 4 vols. (London: Woodfall/Griffin Bohn, 1851–62; repr. Harmondsworth: Penguin, 1985), IV (1862), pp. 492–9.

8. Mike Dash, *Thug: The True Story of India's Murderous Cult* (London: Granta Books, 2005), p. 289.

9. Quoted in Kevin Rushby's *The Children of Kali: Through India in Search of Bandits, the Thug Cult and the British Raj* (London: Constable, 2002), p. 10.

2 The Ticket-of-Leave Man

1. Davis, 'London Garotting Panic', p. 201.
2. Daniel Pick, *Faces of Degeneration: A European Disorder, c. 1848–1918* (Cambridge University Press, 1996), p. 195.
3. Jennifer Jones, 'The Face of Villainy on the Victorian Stage', *Theatre Notebook*, 50 (1996), 95–108 (p. 98).
4. Watts Phillips, *A Ticket of Leave: A Farce in One Act* (1862; hereafter *A Ticket of Leave*), *Lacy's Acting Edition of Victorian Plays*, http://www.worc.ac.uk/victorian/victorianplays/editorialnote.htm, accessed 8 May 2010, p. 13.
5. See Wood, 'A Useful Savagery' and *Violence and Crime*.
6. *All the Year Round*, 8 (11 October 1862), p. 113 and *Illustrated London News*, 6 December 1862, p. 589.
7. Anne McClintock, *Imperial Leather: Race, Gender and Sexuality in the Colonial Contest* (London: Routledge, 1995), pp. 71–2.
8. John Binney, 'Thieves', p. 49.
9. Michael R. Booth, *Theatre in the Victorian Age* (Cambridge University Press, 1991), p. 13.
10. *Athenaeum*, 6 June 1863, p. 753.
11. This amendment of the original Penal Servitude Act of 1853 lengthened sentences to five years for a first offence and seven years for repeat offences. As regards the Security Against Violence Act of 1863, only under the Criminal Justice Act of 1948 was flogging restricted to crimes of prisoner mutiny and aggression towards prison officers. Sindall, *Street Violence*, pp. 41 and 146.
12. Davis, 'London Garotting Panic', p. 208.
13. Dennis W. Allen, 'Young England: Muscular Christianity and the Politics of the Body in "Tom Brown's Schooldays"', in Donald E. Hall (ed.), *Muscular Christianity: Embodying the Victorian Age* (Cambridge University Press, 1994), pp. 114–32 (p. 119).
14. Simpson, 'Dandelions', p. 108.
15. Samuel Smiles, *Self-Help: With Illustrations of Conduct and Perseverance* (London: John Murray, 1958), p. 50.
16. Sindall, 'Garotting 1856 and 1862', p. 356.
17. Robbery, trial reference number, t18570105-243, 5 January 1857, http://www.Oldbaileyonline.org.
18. R.W. Connell, *Masculinities* (Cambridge: Polity, 2006), p. 100.
19. *The Garotters* (1873), B.L. Lord Chamber. M. S. Coll, M53117, pp. 2–3.
20. Watts Phillips, *A Ticket of Leave*, p. 12.
21. *Illustrated London News*, 6 December 1862, p. 598.

3 Tooled Up: The Pedestrian's Armoury

1. Joseph Kestner, *Masculinities in Victorian Painting* (Aldershot: Scholar Press, 1995), p. 97.
2. Letter written by Mrs Gaskell in 1856, quoted in Guy Wilson, '"To Save Our Brave Men"', *Royal Armouries Yearbook*, 4 (1999), 71–5 (p. 71).
3. Sennett, *Conscience of the Eye*, p. xii.

4. Armour is worn on or carried close to the body. See Robert Woosnam-Savage and Anthony Hall, *Body Armour* (Virginia: Brassey's, 2001), p. 11.
5. G. Charter Harrison Jr., 'The Anti-Garotter', *The Gun Report* 2 (1956), 22.
6. Collins, *The Anti-Garotte* (1857), B.L. Lord Chamber. M.S. Coll, L52964, p. 4. With the assistance of Kathryn Johnson of the British Library Manuscript Collection, I was able to make a link between *The Antigarotte* (1863), B.L. Lord Chamber. M.S. Coll, M53019 and a play called *My Knuckleduster*, which, according to Donald Mullin, was shown at the Strand in 1863 – Donald Mullin, *Victorian Plays: A Record of Significant Productions on the London Stage, 1837–1901* (London: Greenwood, 1987), p. 258. The same Strand play of 1863 is referred to as *The Knuckleduster* (with John Crawford Wilson as the author) in Allardyce Nicoll's *A History of English Drama: 1660–1900: Late Nineteenth Century Drama, 1850–1900*, 6 vols. (Cambridge University Press, 1946), v, p. 628. On first glance, neither *My Knuckleduster* nor *The Knuckleduster* feature on the British Library's Manuscript Collection database and appeared to be missing. However, *My Knuckleduster* resurfaced unexpectedly.
   It is essential to point out that *The Antigarotte* (1863) was revised and shown at the Strand in 1863. It bears virtually the same title as the earlier farce *The Anti-Garotte* [L52964], which was licensed on 8 April 1857 and was shown at the Strand in the same year. However, apart from their interest in anti-garotting equipment, the plays are completely different in style, plot and characterization. *The Anti-Garotte* (1857) features characters such as Harry Datum and Commodore Rattlin, and tells the story of Tomkins, who invents an anti-garotte device. *The Antigarotte* (1863) describes the ways in which a Mr Augustus Herbert Smith repeatedly injures himself with pistols and life-preservers in his desperate attempt to defend himself from garotters in Highgate, London. According to *The Times*, *My Knuckleduster* was shown at the Royal Strand Theatre. See *The Times*, 20 February 1863, p. 8. The *Athenaeum* review of a play entitled *My Knuckleduster* (February 1863), purportedly written by a 'Mr Crawford Wilson', corresponds with the plot of *The Antigarotte* (1863), except the man lodging at Highgate is not referred to in the review as A.H. Smith but as Mr Rodgers. I have not found an explanation as to why the surnames do not match. However, the way in which the names of the authors, the locations, the plots and stage directions in *The Antigarotte* (1863) and *My Knuckleduster* correlate strongly suggests that *The Antigarotte* (1863) is not a revision of *The Anti-Garotte* (1857) and consequently that *The Antigarotte* (1863) and *My Knuckleduster* are the same play, despite the different titles.
7. Collins, *The Anti-Garotte* (1857), B.L. Lord Chamber. M.S. Coll, L52964, p. 4.
8. Wilson, *The Antigarotte* (1863), B.L. Lord Chamber. M.S. Coll, M53019, p. 17.
9. Metropolitan Police Stores, Woolwich, Stocks, Item 17.
10. *Athenaeum*, 14 February 1863, p. 235.
11. *Punch*, 27 December 1856, p. 251.
12. See Norman Vance, *The Sinews of Spirit: The Ideal of Christian Manliness in Victorian Literature and Religious Thought* (Cambridge University Press, 1985) and Mark Girouard's classic text, *The Return to Camelot: Chivalry and the English Gentleman* (London: Yale University Press, 1981).
13. Girouard, *Camelot*, p. 103.

14. 'The Uncommercial Traveller', 'The Ruffian', *All the Year Round*, 20 (1868), 421–4

15. Charles Dickens, 'On an Amateur Beat' (*All the Year Round*: 1869), in David Pascoe (ed.), *Charles Dickens: Selected Journalism, 1850–1870* (London: Penguin, 1997), pp. 386–92 (p. 386).

16. Elaine Freedgood, *Victorian Writing about Risk: Imaging a Safe England* (Cambridge University Press, 2000), p. 77.

17. Dickens, 'Amateur Beat', p. 386.

18. *Illustrated London News*, 26 January 1856, p. 83.

19. *The Garotters* (1873), B.L. Lord Chamber. M.S. Coll, 53117, p. 6.

20. Simpson, 'Dandelions', p. 108.

21. *The Times*, 9 January 1857, p. 8.

22. *Punch*, 20 December 1862, p. 249.

4   Threats from Above and Below

1. Mark W. Turner, *Trollope and the Magazines: Gendered Issues in Mid-Victorian Britain* (London: Macmillan, 2000), p. 144.

2. Arthur Conan Doyle, *Memories and Adventures* (London: John Murray, 1930), p. 306.

3. Waters, *Perfect Gentleman*, p. 24.

4. James Fitzjames Stephen, 'Gentlemen', *Cornhill Magazine*, 5 (March 1862), 327–42 (p. 331).

5. Samuel Smiles, *Character* (London: John Murray, 1871), p. 243.

6. 'Our Police', *Saturday Review of Politics, Literature, Science and Art*, 24 October 1868, 553–4 (p. 553).

7. Pamela Gilbert, *The Citizen's Body: Desire, Health, and the Social in Victorian England* (Ohio State University Press, 2007), p. 24.

8. Gay, *Cultivation of Hatred*, p. 4.

9. Martin Wiener, 'Alice Arden to Bill Sikes: Changing Nightmares of Intimate Violence in England, 1558–1869', *Journal of British Studies*, 40 (2001), 184–213 (pp. 195–6).

10. Quoted in *Gentlemen's Blood: A History of Duelling, From Swords at Dawn to Pistols at Dusk* (New York: Bloomsbury, 2003), p. 3.

11. Donna. T. Andrew, 'The Code of Honour and its Critics: The Opposition to Duelling in England, 1700–1850', *Social History*, 5 (1980), 409–34 (p. 415).

12. Simpson, 'Dandelions', p. 107.

13. Robin Gilmour, *The Idea of the Gentleman in the Victorian Novel* (London: George Allen & Unwin, 1981), p. 29.

14. Simpson, 'Dandelions', p. 140.

15. Wiener, *Men of Blood*, p. 41.

16. Wiener, *Men of Blood*, p. 41.

17. '*The Romance of Duelling in all Times and Countries*: Review', *Contemporary Review*, 10 (1869), 449–50 (p. 449).

18. Robert B. Shoemaker, 'The Taming of the Duel: Masculinity, Honour and Ritual Violence in London, 1660–1800', *Historical Journal*, 3 (2002), 525–45 (p. 545).

19. John. E. Archer, 'Men Behaving Badly? Masculinity and the Uses of Violence, 1850–1900', in D'Cruze, *Everyday Violence*, pp. 41–54 (p. 43).
20. Jerome K. Jerome, *Three Men on the Bummel* (1900), pp. 205–6, quoted in Gay, *Cultivation of Hatred*, p. 11.
21. 'Code of Duelling, The', *Chambers's Journal of Popular Literature, Science and Art*, 177 (18 May 1867), 305–8 (p. 305).
22. '*Romance of Duelling*: Review', *Contemporary Review*, p. 450.
23. Victoria Glendinning, *Trollope* (London: Pimlico, 1993), p. 173.
24. Hughes, *Tom Brown*, p. 302.
25. Jerome, *Three Men*, p. 208, quoted in Gay, *Cultivation of Hatred*, p. 12.
26. Turner, *Trollope and the Magazines*, p. 169.

5 Lord Chiltern and Mr Kennedy

1. 'Phineas Finn: Review', *Spectator*, 20 March 1869, pp. 356–7, quoted in Donald Smalley (ed.), *Anthony Trollope: The Critical Heritage* (London: Routledge, 1995), pp. 309–313 (p. 312).
2. 'Phineas Finn: Review', *Spectator*, quoted in Donald Smalley, *Trollope*, p. 313.
3. Simpson, 'Dandelions', pp. 107–8.
4. Philip Mason, *The English Gentleman: The Rise and Fall of an Ideal* (London: André Deutsch, 1982), p. 13.
5. 'Phineas Finn: Review', *Spectator*, quoted in Donald Smalley, *Trollope*, p. 313.
6. Andrew Dowling, *Manliness and the Male Novelist in Victorian Literature* (Aldershot: Ashgate, 2001), p. 85.
7. Huggins, *Victorians and Sport*, p. 6.
8. Waters, *Perfect Gentleman*, p. 86.
9. Wilkie Collins, *Man and Wife* (Oxford: Oxford World's Classics, 1995), p. 211.
10. Wilkie Collins, *Man and Wife*, p. 219.
11. Waters, *Perfect Gentleman*, p. 87.
12. Wilkie Collins, *Man and Wife*, p. 220.
13. 'Physical Training', *St James's Magazine*, February 1863, pp. 322–8 (p. 324).
14. *Punch*, 20 December 1862, p. 247.
15. Trollope, *Phineas Redux*, I, p. 61.
16. Trollope, 'The Uncontrolled Ruffianism of London as Measured by the Rule of Thumb', *Saint Paul's Magazine*, 1 (1868), 419–24 (p. 419).
17. Davis, 'London Garotting Panic', p. 190.
18. *Daily News*, 18 July 1862, p. 2.
19. *Daily News*, 18 July 1862, p. 2.
20. *Daily News*, 18 July 1862, p. 2.
21. *Punch*, 27 December 1862, p. 259.
22. *The Times*, 24 June 1854, p. 12.
23. Juliet McMaster, *Trollope's Palliser Novels: Theme and Pattern* (London: Macmillan, 1978), p. 67.
24. Hughes, *Tom Brown*, p. 283.
25. *Habits of Good Society: A Handbook of Etiquette for Ladies and Gentlemen* (London: James Hogg & Sons, 1859), p. 193.
26. Anthony Trollope, *An Autobiography* (Adamant Media Corporation, 2006), p. 24.

27. Mason, *English Gentleman*, p. 142.
28. Smiles, *Self-Help*, p. 306.
29. *Thoughts on Duelling and its Abolition* (London: G.W. Nickisson, 1844), p. 25.
30. Pierce Egan, *Every Gentleman's Manual: A Lecture on the Art of Self-Defence* (London: Flintoff, 1851), pp. 16–18.
31. 'Our Police', *Saturday Review of Politics, Literature and Art*, 24 October 1868, pp. 553–4 (p. 554).
32. *Habits of Good Society*, pp. 190–1.
33. 'Physical Training', *St James's Magazine*, p. 324.
34. Wood, *Violence and Crime*, p. 72.
35. Brookes, John Brookes, *Manliness: Hints to Young Men* (London: James Blackwood, 1859), p. 10.
36. 'Pugilism in High Quarters', *London Review*, 5, 127 (6 December 1862), pp. 492–3 (p. 492).
37. 'Pugilism in High Quarters', p. 493.
38. Both quotations from 'Physical Training', *St James's Magazine*, pp. 322 and 323.
39. 'Prize-Fighting', *Pall Mall Gazette*, 6 November 1866, p. 5.
40. 'Prize-Fighting', *Pall Mall Gazette*, 6 November 1866, p. 5.
41. John Halperin, *Trollope and Politics: A Study of the Pallisers and Others* (London: Macmillan, 1977), p. 71.
42. Turner, *Trollope and the Magazines*, p. 8.
43. Turner, *Trollope and the Magazines*, pp. 48 and 71.
44. Henry W. Holland, 'The Art of Self-Protection against Thieves and Robbers', *Good Words*, 7 (1866), 847–51, p. 851.
45. *The Times*, 9 January 1857, p. 8.
46. Catherine Hall, 'A Nation Within and Without', in Catherine Hall, Keith McClelland and Jane Rendall (eds), *Defining the Victorian Nation: Class, Race and the British Reform Act of 1867* (Cambridge University Press, 2000), pp. 179–233 (p. 181).
47. Waters, *Perfect Gentleman*, pp. 39–40.
48. McMaster, *Palliser Novels*, p. 48.
49. Gay, *Cultivation of Hatred*, p. 105.
50. Glendinning, *Trollope*, p. 400.
51. Turner, *Trollope and Magazines*, p. 175.
52. 'Phineas Finn: Review', *Spectator*, quoted in Donald Smalley, *Trollope*, p. 313.
53. Trollope, 'Uncontrolled Ruffianism', p. 420.

6   *Phineas Redux*

1. Halperin, *Trollope and Politics*, p. 165.
2. Halperin, *Trollope and Politics*, p. 166.
3. Trollope, *Autobiography*, p. 14.
4. Charles Dickens, *Great Expectations* (London: Everyman, 1994), p. 318.
5. Walkowitz, *City of Dreadful Delight*, p. 90.
6. Wilkie Collins, *Man and Wife*, p. 104.
7. *Archbold's Pleading and Evidence in Criminal Cases; with the Statutes, Precedents of Indictments and Evidence Necessary to Support Them* (London: William Bruce, 1867), p. 612.

8. James Paterson, *Commentaries on the Liberty of the Subject and Laws of England Relating to the Security of the Person*, 2 vols. (London: 1877) I, p. 441, quoted in Malcolm, *Guns and Violence*, p. 132.
9. Malcolm, *Guns and Violence*, p. 132.
10. Paterson, *Commentaries on the Liberty*, p. 442. Paterson aimed to make English law accessible to larger numbers of educated readers.
11. *Pall Mall Gazette*, 26 April 1865.
12. *The Times*, 29 April 1865, p. 9.
13. *The Times*, 2 May 1865, p. 7.
14. Trollope, 'Uncontrolled Ruffianism', p. 422.
15. Turner, *Trollope and the Magazines*, p. 169.
16. Joseph Kestner, *Sherlock's Men: Masculinity, Conan Doyle, and Cultural History* (Aldershot: Ashgate, 1997), p. 48.
17. Shirley Letwin, *The Gentleman in Trollope: Individuality and Moral Conduct* (Basingstoke: Macmillan, 1982), p. 258.
18. *Archbold's Snowden's Magistrates Assistant, and Police Officers and Constables' Guide* (London: Shaw & Sons, 1859), p. 251.
19. Dickens, *Our Mutual Friend*, 2 vols. (London: Penguin, 1997), II, p. 536.
20. Dickens, *Our Mutual Friend*, II, p. 534.
21. Trollope, 'Uncontrolled Ruffianism', p. 423.
22. This information on truncheons was gleaned from Martin Fido and Keith Skinner, *The Official Encyclopedia of Scotland Yard* (London: Virgin Books, 1999), p. 271.
23. Smiles, *Character*, p. 30.
24. Henry W. Holland, 'Professional Thieves', *Cornhill Magazine*, 6 (1862), 640–53 (p. 646). See also Holland, 'Science of Housebreaking and Housebreaking', *Cornhill* Magazine, 7 (1863), 79–92, p. 82.
25. Tom Taylor, *The Ticket of Leave: A Drama in Three Acts and a Prologue* (1863), Lord Chamberlain's Manuscript Collection, AA53002, p. 56. This play later became known as *The Ticket-of-Leave Man*.
26. 'The Black Museum', *Observer*, 8 April 1877, p. 3.
27. 'Phineas Redux: Review', *Spectator*, in 3 January 1874, pp. 15–17, quoted in Donald Smalley, *Anthony Trollope*, p. 380.
28. Glendinning, *Trollope*, p. 173.
29. Kestner, *Sherlock's Men*, p. 40.
30. Fergus Hume, *The Mystery of a Hansom Cab* (London: The Hansom Cab Publishing Company, 1888) pp. 144–8.
31. Ellen Moody, 'Trollope's Comfort Romances for Men: Heterosexual Male Heroism in his Work', *The Victorian Web: Literature, History and Culture in the Age of Victoria*: http://www.victorianweb.org/authors/trollope/moody2/comfort.html, p. 2. Accessed 8 May 2010.

7   Exotic Enemies

1. E.W. Hornung, 'Gentlemen and Players', *Raffles: The Amateur Cracksman* (London: Penguin, 2003), p. 39.
2. Doyle, 'AFP', p. 472.
3. Doyle, 'The Adventure of Charles Augustus Milverton' (1904; hereafter 'ACAM'), p. 572.

4. 'Zigzags at the Zoo: The Ophidian', *Strand*, 5 (1892), 407–14 (p. 409).
5. Joseph Conrad, *Heart of Darkness* (London: Penguin/Daily Telegraph, 1973), p. 12.
6. Julia Kristeva, *Powers of Horror: An Essay on Abjection*, Leon S. Roudiez (trans.) (New York: Columbia University Press, 1982), p. 4.
7. Elaine Showalter, *Sexual Anarchy: Gender and Culture at the Fin de Siècle* (London: Virago, 2001), p. 189.
8. Showalter, *Sexual Anarchy*, p. 200.
9. Showalter, *Sexual Anarchy*, p. 199.
10. Catherine Wynne, *The Colonial Conan Doyle: British Imperialism, Irish Nationalism and the Gothic* (Westport, CT: Greenwood Press, 2002), p. 121.
11. Angus McLaren, *The Trials of Masculinity: Policing Sexual Boundaries 1870–1930* (University of Chicago Press, 1997), p. 36.
12. Wiener, *Men of Blood*, p. 290.
13. Diana Barsham, *Arthur Conan Doyle and the Meaning of Masculinity* (Aldershot: Ashgate, 2000), p. 106.
14. Wiener, *Men of Blood*, p. 290.
15. Frederick Wilkinson, *Those Entrusted with Arms: A History of the Police, Post, Customs and Private Use of Weapons in Britain* (Leeds: Royal Armouries/ Greenhill Books, 2002), p. 235.
16. Peter Hitchens, *A Brief History of Crime: The Decline of Order, Justice and Liberty in England* (London: Atlantic Books, 2003), p. 149.
17. Interview conducted with Donald Rumbelow, 'Jack the Ripper Haunts' tour, *London Walks*, 30 March 2007.
18. J. B. Shaw, 'A Final Word', p. 33.
19. Rudyard Kipling, *From Sea to Sea* (1899), available at http://ghostwolf.dyndns. org/words/authors/K/KiplingRudyard/prose/FromSeaToSea/index.html, accessed 8 May 2010.
20. 'Pistols Bill', *Hansard*, 27 February 1895, coll. 1657–8 (1658).
21. *Health and Strength*, 4 (1902), p. 337.
22. Students and followers of Steampunk might be familiar with Ian Crichton's acid- and water-powered pistol which contains round bullets for shooting humans and more destructive square bullets to tackle aliens such as the Martians that descend on London in H.G. Wells's *The War of the Worlds* (1898). Crichton's visually arresting contraption is a modern interpretation of the nineteenth-century firearm, intricately constructed but, being designed with modern values in mind, thankfully a non-functional prototype. However, the outlandish firearm that is aimed at Holmes is expressly enhanced to ensure the detective's absolute destruction with the actual Victorian equivalent of Crichton's square bullet, the dum-dum.
23. Stephen, Farrell, 'A Treatise upon Sherlockian Firearms', *Sherlock Holmes Journal*, 23 (1993), 88–9 (p. 89).
24. Doyle, 'AEH', p. 484.
25. *The Times*, 10 November 1888, p. 7.
26. *Star*, 1 October 1888, p. 1.
27. Wynne, *Colonial Conan Doyle*, p. 40.
28. Wynne, *Colonial Conan Doyle*, p. 53.
29. Geoffrey G. Butler and Simon Maccoby, *The Development of International Law* (London: Longmans and Co, 1928), p. 420.

30. 'Dr Conan Doyle on his Defence', *Daily News*, 31 January 1902, p. 6, quoted in Michael Gibson and Richard Lancelyn Green (eds), *The Unknown Conan Doyle: Letters to the Press* (London: Secker and Warburg, 1986), p. 84.
31. Arthur Eyffinger, *The 1899 Hague Peace Conference: 'The Parliament of Man, the Federation of the World'* (The Hague: Kluwer Law International, 1999), p. 180.
32. Paula Krebs, *Gender, Race and the Writing of Empire* (Cambridge University Press, 1990), p. 108.
33. Francis Galton, 'Africa for the Chinese', *The Times*, 5 June 1873, p. 8.
34. I am indebted to Mark Murray-Flutter of the Royal Armouries in Leeds for this information.
35. Catherine Dike, *Cane Curiosa: From Gun to Gadget* (Geneva: Les Editions de L'Amateur, 1983), p. 283.
36. Peter Brooks, *The Melodramatic Imagination: Balzac, Henry James, Melodrama, and the Mode of Excess* (London: Yale University Press, 1995), p. 17.
37. Harvey, *Men in Black*, p. 239.
38. Harvey, *Men in Black*, p. 156.
39. Brooks, *The Melodramatic Imagination*, p. 31.
40. Richard Lancelyn Green, 'Introduction', in E.W. Hornung, *Raffles: Amateur Cracksman* (London: Penguin, 2003), pp. xxvii–lvi (p. xxii).
41. Marie Belloc Lowndes, *The Lodger* (Wildside Press, 2009), p. 65.

8   Urban Knights in the London Streets

1. Eugen Sandow, 'Physical Culture: What is it?', *Sandow's Magazine*, 1 (1898), 3–7 (p. 7).
2. 'Health is a Duty', taken from 'Herbert Spencer's Education', *Health and Strength*, 1 (1900), 11.
3. Pick, *Faces of Degeneration*, p. 184.
4. Harry Law, 'A Day with Dr. Conan Doyle' *Strand*, 4 (1892), 182–8 (p. 183).
5. Doyle, *Memories and Adventures*, p. 316.
6. Doyle, *Memories and Adventures*, p. 316.
7. Peter Lovesey, 'Conan Doyle and the Olympics', *Journal of Olympic History*, 10 (2001–2), 1–9 (pp. 1–2).
8. Doyle, 'A Study in Scarlet' (1887), p. 22. Single-stick play had working-class origins and was adopted by the middle classes in the nineteenth century. See Tony Wolf, 'The Manly Arts of Self Defence in Victorian and Edwardian England', in *Bartitsu Compendium*, pp. 21–40 (p. 32).
9. J. Frank Bradley, *The Boxing Referee: An Exhaustive Treatise on the Duties of a Referee and an Explanation of the Queensberry Rules Relating to Boxing Contests and Competitions* (London: The Queenhithe Printing and Publishing Co., 1910), p. 57.
10. Douglas Kerr, 'The Straight Left: Sport and the Nation in Arthur Conan Doyle', *Victorian Literature and Culture*, 38 (2010), 187–206 (p. 193).
11. Doyle, 'ASC', p. 536.
12. Joseph McLaughlin, *Writing the Urban Jungle: Reading Empire in London from Doyle to Eliot* (University of Virginia Press, 2000), p. 50.
13. The symbolic importance of Japanese martial arts in defending the realm and keeping up morale is even reflected in a book by James Hipkiss which

was written during the Second World War entitled *Your Answer to Invasion – Ju-Jitsu* (London: F.W. Bridges, 1941).

14. Hirayama and Hall, 'Some Knowledge', p. 38.
15. Richard Bowen, 'Further Lessons in Baritsu', *The Ritual Bi-Annual Review: The Northern Musgraves Sherlock Holmes Society*, 20 (1997), 22–26.
16. Tony Wolf, 'Barton-Wright's Misadventures in Electrotherapy', in *Bartitsu Compendium*, pp. 63–4.
17. Tony Wolf, 'Foreword', in *Bartitsu Compendium*, pp. 13–14.
18. S. Shipley, 'Tom Causer of Bermondsey: A Boxer Hero of the 1890s', *History Workshop*, 15 (1983), 28–59 (p. 43).
19. Mary Nugent, 'Barton-Wright and his Japanese Wrestlers: A Man and his Method', *Health and Strength*, 3 (1901), 336–41 (p. 337).
20. Barton-Wright, 'The New Art of Self-Defence' (Part 1), *Pearson's Magazine*, 7 (1899), 268–75 (p. 268).
21. Barton-Wright, 'New Art' (Part 1), p. 270
22. Barton-Wright, 'New Art' (Part 1), p. 270.
23. Barton-Wright, 'New Art' (Part 1), p. 269.
24. Hume, *Hansom Cab* (1888), p. 102.
25. 'Jujitsu: Some Means of Attack and Defence', *Pall Mall Gazette*, 23 October 1900, p. 10.
26. Pearson, *Hooligan*, p. 102.
27. *Newcastle Weekly Courant*, 22 July 1899, p. 2.
28. Pierce Egan, *Every Gentleman's Manual: A Lecture on the Art of Self-Defence* (London: Flintoff, 1851), p. 4.
29. J. St. A. Jewell, 'The Gymnasiums of London: Pierre Vigny's', *Health and Strength*, 7 (1904), 173–7 (p. 173).
30. Barton-Wright, 'New Art' (Part 1), p. 269.
31. W.H. Collingridge, *Tricks of Self-Defence* (London: Health and Strength Limited, 1914), p. 9.
32. 'Dan Leno on Physical Culture', *Sandow's Magazine*, 5(6) (1900), 69–70.
33. Barton-Wright, 'New Art' (Part 1), p. 269.
34. *The Era*, 20 October 1900, p. 54.
35. *Sandow's Magazine of Physical Culture*, 2 (1899), p. 241.
36. C. B. Fry, 'The Athlete in Bronze and Stone', *Strand*, 14 (1902), 531–541.
37. Advertisement for a physical culture institute, *Health and Strength*, 14 (1907), p. 3.
38. Barton-Wright, 'New Art' [Part 1], p. 269.
39. Doyle, *Memories and Adventures*, p. 318.
40. Barton-Wright, 'Strong Man', pp. 61–5.
41. Barton-Wright, 'Self-Defence with a Walking-Stick: The Different Methods of Defending Oneself with a Walking-Stick or Umbrella when Attacked under Unequal Conditions' (Part 1), *Pearson's Magazine*, 11 (1901), 11–20, p. 11.
42. Barton-Wright, 'New Art' (Part 1), p. 270.
43. Barton-Wright, 'Walking-Stick Self-Defence with a Walking-Stick: The Different Methods of Defending Oneself with a Walking-Stick or Umbrella when Attacked under Unequal Conditions' (Part 2), *Pearson's Magazine*, 11 (1901), 130–9 (p. 132).
44. Barton-Wright, 'New Art' (Part 1), p. 269.
45. *Star*, 8 September 1888, p. 2.

46. E.T. Cook, *Highways and Byways in London* (London: Macmillan and Co., 1902), p. 174.
47. *St James's Gazette*, 21 August 1889, Toynbee Hall, Ephemera Collection.
48. McLaughlin, *Urban Jungle*, p. 84.
49. As a discussion on the Victoria List shows, there appear to be few Victorian works of fiction which allude to the Ripper directly: See 'Ripper in Fiction', Victoria List, Indiana University: https://listserv.indiana.edu/cgibin/waiub. exe?S2=VICTORIA&m=66224&q=Ripperdiscussion, accessed 8 May 2010.
50. Andrew, 'Code of Honour', p. 409.
51. Marie Corelli, *The Sorrows of Satan, Or the Experience of One Geoffrey Tempest, Millionaire* (London: Methuen and Co, 1898), p. 188.
52. Wiener, *Men of Blood*, p. 41.
53. R.G. Allanson-Winn and C. Phillipps-Wolley, *Broad-Sword and Single-Stick* (London: George Bell and Sons, 1890), p. 106.
54. Allanson-Winn and Phillipps-Wolley, *Broad-Sword and Single-Stick*, p. 116.
55. Allanson-Winn and Phillipps-Wolley, *Broad-Sword and Single-Stick*, pp. 108–9.
56. Percy Longhurst, *Jiu-Jitsu and Other Methods of Self-Defence* (London: L. Upcott Gill, 1906) p. 97.
57. A holder of black belts in jujitsu, judo and weaponry, Kevin Garwood is featured in a variety of British newspapers, including the *Daily Telegraph*: http://www.telegraph.co.uk/news/uknews/7404905/Pensioners-taught-to-use-walking-stick-in-self-defence.html, accessed 8 May 2010.
58. Trollope, 'Uncontrolled Ruffianism', p. 422.
59. Judith Walkowitz, 'The Indian Woman, the Flower Girl, and the Jew: Photojournalism in Edwardian London', *Victorian Studies*, 42 (1998–9), 3–46 (p. 5).
60. Michel de Certeau, 'Walking in the City', in Gary Bridge and Sophie Watson (eds), *The Blackwell City Reader* (Oxford: Blackwell, 2002), pp. 383–92 (p. 387).
61. Girouard, *Camelot*, pp. 217–18.
62. Barton-Wright, 'New Art' (Part 1), p. 271.
63. The 'flight from domesticity' is discussed at length in John Tosh's *A Man's Place: Masculinity and the Middle-Class Home in Victorian England* (Yale University Press, 1999).
64. Barton-Wright, 'Walking-Stick' (Part 2), p. 139.
65. Kerr, 'Straight Left', p. 190.
66. Barton-Wright, 'Walking-Stick' (Part 1), p. 11.
67. Barton-Wright, 'The New Art of Self-Defence' (Part 2), *Pearson's Magazine*, 7 (1899), 402–10 (p. 402).
68. Jewell, 'Vigny's', p. 174

9   Foreign Friends

1. Information in an article by Tsukasa Kobayashi, Japan Sherlock Holmes Society website: http://www.holmesjapan.jp/english/koba01.htm, accessed 8 May 2010. Many thanks to Yuichi Hirayama of the Japan Sherlock Holmes Club for updating this information for me.
2. For instance, Wynne's *Colonial Conan Doyle* and *Urban Jungle* by Joseph McLaughlin.

3. Olive Checkland, *Japan and Britain after 1859: Creating Cultural Bridges* (London: Routledge Curzon, 2003), p. 122.
4. Kipling, *From Sea to Sea*.
5. Harry Ricketts, 'A Short Walk on the Wilde Side: Kipling's First Impressions of Japan', *New Zealand Journal of Asian Studies*, 5 (2003), 26–32 (p. 30).
6. Checkland, *Japan*, p. xii.
7. Hirayama and Hall, 'Some Knowledge', p. 41.
8. Connell, *Masculinities*, p. 77–86.
9. McLaughlin, *Urban Jungle*, p. 3.
10. McLaughlin, *Urban Jungle*, p. 29.
11. McLaughlin, *Urban Jungle*, p. 60.
12. Eustace Fry, 'The Peril of the East', *Health and Strength*, 9 (1904), 198–200 (p. 198).
13. Fry, 'Peril of the East', p. 199.
14. Quotation from *Penny Guide* (1910), p. 10 in Checkland, *Japan*, pp. 182–3.
15. Hirayama and Hall, 'Some Knowledge', p. 47.
16. *Health and Strength* editor, in *Text-Book*, p. 100.
17. Kestner, *Sherlock's Men*, pp. 63–4.
18. Kestner, *Sherlock's Men*, p. 63.
19. Lafcadio Hearn, *Glimpses of an Unfamiliar Japan*, 2 vols. (Boston: The Riverside Press, 1894), I, p. vii.
20. Leonard Larkin, 'The Japanese Jack the Giant Killer', *Strand*, 22 (1901), 150–8 (p. 150).
21. Toshio Yokoyama, *Japan in the Victorian Mind: A Study of Stereotyped Images of a Nation 1850–80* (Basingstoke: Palgrave, 1987), pp. 13–16.
22. 'London Women of the Upper Tendon Are Learning Protection Against Ruffians', *Stevens Point Daily Journal*, Wisconsin, 24 December 1903 (no page reference given), reprinted in *Bartitsu Compendium*, pp. 117–18 (p. 117).
23. Checkland, *Japan*, pp. 173–82.
24. Bill Tonkin, 'Japan-British Exhibition, 1910', http://www.studygroup.org.uk/Exhibitions/Pages/1910%20Japan-British.htm, accessed 8 May 2010.
25. Maurice Leblanc, 'The Escape of Arsène Lupin', in *The Exploits of Arsène Lupin*, Alexander Teixeiria de Mattos (trans.) (London: Cassell and Co., 1909), p. 156.
26. Aaron Freundschuh, '"New Sport" in the Street: Self-Defence, Security and Space in Belle Epoque Paris', *French History*, 20 (2006), 424–41 (p. 429).
27. Uyenishi, *Text-Book*, p. 8.
28. H.G. Wells, *The History of Mr Polly* (London: Everyman, 2003), p. 115.
29. Stephen Wright, 'The Non-PC Guide to Policing: How to Apprehend a Criminal, 1907-Style', http://www.dailymail.co.uk/news/article-1239754/The-non-PC-guide-policing-How-apprehend-criminal-1907-style.html, accessed 7 April 2010.
30. Freundschuh, '"New Sport"', p. 427.
31. See Antonia Raeburn, *The Militant Suffragettes* (London: Michael Joseph, 1973); Joe Svinth, 'The Evolution of Women's Judo, 1900–1945', in *InYo: The Journal of Alternative Perspectives on the Martial Arts and Sciences* http://ejmas.com/jalt/jaltart_svinth_0201.htm, accessed 8 May 2010; Tony Wolf, *Edith Garrud: The Suffragette Who Knew Jujutsu* (Raleigh, NC: Lulu.com, 2009). For a literary stance on this topic, see Gillian Linscott's novel *The Perfect*

Daughter: A Nell Bray Mystery (London: Virago Press, 2000) and Emelyne Godfrey, 'Uses for a Hat Pin: Women's Self-Defence as Pioneered in the Fiction of H.G. Wells', *Times Literary Supplement*, 5 February 2010, pp. 14–15.

32. Jill Greenfield, Sean O'Connell and Chris Reid, 'Gender, Consumer Culture and the Middle-Class Male, 1918–1939', in Alan Kidd and David Nicholls (eds), *Gender, Civic Culture and Consumerism: Middle-class Identity in Britain 1800–1940* (Manchester University Press, 1999), pp. 183–97 (p. 183).

Bibliography

Adams, James Eli, *Dandies and Desert Saints: Styles of Victorian Masculinity* (Ithaca, NY: Cornell University Press, 1995).

Ainsworth, Harrison, *The Tower of London: A Historical Romance* (London: Richard Bentley, 1840).

Allanson-Winn, R.G. and C. Phillipps-Wolley, *Broad-Sword and Single-Stick* (London: George Bell and Sons, 1890).

Allen, Dennis W., 'Young England: Muscular Christianity and the Politics of the Body in "Tom Brown's Schooldays"', in Donald E. Hall (ed.), *Muscular Christianity: Embodying the Victorian Age* (Cambridge University Press, 1994), pp. 114–32.

Alpert, Michael, *London, 1849: A Murder Story* (Harlow: Pearson/Longman, 2004).

André, Émile, *100 Façons de se Défendre dans la Rue Sans Armes* (Paris: Ernest Flammarion, 1905).

Andrew, Donna. T., 'The Code of Honour and its Critics: The Opposition to Duelling in England, 1700–1850', *Social History*, 5 (1980), 409–34.

'Another Chamber of Horrors: The Police Museum of Scotland Yard', *Black and White Budget*, 4 (1900), 138–9.

Anstruther, Ian, *The Knight and the Umbrella: An Account of the Eglinton Tournament 1839* (London: Geoffrey Bles, 1963)

Archbold's Pleading and Evidence in Criminal Cases; with the Statutes, Precedents of Indictments and Evidence Necessary to Support Them (London: S. Sweet, 1846; London: William Bruce, 1867; London: S. Sweet, 1853; London: H. Sweet and Sons, 1886; London, Henry Sweet, 1871; London: Stevens and Sons, 1900).

Archbold's Snowden's Magistrates Assistant, and Police Officers and Constables' Guide (London: Shaw and Sons, 1859).

Archer, John. E., 'Men Behaving Badly? Masculinity and the Uses of Violence, 1850–1900', in Shani D'Cruze (ed.), *Everyday Violence in Britain, 1850–1950: Gender and Class* (Harlow: Longman/Pearson, 2000), pp. 41–54.

Arnold, Matthew, *Culture and Anarchy* (Oxford: Oxford World's Classics, 2006).

Atkinson, John, A., *Duelling Pistols and Some of the Affairs They Settled* (London: Cassell, 1964).

Baden-Powell, Lieutenant, *Scouting for Boys: A Handbook for Instruction in Good Citizenship* (London: Horace Cox, 1908).

Banham, Martin (ed.), *Plays by Tom Taylor* (Cambridge University Press, 1985).

Barker, Juliet, *The Brontës* (London: Weidenfeld & Nicholson, 1994).

Barsham, Diana, *Arthur Conan Doyle and the Meaning of Masculinity* (Aldershot: Ashgate, 2000).

Barthes, Roland, 'The World of Wrestling', in *Mythologies*, Annette Lavers (trans.) (New York: Hill and Wang, 2000), pp. 15–25.

Barton-Wright, E.W., 'How to Pose as a Strong Man', *Pearson's Magazine*, 7 (1899), 59–66.

——, 'The New Art of Self-Defence: How a Man may Defend Himself against every Form of Attack' (Part 1), *Pearson's Magazine*, 7 (1899), 268–75.

——, 'The New Art of Self-Defence' (Part 2), *Pearson's Magazine*, 7 (1899), 402–10.
——, 'Self-Defence with a Walking-Stick: The Different Methods of Defending Oneself with a Walking-Stick or Umbrella when Attacked under Unequal Conditions' (Part 1), *Pearson's Magazine*, 11 (1901), 11–20.
——, 'Self-Defence with a Walking-Stick: The Different Methods of Defending Oneself with a Walking-Stick or Umbrella when Attacked under Unequal Conditions' (Part 2), *Pearson's Magazine*, 11 (1901), 130–9.
——, 'Ju-Jitsu and Ju-Do', *The Transactions of the Japan Society of London*, 5 (1901), 261–4.
Barwick Lloyd Baker, Thomas, *'War with Crime': Being a Selection of Reprinted Papers on Crime, Reformatories, etc* (London: Longmans and Co., 1889).
Beauman, Nicola, *A Very Great Profession: The Woman's Novel 1914–39* (London: Virago, 1983).
Bensley, D.F., 'A Question of Ballistics?', *Baker Street Journal: An Irregular Quarterly of Sherlockiana*, 44 (1994), 173–8.
Binney, John, 'Thieves' (1862), in Henry Mayhew, 'Those That Will Not Work', *London Labour and the London Poor*, Victor Neuburg (ed.), 4 vols. (London: Woodfall/Griffin Bohn, 1851–62; reprinted Harmondsworth: Penguin, 1985), IV (1862), pp. 492–9.
'Bird-Garotters', *All the Year Round*, 30 May 1863, 320–3.
'Black Museum, The', *Observer*, 8 April 1877, p. 3.
Blackmore, Howard, L., *English Pistols* (London: The Trustees of the Armouries, 1985).
Blackwell, Elizabeth, 'Extracts From the Laws of Life, with Special Reference to the Physical Education of Girls', *Englishwoman's Journal*, 1 (1858), 189–90.
Bland, Lucy, *Banishing the Beast: English Feminism and Sexual Morality 1885–1914* (London: Penguin, 1995).
Bloom, Clive, 'The Ripper Writing: A Cream of a Nightmare Dream', in Alexandra Warwick and Martin Willis (eds), *Jack the Ripper: Media, Culture, History* (Manchester University Press, 2007), pp. 91–109.
——, *Violent London: 2000 Years of Riots, Rebels and Revolts* (London: Sidgwick and Jackson, 2003).
Boddice, Rob., 'Manliness and the "Morality of Field Sports": E. A. Freeman and Anthony Trollope, 1869–71', *The Historian*, 1(70) (2008), 1–29.
Boddy, Kasia, *Boxing: A Cultural History* (London: Reaktion Books, 2008).
Bondeson, Jan, *The London Monster: A Sanguinary Tale* (Cambridge: University of Pennsylvania Press/Da Capo Press: 2002).
Booth, Michael R., *Theatre in the Victorian Age* (Cambridge University Press, 1991).
Bourke, Joanna, *Dismembering the Male: Men's Bodies, Britain and the Great War* (London: Reaktion Books, 1996).
——, *Fear: A Cultural History* (London: Virago, 2005).
Bowen, Richard, 'Further Lessons in Baritsu', *The Ritual Bi-Annual Review: The Northern Musgraves Sherlock Holmes Society*, 20 (1997), 22–6.
——, 'Various Rough Notes; Edward William Barton-Wright and Tani', University of Bath Library, Richard Bowen Archive, Item 21, pp. 1–13.
Boyle, Thomas, *Black Swine in the Sewers of Hampstead: Beneath the Surface of Victorian Sensationalism* (London: Hodder & Stoughton, 1990).

Bradley, Frank J., *The Boxing Referee: An Exhaustive Treatise on the Duties of a Referee and an Explanation of the Queensberry Rules Relating to Boxing Contests and Competitions* (London: The Queenhithe Printing and Publishing Co., 1910).

Brake, Laurel, 'The Old Journalism and the New: Forms of Cultural Production in London in the 1880s', in Joel H. Wiener (ed.), *Papers for the Millions: Journalism in Britain, 1850s to 1914* (Westport, CT: Greenwood Press, 1988), pp. 1–24.

Brake, Laurel and Julie F. Codell (eds), *Encounters in the Victorian Press: Editors, Authors, Readers* (Basingstoke: Palgrave Macmillan, 2005).

Breward, Christopher, *The Hidden Consumer: Masculinities, Fashion and City Life, 1860–1914* (Manchester University Press, 1999).

Briggs, Asa, 'Centenary Introduction', in Samuel Smiles, *Self-Help with Illustrations of Conduct and Perseverance* (London: John Murray, 1958).

——, *Victorian Cities* (London: Odhams Press, 1963).

——, *Victorian Things* (Bath: B.T. Batsford, 1988).

Briggs, Asa and Anne Macartney, *Toynbee Hall: The First Hundred Years* (London: Routledge & Kegan Paul, 1984).

British Boxer, The; Or Guide to Self-Defence (London: W. Winn, c. 1850).

Brontë, Anne (Acton Bell), *The Tenant of Wildfell Hall* (London: Penguin, 2003).

Brontë, Emily, (Ellis Bell), *Wuthering Heights,* Linda H. Peterson (ed.) (Boston: Bedford/St Martin's Press, 2003).

Brookes, John, *Manliness: Hints to Young Men* (London: James Blackwood, 1859).

Brown, Bill, 'Thing Theory', *Critical Inquiry*, 28 (2001), 1–22.

Burgin, G.B., 'Japanese Fighting (Self-Defence by Sleight of Body)', *Idler*, 2 (1892–3), 281–6.

Burn, W.L., *The Age of Equipoise: A Study of the Mid-Victorian Generation* (London: George Allen, 1964).

Burnett, Frances Hodgson, *Editha's Burglar. A Story for Children* (Boston: Jordan, Marsh and Company, 1888).

Butler, Geoffrey G. and Simon Maccoby, *The Development of International Law* (London: Longmans and Co, 1928).

Caird, Mona, *The Wing of Azrael* (London: Truebner and Co, 1889).

Cantlie, J., *Degeneration Amongst Londoners* (London, Field and Tuer, 1885; reprinted by Lee Jackson) http: www.victorianlondon.org, accessed 8 May 2010.

Carlyle, Thomas, *On Heroes, Hero-Worship and the Heroic in History* (London: James Fraser, 1841).

——, *Past and Present* (London: Chapman & Hall, 1843).

Cassell's Book of Sports and Pastimes: Being a Compendium of Out-Door and In-Door Amusements (London: Cassells and Co., 1893).

Catron, Douglas M., "Jiu-Jitsu" in Lawrence's "Gladiatorial"', *The South Central Bulletin*, 43 (1983), 92–4.

de Certeau, M., 'Walking in the City', in Gary Bridge and Sophie Watson (eds), *The Blackwell City Reader* (Oxford, Blackwell, 2002), pp. 383–92.

'Champion Lady Mountaineer, The', *Pearson's Magazine*, 7 (1903), 354–64.

Chatterton, G.G., 'The Gentle Art of Ju-Ju-Tsu', *Chamber's Journal*, 10 (1907), 751–2.

Checkland, Olive, *Japan and Britain after 1859: Creating Cultural Bridges* (London: Routledge Curzon, 2003).

Clark, Anna, 'Humanity or Justice? Wifebeating and the Law in the Eighteenth and Nineteenth Centuries', in Carol Smart (ed.), *Regulating Womanhood: Historical Essays on Marriage, Motherhood and Sexuality* (London: Routledge, 1992).

——, 'Rape or Seduction? A Controversy Over Sexual Violence in the Nineteenth Century', in London Feminist History Group (ed.), *The Sexual Dynamics of History: Men's Power, Women's Resistance* (London: Pluto Press, 1983), pp. 13–27.

——, *Women's Silence, Men's Violence: Sexual Assault in England 1770–1845* (London: Pandora, 1987).

Clark, John W., *The Language and Style of Anthony Trollope* (London: André Deutsch, 1975).

Clarke, William, *The Boy's Own Book: A Complete Encyclopaedia of Sports and Pastimes* (London: Crosby, Lockwood and Co., 1880).

'Code of Duelling, The', *Chambers's Journal of Popular Literature, Science and Art*, 177 (18 May 1867), 305–8.

Cohen, Stanley, *Folk Devils and Moral Panics: The Creation of the Mods and Rockers* (London: MacGibbon and Kee, 1972).

Collingridge, W.H., *Tricks of Self-Defence* (London: Health and Strength Limited, 1914).

Collins, C.J., *The Anti-Garotte: A Farce in One Act* (1857), British Library, Lord Chamberlain's Manuscript Collection, L52964.

Collins, Wilkie, *Man and Wife* (Oxford: Oxford World's Classics, 1995).

Connell, R.W., *Masculinities,* rev. edn (Cambridge: Polity, 2006).

Conrad, Joseph, *Heart of Darkness* (London: Penguin/*Daily Telegraph*, 1973)

Cook, E.T., *Highways and Byways in London* (London: Macmillan and Co., 1902).

Corelli, Marie, *The Sorrows of Satan, Or the Experience of One Geoffrey Tempest, Millionaire,* (London: Methuen and Co., 1898).

Coren, Michael, *The Invisible Man: The Life and Liberties of H.G. Wells* (Toronto: McArthur and Company, 2005).

Craik, Dinah Mulock, 'A Woman's Thoughts about Women' (London: Bungay, 1858), in Elaine Showalter (ed.), *Maude/Christina Rossetti. On Sisterhoods; A Woman's Thoughts About Women/Dinah Mulock Craik* (New York University Press, 1993).

——, *A Woman's Thoughts about Women* (London: Hurst and Blackett, 1858).

Crawford, Elizabeth, *The Women's Suffrage Movement: A Reference Guide, 1866–1928* (London: UCL Press, 1999).

'Crime and Criminals: Burglars and Burgling', *Strand*, 7 (1894), 273–84.

'Crime and Criminals: Dynamite and Dynamiters', *Strand*, 7 (1894), 118–32.

Cunningham, Gail, 'Masculinities in the Age of the New Woman: From She to "Vee"', in Alcinda Pinheiro de Sousa, Luisa Maria Flora and Teresa de Ataíde Malafaia (eds), *The Crossroads of Gender and Century Endings* (Lisbon: Colibri, 2000), pp. 111–24.

Curtis, L. Perry, *Jack the Ripper and the London Press* (London: Yale University Press, 2001).

'Dan Leno on Physical Culture', *Sandow's Magazine*, 5(6) (1900), 69–70.

Darwin, Charles, *On the Origin of Species by Means of Natural Selection, or The Preservation of Favoured Races in the Struggle for Life* (London: Collection Library, 2004).

Dash, Mike, *Thug: The True Story of India's Murderous Cult* (London: Granta Books, 2005).

Davies, A., 'Youth Gangs, Masculinity and Violence in Late Victorian Manchester and Salford', *Journal of Social History*, 32 (1998), 349–69.

Davies, Stevie, 'Introduction', in Anne Brontë, *The Tenant of Wildfell Hall* (London: Penguin, 2003), pp. viii–xxx.

Davis, Jennifer, 'The London Garotting Panic of 1862: A Moral Panic and the Creation of a Criminal Class in Mid-Victorian England', in V.A.C. Gatrell, Bruce Lenman and Geoffrey Parker (eds), *Crime and the Law: The Social History of Crime in Western Europe Since 1500* (London: Europa, 1980), pp. 190–213.

D'Cruze, Shani, 'Introduction: Unguarded Passions: Violence, History and the Everyday', in *Everyday Violence in Britain, 1850–1950, Class and Gender* (Harlow: Longman/Pearson, 2000), pp. 1–19.

D'Cruze, Shani (ed.), *Everyday Violence in Britain, 1850–1950, Class and Gender* (Harlow: Longman/Pearson, 2000).

De Quincey, Thomas, 'Travelling in England in Old Days', in David Masson (eds), *Collected Writings of Thomas de Quincey*, 14 vols. (London: A&C Black, 1896), I, pp. 280–2.

Dennis, R., *Cities in Modernity: Representations and Productions of Metropolitan Space, 1840–1930* (Cambridge University Press, 2008).

Dettman, Bruce and Michael Bedford, *Compendium of Canonical Weaponry: Being a Catalogue and Description of the Implements of Foul Play and Justice in the Writings of John H Watson, M.C.* (California: Luther Norris, 1969).

Dickens, Charles, *Bleak House* (Oxford University Press, 1996).

——, *Great Expectations* (London: Everyman, 1994).

——, *Oliver Twist* (London: Everyman, 1999).

——, 'On an Amateur Beat' (1869) in David Pascoe (ed.), *Charles Dickens: Selected Journalism, 1850–1870* (London: Penguin, 1997), pp. 386–92.

——, *Our Mutual Friend* (London: Penguin Classics, 1997).

Dike, Catherine, *Cane Curiosa: From Gun to Gadget* (Geneva: Les Editions de L'Amateur, 1983).

Disher, Maurice Willson, *Blood and Thunder: Mid-Victorian Melodrama and Its Origins* (London: Frederick Muller, 1949).

Dowling, Andrew, *Manliness and the Male Novelist in Victorian Literature* (Aldershot: Ashgate, 2001).

Doyle, Arthur Conan, *The Great War* (London: Smith, Elder and Co., 1901).

——, *Memories and Adventures* (London: John Murray, 1930).

——, *Rodney Stone* (London: Smith and Elder, 1896).

——, *The Penguin Complete Sherlock Holmes* (London: Penguin, 1981).

——, *The War in South Africa; Its Cause and Conduct* (Leipzig: Bernhard Tauchnitz, 1902).

'Dr Conan Doyle on his Defence', *Daily News*, 31 January 1902, p. 6.

Dudink, Stefan, Karen Hagenamm and John Tosh (eds), *Masculinities in Politics and War: Gendering Modern History* (Manchester University Press, 2004).

Dunlop, Barbara, 'The Idler', in Alvin Sullivan (ed.), *British Literary Magazines: The Victorian and Edwardian Age, 1837–1913* (London: Greenwood, 1984), pp. 178–82.

Egan, Pierce, *Every Gentleman's Manual: A Lecture on the Art of Self-Defence* (London: Flintoff, 1851).

——, *Life in London; or, the Day and Night Scenes of Jerry Hawthorn, Esq, and his Elegant Friend Corinthian Tom, accompanied by Bob Logic, The Oxonian, in their Rambles and Sprees through the Metropolis* (London: Sherwood, Neely and Jones, 1820/1821).

Eissler, M., *A Handbook of Modern Explosives: Being a Practical Treatise on the Manufacture and Application of Dynamite, Gun-Cotton, Nitro-Glycerine, and other Explosive Compounds, Including the Manufacture of Collodion-Cotton* (London, Crosby Lockwood and Son, 1890).

Elias, Norbert, *The Civilizing Process: State Formation and Civilization*, Edmund Jephcott (trans.) (Oxford: Blackwell, 1982).

Ellett, Wade, 'The Death of Dueling', *Historia* (2004), 59–67, http://www.eiu.edu/~historia/2004/death%20of%20dueling.pdf, accessed 8 May 2010.

Emsley, Clive, *Crime and Society in England, 1750–1900*, rev. edn (London: Pearson/ Longman, 2005).

——, *The English Police: A Political and Social History* (London: Longman/Pearson, 1996).

——, *The Great British Bobby: A History of British Policing from the 18th Century to the Present* (London: Quercus, 2009).

——, *Hard Men: The English and Violence since 1750* (London: Hambledon and London, 2005).

——, '"The Thump of Wood on a Swede Turnip": Police Violence in Nineteenth-Century England', *Criminal Justice History*, 6 (1985), 125–49.

Epstein-Nord, Deborah, *Walking the Victorian Streets, Women, Representation and the City* (Ithaca: Cornell University Press, 1995).

Evans, B.J., 'Is Ju-Jitsu of Use to Women?', *Health and Strength*, 7 (20 August 1910), 202.

Evans, Stewart P. and Keith Skinner, *Jack the Ripper and the Whitechapel Murders* (London: P.R.O. Publications, 2002).

Evans, Stewart P. and Keith Skinner (eds), *The Ultimate Jack the Ripper Sourcebook: An Illustrated Encyclopedia* (London: Constable & Robinson, 2000).

Ewing-Ritchie J., *The Night Side of London* (London: William Tweedie, 1857).

Eyffinger, Arthur, *The 1899 Hague Peace Conference: 'The Parliament of Man, the Federation of the World'* (The Hague: Kluwer Law International, 1999).

Farrell, Stephen, 'A Treatise upon Sherlockian Firearms', *Sherlock Holmes Journal*, 23 (1993), 88–9.

'Fatal Duel, The', *Derby Mercury*, 6 March 1867, p. 3.

Fido, Martin and Keith Skinner, *The Official Encyclopedia of Scotland Yard* (London: Virgin Books, 1999).

Fletcher, Sheila, *Women First: The Female Tradition in English Physical Education, 1880–1980* (London: Athlone Press, 1984).

Foot, Michael, *H.G.: The History of Mr Wells* (London: Black Swan, 1996).

Freedgood, Elaine, *The Ideas in Things: Fugitive Meaning in the Victorian Novel* (University of Chicago Press, 2006).

——, *Victorian Writing about Risk: Imaging a Safe England* (Cambridge University Press, 2000).

Freundschuh, Aaron, '"New Sport" in the Street: Self-Defence, Security and Space in Belle Epoque Paris', *French History*, 20 (2006), 424–41.

Furnivall, F.J. (ed.), *Harrison's Description of England in Shakspere's Youth* (London: New Shakspeare Society, 1877) adapted from William Harrison, *Description of Britaine and Englande* (1577), 3 vols, II.

Fry, C.B., 'The Athlete in Bronze and Stone', *Strand*, 14 (1902), 531–41.

Fry, Eustace, 'The Peril of the East', *Health and Strength*, 9 (1904), 198–200.

Galton, Francis, 'Africa for the Chinese', *The Times*, 5 June 1873, p. 8.

'Garotte, Or Garrotte', *Notes and Queries*, 2 (11 December 1862), 159.

Garotters, The (1873), British Library, Lord Chamberlain's Manuscript Collection, M53117.

'Garotters', *The Saturday Review of Politics, Literature and Art*, 22 November 1862 (14: 369), 620.

Garrud, Edith, 'Damsel versus Desperado', *Health and Strength*, 7 (23 July 1910), in Tony Wolf (ed.), *The Bartitsu Compendium: Volume 1: History and Canonical Syllabus* (Raleigh, NC: Lulu.com, 2005), pp. 161–3.

——, 'The World We Live In', *Votes for Women*, 4 March 1910, 355.

Gaskell, Elizabeth, *The Life and Works of Charlotte Brontë and Her Sisters*, 7 vols. (London: Smith, Elder and Co., 1857; London: Smith, Elder and Co., 1882), VII, pp. 30–40.

Gay, Peter, *The Cultivation of Hatred in The Bourgeois Experience: Victoria to Freud*, 5 vols. (London: HarperCollins, 1994), III.

Gee, Tony, *Up to Scratch: Bareknuckle Fighting and Heroes of the Prize-Ring* (Hertfordshire: Queen Anne Press, 2001).

Gent, Helena, 'Does Physical Culture Retard Mental Culture?', *Health and Strength*, 7 (6 August 1910), 156–7.

——, 'Why Women Should Learn Ju-Jutsu', *Health and Strength*, 11 (31 January 1914), 116.

The Gentleman's Book of Manners: Showing How to Become a Perfect Gentleman (London: William Nicholson and Sons, c. 1881).

Gibbon, John Michael and Richard Lancelyn Green (eds), *The Unknown Conan Doyle: Letters to the Press* (London: Secker and Warburg, 1986).

Gilbert, Pamela, *The Citizen's Body: Desire, Health, and the Social in Victorian England* (Ohio State University Press, 2007).

Gilbert, William S., *London Characters and the Humorous Side of London Life* (c. 1871), http://www.victorianweb.org/books/mcdonnell/streets1.html, accessed 8 May 2010.

Gilmour, Robin, *The Idea of the Gentleman in the Victorian Novel* (London: George Allen & Unwin, 1981).

Girouard, Mark, *The Return to Camelot: Chivalry and the English Gentleman* (London: Yale University Press, 1981).

Gissing, George, *The Odd Women* (1893; reprint London: Penguin, 1993).

Glendinning, Victoria, *Trollope* (London: Pimlico, 1993).

Godfrey, Emelyne, 'Bartitsu: A Martial Art Tailor-Made for the Late-Victorian and Edwardian English Gentleman', in Tony Wolf (ed.), *The Bartitsu Compendium: Volume 1: History and Canonical Syllabus* (Raleigh, NC: Lulu.com, 2005), pp. 69–76.

——, 'The Perfect Gentleman and his Villainous Double in Selected Fin-de-Siècle Fiction, 1889–1906' (unpublished Master's thesis, University of London, Birkbeck College, 2002).

——, 'Uses for a Hat Pin: Women's Self-Defence as Pioneered in the Fiction of H.G. Wells', *Times Literary Supplement*, 5 February 2010, pp. 14–15.

Gorham, Deborah, *The Victorian Girl and the Feminine Ideal* (London: Croom Helm, 1982).

Grand, Sarah, *The Heavenly Twins* (Ann Arbor: University of Michigan Press, 1992).

Gravett, Christopher, 'The Spanish Armoury', *Royal Armouries Yearbook*, 4 (1999), 10

Green, Richard Lancelyn (ed.), *The Sherlock Holmes Letters* (London: Secker and Warburg, 1986).

Greenfield, Jill, Sean O'Connell and Chris Reid, 'Gender, Consumer Culture and the Middle-Class Male, 1918–1939', in Alan Kidd and David Nicholls (eds), *Gender, Civic Culture and Consumerism: Middle-class Identity in Britain 1800–1940* (Manchester University Press, 1999), pp. 183–97.

Greenwood, Colin, *Firearms Control: A Study of Armed Crime and Firearms Control in England and Wales* (London: Routledge & Kegan Paul, 1972).

Greenwood, James, *The Policeman's Lantern: Strange Stories of London Life* (London: Walter Scott, 1888).

Guernsey, A.H., 'Robbery as a Science', *Harper's New Monthly Magazine*, 26 (1863), 738–47.

Habits of Good Society: A Handbook of Etiquette for Ladies and Gentlemen (James Hogg and Sons, 1859).

Halford, Sir Bart. Henry St John, *The Art of Shooting with the Rifle* (London: Land and Water, 1888).

Hall, Catherine, 'A Nation Within and Without', in Catherine Hall, Keith McClelland and Jane Rendall (eds), *Defining the Victorian Nation: Class, Race and the British Reform Act of 1867* (Cambridge University Press, 2000), pp. 179–233.

Hall, Catherine, Keith McClelland and Jane Rendall (eds), *Defining the Victorian Nation: Class, Race and the British Reform Act of 1867* (Cambridge University Press, 2000).

Halperin, John, *Trollope and Politics: A Study of the Pallisers and Others* (London: Macmillan, 1977).

Hammond, Peter, '"Epitome of England's History": The Transformation of the Tower of London as Visitor Attraction in the Nineteenth Century', *Royal Armouries Yearbook*, 4 (1999), 144–74.

Hancock, H. Irving, 'Jiu-Jitsu, The Japanese Mode of Self-Defense: The Description of a Course in a System that Makes the Japanese the Most Formidable Antagonists in the World', *Macfadden's Physical Development Magazine*, 7 (1904), 57–60.

——, *Physical Training for Women by Japanese Methods* (London: G.P. Putnam's Sons/The Knickerbocker Press, 1904).

Hardy, Sylvia, 'A Feminist Perspective on H. G. Wells', *Wellsian*, 1997, 49–64.

Harkness, Margaret (John Law), *Captain Lobe: A Story of the Salvation Army* (London: Hodder & Stoughton, 1889).

Harrison Jr, G. Charter, 'The Anti-Garotter', *Gun Report*, 2 (1956), 22.

Harrison, J.F.C., *Late Victorian Britain, 1870–1901* (Glasgow: Fontana Press, 1990).

Hart-Davis, Adam, *What the Victorians Did For Us* (London: Headline/BBC, 2001).

Harvey, John, *Men in Black* (London: Reaktion Books, 1997).

Hearn, Lafcadio, *Glimpses of an Unfamiliar Japan*, 2 vols. (Boston: The Riverside Press, 1894), I.

'Herbert Spencer's Education', *Health and Strength*, 1 (1900), 11.

Higgins, Lynn A., and Brenda R. Silver (eds), *Rape and Representation* (Columbia University Press, 1991).

——, 'Introduction: Rereading Rape', in Lynn A. Higgins and Brenda R. Silver (eds), *Rape and Representation* (Columbia University Press, 1991), pp. 1–11.

Hipkiss, James, *Ju-Jitsu: Your Answer to Invasion, Unarmed Combat, The Art of Physical Defence and Attack* (London: F.W. Bridges, 1941).

Hirayama, Yuichi and John Hall, 'Some Knowledge of Baritsu: An Investigation of the Japanese System of Wrestling used by Sherlock Holmes', *Musgrave Monographs*, 7 (The Northern Musgraves, 1996).

Hitchens, Peter, *A Brief History of Crime: The Decline of Order, Justice and Liberty in England* (London: Atlantic Books, 2003).

Holland, Barbara, *Gentlemen's Blood: A History of Duelling, From Swords at Dawn to Pistols at Dusk* (New York: Bloomsbury, 2003).

Holland, Henry W., 'The Art of Self-Protection against Thieves and Robbers', *Good Words*, 7 (1866), 847–51.

——, 'Professional Thieves', *Cornhill Magazine*, 6 (1862), 640–53.

——, 'The Science of Garotting and Housebreaking', *Cornhill Magazine*, 7 (1863), 79–92.

Hornung, E.W., *Raffles: Amateur Cracksman* (London: Penguin, 2003).

——, 'A Bad Night' in *A Thief in the Night* (Leipzig: Bernhard Tauchnitz, 1905).

Howells, William D., *The Garotters* (Edinburgh: David Douglas, 1897).

Hughes, Thomas, *Tom Brown's Schooldays: By an Old Boy* (Oxford University Press, 1999).

Huggins, Mike, *The Victorians and Sport* (London: Hambledon and London, 2004).

Hume, Fergus, *The Mystery of a Hansom Cab* (London: The Hansom Cab Publishing Company, 1888).

Hunt, Tristram, *Building Jerusalem: The Rise and Fall of the Victorian City* (London: Weidenfeld & Nicolson, 2004).

'If You Want to Earn Some Time Throw a Policeman', *Sketch*, 6 July 1910, 425.

Ibsen, Henrik, *Ghosts in Henrik Ibsen: Three Plays: The Wild Duck, Ghosts and A Doll's House* (Harlow: Longman Literature, 1995), pp. 123–201.

Idler (1900), in 'Arms and Armour: 'Paper Cuttings: 1896–1905', Royal Armouries Library, Leeds.

James, G.P.R., 'The Garrote', *Harper's New Monthly Magazine*, 8 (1854), 330–7.

Jerome, Jerome K., *Three Men on the Bummel* (Bristol: J.W. Arrowsmith, 1900).

Jewell, J. St A., 'The Gymnasiums of London: Pierre Vigny's', *Health and Strength*, 8 (1904), 173–7.

John, Kevin, 'Sherlock Holmes, the Napoleon of Crime?', *Baker Street Journal: An Irregular Quarterly of Sherlockiana*, 31 (1981), 75–6.

Jones, Jennifer, 'The Face of Villainy on the Victorian Stage', *Theatre Notebook*, 50 (1996), 95–108.

'Jujitsu: Some Means of Attack and Defence', *Pall Mall Gazette*, 23 October 1900, 10.

Ju-Jitsu, or the Japanese Wrestler: A Farce in One Act, British Library, Lord Chamberlain's Manuscript Collection, 25/08.

'Ju-Jutsu as a Husband-Tamer: A Suffragette Play with a Moral', *Health and Strength*, 8 (8 April 1911), 339.

'Ju-jutsuffragettes, A New Terror for the London Police', *Health and Strength*, 6 (24 April 1909), 421.

Kelly, James, *'That Damn'd Thing Called Honour': Duelling in Ireland 1570–1860* (Cork University Press, 1995).

Kern, Stephen, *Eyes of Love: The Gaze in English and French Paintings and Novels, 1840–1900* (London: Reaktion Books, 1996).

Kerr, Douglas, 'The Straight Left: Sport and the Nation in Arthur Conan Doyle', *Victorian Literature and Culture*, 38 (2010), 187–206.

Kestner, Joseph, *Masculinities in Victorian Painting* (Aldershot: Scholar Press, 1995).

——, *Sherlock's Men: Masculinity, Conan Doyle, and Cultural History* (Aldershot: Ashgate, 1997).

Kidd, Alan, and David Nicholls (eds), *Gender, Civic Culture and Consumerism: Middle-Class Identity in Britain, 1800–1940* (Manchester University Press, 1999).

Kipling, Rudyard, *From Sea to Sea* (1899), available at http://ghostwolf.dyndns.org/words/authors/K/KiplingRudyard/prose/FromSeaToSea/index.html, accessed 7 May 2010.

Kobayashi, Tsukasa, 'Sherlock Holmes and Japan', Japan Sherlock Holmes Club website, http://www.holmesjapan.jp/english/koba01.htm, accessed 6 March 2010.

Krebs, Paula, *Gender, Race and the Writing of Empire* (Cambridge University Press, 1990).

Kristeva, Julia, *Powers of Horror: An Essay on Abjection,* Leon S. Roudiez (trans.) (New York: Columbia University Press, 1982).

'"Ladies" Night at the Bath Club: A Varied Entertainment: "Bartitsu"', *Graphic*, 18 March 1899, 324.

Larkin, Leonard, 'The Japanese Jack the Giant Killer', *Strand*, 22 (1901), 150–8.

Law, Harry, 'A Day with Dr. Conan Doyle' *Strand*, 4 (1892), 182–8.

'The Latest Fashionable Pastime: The Bartitsu Club', *Black and White Budget*, 4 (29 December 1900), 402–4.

'Laws of War: Declaration on the Use of Bullets Which Expand or Flatten Easily in the Human Body: July 29, 1899', *The Avalon Project at Yale Law School*, http://www.yale.edu/lawweb/avalon/lawofwar/dec99-03.htm, accessed 8 May 2010.

Leapman, Michael, *The World for a Shilling: How the Great Exhibition of 1851 Changed a Nation* (London: Headline, 2001).

Leblanc, Maurice, *Arsène Lupin: Gentleman Cambrioleur* (Paris: Pierre Lafitte and Co., 1907).

——, *The Exploits of Arsène Lupin,* Alexander Teixeira de Mattos (trans.) (London: Cassell and Co., 1909).

Ledger, Sally, *The New Woman: Fiction and Feminism at the Fin de Siècle* (Manchester University Press, 1997).

Ledger, Sally and Roger Luckhurst (eds), *The Fin de Siècle: A Reader in Cultural History, 1880–1900* (Oxford University Press, 2000).

Letwin, Shirley, *The Gentleman in Trollope: Individuality and Moral Conduct* (Basingstoke: Macmillan, 1982).

Lindgren, Charlotte, 'Nathaniel Hawthorn, Consul at Liverpool', *History Today*, 26 (1976), 516–24.

Linscott, Gillian, *The Perfect Daughter: A Nell Bray Mystery* (London: Virago, 2000).

Linton, Eliza Lynn, 'Out Walking', *Temple Bar*, 5 (1862), 132–41.

'The London Parks', *The Saturday Review of Politics, Literature, Science and Art*, 3 August 1867, 137–8.

Longhurst, Percy, 'A Few Practical Hints on Self-Defence', *Sandow's Magazine*, 4 (1900), 121–7.

——, *Jiu-Jitsu and Other Methods of Self-Defence* (London: L. Upcott Gill, 1906).

Lovesey, Peter, 'Conan Doyle and the Olympics', *Journal of Olympic History*, 10 (2001–2), 1–9.

Lowndes, Marie Belloc, *The Lodger* (Wildside Press, 2009)

Malcolm, Joyce Lee, *Guns and Violence: The English Experience* (London: Harvard University Press, 2002).

Mangan, J.A. and James Walvin (eds), *Manliness and Morality: Middle-Class Masculinity in Britain and America 1800–1940* (Manchester University Press, 1987).

Marks, Patricia, *Bicycles, Bangs and Bloomers: The New Woman in the Popular Press* (University of Kentucky Press, 1990).

——, '*Household Words*', in Alvin Sullivan (ed.), *British Literary Magazines: The Victorian and Edwardian Age, 1837–1913* (London: Greenwood, 1984), pp. 170–5.

Marsh, Richard, *The Beetle: A Mystery* (London: Skeffington & Son, 1897).

Mason, Philip, *The English Gentleman: The Rise and Fall of an Ideal* (London: André Deutsch, 1982).

Mayhew, Henry, 'Those That Will Not Work', in Victor Neuburg (ed.), *London Labour and the London Poor*, 4 vols. (Harmondsworth: Penguin, 1985), IV (1862).

Mayne, Richard, Douglas Johnson and Robert Tombs (eds), *Cross Channel Currents: 100 Years of the Entente Cordiale* (London: Routledge, 2004).

McClintock, Anne, *Imperial Leather: Race, Gender and Sexuality in the Colonial Contest* (London: Routledge, 1995).

McCrone, Kathleen, *Sport and the Physical Emancipation of English Women, 1870–1914* (London: Routledge, 1988).

McEwan, Ian, *Saturday* (London: Jonathan Cape, 2005).

McLaren, Angus *The Trials of Masculinity: Policing Sexual Boundaries 1870–1930* (University of Chicago Press, 1997).

McLaughlin, Joseph, *Writing the Urban Jungle: Reading Empire in London from Doyle to Eliot* (University of Virginia Press, 2000).

McLelland, Keith, 'England's Greatness, the Working Man', in Catherine Hall, Keith McClelland and Jane Rendall (eds), *Defining the Victorian Nation: Class, Race and the British Reform Act of 1867* (Cambridge University Press, 2000), pp. 71–118.

McMaster, Juliet, *Trollope's Palliser Novels: Theme and Pattern* (London: Macmillan, 1978).

McPhee, C. and A. FitzGerald (eds), *The Non-Violent Militant: Selected Writings of Teresa Billington-Greig* (London: Routledge & Kegan Paul, 1987).

Meserve, Walter J. (ed.), *The Complete Plays of W.D. Howells* (New York University Press, 1960).

Metropolitan Police Crime Museum: http://www.met.police.uk/history/crime_museum.htm, accessed 8 May 2010.

Mills, Victoria, 'Introduction: Victorian Fiction and the Material Imagination', *19: Interdisciplinary Studies in the Long Nineteenth Century*, 6 (2008), http://www.19.bbk.ac.uk/index.php/19/issue/view/69, accessed 17 March 2010.

Mitchell, Sally, *Dinah Mulock Craik* (Massachusetts: G.K. Hall and Co., 1983).

Moody, Ellen, 'Trollope's Comfort Romances for Men: Heterosexual Male Heroism in his Work', *The Victorian Web: Literature, History and Culture in the Age of Victoria*, http://www.victorianweb.org/authors/trollope/moody2/comfort.html, accessed 8 May 2010.

'The Moral Philosophy of Garotting', *Fraser's Magazine*, 67 (1863), 258–63.

'Mr Conan Doyle on Army Reform', *Westminster Gazette*, 12 November 1900, 2.

Mullin, Donald, *Victorian Plays: A Record of Significant Productions on the London Stage, 1837–1901* (London: Greenwood, 1987).

Murphy, Cliona, 'H. G. Wells and Votes for Women', *Wellsian*, 10 (1987), 11–19.

Muybridge, Eadweard, *The Human Figure in Motion: An Electro Photographic Enbestigation of Consecutide Phases in Muscular Actions* (London: Chapman & Hall, 1901).

Nead, Lynda, *Victorian Babylon: People, Streets and Images in Nineteenth-Century London* (London: Yale University Press, 2000).

Newcastle Weekly Courant, 22 July 1899, 2.

Nicoll, Allardyce, *A History of English Drama: 1660–1900: Late Nineteenth Century Drama, 1850–1900*, 6 vols. (Cambridge University Press, 1946), V.

Nordstrom, Carolyn, *A Different Kind of War Story* (Philadelphia: University of Pennsylvania Press, 1997).

Nugent, Mary, 'Barton-Wright and his Japanese Wrestlers: A Man and his Method', *Health and Strength*, 3 (1901), 336–41.

O'Keefe, Jamie, *Dogs Don't Know Kung Fu: A Guide to Female Self-Protection* (Dagenham: New Breed, 1996).

Onslow, Lady, 'The Call for a New Chivalry', *New Age*, 21 October 1909, 460.

'Our Police', *Saturday Review of Politics, Literature and Art*, 24 October 1868, 553–4.

Palmegiano, E.M., *Crime in Victorian Britain: An Annotated Bibliography from Nineteenth-Century British Magazines* (London: Greenwood Press, 1993).

Pankhurst, Christabel, 'In Fear of Women', *The Suffragette*, 2 (19 December 1913), 225.

Parsons, Deborah L., *Streetwalking the Metropolis: Women, the City, and Modernity* (Oxford University Press, 2000).

Pascoe, David (ed.), *Charles Dickens: Selected Journalism, 1850–1870* (London: Penguin, 1997).

Paterson, James, *Commentaries on the Liberty of the Subject and Laws of England Relating to the Security of the Person*, 2 vols. (London: Macmillan and Co., 1877).

Paxton, Nancy, L., 'Mobilizing Chivalry: Rape in British Novels about the Indian Uprising of 1857', *Victorian Studies*, 36 (1992), 5–30.

Pearson, Geoffrey, *Hooligan: A History of Respectable Fears* (London: Macmillan, 1983).

Peterson, Linda, H. (ed.), *Wuthering Heights: Case Studies* (Boston: Bedford/St Martin's Press, 2003).

Philips, Mary, 'The Typical Suffragist', *Votes for Women*, December 1907, p. 35.

Phillips, Watts, *A Ticket of Leave: A Farce in One Act* (1862), British Library, Lord Chamberlain's Manuscript Collection, 53017P.

Phillips, Watts, *A Ticket of Leave: A Farce in One Act* (1862), *Lacy's Acting Edition of Victorian Plays*, http://www.worc.ac.uk/victorian/victorianplays/editorialnote.htm, accessed 8 May 2010.

'*Phineas Finn*: Review', *Saturday Review of Politics, Literature and Art*, 27 March 1869, 431–2.

'*Phineas Redux*: Review', *Saturday Review of Politics, Literature and Art*, 7 February 1874, 186–7.

'*Phineas Redux*: Review', *Academy*, 7 February 1874, pp. 141–3.

'Physical Training', *St James's Magazine* (February 1863), 322–8.

Pick, Daniel, *Faces of Degeneration: A European Disorder, c. 1848–1918* (Cambridge University Press, 1996).

'Pistols Bill', *Hansard*, 27 February 1895, coll. 1658–86.

'Prize-Fight, The', *Saturday Review of Politics, Literature, Science and Art*, 29 November 1862, pp. 650–1.

'Prize-Fighting', *Pall Mall Gazette*, 6 November 1866, p. 5.

'Professional Thieves', *Cornhill Magazine*, 6 (1862), 640–53.

'Professor Vigny's Third Great Tournament and Assault-at-Arms', *Health and Strength*, 8 (1904), p. 20.

'Provisional Patents', *Mechanics' Magazine*, 6 December 1856, p. 549.

Pound, Reginald, *Strand Magazine: 1891–1950* (London: Heinemann, 1966).

'Pugilism in High Quarters', *London Review*, 5, 127 (6 December 1862), 492–3.

R v Rose (1884) 15 Cox CC 540 (Assizes).

Raeburn, Antonia, *The Militant Suffragettes* (London: Michael Joseph, 1973).

Rahill, Frank, *The World of Melodrama* (London: Pennsylvania State University Press, 1967).

Reid, J.C., *Bucks and Bruisers: Pierce Egan and Regency England* (London: Routledge & Kegan Paul, 1971).

'Revolver Fiend Abroad and How to Baffle Him, The', *Health and Strength*, 6 (6 February 1909), 127.

Richardson, Angelique, *Love and Eugenics in the Late Nineteenth Century: Rational Reproduction and the New Woman* (Oxford University Press, 2003).

Ricketts, Harry, 'A Short Walk on the Wilde Side: Kipling's First Impressions of Japan', *New Zealand Journal of Asian Studies*, 5, 2 (December, 2003), pp. 26–32.

Rider-Haggard, H., *King Solomon's Mines* (Oxford: Oxford World's Classics, 1998).

Riley, Peter, *The Highways and Byways of Jack the Ripper* (Cheshire: P&D Riley, 2001).

'Ripper in Fiction', Victoria List Archives, Indiana University, https://listserv.indiana.edu/cgi-bin/waiub.exe?S2=VICTORIA&m=66224&q=Ripperdiscussion, accessed 8 May 2010.

Robbery, trial reference number, t18570105-243, 5 January 1857, http://www.Oldbaileyonline.org, accessed 8 May 2010.

Robins, Elizabeth, *Both Sides of the Curtain* (London: Heinemann, 1940).

Roland, Paul, *The Crimes of Jack the Ripper* (London: Arcturus, 2006).

'Rooks and Herons', *All the Year Round*, 10 (1864), 136–41.

Rooney, Ellen, '"A Little More than Persuading": Tess and the Subject of Sexual Violence', in Lynn A. Higgins and Brenda R. Silver (eds), *Rape and Representation* (New York: Columbia University Press, 1991), pp. 87–114.

Rønning, Ann Holden, *Hidden and Visible Suffrage: Emancipation and the Edwardian Woman in Galsworthy, Wells and Forster* (Berne: Peter Lang, 1995).

Rosa, Joseph G., *Colt Revolvers and the Tower of London* (London: The Trustees of the Royal Armouries, 1988).

Rotundo, Anthony E., 'Learning about Manhood: Gender Ideals and the Middle-Class Family in Nineteenth-Century America', in J.A. Mangan, and James Walvin (eds), *Manliness and Morality: Middle-Class Masculinity in Britain and America, 1800–1940* (Manchester University Press, 1987).

Rowbotham, Judith and Kim Stevenson (eds), *Criminal Conversations: Victorian Crimes, Social Panic, and Moral Outrage* (Ohio State University Press, 2005).

Rushby, Kevin, *The Children of Kali: Through India in Search of Bandits, the Thug Cult and the British Raj* (London: Constable, 2002).

Said, Edward, *Orientalism: Western Conceptions of the Orient* (Harmondsworth: Penguin, 1995).

Sala, George Augustus, *Twice Round the Clock; or The House of the Day and Night in London* (London: George Robert Maxwell, 1878).

Sandow, Eugen, 'Physical Culture: What Is It?', *Sandow's Magazine*, 1 (1898), 3–7.

Scott, James Brown, *The Proceedings of the Hague Peace Conferences (Translation of the Official Texts): The Conference of 1899* (New York: Oxford University Press, 1920).

Sedgwick, Eve Kosovsky, *Between Men: English Literature and Male Homosocial Desire* (New York: Columbia University Press, 1985).

'Self-Defence Against the Strong: Bartitsu at the Bath Club', *Daily News*, 11 March 1899, 9.

Sennett, Richard, *Flesh and Stone: The Body and the City in Western Civilization* (London: Faber & Faber, 1994).

——, *The Conscience of the Eye: The Design and Social Life of Cities* (London: Faber & Faber, 1991).

Sharpe, Gene, 'Beyond Just War and Pacifism: Nonviolent Struggle towards Justice, Freedom and Peace' (1996), in Manfred B. Steger and Nancy S. Lind (eds), *An Interdisciplinary Reader: Violence and Its Alternatives* (Basingstoke: Macmillan, 1999), pp. 317–33.

Shoemaker, Robert, 'Male Honour and the Decline of Public Violence in Eighteenth-Century London', *Social History*, 2 (2001), 190–208.

——, 'The Taming of the Duel: Masculinity, Honour and Ritual Violence in London, 1660–1800', *Historical Journal*, 3 (2002), 525–45.

Shidachi, T., '"Jujitsu", The Ancient Art of Self-Defence by Sleight of Body', *Proceedings of the Japan Society*, 1892, Richard Bowen Collection, Item 7, 4–21.

Shipley, S., 'Tom Causer of Bermondsey: A Boxer Hero of the 1890s', *History Workshop*, 15 (1983), 28–59.

'Should Women Wrestle?', *Health and Strength*, 14 (1907), 182–3.

Showalter, Elaine, *A Literature of their Own* (London: Virago, 1999).

——, *Sexual Anarchy: Gender and Culture at the Fin de Siècle* (London: Virago, 2001).

——, (ed.), *Maude/Christina Rossetti. On Sisterhoods; A Woman's Thoughts about Women/Dinah Mulock Craik* (New York University Press, 1993).

Simmel, G., The Metropolis and Mental Life, in Donald N. Levine (ed.), *On Individuality and Social Forms: Selected Writings of Georg Simmel* (University of Chicago Press, 1972), pp. 324–39.

Simpson, Antony E. '"Dandelions on the Field of Honor": Duelling, the Middle Classes and the Law in Nineteenth-Century England', *Criminal Justice History*, 9 (1988), 99–155.

Sindall, Rob, 'The London Garotting Panics of 1856 and 1862', *Social History*, 12 (1987), 351–359.

——, *Street Violence in the Nineteenth-Century: Media Panic or Real Danger?* (Leicester University Press, 1990).

Sleeman, James, *Thug: A Million Murders* (London: Sampson Low, Marston & Co., 1933).

Smalley, Donald (ed.), *Anthony Trollope: The Critical Heritage* (London: Routledge, 1995).

Smiles, Samuel, *Character* (London: John Murray, 1871).

——, *Self-Help: With Illustrations of Conduct and Perseverance* (London: John Murray, 1958).

Smith, David Clayton (ed.), *The Correspondence of H.G. Wells: 1904–1918*, 4 vols. (London: Pickering & Chatto, 1998), II.

Smith, Frederick Edwin (Earl of Birkenhead) (ed.), *Fifty Famous Fights in Fact and Fiction* (London: Cassell and Co., 1932).

Spierenberg, Pieter (ed.), *Men and Violence: Gender, Honor, and Rituals in Modern Europe and America* (Ohio University Press, 1998).

Spraggs, Gillian, *Outlaws and Highwaymen: The Cult of the Robber in England from the Middle Ages to the Nineteenth Century* (London: Pimlico, 2001), http://www.outlawsandhighwaymen.com/harrison.htm#hanger, accessed 30 September 2007.

Stanko, Elizabeth, *Everyday Violence: How Women and Men Experience Sexual and Physical Danger* (London: HarperCollins, 1990).

Stanton, Mary Olmstead, *Physiognomy: A Practical and Scientific Treatise* (San Francisco: the author, 1881).

Stephen, James Fitzjames, *A General View of the Criminal Law of England* (New York: Macmillan and Co, 1890).

——, 'Gentlemen', *Cornhill Magazine*, 5 (March 1862), 327–42.

Stevenson, Robert Louis, 'Gentlemen', *The Works of Robert Louis Stevenson*, Tusitala Edition, 35 vols. (London: William Heinemann, 1924), XXVI, pp. 91–112.

——, *The Strange Case of Dr Jekyll and Mr Hyde* (London: Penguin, 2000).

Storey, Neil, R., *The Grim Almanac of Jack the Ripper, London 1870–1900* (Stroud: Sutton, 2004).

'Stories for the First of April', *Household Words*, 15 (7 March 1857), 217–22.

Strachan, John., 'Poets and Pugilists', *History Today*, 59 (2009), 17–23.

Strong, Roy, *The Spirit of Britain: A Narrative History of the Arts* (London: Pimlico, 2000).

Sue, Eugène, *The Wandering Jew* (London: Chapman & Hall, 1845).

Sullivan, Alvin (ed.), *British Literary Magazines, Vol 3: The Victorian and Edwardian Age, 1837–1913* (London: Greenwood, 1984).

Sutherland, Bruce, W., *Ju-Jitsu: Self-Defence* (Edinburgh: Thomas Nelson and Sons, 1916).

Svinth, Joe, 'The Evolution of Women's Judo, 1900–1945' in *InYo: The Journal of Alternative Perspectives on the Martial Arts and Sciences*, http://ejmas.com/jalt/jaltart_svinth_0201.htm, accessed 8 May 2010.

——, 'Women Who Would Not Be Sheep: Women's Combative Sports in the Twentieth Century' in *InYo: Journal of Alternative Perspectives on the Martial*

Arts and Sciences, http://ejmas.com/jalt/jaltart_svinth4_1199.htm, accessed 8 May 2010.

Tani, Yukio and Taro Miyake, *The Game of Ju-Jitsu, for the Use of Schools and Colleges* (London: Hazell, Watson and Viney, 1906).

Taylor, David, *Crime, Policing and Punishment in England, 1750–1914* (London: Macmillan, 1998).

Taylor, Irene and Alan (eds), *The Assassin's Cloak* (Edinburgh: Canongate, 2000).

Taylor, Philip Meadows, *Confessions of a Thug* (London: Richard Bentley, 1858).

Taylor, Tom, *The Ticket of Leave Man* (1863) in 'The Victorian Plays Project: Electronic Archive of Rare Victorian Plays', University of Worcester, http://www.worc.ac.uk/victorian/victorianplays/resources.htm, accessed 20 May 2010.

——, *The Ticket of Leave: A Drama in Three Acts and a Prologue* (1863), Lord Chamberlain's Manuscript Collection, AA53002.

Terry, T. Philip, 'Jiujitsu: Japanese Self-Defense without Weapons', *Outing Magazine*, 41 (1902), 12–18.

Thackerey, William Makepeace, *Vanity Fair: A Novel Without a Hero* (Leipzig: Bernhardt Tauchnitz, 1848).

Thoughts on Duelling and its Abolition (London, 1844, G.W. Nickisson).

Tidrick, Kathryn, *Empire and the English Character* (London: I.B. Tauris, 1990).

Tindal, Marcus, 'Self Protection on a Cycle', *Pearson's Magazine*, 11 (1901), 425–31.

Todd, Jan, 'From Milo to Milo: A History of Barbells, Dumbells, and Indian Clubs', *Iron Game History*, 3 (1995), 4–16.

Tonkin, Bill, 'Japan-British Exhibition, 1910', http://www.studygroup.org.uk/Exhibitions/Pages/1910%20Japan-British.htm, accessed 8 May 2010.

Torrese, Dante, M., 'Firearms in the Canon: The Guns of Sherlock Holmes and John H. Watson', *Baker Street Journal: An Irregular Quarterly of Sherlockiana*, 42 (1992), 154–8.

Tosh, John, *A Man's Place: Masculinity and the Middle-Class Home in Victorian England* (Yale University Press, 1999).

Torture and Punishment (Leeds: The Trustees of the Armouries, 2003).

Toynbee Hall, Ephemera Collection.

Trollope, Anthony, *An Autobiography* (Adamant Media Corporation, 2006).

——, (ed.), *British Sports and Pastimes* (London: Virtue and Co., 1868).

——, *Can You Forgive Her?*, 2 vols. (London: Chapman & Hall, 1865).

——, *The Duke's Children*, 3 vols. (London: Chapman & Hall, 1880).

——, *Eustace Diamonds, The*, 3 vols. (London: Chapman & Hall, 1873).

——, *Phineas Finn*, 2 vols. (Oxford: Oxford World's Classics, 1999).

——, 'Phineas Finn', *Saint Paul's Magazine*, October 1867 to May 1869.

——, *Phineas Redux*, 2 vols. (Oxford: Oxford World's Classics, 2000).

——, 'Phineas Redux', *Graphic*, 19 July 1873 to 10 January 1874.

——, *The Prime Minister*, 4 vols. (London: Chapman & Hall, 1876).

——, 'The Uncontrolled Ruffianism of London as Measured by the Rule of Thumb', *Saint Paul's Magazine*, 1 (1868), 419–24.

Tropp, Martin, *Images of Fear: How Horror Stories Helped Shape Modern Culture* (London: McFarland Classics, 1999).

Trotter, David, 'Household Clearances in Victorian Fiction', *19: Interdisciplinary Studies in the Long Nineteenth Century*, 6 (2008), http://www.19.bbk.ac.uk/index.php/19/issue/view/69, accessed 8 May 2010.

Turner, Mark W., *Trollope and the Magazines: Gendered Issues in Mid-Victorian Britain* (London: Macmillan, 2000).

——, 'Urban Encounters and Visual Play in the Yellow Book', in Laurel Brake and Julie F. Codell (eds), *Encounters in the Victorian Press: Editors, Authors, Readers* (Basingstoke: Palgrave Macmillan, 2005), pp. 138–60.

Uncommercial Traveller, The, 'The Ruffian', *All the Year Round*, 20 (1868), 421–4.

Uyenishi, S.K., *The Text-Book of Ju-Jutsu as Practised in Japan* (London: Health and Strength, 1906).

VanArsdel, Rosemary T., 'Women's Periodicals and the New Journalism: The Personal Interview', in Joel H. Wiener (ed.), *Papers for the Millions: The New Journalism in Britain, 1850s–1914* (Westport, CT: Greenwood Press, 1988), pp. 243–56.

Vance, Norman, *The Sinews of Spirit: The Ideal of Christian Manliness in Victorian Literature and Religious Thought* (Cambridge University Press, 1985).

Walkowitz, Judith, *City of Dreadful Delight: Narratives of Sexual Danger in Late-Victorian London* (London: Virago, 1992).

——, 'Going Public: Shopping, Street Harassment, and Streetwalking in Late Victorian London', *Representations*, 62 (1998), 1–30.

——, 'The Indian Woman, the Flower Girl, and the Jew: Photojournalism in Edwardian London', *Victorian Studies*, 42 (1998/9), 3–46.

——, 'Jack the Ripper and the Myth of Male Violence', *Feminist Studies*, 8 (1982), 542–74.

Walter, John, D., *Secret Firearms: An Illustrated History of Miniature and Concealed Handguns* (London: Cassell/Arms and Armour, 1997).

'Wanderings in India', *Household Words*, 16 (7 November 1857), 457–463.

Warwick, Alexandra and Martin Willis (eds), *Jack the Ripper: Media, Culture, History* (Manchester University Press, 2007).

Waterloo Directory, 1800–1900 (Waterloo, Ontario: North Waterloo Academic Press, 2003).

Waters, Karen Volland, *The Perfect Gentleman: Masculine Control in Victorian Men's Fiction, 1870–1901* (New York: Peter Lang, 1997).

Watters, Daniel E., 'The Truth about Dum Dums: A Learned Monograph on the Origins of a Much Mis-used [sic] Term of Today', *Gun Zone*, http://www.the gunzone.com/dum-dum.html, accessed 8 May 2010.

Watts, Emily Diana, *The Fine Art of Jujutsu* (London: William Heinemann, 1906).

Wells, H.G., *Experiment in Autobiography: Discoveries and Conclusions of a Very Ordinary Brain (since 1866)* (London: Victor Gollancz, 1934).

——, *The History of Mr Polly* (London: Everyman, 2003).

——, *The Time Machine* (London: Everyman, 1995).

——, *The War of the Worlds* (London: Everyman, 1993).

Westney, Eleanor, D., *Imitation and Innovation: The Transfer of Western Organizational Patterns to Meiji Japan* (London: Harvard University Press, 1987).

Westwood, Jennifer, *The Lore of the Land: A Guide to England's Legends from Spring-Heeled Jack to the Witches of Warboys* (London: Penguin, 2005).

White, J., *London in the Twentieth Century: A City and its People* (London: Vintage, 2008).

Wiegers, Yvonne, 'Male Bodybuilding: The Social Construction of a Masculine Identity', *Journal of Popular Culture*, 32 (1998), 147–61.

Wiener, Joel, H., *Papers for the Millions: The New Journalism in Britain, 1850s to 1914* (Westport, CT: Greenwood Press, 1988).

Wiener, Martin, 'Alice Arden to Bill Sikes: Changing Nightmares of Intimate Violence in England, 1558–1869', *Journal of British Studies*, 40 (2001), 184–213.

——, *Men of Blood: Violence, Manliness and Criminal Justice in Victorian England* (Cambridge University Press, 2004).

——, 'New Women vs. Old Men? Sexual Danger and "Social Narratives" in Later-Victorian England', *Journal of Victorian Culture*, 2 (1997), 302–9.

——, *Reconstructing the Criminal: Culture, Law, and Policy in England, 1830–1914* (Cambridge University Press, 1990).

Wilkinson, Frederick, *Those Entrusted with Arms: A History of the Police, Post, Customs and Private Use of Weapons in Britain* (Leeds: Royal Armouries/Greenhill Books, 2002).

Wilson, Evan M., 'Sherlock Holmes and A.J. Raffles', *The Baker Street Journal: An Irregular Quarterly of Sherlockiana*, 34 (1984), 155–8.

Wilson, Gretchen, *With All Her Might: The Life of Gertrude Harding, Militant Suffragette* (Fredericton, Canada: Goose Lane, 1996).

Wilson Guy, '"To Save Our Brave Men"', *Royal Armouries Yearbook*, 4 (1999), 71–5.

Wilson, John Crawford, *The Antigarotte/My Knuckleduster* (1863), British Library, Lord Chamberlain's Manuscript Collection, M53019.

Winant, Lewis, *Firearms Curiosa* (New York: Greenberg, 1955).

Winder, Robert, *Bloody Foreigners: The Story of Immigration to Britain* (London; Abacus, 2004).

Winn, Godfrey, 'Dear Mrs Garrud – I Wish I'd Known You Then...', *Woman*, 19 June 1965, pp. 22–5.

Winnett, Susan, 'The Marquise's "O" and the Mad Dash of Narrative', in Lynn Higgins and Brenda R. Silver (eds), *Rape and Representation* (New York: Columbia University Press, 1991), pp. 67–86.

Wood, John Carter, 'A Useful Savagery: The Invention of Violence in Nineteenth-Century England', *Journal of Victorian Culture*, 9, 1 (2004), 22–42.

——, *Violence and Crime in Nineteenth-Century England: The Shadow of Our Refinement* (London: Routledge, 2004).

Wolf, Tony, 'Barton-Wright's Misadventures in Electrotherapy', in Tony Wolf (ed.), *Bartitsu Compendium: Volume 1: History and Canonical Syllabus* (Raleigh, NC: Lulu.com, 2005), pp. 63–4.

——, *Edith Garrud: The Suffragette Who Knew Jujutsu* (Raleigh, NC: Lulu.com, 2009).

——, 'Foreword', *Bartitsu Compendium: Volume 1: History and Canonical Syllabus*, Tony Wolf (ed.) (Raleigh, NC: Lulu.com, 2005), pp. 13–14.

——, '"A Grand Assault-at-Arms": Combative Exhibitions in Victorian England', *E-Journal of Manly Arts: European and Colonial Combatives 1776–1914*, August 2001, http://ejmas.com/jmanly/jmanlyframe.htm, accessed 8 May 2010.

——, 'A System Which He Termed Bartitsu', *E-Journal of Manly Arts: European and Colonial Combatives 1776–1914*, May 2006, http://ejmas.com/jmanly/jmanly frame.htm, accessed 8 May 2010.

Woosnam-Savage, Robert and Anthony Hall, *Body Armour* (Virginia: Brassey's, 2001).

Wright, Stephen, 'The Non-PC Guide to Policing: How to Apprehend a Criminal, 1907-Style', *Daily Mail*, http://www.dailymail.co.uk/news/article-1239754/ The-non-PC-guide-policing-How-apprehend-criminal-1907-style. html, accessed 8 May 2010.

Wynne, Catherine, *The Colonial Conan Doyle: British Imperialism, Irish Nationalism and the Gothic* (Westport, CT: Greenwood Press, 2002).

Yokoyama, Toshio, *Japan in the Victorian Mind: A Study of Stereotyped Images of a Nation 1850–80* (Basingstoke: Palgrave, 1987).

Young, Arlene, *Culture, Class and Gender in the Victorian Novel: Gentlemen, Gents and Working Women* (Basingstoke: Macmillan, 1999).

'Zigzags at the Zoo: The Ophidian', *Strand*, 5 (1892), 407–14.

Index

194